Naughty or Nerdy?

"The kiss we shared wasn't a lie.

"And while I take full responsibility for having started it—" Judd moved toward her again.

This time when Lucy backed up, she fell onto his bed.

"You, Lucy Weston, contributed your full share."

"You...you caught me...off guard."

"I'll grant you that. For the first few seconds," he added with a teasing smile. Ten years ago, he'd convinced himself he didn't stand a chance with her.

Well, this time around, he was going for the gold.

"Will you take those dumb braces off," she muttered.

He gladly complied, tossing the sham metalwork onto the bedside table. "Better?"

"I can't figure you out. One minute you're this...this—"

"Nerd?"

"And the next minute, you're...Don Juan."

"I guess you could say I'm a man of many sides."

"And I'm not sure I care for any of them."

"Liar."

For more, turn to page 9

Tara Patterson: The Husband Hunter

And as wet as a fish, no less, having just taken an accidental dunk in the hotel's hot tub—in full managerial attire.

"I'm Jay Overman...here for the maintenance job."

Tara just stared at him, dripping. "You sure don't look like any maintenance man I've ever seen."

Jay jiggled the tool belt around his hips.

"Yep, that's me. The maintenance man." As he shook her hand he tried to ignore the feeling that shot through him. She looked good soaking wet. Damn good.

Tara glanced down at herself and gasped in dismay. "Just give me a few minutes to change and I'll meet you in my office."

As she hurried away, Jay thought maybe he should suggest she not bother to change out of her clinging clothes for him. Or maybe he'd offer to help her out of those things. And while he was at it, he could personally measure her for an *Impeccabra*. He watched Tara until she disappeared from sight, no longer thinking about bras, now he had breasts on the brain. Naked ones, at that.

For more, turn to page 197

HARLEQUIN DUETS

ISBN 0-373-44134-7

Copyright in the collection:
Copyright © 2002 by Harlequin Books S.A.

The publisher acknowledges the copyright holders
of the individual works as follows:

NAUGHTY OR NERDY?
Copyright © 2002 by Elise Title

THE HUSBAND HOTEL
Copyright © 2002 by Darlene Hrobak Gardner

Visit us at www.eHarlequin.com

Printed in U.S.A.

Naughty or Nerdy?

Elise Title

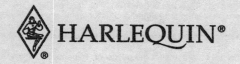

HARLEQUIN®

TORONTO • NEW YORK • LONDON
AMSTERDAM • PARIS • SYDNEY • HAMBURG
STOCKHOLM • ATHENS • TOKYO • MILAN • MADRID
PRAGUE • WARSAW • BUDAPEST • AUCKLAND

Dear Reader,

How nice to be back with a new romantic comedy. Many of you may remember my Temptation books, and how much I enjoy bringing smiles to my readers' faces. I hope *Naughty or Nerdy?* will be no exception! Having spent many winters in glorious South Beach, I couldn't imagine a more entrancing setting for this funny, rollicking romance. While I've never leapt off tall buildings as my heroine nearly does, or gotten trapped in a hotel room with a couple of hoodlums as my heroine most definitely does, I like to think I've had my fair share of adventure. As well as my fair share of reunions! Oh, the fretting, the agonizing, the dieting, the search for the *perfect dress*. The desire— no, the determination—to look as good—no, better— than I did back then. Take it from my hero, who transformed himself from ugly duckling into dashing swan, that there are great rewards to be had from all the effort!

Another reunion beckons me next fall. Will I go?

I'll let you know....

Happy reading,

Elise Title

To Jeff
and our glorious days and nights in South Beach

1

"NO WAY. FORGET IT, ROZ." Judd Turner raised his right hand like a cop attempting to stop traffic. Traffic was a lot easier to stop than Roz Morrisey. "Find someone else."

"There's no one else better, Judd. Especially for this one." The elegant forty-three-year-old head of Morrisey Associates, a top Florida private investigation agency specializing in white-collar crime, let her gaze shift from her darkly handsome, six-foot-two thirty-one-year-old operative to the college yearbook photo on her desk. "It's hard to believe, Judd. How'd you manage to go from ugly duckling to a totally hunky swan?"

"I grew up," he said sardonically.

Roz grinned. "And filled out."

"College was not a happy time for me, Roz. I was skinny, wore glasses, had braces..."

"And the world's worst haircut. It looks like you were ambushed by a lawn mower."

"I thought it made me look older, more sophisticated."

Roz tried to hide her smile.

He didn't hide his. "Go on and laugh. Even I can laugh now. But, believe me, I didn't do a lot of laughing back when I was at Florida State."

"Well, now you'll get to have the last laugh." She flicked through the pages of his yearbook until she got to the photo of the man of the hour, Kyle Warner.

Judd gave the pic a quick glance, not that he really

needed any reminders of what Warner looked like back then. Nothing geeky about Florida State's blond Adonis football star. Where Judd had stared glumly off into the distance during his photo shoot, twenty-one-year-old Kyle had beamed at the camera as if he owned the world. And why not? Judd thought. He was handsome, popular, rich, a star athlete. The young man who had everything.

Including Lucy Weston, whose yearbook picture was two photos below Kyle's. Beautiful, beguiling Lucy. Judd had met her their freshman year. Well, *met* was an exaggeration. She was in his Introduction to Psychology class. She sat two rows over, one row up from him. For the first few weeks of class, he could barely concentrate on the lectures. All of his attention was used up taking surreptitious glances at Lucy interspersed with losing himself in hot fantasies about her. And him. In bed. On a picnic blanket. On the living-room carpet. In a steamy shower. Oh, yes, the steamy-shower fantasy was really something. He had that one quite frequently.

How many times did he have to stay in his seat after the class ended? Or had to leave with a textbook strategically covering the *hard* evidence of his mental workout?

He could still remember in absolute detail every second of their first encounter. Partly because it lasted all of fifteen seconds.

"Hey, Jude, isn't it?" Lucy said.

Judd stared at the willowy, five-foot-eight auburn-haired beauty, dumbfounded. Lucy Weston was addressing him. This dream goddess knew his name. Well, almost. Was he still daydreaming?

"Uh…yeah. Right. Uh…no, not exactly. But…close. It's…Judd. But you can call me…Jude." Cool, man. Really cool! Babble like an idiot a little more. Just in case she hasn't already written you off as nerd of the year.

But she wasn't giving him the write-off. She was smil-

ing. Lucy Weston was smiling. At him. And it wasn't one of those you're-pathetic-I-feel-sorry-for-you smiles. It was more like a you're-sweet smile. He had to be dreaming.

"Did you catch the homework assignment, Judd? I must have been spacing when Gorman gave it out." Her voice had just a hint of a Southern accent. Later he learned she was from Mississippi and that she was working hard to lose the accent because she wanted to be a TV news anchorwoman.

But at the moment, he was conscious only of her alluring presence and the warm rush of blood working its way up from his neck to his cheeks. Here it was. The golden opportunity to make a connection with, literally, the girl of his dreams. His mind was racing with replies—"Sure, I've got the assignment. Why don't we go have some coffee and I'll give it to you?" Or "Hey, I've got a great idea. Let's get together tonight and do the assignment together." Or—

"So, do you have it, Judd?"

"Um...uh, not exactly. I mean...I guess I was...uh...a little distracted..." He was mesmerized by her eyes. From a distance, they looked simply brown. But close up, he saw that they were the color of bittersweet chocolate with flecks of cinnamon around the pupils. Extraordinary eyes. He could lose himself in Lucy's eyes forever....

"Judd? Are you okay?"

"Uh...well...I think..." That was the problem. He couldn't think clearly.

Before he could finish making a fool of himself, which included not only stammering but dropping his books on the floor, Kyle Warner sauntered over. While Judd lamely began retrieving his books, Kyle was making his slick moves on Lucy.

"Hey, I've got the assignment, Lucy. Let's go over to the coffee bar and get some mocha latte and you can copy

*it down. Better still, why don't you come over to my dorm
tonight and we can work on it together?''*

Until that moment, Judd hadn't even noticed that Kyle
was also in their psych class. But one look at Lucy—make
that one look at Lucy looking adoringly at Kyle—told
Judd his dream girl had noticed Kyle Warner plenty.
She'd probably missed hearing the homework assignment
for the same reason Judd had. The difference being that
she wasn't wrapping her lithe, lovely body around him in
the steamy hot shower. She was wrapped up in Kyle Warner's broad, muscular, he-man arms—

"I can't make out what Kyle inscribed to you." Roz
was squinting at the yearbook photo, her reading glasses
tucked away, as usual, in her purse.

Judd gave the photo another glance. "With your brains
and my looks, we're going to go far."

"So you two were real buddies."

He laughed harshly. "I was like his mascot, Roz. I
wrote his papers, did errands for him, let him crash at my
dorm when he was too drunk to make it back to his frat
house. We were never *friends.*" What he deliberately
omitted mentioning was that the primary reason he'd
stuck around Kyle all through college was so he could
also be around Lucy. She and Kyle had gone steady off
and on right until a few months before graduation when
Kyle unceremoniously dumped her for a hot little Parisian
number who'd transferred to Florida State that year. Lucy
had been devastated. Judd had done his best to console
her. She even let him drag her out to a few movies and
a couple of concerts, but he knew he was never more than
a pleasant diversion. He wondered if she even remembered those *dates.*

"But Kyle thought you were best buds," Roz was saying. "Guys like Kyle Warner lack the depth for real

friendships. You show up at the ten-year reunion and he'll act as though you two are long-lost blood brothers.''

"No, he won't," Judd argued. "Back in college I wasn't a threat." A faint flush colored his cheeks. "Not that I'm the best-looking guy out there, but I'm just not as dorky as I used to be——"

"Honey, you're a hottie and you damn well know it," she said, giving him a long, slow, assessing study. "And that's precisely what we're going to have to work on."

He gave his boss a wary look. "Meaning?"

"You said it yourself, Judd. Kyle won't open up to you unless he can trust you. And he can't trust you if he sees you as competition, another Alpha Man. His ego can't handle it. So, if we're going to get the goods on our college heartthrob turned investment broker turned sneaky low-life embezzler, you're going to have to go undercover.''

"Forget it, Roz. My nerd days, thankfully, are behind me.''

She wasn't listening. She rarely did when she had a bee in her bonnet. "I don't suppose you could lose thirty pounds of muscle by Saturday. Four days? No. So, we'll go the other way. A fat suit——"

"A what?"

"Okay, relax. Not a whole suit. Some padding in the right places should do it. Like your butt——"

"My what?"

"And your gut. Hey, I'm a poet——"

"I'm not doing this, Roz. I have not spent endless hours at a gym over the past ten years to walk into my college reunion looking like…like a fat geek——"

"Now, Judd. Women use padding all the time. Check out any Victoria's Secret catalog and there's pages upon pages of padded bras——"

"The women I date don't wear padded bras, Roz. And

I don't browse through women's lingerie catalogs in my spare time.''

She grinned. "I know, darling. You're too busy removing women's lingerie."

"And I happen to be very adept at it," he said. Not that it hadn't taken a lot of practice.

"Of course you are," she said distractedly, continuing to be absorbed in her critical survey of her investigator. "Do you still have your old glasses? That would be a nice touch. We could even put some white tape on the bridge so it looks like you've been wearing them since college."

"I did not switch to contact lenses only to have to start wearing glasses again—"

"And we'll have to do something about your teeth—"

"These teeth cost my folks five grand. You are not touching my pearly whites."

"I have an orthodontist friend— Well, actually we dated a few times. That was in between Fred and Barry. You remember them. Husbands number three and four."

"It's hard to keep the numbers straight," Judd said with a mix of sarcasm and affection. His much-married boss was now working on husband number six. Or was it seven? Depended on whether you counted husband of the moment, Orson Royce, once or twice—he'd also been husband number two.

"I'm sure Dr. Darren could fix you up with temporary braces."

"No one wears braces for fourteen years, Roz."

"Of course not. You can just say they didn't take the first time around. Not that anyone will ask."

"Uh-uh. I'm not wearing braces again. Not in this life. No way. Look, you want me to take this assignment, fine. But, I'm not going undercover. It's either I go as I am or—"

Ignoring his protestations, she opened her desk drawer and retrieved an electric shaver. "We'll start with the hair."

Judd backed up, his hand instinctively shooting up to his dark wavy locks. A week ago, he'd paid a top-rated Fort Lauderdale beautician seventy-five bucks for this perfect trim. "No. No way, Roz. I've got a hot date to-night—"

She flicked on the electric shaver and started toward him, her blue-gray eyes glinting. "You've got a hot date every night, Judd. One of these days you're going to have to settle on one of those goddesses and marry her."

He shivered, only half putting it on for effect. "Marry? That's not a word in my vocabulary. I like playing the field. I like my life just the way it is. Anyway, you're a fine one to talk—"

"Exactly. I've done the wedding march enough times to know how great it is with the right mate. You just haven't met your Ms. Right yet."

That was the problem, Judd thought. He had met her....

Even after all these years, Judd Turner was still carrying a torch for Lucy Weston.

"COME ON, LUCY. Of course we're going."

"No, Kyle. I can't. I'm covering the MacKenzie political scandal out in L.A., and I've got a flight booked first thing Monday morning out of Kennedy."

"That's Monday. The reunion is Saturday afternoon through Sunday brunch. And it's being held at one of those ultrachic South Beach art deco hotels on Ocean Drive. It's a happening scene down there. Totally cool. You'll love it. Everyone loves Miami Beach in the dead of winter. And you tan so beautifully, Luce."

"Not in twenty-four hours I don't. I put this pale New

York City skin of mine in the Southern sun for one afternoon and I'll look like a lobster.''

"I keep telling you to hit the tanning salon at the club." Kyle was very diligent about keeping up his bronze glow throughout the year. She suspected that he was also diligent about keeping his hair that golden shade of blond. Not that he'd admit it. Only his hairdresser knew for sure.

"I just don't think I can spare the time, Kyle."

"Sure you can. We'll fly down on Friday, check into the best suite at the Royal Palm, get a little sun, have a romantic dinner—I can ask Jim Pearsall which is the hottest restaurant on the beach—and you can leave for L.A. first thing Monday morning. Just switch your flight from Kennedy to Miami." He smiled. "See how simple it is."

Everything always seemed so simple to Kyle. Lucy knew if she said that to her fiancé he'd simply argue that she always made everything too complicated.

"I need to use the weekend to go over a ton of notes, prep myself—"

Kyle perched his muscular frame on the edge of her desk, absently pushing aside numerous piles of papers.

"Kyle, you're—"

"I know. I'm messing up all your notes."

"That, too."

He gave her a puzzled look.

"You just sat down on my jelly doughnut."

He leaped up, his hand going to the seat of his light-gray wool trousers. He came away with a squished pastry oozing red jam. He twisted his neck trying to assess the damage, but he couldn't crane it far enough. He turned his back to Lucy. "How bad is it?"

"Well…"

"Damn. These are my favorite Armanis. Now I'm going to have to scoot home and change before I go to my meeting," he grumbled.

"I've got to get back to work anyway, Kyle." She was already trying to reorganize her paper piles.

"Lucy, Lucy, Lucy." He gave it his best Cary Grant impersonation. It wasn't great, but he got the onetime screen idol's movie-star smile down just right. A smile that launched a thousand hearts. Which, she mused, was one of the problems. Not that he had been unfaithful to her during their recent courtship and subsequent engagement. Not that she knew about, anyway. But Kyle, as he oh so jokingly liked to put it, was a *babe magnet*. Women were drawn to him like bees were drawn to honey. He'd then teasingly follow up his babe magnet claim with a phrase from a popular hair commercial— "Don't hate me 'cause I'm beautiful." The first time he said it, she got irritated. Told him beauty was skin deep. And he was looking mighty thin-skinned. Kyle told her she was too serious. He was always telling her she was too serious.

She, in turn, worried that he wasn't serious enough. He was the only stockbroker she knew who rarely made it into his office before eleven, routinely took two-hour lunches, put in a couple of hours in the afternoon and was ready to party most nights. But, in the end, she always came to the conclusion that he must really be a boy wonder—another of his claims—because he certainly had all the accoutrements of wealth and success. A bright red Beemer, a wardrobe stocked with designer wear, a two-bedroom condo on Central Park West, even a getaway cottage in the Hamptons. And whenever she complained that he was spending all his money, he'd assure her that he was also stashing plenty away for rainy days.

Kyle retrieved a bunch of tissues from the box on her desk and cleaned off his pants as best he could. When he'd finished his fruitless ministrations, he refocused his attention back on his fiancée. "Come on, Luce. We've got to go to the reunion. Everyone'll be expecting us."

"I'm sure they'll all carry on somehow without us. Now, please go home and change, and let me get on with my report on breast health awareness. Marc Arden hits the air with it on the six-o'clock broadcast."

Kyle smiled crookedly. "I'm mighty aware of your lovely breasts, Lucy." He reached out to sample the merchandise, but she swatted his hand away from her gray cashmere sweater. "I'm working, Kyle."

"All work and no play makes Lucy a dull girl."

"You know I hate it when you call me a girl."

"Okay, woman. A dull woman."

"That's better," she said dryly.

He toyed with a strand of her auburn hair. "You're not really dull, Lucy. You're supremely intelligent, and sublimely beautiful. I still say you were nuts to give up a shot at being on TV. You'd be the hottest-looking anchorwoman on the air."

"Precisely. I learned real fast that being an anchorwoman had very little to do with what you had up here." She tapped her head. "It was all about appearance. Looking good. Having a hairstyle that pleased your viewers. Wearing the right clothes that showed off your figure. But if you bulked up a bit, you'd be getting not too discreet little memos from the management about the 'proper image' an anchorwoman needed to project. Well, I am not interested in image, Kyle. I'm interested in analyzing news, getting in on breaking stories, letting John Q. Public know what's going on in this world."

"Will you change your mind about coming with me to the Pearsall party tonight?"

"You know how I feel about that crowd. All they ever talk about is their latest sports cars, their interior decorators, the hot new restaurant they got special invites to, which five-star hotel is more chic—the new whatever versus the other new whatever."

"I know it can be tedious, but Jim Pearsall is one of my biggest clients, Luce."

"I know. Okay. Fine, I'll go. But I'm going to cut out early. I really have a ton of work—"

"Ooh, there's that word again—*work*."

"Kyle, if my being a workaholic bothers you so much, why do you want to marry me?" It was a question she'd asked herself on numerous occasions. Her best friend, Gina Reed, was of the opinion Lucy asked that question to avoid the one she should be asking herself. Why was *she* marrying Kyle? There was no love lost between Kyle and Gina, which was awkward since not only had Gina and she been best friends since grade school, but Gina and Kyle worked as brokers for the same brokerage firm.

Kyle gently lifted her chin, staring deep into her eyes. "You know you're everything to me, Lucy. I wish you'd set the date and make me the happiest man on this planet. Hey, I've got a great idea. Why not announce the date at the reunion?"

"No," she said so sharply she flushed scarlet. "I didn't mean it like that. It's just…I'd really rather not go to the reunion, Kyle. College wasn't all fun and games for me." Deliberately implying that it had been for him.

"You're not still holding Danielle against me, are you? She was a big mistake."

Lucy decided not to point out that while Danielle was a big mistake, there'd been other, smaller *mistakes*. Which was why she kept breaking up with him during their college years. But then, after he'd sown some of his wild oats, he'd invariably come sauntering—never crawling, that wasn't Kyle's style—back to her. And, almost out of habit, she'd take him back. Until Danielle. What had been different about the French bombshell was that Kyle had been the one to break it off with her that time. And he hadn't come sauntering back into her life for almost eight years.

He started for the door. Lucy couldn't help smiling as he tried unsuccessfully to conceal the jelly stain by tugging on his navy blazer. She quickly lost the smile when he glanced back at her.

"What about your old buddy, Judd Turner? He's probably going to show at the reunion. Bet he's dying to see you again. Probably the main reason he's going. You know he had a wicked crush on you all through school."

A mental image of Judd flashed in her mind. She saw the old-fashioned horn-rimmed glasses, the mouthful of braces, the disastrous haircuts. She also saw Judd's piercing, inquisitive blue eyes, the sexy cleft in his chin, the warmth of his smile. But it really wasn't so much his physical image she recalled, it was his intelligence and his sweetness. And she remembered, once he got over his painful shyness around her, how much she used to enjoy their intellectual bouts on everything from the pros and cons of being a vegetarian to national politics, the ozone layer, whether cats or dogs made the better pets. Both she and Judd loved taking on the role of devil's advocate.

Lucy found herself smiling again.

Kyle scowled. "Hey, Luce. Don't tell me there was something going on between the two of you."

She glanced over at her fiancé. "Me and Judd?"

Kyle gave it a moment's thought and chuckled. "Right. What was I thinking? You and Judd. Now that's one for the books all right." He was still laughing as he pulled open her office door.

He was halfway out when she called to him.

"You know what, Kyle. Maybe we should go to the reunion. I mean…how many times do you get a chance to go to your ten-year college reunion?"

He gave her a thumbs-up sign as he exited. "That's my girl."

"Woman, Kyle. That's my *woman*."

But her fiancé was out of earshot.

"GREAT," JUDD GROUSED, running his hand over his prickly flat-top as he tried to check himself out in his boss's compact mirror. "I look like a porcupine."

Roz frowned. "Yeah, but a damn cute one. You're going to need more work." She plucked a pair of black-rimmed glasses from her purse. "Here, try these."

Before he made a move to protest, she'd already popped them on over his electric blue eyes. The lenses were so thick and distorted, he felt as though he was looking through a kaleidoscope. There were a good six of Roz. Six too many. He resolutely removed the glasses and chucked them unceremoniously in her wicker trash basket.

She sighed. "Okay, maybe they're a little extreme. But they did help you look less…yummy."

"You make me sound like a candy bar."

"I wonder if we could fabricate a few pimples—"

"Roz," he said sternly.

"Okay, okay. I'm just trying—"

"Your 'trying' time is over. I'll get myself in shape for Warner. Trust me. He won't feel threatened. If anything, he'll be feeling sorry for me just like he did back when we were in college."

"Especially when he learns you ended up running a chain of Laundromats. There's nothing less sexy than a Laundromat czar."

"Why Laundromats?"

"Look, if Kyle is surreptitiously skimming money off his clients' accounts, he's going to need safe places to launder that money." Roz smiled broadly. "And I ask you, what better place to launder money than—"

"A Laundromat," he finished for her, smiling half-heartedly at her cleverness. Great, he thought. A fat nerd with a string of Laundromats. If he tried he wouldn't have been able to come up with a more unglamorous cover. Not that he cared what most of his former classmates thought of him. But there were a few— Well, there was at least one…

"My bet is, before the weekend is out, if Warner buys your cover, he'll be trying to invest in your business." She held him with her gaze, reiterating, "If he buys your cover."

"Have I ever let you down, Roz?"

"Never, Judd. Like I said before, you're the best."

He knew she believed that, but he picked up something in her voice, something that told him she was troubled. He was beginning to get the distinct feeling there was more to this assignment than met the eye. Certainly more than she was telling him. He knew his boss better than to imagine he'd get anywhere by confronting her directly. No, he'd have to play it more subtle.

"Tell me something, Roz. What makes you so sure Kyle Warner is skimming money off his firm's clients?"

She hesitated—a red-letter sign that told Judd he was getting warmer.

"An investor who works for the same brokerage house as Warner has been doing some digging. But she's worried our boy's getting suspicious and she feels she needs to pull back. Leave it for the pros to ferret out his dirty deeds."

"*She?*"

Again, a pause. He waited, feeling as if a shoe was about to be dropped.

"Gina Reed," she said finally, watching him in anticipation.

Judd stared reflectively past Roz. *Gina Reed.* Now why

did that name ring a bell? Someone from his past? Someone he once dated? And then the shoe dropped.

"Wait. Hold it. Gina Reed. I know her. Well, I know about her. She used to be the best friend of a..." he hesitated. How did he describe his past relationship with Lucy Weston? Even using the word *relationship* seemed somewhat of an exaggeration.

"The best friend of Lucy Weston." Roz was observing him closely.

"How did you know?"

She retrieved Judd's college yearbook from her desk. It was still open to the page that held Kyle Warner's photo. And Lucy's.

He eyed her accusingly. "You read what she wrote me."

"Hard not to," she said with a touch of apology—and a hint of sympathy—in her voice. She glanced down at the fine, graceful penmanship and read the inscription aloud. "To Judd. Remember, it's what's inside that counts. You'll always be someone I think of fondly. And I know you're going to do great things. Lucy."

He folded his arms across his broad chest, shifting uneasily from one foot to the other. "It's what a beautiful girl writes to a nerd she feels sorry for."

"Gina Reed says Lucy liked you a lot."

He gave Roz a dubious look.

"Really," she insisted. "Gina told me that when she was at Vassar she'd get letters from Lucy at Florida State and your name came up all the time."

Judd frowned, realizing this was one of her diversions. "And exactly why were you and Gina Reed discussing Lucy Weston's feelings about me? How did Gina even know I worked here? We've never even met."

"Derek Foster referred her. You remember. He's an investigator with the Youngman Agency in Manhattan.

The two of you worked on the Edwards case back in '99. The New York investment banker who had that fabulous duplex penthouse getaway on Fisher Island off Miami Beach. *Had* being the operative word. Thanks to you and Foster, Edwards's current address is decidedly less chic.

"Anyway, when Gina learned that Kyle Warner would be down here for his college reunion, she suspected that he might be planning to make some underworld contacts for laundering his ill-gotten gains and she thought it would be a good idea if Foster followed him. Foster came up with a better idea. You. And he didn't even know you were a classmate of Kyle's and had the perfect cover for being at the reunion. Gina couldn't believe her stroke of good luck."

So far, he had the picture. But he knew it wasn't the *whole* picture. "Where does Lucy fit into this business?"

Roz dropped the other shoe. "They're engaged, Judd."

For a moment he foolishly hoped she meant Gina and Kyle. But he knew she was talking about Kyle and Lucy. He looked away, remembering a long-ago conversation between them.

"You don't understand, Judd. I've never been serious about anyone but Kyle. He's the only man I've ever—"

"I get the picture, Lucy. But it doesn't change the fact that the guy's a bastard. Not to mention a fool. He has to be to dump you for Danielle. Hell, for any woman."

She lightly touched his cheek. The contact was like an electric charge. "You're sweet, Judd. But the thing is, I know, in the end, Kyle will come back to me. I guess it's just fate. We were meant to get married someday."

"Is it fate, Lucy? Or is it fear of the unknown?"

"I'm sorry," Roz said softly.

Judd pulled himself from his reverie, quickly waving off the apology. "Hey, don't be ridiculous. She meant nothing to me back then. And she means even less to me now.''

Roz didn't bother pretending to look convinced. ''Gina thought you might still have a thing for Lucy.'' She didn't add that she'd gotten the distinct impression that Gina Reed had been particularly pleased that Judd was the investigator for that very reason. If he did get the goods on Kyle, his lovely fiancée was going to need a friendly shoulder to cry on. According to Gina, Lucy had cried on his shoulder several times back when they were in college.

Roz had other worries, such as what would Judd do if it turned out that Lucy Weston was in cahoots with her husband-to-be? Gina insisted she wasn't involved—didn't have so much as a clue about Warner's sticky fingers— but what if Gina was wrong?

Normally Judd would have quickly tuned into the fact that Roz was troubled and he'd have wheedled those worries out of her. But he was too intent on disavowing his boss—not to mention himself—of any past, present or future emotional attachment to Lucy Weston. ''I do not have a *thing* for her,'' he said emphatically. ''I haven't seen her in ten years. I haven't had so much as a passing thought about her.''

Roz smiled crookedly. ''Fine. That's great, Judd. Because I admit I was a bit worried you might have some difficulty getting into character with Lucy Weston on the scene. You know, not wanting her to see you not looking...your best. But, obviously I was wrong.''

''Right. I mean...wrong. You were right to be wrong. You are...wrong. Right, that's it.'' He exhaled heavily. It had been a lot of years since he'd found himself tongue-tied. Ten, to be precise. ''It's this dumb buzz cut. I can't think straight with all my hair shaved off.''

''I'M GLAD YOU'RE GOING to your reunion,'' Gina told Lucy when she dropped by her Upper West Side apartment around ten that evening. Lucy had beaten her there by fifteen minutes, having bowed out of the Pearsall dinner party early with the excuse of a migraine that was not totally fabricated. She found those business gatherings thuddingly tedious. She tried to be a good sport, knowing Kyle had to suffer through these engagements because they were work-related, but he never did seem to mind them all that much even though he assured her he did. And although he'd been very solicitous when she'd begged off early with a headache, offering to leave with her, he knew, of course, she would insist he stay. And he seemed perfectly happy to remain behind.

"You're the one who really talked me into going to the reunion," Lucy admitted. "You've been on my case about attending since the invitation arrived. All this talk about how enriching it would be for me to revisit my past. I have no idea exactly what that means, but I confess I started to get curious about some of the people I knew back then. And lost touch with." She caught the faint smile on Gina's face and quickly went on. "Besides, Kyle really wants to go." She didn't add that he wanted them to announce the date for their wedding at the reunion. It would only get Gina going again about what a big mistake it would be for her to marry Kyle. She knew Gina still held out hope that she would wise up and call off the engagement. But Lucy was comfortable with him. She felt she knew him—his good points as well as his bad. With Kyle, there would be no surprises. And Lucy didn't particularly like surprises.

"You didn't tell Kyle I'd influenced your decision to go to the reunion, did you?" Gina asked.

"No," Lucy said, unaware of her friend's anxiety, partly because she had some anxiety of her own. "Every time I mention your name lately, Kyle gets his dander up.

I know you and Kyle have never been exactly bosom buddies, but it seems as though the two of you are entering an all-time low.''

Gina did not want to be the one to drop the bomb about Kyle's nefarious activities. Besides, there was still no concrete proof. Hopefully, that would change at the reunion. "I just think you can do better and he knows it," she said evasively.

"Let's not go there again," Lucy sighed, slipping off her black leather pumps and dropping onto her taupe suede couch. On the glass coffee table lay her old college yearbook. While Gina went off to the kitchen to get them a couple of glasses of white wine, she picked up the yearbook and began idly riffling through it, skimming over the faces of her classmates. She stopped when she came to the photo of Judd Turner.

She smiled. What a god-awful picture. Judd really wasn't nearly that goofy looking in person. If he ditched the glasses, finished up with the orthodontist, let his hair grow, filled out a bit, she suspected he wouldn't look half-bad. Not half-bad at all.

JUDD STARED GLUMLY at his reflection in the full-length mirror in his bedroom. He squinted through the too-strong lenses, making a mental note to have them replaced with clear glass first thing tomorrow, and thinking ruefully how tickled pink Roz would be if she knew he still did have his old glasses. One of his problems was holding on to things from his past. As well as feelings from his past.

And now here he was—Judd Turner, Laundromat mogul—looking painfully like a grown-up and unpleasantly fattened-up version of that geeky boy he'd thought he'd left behind forever.

He eyed the padding that effectively gave him a sizable paunch. Next he turned to the side, checking out the buttocks-shaped wedge of foam fitted into the seat of his pants. Where in God's name had Roz purchased such a bizarre item?

He supposed he should feel proud of himself. He'd done a top-notch job of getting into character. Even Jenna, the woman he'd taken out for dinner twice that past week, wouldn't recognize him. More to the point, the beautiful five-foot-ten brunette wouldn't so much as give him the time of day. Which, he told himself, was why he'd canceled their date for that evening. But the truth was his mind was elsewhere.

So much for those secret fantasies of meeting up with Lucy again at some point, showing her how well he'd turned out—far better than she would ever have imagined—and sweeping her off her feet.

Now he'd be lucky if she asked him to fluff and fold her laundry!

2

"JUDD TURNER. I'd know you anywhere." Kyle Warner's greeting was preceded by a resounding slap on Judd's back, which sent his glasses flying off his face. As he bent to pick them up, Kyle chuckled.

"Hey, Sport, life must be treating you good. Put on a bit of weight there."

Since Judd's derriere was in Kyle's direct line of vision at the moment, Judd was glumly assured the padding was as effective as Roz had promised. Why had he ever let her talk him into this ludicrous charade?

Judd rose, glasses askew, and turned to face his quarry. He'd have known Kyle Warner anywhere, as well. Damn him, Kyle really hadn't changed one iota. He was still as muscular, as tanned, as blond as ever. Not even a hint of a love handle in sight. Judd's only measure of relief was seeing that Kyle was standing alone in the all-white art deco lobby of the Regale, one of South Beach's hottest hotels. Maybe Lucy hadn't come down with him. Maybe she wasn't coming at all.

His hopes were quickly dashed. "Wait till Luce sees you, man." Kyle gave him an unpleasant nudge in the ribs. "She's going to be so pleased."

"I bet," Judd muttered under his breath.

"What's that?"

"Nothing. Where...is she?"

"She's out at the pool, probably hiding under a big umbrella so she won't broil. Let's go find her." Kyle, ever so stylishly dressed in perfectly tailored ecru slacks, a blue-and-tan-striped yachting jersey and Gucci loafers worn voguishly sockless, slung a meaty arm around Judd's shoulder. "Hey, Sport, is that muscle I feel here? Not bad. You know, a little more ab work and you'd be kissing that ho-ho-ho belly good bye. What do you say we hit the gym here at the hotel later this afternoon and I'll give you a few pointers. I know a few exercises for those glutes, too." Judd edged away before Kyle managed to give his padded butt a friendly pat.

"Right. Yeah. Great," he mumbled as Kyle began leading him across the crisp white-and-silver lobby that had been designed to resemble the interior of a 1920s ocean liner.

"So what have you been up to all these years, man?" Kyle smiled crookedly as he pulled open the French doors that led to the patio and, just past that, to the sumptuous palm-lined scallop-shaped pool. "Bet it's got nothing to do with the fashion industry," he added with a chuckle, giving Judd's loud Hawaiian shirt plastered with multi-colored parrots, and roomy white pleated slacks the once-over. "No offense, man, but that outfit shouts *tourist*."

Judd shrugged. "I am a tourist." He'd used a fictitious Cincinnati, Ohio, address when he'd signed up for the reunion.

"When in Rome, Sport." Kyle ushered him through the French doors. "I shiver to think of what color the tux is you brought to wear to the banquet."

"Blue," Judd muttered. "Sky-blue." Another of Roz's little touches.

Kyle rolled his eyes. "What do you say we stop at the men's shop off the lobby and get you fixed up with a nice black tux instead? Maybe Armani or Calvin Klein. Yeah, I'd say you're more of a Calvin."

"Thanks, but—"

"Hey, Sport, if it's dough you're worried about, I owe you."

"You do?"

Kyle gave his shoulder a squeeze. "Yeah, for all those assignments you did for me back in college."

"Oh, well, that's okay. I've got plenty of money. Actually, I'm doing real well these days."

Kyle glanced over at him. "You are?"

"Yeah, I'm running a pretty big operation."

Kyle was definitely looking interested. "Is that right? What kind of operation?"

Judd took a deep breath. "Laundromats."

"Huh?"

"You know…washers and dryers. Coin-op. I've got close to fifty of them. Laundromats. Nationwide."

"Fifty Laundromats." Judd could see Kyle mulling this over.

"It's pretty much a…cash operation," Judd added, trying to keep his tone casual and offhanded.

Kyle's gaze fixed on Judd's face. Judd could practically see dollar signs in the jerk's hazel eyes.

"Say, are you here by your lonesome or is there a *Mrs. Sport?*"

"I'm…unattached," Judd said.

"Man, I envy you."

Judd looked at him sharply. "You do?"

"Hey, some of the luscious babes down here strutting around in their teeny-weeny bikinis—and I'm not talking about our old classmates, but who knows. Some of the gals who were hot then might be even hotter now. We'll have to see."

Judd wondered if one of those gals Kyle was thinking about was his old flame, Danielle Brunaud. According to the guest list Roz had managed to get for him, Danielle was expected to be attending the reunion.

"Of course, that's all I can do. *Look*. But you, man—" Kyle gave him a broad wink. "Man, if I were unattached I'd be having myself a field day." Kyle chuckled again. Judd could get to seriously hate that laugh.

"There she is. My future ball and chain." Kyle pointed to a breathtaking vision in a clinging, almost transparent one-piece white bathing suit stepping out of the pool. As the svelte beauty stepped onto terra firma, she shook her head, drops of water spraying off her luxurious wet hair, forming a shimmering aura around her.

Judd felt light-headed. *Lucy*. How was it possible the most beautiful girl in the world could have become an even more exquisite woman? How was he ever going to concentrate on this assignment with her in the picture? Staring out at her from the patio, everyone else around the pool vanished. The world as he knew it no longer existed. It might never be the same again.

Another slap on his back, courtesy of Kyle Warner, brought him rudely back to reality. "She's really something, isn't she?" Kyle sounded like a man proud of a prize possession.

Judd didn't trust his voice so he merely nodded. *Oh, Lucy, if you could only see me as I really am.*

Lucy spotted them—at least she spotted Kyle—and waved brightly. Kyle waved back with his free hand, his other arm still firmly wrapped around Judd's shoulder, nudging him inexorably in her direction.

Judd didn't feel ready. He felt as nervous and tongue-tied as he had back in college when he'd first met Lucy. How could ten years of being a desirable and desired bona fide hunk suddenly evaporate? He felt as though those years had been nothing but pure fantasy. Ironically, he felt more like the fat, geeky Laundromat mogul he was pretending to be than who he truly was—a reasonably handsome, well-built, sharp-witted private eye.

"Judd Turner. Wow. What a nice surprise," Lucy said as the two men approached.

He awkwardly stuck out his right hand to shake hers, but she blithely leaned toward him and planted a light kiss on his lips. He was so taken aback that his mouth dropped open as her lips landed, the tip of his tongue inadvertently skimming her salty-tasting lips. *Elixir in a desert.*

He found himself glad he was wearing those baggy slacks.

"You look…good, Judd."

He smiled. "Liar."

"We're going to hit the weights together later on, Luce. Give the guy a few months on my regimen and you won't recognize him," Kyle bragged.

"You look terrific, Lucy," Judd said.

Kyle chuckled. "And we know you're not lying, *Sport.*"

"His name is Judd, Kyle. I hate when you call other men *Sport,*" Lucy chided.

"Hey, it's a term of endearment. I only call guys I like *Sport.*"

This earned Judd another playful smack on the back.

All the negative feelings about Kyle Warner he'd been carrying around for the past ten years took a soaring leap. If nothing else, he decided he'd be doing Lucy the biggest favor of her life, nailing the narcissistic jerk for embezzlement and getting him sent up the river for a few years. Let him try swatting his fellow inmates on the back. Better yet, on the butt.

Lucy tugged lightly on his shirt. "Do you have swim trunks on under those slacks?"

Kyle was already slipping his jersey over his head, revealing a brawny, deeply tanned chest. Inwardly, Judd was thinking he could easily hold a candle, if not two, to

him. And then it hit him that he had a problem. No way
could he maintain the geek charade in a pair of swim
trunks. No place to conceal all the padding.

"I'm…uh…allergic to…the sun," he stammered.

"I've got some great sunscreen," Lucy offered. "In
fact, I need to put some more on, myself."

As she reached into the tote bag resting on the ground
next to a sleek blue-and-white striped lounge chair, Kyle's
cell phone went off.

"Damn. I've got to take this," he muttered, after
checking the phone number that popped up on the screen.
"Be back in a few minutes."

Judd was more than a bit curious as to who was on the
other end of the line, but Kyle didn't click on until he
was several yards away from them, heading back into the
lobby.

"Will you?" Lucy asked. She was holding out a tube
of sun screen.

Judd swallowed hard. "Oh…oh, yeah." But somehow
he couldn't get himself to take hold of the tube.

"You look a bit flushed, Judd. Come sit here." She sat
first, then tapped a spot beside her farther up on the lounge
chair.

"I…uh…really should get out of…the sun."

"And leave a damsel in distress?" She reached over
her shoulder and touched her back. "You don't want me
to ask a total stranger to do this for me." She took firm
hold of his wrist and tugged him down beside her. Then
she deposited the sun screen in his lap and turned her back
to him. She undid the straps to her suit and tipped her
chin toward her chest.

Judd stared at the beautiful, flawless expanse of skin.
He couldn't help wondering if Lucy would have been so
comfortable about having him carry out these ministra-

tions on her if she saw him as a hottie, as Roz had so inimitably put it.

Lucy glanced back at him. He was still clutching the unopened tube of sunscreen in his hands. She smiled. "Still shy, huh."

"Around you...yeah," he admitted.

"I'm glad you're here, Judd. It's nice touching base with you again. I want to hear all about what you're doing now, what you've been up to, whether you've found someone special—"

Judd pulled his gaze away from her face. "Not exactly."

She placed her hand lightly over his. "Ah, but you've got someone in mind."

"It's too soon to tell."

Her hand rose to his chin and, with her index finger, she tightly traced the indentation there. "I always found that cleft very sexy. I bet this woman you're keen on does, too."

Judd grabbed hold of Lucy's hand and pressed it to his chest. He could see from her expression she was surprised by his bold move. He immediately released her and busied himself unscrewing the cap on the tube of lotion. It bore the fragrant scent of bougainvillea.

He tried to pretend it would be like slathering oil on an uncooked turkey.

But he knew the attempt at pretense was futile.

Even the thought of touching Lucy was heaven and hell combined.

"TURN AROUND."

Lucy wasn't particularly affronted by Judd's brusque tone, but she was surprised. Back in school he had always been so cautious around her, so reserved. But even then she'd sensed a hidden fire in him. And now she caught a glint of that fire in those brilliant blue eyes. She felt tempted to remove his corny, old-fashioned glasses and get a clearer look. Instead, she turned her back to him as ordered.

After a few moments' wait—moments oddly filled with an inexplicable sense of expectation—she felt a long, cold squirt of sunscreen on her back. It sent an icy tingle down her spine.

And then she felt Judd's cool fingers on her warm skin. Immediately, a second tingle followed the trail of the first. Only this one wasn't icy. It was hot. Sizzling.

This is crazy, Lucy thought. Why was she having this reaction to the touch of a man who, appearance-wise, wasn't even in the same ballpark as Kyle? Lucy wasn't blind. She hadn't failed to notice that Judd had put on some weight in all the wrong places. She certainly hadn't missed the disastrous outfit he was wearing. And that buzz cut. Why hadn't someone taken Judd Turner in hand before now?

Lucy lost momentary track of her thoughts as Judd's fingers moved down her back, the deep, low cut of the bathing suit offering no hindrance to his ministrations. Her eyelids fluttered closed. Judd's touch was firm yet gentle. He took his time, as though he was getting something out of the task.

Lucy's eyes shot open. *Was he?*

She spun around to face him so abruptly that Judd's palms, seconds ago on her back, ended up settled unwittingly on her breasts. His hands flew off her.

It was a toss-up who was more embarrassed.

And thanks to the greasy sunscreen congealing on Judd's hands, the telltale sign of that unintentional contact was emblazoned on the bra section of Lucy's white bathing suit.

She wasn't aware of the grease stains until she saw Judd's eyes fix on her breasts.

"Oh," she murmured, following his gaze.

"Lucy...I'm...I didn't mean..."

Lucy was smiling. "Well, you've got me covered now."

Judd glanced at her face. A smile slowly spread across his lips, too.

Lucy's smile broadened. "You're still wearing braces."

Judd clamped his lips shut.

"Don't, Judd. I didn't mean to make you feel self-conscious. They don't detract from your appearance. Honestly."

He gave her a rueful look.

"I didn't mean it that way." Her eyes locked with his. Funny, but she really meant what she'd said. She didn't exactly understand *why* she meant it, but for it all—the outlandish clothes, the dreadful haircut, the glasses, even the braces—there was something about Judd Turner that drew her to him. A fierce impulse to remove his glasses overtook her.

Judd looked startled when she followed her impulse, but his gaze remained fixed on hers even after the glasses came off. Lucy stared into his penetrating blue eyes, knowing somewhere in the back of her mind that this was ridiculous. She was in love with another man, she was about to be married, or would be as soon as she set the date, but she couldn't pull her gaze away from Judd's eyes.

Judd found himself equally lost in Lucy's eyes. He'd almost believed he'd made up that unique color. Surely, no actual person had shimmering flecks of cinnamon in pools of deep dark chocolate. But it was true.

"Hey, I see you two are getting better acquainted." Kyle's voice startled them both.

"I'm hot. Need a dip— "Lucy flung her arms across her chest as she jumped up from the lounge chair.

The chair, and Judd, went flying backward, Lucy's weight no longer serving to balance it.

"Oh," she cried, as the back of Judd's head made thudding contact with the polished pink-terrazzo deck.

JUDD WAS SEEING six Lucys. It was better than six Rozes. Much better.

"Oh, Judd, I'm so sorry. Please, say something," all six Lucys pleaded.

"My...glasses..."

"I've got them right here. Do you want them?" she asked anxiously.

He started to shake his head, but it sent a shooting pain across the back of his skull. Besides, he thought he was wearing the glasses. The thick-lensed ones that Roz had tried to get him to wear. Then he remembered. He'd tossed them out.

So why was he seeing six—?

Wait. Oh, no. Now he was also seeing a half-dozen Kyles swimming around behind all the Lucys. Damn.

"You hit your head, Judd. It was all my fault," Lucy said. She was racked with guilt. And not only because she'd been the cause of Judd's possible concussion. It was also all the emotions that had coursed through her just prior to his fall.

Judd smiled drunkenly. "It was worth it."

Lucy felt her face get hot. She was sure she was blushing. Luckily she could blame it on the sun.

Kyle scowled. "The man's hallucinating. Maybe we should get him to the hospital."

"No, he'll be okay. We just want to keep him awake

for the next few hours. Why don't we get him up to his room?''

Judd's vision was starting to clear. He tried to focus on the man who was talking. There was something vaguely familiar about the voice. "Do I...know you?"

"Gary Burke. We were lab partners in organic chemistry, junior year.''

"Oh...yeah. Yeah...right. I remember. You were going to be a doctor.''

Gary, a slight man with thinning brown hair, smiled. "And now I am a doctor." There was a brief pause. "A gynecologist actually.''

Kyle chuckled. "Uh oh, Houston, we have a problem.''

Judd gritted his teeth, the sound of Kyle's laugh going through him like chalk screeching across a blackboard.

"Does it hurt very much, Judd?" Lucy asked anxiously as her hand lightly stroked his forehead.

"Not now," Judd murmured.

"Okay, Kyle, let's get him on his feet," Gary ordered. "Nice and easy does it.''

As the two men lifted him, Judd's gaze stayed fixed on Lucy. Pity there was only one of her now.

And that one didn't belong to him.

"CAN I GET YOU SOME WATER?''

"I'm okay, Lucy. Really," Judd assured her.

She smiled a bit nervously as she looked around the deco-meets-Dali hotel room. The spare, all-white twentieth-century moderne furnishings sat in sharp contrast to the wild pink-and-gray floral murals painted on the walls as well as the floor. An immense lime green planter fitted with a lush miniature palm tree rested beside the French doors, which opened onto a narrow balcony overlooking the aqua sea. The king-size bed, covered with a vintage pink chenille spread faced the ocean view. Closer to the door were two pink-and-lime-green-striped club chairs separated by a whimsical metal table in the shape of a butterfly.

Judd sat on the edge of the bed watching Lucy, who was standing in the center of the room surveying the space. She was wearing a loose-fitting white cotton beach dress, but the material was transparent enough for him to make out the bathing suit beneath. And the divine shape of her lusciously curved body.

Concussion or not, Judd felt an alarming rush of desire.

"You really don't have to stay here with me, Lucy."

"Oh, no, I want to." She practically jumped on his words. Then quickly realizing he might misinterpret her meaning—at least she told herself it would be a misinterpretation—she hastened to add, "It's my fault it happened."

Judd began to rise.

Lucy looked nervous. "You...shouldn't..."

He got to his feet and started toward her.

"Gary said...you should...take it easy, Judd."

"That's not so easy to do, Lucy."

As he got within a few feet of her, he started to sway. She rushed to his side. "Here, let me help you. Put your arm around me. Lean your weight—" She half steered, half dragged him over to one of the club chairs.

He sank into the seat, still holding onto her. Lucy found herself toppling on to Judd's lap.

"Oh," she gasped. It wasn't only her position that shook her, it was her awareness of the very solid evidence of Judd's arousal.

She sprang to her feet. "Water. I...definitely think...we need some...water." There was a tray with a bottle of mineral water and two wineglasses on the low-slung white bureau. She snatched up the bottle, unscrewed it and hurriedly filled both glasses. When she turned back to Judd, she saw that he had removed his glasses and his eyes were closed.

"No. No," she cried, grabbing one of the full glasses before she rushed over to him. Gary Burke, their former classmate turned doctor, had been adamant about her not letting Judd fall asleep.

Judd's eyes were just starting to flutter open when he felt the bubbly cold water hit him square in the face.

"Oh…sorry," Lucy stammered as she watched the water stream down his chin onto his shirt.

He blinked the water from his eyes, looked up at her and grinned. "Thanks. I needed that."

It took a few seconds, but then Lucy grinned, too.

Next thing Judd knew, she was kneeling beside him, her hands reaching out to the buttons of his Hawaiian shirt.

His hand clutched hers. "What are you doing?"

"Your shirt's all wet."

"No…it's…fine," he said, still clutching her hands. No way could he let her undress him. She'd discover his padded belly. And he'd go from geek to weirdo in her eyes in no time flat.

"Okay, Judd. Relax. I don't want to make you feel uncomfortable," Lucy soothed.

Good luck there.

"It's just…the wetness feels…good. It's…uh… keeping me…alert." He let go of her hands, but they remained on his damp shirt.

Lucy smiled. "Well, we definitely need to have you alert. So what do you suggest we do to…keep you that way for the next few hours?"

She was so close to him, Judd could feel her warm, slightly mint-scented breath on his face. And he noticed, with pleasure, the return of that sexy Mississippi drawl in her voice. During the past ten years, Judd had made many conquests—each woman lovely and desirable in her own inimitable way. But never—never—had Judd found anyone as lovely or as desirable as the woman filling his gaze, his loins and his heart at that moment. There was no getting around it, no denying it, no escaping it. He was in love with Lucy Weston.

And if his mission down here was accomplished, he'd very likely put the kibosh on Kyle's and Lucy's wedding plans. She'd be free.

Free to hate him forever.

"Cards."

Lucy gave Judd a puzzled look. "What?"

"Cards. Let's play cards. To keep me alert. You know...like gin rummy."

"Oh," Lucy said. "Great. Cards. What a...good idea. Just what...I had in mind."

3

"LAUNDROMATS. Hmm. That sounds…"

Judd smiled at Lucy's hesitation. "Dull."

"No. No, really." A slow smile curved her luscious lips. "I guess I just imagined you'd be doing something more…" Again she was at a loss for the right word.

This time, so was Judd.

"Daring," she finally finished, her eyes lighting with satisfaction at her selection.

"Daring? Me?" This assessment truly amazed him. How could Lucy have seen so deeply—and so accurately—beneath his surface nerdiness all those years back?

"Remember that James Bond retrospective you took me to over at the Alliance? You were so charged by the action and excitement," Lucy recalled. She also remembered that those movie dates had occurred shortly after her split with Kyle. Judd had been so solicitous, so caring, so surprisingly…appealing.

Judd looked uneasy. She was right. He always had been charged by action and excitement. Even more so after he met Lucy. But he certainly didn't think it showed back in his college days. What would it be like if Lucy knew how close she was to the mark? There was a part of him that wanted to blurt it out. That wanted to blow his cover. He even had the fleeting fantasy that they could work this case together. Now that was a fantasy, all right. *Lucy, how about you and I join forces to nail this slimy, good-for-nothing embezzler?*

An embezzler who just happened to be Lucy's fiancé.

Different, but no less disturbing thoughts were ricocheting through Lucy's mind. There was something off-kilter about Judd. Or maybe it was that she was feeling off-kilter around him. But why should that be? It was this…this *aura* that seemed to be emanating from him. Filling the room. Making it hard for her to breathe normally. She sensed…danger. But that was ridiculous. Judd owned a slew of Laundromats, for heaven's sake. What could be more benign than that?

And just look at him. That same old ridiculous haircut. And those glasses. If not the same ones from college, a carbon copy. And braces. Braces?

Lucy's antennae shot up. Surely, someone who'd worn braces from the age of eighteen to twenty-one would not end up with teeth that would *disalign* themselves ten years later to such an extent that braces would be required again. Even his weight gain was perplexing. In fact, it was odd. For instance, why would a man with a distinct potbelly have such well-defined pecs? She'd spotted Judd's muscular chest when she'd started to unbutton his shirt. Muscles like that didn't come from…from watching spin cycles.

The silence between them was both awkward and long.

"Maybe I should run down to the gift shop and see if they have a deck of cards," Lucy said finally.

Before Judd could respond, the phone rang.

"I bet that's Kyle checking to see how you're doing," she said, picking up.

Before she got a chance to say hello, a familiar voice greeted her. Well, actually the caller thought she was greeting Judd.

Lucy looked completely perplexed. "Gina? Gina, is that you?"

Judd leaped to his feet and grabbed for the phone. "Oh, oh that must be Roz."

Lucy wouldn't release her grip on the receiver. "No, it's my friend, Gina. I'd recognize her voice—"

"No, no, it's Roz," he shouted, praying that Gina would hear him. There'd be no explaining why Lucy's best friend would be calling a man she'd supposedly never even met.

Lucy was not convinced. She snatched the receiver away from Judd's grasp and put it back to her ear. "Gina?"

"Who?" Gina's husky response was accompanied by a cough.

"Gina, I know that's you," Lucy insisted.

More coughing on the other end of the line. "This is Roz."

Judd hovered anxiously over Lucy. She looked at him. "She says it's Roz."

"See, I told you." Again he reached for the phone. This time, Lucy reluctantly handed it over.

"Roz," Judd greeted his caller overenthusiastically. "How great to hear from you. How are you...darling?"

"What is Lucy doing in your room, Judd?" Gina asked. She didn't sound so much alarmed as surprised. *Pleasantly* surprised. In an earlier conversation with Judd, Gina had made it very clear that her best friend deserved someone a lot better than Kyle Warner. As she'd said, "Even if he wasn't a crook, he's a no-good womanizer and a first-class creep." Gina had been trying to convince Lucy of this all through college, and even more vociferously since Kyle had reappeared in Lucy's life over a year ago.

Judd, still rattled, put his hand over the phone, eyeing Lucy awkwardly. "She's the...uh...jealous type, Roz is."

"Judd, are you there?" Gina was still keeping her voice pitched low.

"Yes, Roz, I'm here, darling. I just…it's the maid. The maid picked up the phone. My room wasn't quite ready…"

Lucy arched a brow. Judd pressed the receiver against his chest. "Why don't you dash down to the gift shop for those cards?"

It took a few seconds for Lucy to get the hint that he wanted to talk privately to his girlfriend. "Oh, oh right. Sure." She pursed her lips. Something definitely didn't feel right here. Or was it that she was feeling a flurry of jealousy?

No. Ridiculous.

Judd's back was to her as he practically cooed into the phone. "Well, of course I miss you, too, darling."

Gina laughed. "Aren't you putting it on a bit thick there, Judd?"

He glanced over his shoulder. Lucy was taking her time exiting. He gave her a little wave to hurry her on her way.

"Listen, Judd," Gina was saying, "Two things. One, Kyle's taken his laptop computer down there. I'm willing to bet he's got a locked file with info on his covert financial dealings."

Judd kept an eye on Lucy as she took her time opening his hotel room door.

"I'll be back with those extra towels, sir," Lucy drawled.

Judd smiled crookedly at her.

"Two," Gina continued, "I found a note in his trash. It said, Tango Room, 11 p.m., Rico Morales. Tomorrow's date. I did some checking and it seems this Morales has his fingers in a lot of questionable pies down there in Miami. And he makes a lot of trips each month down to the Cayman Islands."

"I know all about Morales. Believe me, he's into those questionable pies right up to his elbows. He was out of commission for a couple of years, but he's back on the scene again, big time."

"And Kyle's hooking up with him. Well," Gina said snidely, "It takes slime to know slime."

"Tango Room. That's the bar here at the hotel. No problem for Kyle to slip out of the reunion banquet for a quick meet." Judd was quickly jotting down the info on a sheet of hotel notepaper.

"And no problem for you to slip out after him."

"Right," Judd said. "But getting at his laptop might not be so easy. Not to mention figuring out how to break into one of his files. I'd need to know his password."

There was a brief pause. "Maybe Lucy knows. I mean the password. Not that she has any idea what Kyle is up to," she hastened to add.

This time, Judd paused. He didn't want to ask the question, but he had to. "Are you sure about that, Gina?"

"You know Lucy, Judd. Do you imagine for one instant that she would be involved in anything crooked?"

"No," he said. "No, of course not." But his feeling of confidence was less emphatic than his tone. After all, how well did he know Lucy? She might still look and even act much the same as she had back in their college days, but ten years had passed. As he knew firsthand, a lot could happen in ten years.

"You still didn't tell me what she was doing in your room." Gina's tone was lightly teasing.

"She knocked me out."

"Huh?"

"I'm fine now." He rubbed the tender bump on the back of his head.

"You're still nuts about her, aren't you?"

"Come on, Gi—"

The hotel door opened just as he started to say Gina's name. Lucy was back. "No cards," she whispered. And then in a loud voice, "I have your towels, Mr. Turner. Should I run your bath, Mr. Turner, sir?" An impish smile lit up her beautiful face.

Color flooded Judd's face. "Gee, darling, the maid just came back. With towels. I…uh…"

Gina laughed. "Hmm. Sounds like you and Lucy are getting along swimmingly. Hope that tub is big enough for two. Good luck, *darling*." The phone clicked off.

"You, too, darling," he said to the dial tone.

Lucy folded her arms across her chest. "So."

He had trouble meeting her gaze. "So."

"So, you and Roz are…" Lucy looked to him to finish her sentence.

"We're…uh…involved."

"So I gathered. Is it…serious?"

Judd shook his head. "No. I mean…well, not in so many words."

"*Serious* is just one word."

"Right. Well, Roz and I are…kind of finding our way."

"What's she like?"

"Roz?"

And then a light dawned. Lucy gave him a piercing look. "Judd, is Roz married?"

"Yes. I mean, no. Roz? No. No, she's not married."

"Then why are you so nervous? What's going on?"

"Nothing. Really. Nothing."

A shadow of hurt crossed her face. "Fine. It's certainly none of my business."

"That's not true."

"It is my business?"

"No. I mean…" Judd sighed heavily. What did he mean? Good question. "You know what? That bath sounds like a really good idea. Not that…I want you to run it for me. I can do that myself. In fact, I really feel fine now, Lucy.''

"You don't sound like you're fine.''

"Oh, well, it's just that phone call from…from Roz…kind of threw me. I wasn't expecting her to call.''

"Why not?''

He was digging a deeper and deeper hole for himself. "We had…a fight before I left. Not really a fight. A misunderstanding. Relationships. You know…they can be so….complicated.''

"Are you in love with Roz, Judd?''

"No," he said reflexively. "I mean…it's too soon. We haven't really known each other….that long.''

She nodded. "Relationships are complicated.''

Now Judd's antennae shot up. "You and Kyle?''

"No. Well, yes. But, we're doing…fine.''

"Fine?''

"Great.''

"Great?''

"Don't be a parrot," she said sharply.

"Sorry.''

She sighed. "No, I'm sorry. I shouldn't have snapped at you.'' She hesitated. "I guess sometimes it isn't so great between me and Kyle. But, no relationship is great all the time, right?''

Judd met her gaze. "Do you love Kyle?''

A flush crept into her cheeks. She looked away. "What a question. We're…engaged, Judd. We're planning…to get married. At…at some point. Really, that's a ridiculous question.'' She rubbed her palms together vigorously. "You know what. I'm going to run you that bath.''

He watched her dash off to the bathroom. It did not pass his notice that she never did answer his question.

"REALLY, LUCY, you don't have to wait out there. I'm fine," Judd called from the bathroom.

But she was determined to stay put. What if he passed out in the tub? What if he drowned in there? "You sure you don't want me to wash your back?"

"What? Can't hear you."

She smiled. "Nothing." She walked over to the sliding glass door, opened and stepped out onto the balcony that overlooked a wide, smooth sand beach dotted with lounge chairs and colorful violet-and-teal shade umbrellas courtesy of the hotel. Beyond the sand, stretched the shimmering aquamarine Atlantic Ocean. Sailboats, yachts and a couple of glistening cruise ships bobbed on the horizon.

It was just past one in the afternoon and there were dozens of bathers and sun worshippers on the beach. Lucy skimmed the crowd, trying to spot old friends for the reunion.

After a few moments, she did find a familiar face. Only it wasn't an old friend. And it wasn't only the face that she noticed. Danielle Brunaud was stretched out on a lounge chair—topless. Not that the French vamp's skimpy bikini bottom covered much of the rest of her.

Lucy glowered down at her old rival. Damn, the woman still looked fantastic. And was still flaunting it. A glint of jealousy was quickly followed by one of anger. Not so much at Danielle as at Kyle. If he'd really loved her back in college as he'd proclaimed so often and so vociferously, he wouldn't have been so easily seduced by another woman. Even if that other woman was a Parisian femme fatale.

Her anger at Kyle escalated sharply when she spotted him down at the beach making his way over to the near-naked, nubile beauty. Lucy couldn't see his face, but she was sure his eyes were popping as he took in his old girlfriend's considerable assets.

Danielle made no attempt to cover up as Kyle approached.

"Hey, Lucy. Everything okay out there?" Judd called from the bathroom.

Lucy scowled. "Everything's just *peachy*," she shouted back from the terrace.

The phone rang again.

"I'll get it," she said, storming back into the room. "Don't worry. If it's Roz, I'll pretend I'm the maid again."

"No, that's okay. Just let it go," Judd said nervously, worried that it was Gina calling back.

Lucy picked up the receiver just as Judd, dripping wet and clad in a terry robe, yanked open the bathroom door.

"Mr. Turner's room," she drawled into the mouthpiece, winking at him.

"Is Mr. Turner there?" the caller inquired.

Lucy's eyebrow arched. Another woman. This one had a hint of a Southern lilt in her voice.

"Tell him it's Roz," the new caller said brusquely.

Lucy's brow creased. "Excuse me?"

"Who's this?"

"The...maid."

"Well, I'm Roz Morrisey and I need to speak to Judd pronto. So, is he there?"

Lucy shot a glance over at Judd. What was going on here? "No," she lied.

"Well, scribble a note for him. Say, call Roz ASAP. Got that?"

"Oh, yes, right. I'll do that," she drawled. When Roz hung up, Lucy smiled in Judd's direction. "But I really don't think Mr. Turner is interested in purchasing a timeshare in Florida." She saw the shimmer of relief on his face as she hung up. She, however, was feeling anything but relief!

She eyed Judd closely. There was definitely something off here. What was the likelihood that a man would, in the matter of thirty minutes, get two calls from two women with the same name? A name like *Roz*, no less?

"YOU'RE LOOKING at me funny," Judd said uneasily, acutely aware that, beneath his robe, he was minus his padding. Thankfully, Lucy didn't seem to notice.

"You're…uh…still covered with…with suds. I guess I put too much of that bubble bath stuff in the water."

He nodded. "Right. Well, I'll go and rinse off under the shower."

"Right. Good idea."

He started to turn back to the bathroom but then glanced over his shoulder at her. "Where exactly was that time-share?"

"What?"

"The time-share? That phone call?"

Her mouth fell open. "Oh. Oh, right. I think she…I mean he…it was a man. A salesman. Very pushy. Obnoxious, really. Don't you hate telemarketers calling at all hours of the day and night trying to sell you magazine subscriptions, new phone services, a…a whole cow—?"

"A whole cow?"

"Cut up, of course. Steaks, chopped meat, rib…rib roasts."

He cocked his head. "Time-shares?"

She looked puzzled. "In cows?"

He smiled.

"Oh, right." And then, not missing a beat, she said, "Boca."

"Boca?"

"Boca Raton. That time-share the…the guy was selling."

"Hmm," Judd said.

"Isn't that a ridiculous name? Do you know what Boca Raton means? It means *mouth of the rat.* Can you believe that?"

"I certainly would not like to buy a time-share in a rat's mouth," he said, smiling.

"Of course, I have nothing against Boca Raton. I hear it's…very nice there. You can't always tell a book by its cover. Or…or name, in this case."

Judd could see that she was clearly rattled. This caused a flurry of questions to pop into his mind. Had she somehow got on to him? Was she, despite Gina's fervent protestations, involved in Kyle's criminal activities and feeling uneasy because of a guilty conscience? Or was she simply nervous because she was alone in a hotel bedroom with a man who was still wildly attracted to her? He hoped it was the latter. He hoped she felt some of that attraction, as well.

But he knew he had no business hoping any such thing.

"I'd better go…rinse off these suds," he muttered, aware that all the bubbles had burst by now. How apropos!

He went back into the bathroom and ran a very cold shower.

LUCY WALKED BACK OUT to the terrace. Danielle Brunaud was no longer on the beach. Neither was Kyle. She decided to call up to the hotel room she and Kyle were sharing. If Danielle answered…

Well, if Danielle answered, that was it. The final straw. The end.

She picked up the phone and punched in 1620. As she listened to the rings, she spotted a scribbled-on piece of paper on the art-deco mahogany desk. Rico Morales. Tango Room. Saturday, 11 p.m.

Who was Rico Morales?

After four rings to her hotel room, an automated message clicked on. Lucy hung up. Either no one was in the room, or the occupants were too busy—

Lucy shook the image from her mind. Even if Kyle was tempted to cheat on her, he wasn't dumb enough to take Danielle up to the room he was occupying with his fiancée. He'd simply go to Danielle's room.

No. No, Kyle wouldn't do that. Lucy resolutely told herself she had absolutely no call to feel jealous. He loved her. He'd asked her to marry him. He wanted to spend the rest of his life with her. If she couldn't trust him...

Lucy tapped her fingers nervously on the desk. She had to stop letting her imagination run away with itself.

Her gaze fell once again on the piece of paper by the phone. She stared at the name written on it. *Rico Morales.* Hadn't she come across that name sometime in the past? A news story she'd covered? She thought of calling her station and getting her secretary to check the name out, but decided to first do a bit of investigating on her own. Why she felt compelled to do any checking at all was the question. The answer was that for some reason she couldn't quite fathom, she felt there was a clue here. A clue to what? She supposed it was to the mystery that lay beneath the altogether too-mundane-looking Judd Turner.

She cracked open the bathroom door. "Judd, I'm just going to run down to the gift shop for—" Damn, it couldn't be a deck of cards. What could she suddenly need at the gift shop? "For some *female* stuff." So what if her period wasn't due for another two and a half weeks!

LUCY WAS RIFFLING THROUGH the phone book in the lobby. She could have gone up to her hotel room since there was one there, as well, but, despite her efforts, she was still fighting some niggling fears about finding Kyle *entertaining* Danielle up there. She chose to leave it to fate. Judd's room was on the fourteenth floor, hers and Kyle's on the sixteenth. When she left Judd's room, she decided she would take the first elevator that opened, and that would determine whether she went up to her floor or down to the lobby. The first elevator was going up, but it was awfully crowded. There was simply no room for her to squeeze in. So she took the second elevator, it was headed down.

Lucy closed the phone book. There was no Rico Morales listed. Maybe he had an unlisted number. Or maybe he was from out of town.

She scowled. What did it matter who Rico Morales was? What difference did it make to her? Why was she so curious about Judd—a man she hadn't seen for ten years?

But it wasn't merely curiosity. And Judd wasn't just any man. He was an old friend. A dear friend. Someone she'd cared about. Still cared about. What if he was in some kind of trouble? He certainly seemed edgy. And there was that mystery of the two Rozes. When Judd had talked to Roz number one, he hadn't sounded like a man involved in a romantic liaison. Even one that was *complicated*. And then there was Roz number two. Lucy felt a sharp pang of guilt. She'd lied about that call. Which meant Judd didn't know he was supposed to call Roz number two back ASAP. And now she was probably angry as all get-out. Angry enough to—

What?

Lucy stared down at the phone book again. What was Roz number two's last name? Moriarity? Morrison? Mor...Mor...Morrisey. Yes, that was it. Roz Morrisey.

Once again Lucy began flipping through the pages of the phone book. There was no Roz Morrisey listed, but there was a listing for a Morrisey Associates on Brickell

Boulevard in Miami. Lucy hesitated, then dropped in some coins and punched in the number.

"Morrisey Associates. Gail speaking."

"Oh, I'm not sure I have the right number. I'm looking for a Roz Morrisey."

"She's at our main offices in Fort Lauderdale." Lucy got the number and called it, only to find that Roz Morrisey was out for the afternoon.

"Can I have her call you back?"

"Well...no. That's...okay. I'll try again later."

"Would you like to speak to one of our investigators?"

"Investigators?"

"Yes, if you're looking to employ a private investigator, I should tell you Ms. Morrisey only handles a very few select cases."

"Oh. Oh, I...see."

"To be frank," the secretary said pleasantly, "Ms. Morrisey's plate is very full right now. But we have a number of top investigators—"

"No. No, I don't think I'll need her services after all," Lucy said. But obviously Judd did. Why did Judd Turner need the services of the head honcho of a private investigation firm? Down here in Florida no less. Was he in some kind of trouble?

Her nose for news told her that if she found out more about Rico Morales it might provide some answers to her questions about Judd.

Glancing across the lobby, Lucy's gaze fell on the neon sign over a wide double door. Tango Room.

Tango Room! The place Judd had scribbled on that piece of paper.

A long mahogany bar ran down one side of the hotel's cocktail lounge. Tango music oozed from the pricey Bose speakers placed strategically around the room. Large, slowly rotating fans hung from the ceiling and the floor-to-ceiling windows facing the ocean were fitted with louvered doors so that the afternoon sun slipped through the slats, casting stripes of light in the dimness. There was no one in the lounge save for the bartender, a slender young man with spiky bleached-blond hair and pirate-like hoops in his ears.

"Not open until five, miss."

"Oh, that's okay. I didn't want a drink. Just...checking the place out."

"Be my guest," he said amiably.

Lucy strolled aimlessly around the lounge that was reminiscent of those Havana, Cuba, clubs she'd seen in fifties films.

The bartender was dusting off a glass shelf lined with fine single-malt Scotches.

"Have you worked here long?" Lucy asked casually as she sauntered up to the bar.

"A couple of years. I did a stint at a Hyatt in downtown Miami before coming here to South Beach. This is definitely a more happening scene."

"I bet. I...um...guess you know a lot of the regulars who drop in here."

He smiled. "You can't imagine how much better the tips are when you greet a customer by name and have his or her drink of choice poured before they even sit down."

"My name is Lucy, by the way." She extended her hand across the bar.

"Derek," he said, shaking her hand. "So what's your favorite drink, Lucy?"

"Iced tea."

He laughed. "Teetotaler, huh?"

"No, I imbibe on occasion. Even got drunk as a skunk once. Made an absolute fool of myself." Her mind flashed back to that infamous night of debauchery—the debauchery consisting of a bottle of tequila, a huge wad of tissues and a comforting shoulder to cry on. The tequila was Kyle's. He'd left it behind when he dumped her and moved in with Danielle. The tissues were Kleenex brand, if she remembered correctly. One thing she was sure of— the shoulder had belonged to Judd Turner. She'd cried her eyes out on that shoulder. And when she was finally drained dry she'd— Well, she couldn't really remember too much after that.

Liar. She remembered at some point before she'd used up that box of tissues that she and Judd had kissed. It had started out as a peck, the kind of kiss someone would give a grieving friend. But it went on a bit longer than your typical peck. And it somehow transformed into what could only be described as a flat-out kiss. First it was merely lips pressed against lips. But then lips parted, tongues met and explored, arms found their way around necks, breasts crushed against chest—

She also remembered Judd had been the first to pull away. If he hadn't, Lucy wasn't the least bit sure she would have.

The next day, Judd flooded her with abject apologies. She dealt with the folly by pretending she didn't remember that kiss. She'd sometimes wondered afterward what would have transpired between them if she hadn't lied. Would it have been the start of a romantic relationship? Or would Judd simply have felt he was merely filling in for the man she really wanted?

"The only thing I don't drink anymore is tequila. You could say I have an allergy to it," Lucy said.

The bartender gave her a knowing look. "Like I said, we don't officially open until five, but I could get you an iced tea."

"That's really sweet of you, Derek."

He winked. "That's me. Sweet as they come."

She watched as he removed a jug of iced tea from a

cooler beneath the bar, then reached overhead for a tall glass.

"I was wondering, Derek, if an old friend of mine happens to be a regular here. We haven't seen each other for a while. Actually, I'm meeting him here tomorrow night. At eleven. I'm a little nervous. We used to have…well, a thing, if you know what I mean. But it was a long time ago."

"So what's this old beau's name?"

"Rico."

Derek abruptly stopped pouring the iced tea into the glass. He shot her a wary look. "Rico?"

"Yes. Rico Morales."

Even in the dim light of the bar, Lucy could see the color drain from the bartender's face. He set the jug and glass down. "You and Mr. Morales used to be an item?"

"Yes. Well, like I said, it was a long time ago."

She could see his Adam's apple bob as he swallowed. "Are you okay, Derek?"

"Yeah, yeah, I'm fine. It's just…you don't seem the type. I mean…Mr. Morales usually goes for…" He cleared his throat instead of finishing the sentence. "How long has it been since you've seen him?"

"Ages. He was…just getting started back then."

"So you…uh…know what he's into." He was eyeing her carefully.

"Well, I'm sure he's expanded his…operations…since then." Lucy remembered now why the name Rico Morales had rung a bell. She hadn't covered the story, but she'd heard about him quite some time back. Morales was a Miami loan shark who was linked to a mob figure in New York who was under investigation for—

Money laundering.

And Judd, *the Laundromat king,* was meeting with Morales tomorrow night.

Her heart sank. Judd was mixed up with the mob. What better cover for money laundering than a widespread cash-and-carry operation?

"Of course," Derek was saying, "that two-year stint with the Feds slowed him up some. But since he's been out, he's made up for lost time." He picked up the jug and filled the rest of the glass. "You sure I can't give that iced tea a little extra punch for you? I mean, any friend of Mr. Morales's gets special treatment here at the Tango Room. Hell, a special friend of Mr. Morales's gets special treatment anywhere in Miami."

"So...when did he get out? Mr. Morales? Rico?" Maybe he was on parole and Lucy could get Judd to turn state's evidence.

"You knew he was in the joint, right?" Derek looked a little uneasy now.

"Oh...oh sure, I knew. We...corresponded. But then we...we lost touch. You know how it is when...when someone's...in the joint."

Not that she knew what it was like. But she might be finding out since, if she didn't do something about it, Judd might very well end up in residence there.

JUDD STEPPED OUT OF the bathroom, dressed once more in his ludicrous Hawaiian getup, the even more ludicrous padding again in place.

"Lucy?"

The hotel bedroom was empty. He felt a mixture of relief and disappointment that she hadn't yet returned from the gift shop. He rubbed his jaw, thinking about his next move. Time was slipping away and he'd let his mind—not to mention his body—get decidedly off the track.

Briskly he crossed the room and was about to pick up the phone when he spotted Lucy's tote bag. He hesitated for the briefest of moments, then dodged over to the door and threw the chain so that he wouldn't be caught in the act if she returned before his task was completed. Then, carrying the tote bag over to his bed, he dumped out the contents.

Sunscreen, tissues, comb, sunglasses, a romance novel, a small folder containing a hotel room card-key for room 1620, a small red leather wallet some cash and change, and an appointment book. He skimmed through the pages, looking to see if anything alarming popped out at him. He even checked Sunday's listing to see if Lucy, too, had an eleven o'clock appointment with the notorious hood Rico Morales. He was happy to find a blank page.

Tearing off the sheet of paper with Morales's name on it from the hotel notepad and sticking it into a trouser pocket, Judd scribbled a note to Lucy. "Decided I needed a bit of air, so I'm going for a walk along Ocean Drive to soak up the scene. Be back in about an hour. Feeling much better thanks to your TLC." He was about to sign *Love, Judd,* but instead merely signed the note "J."

He read it through once, nodded his satisfaction, then quickly returned all but one of Lucy's belongings to her tote bag, careful to replace the bag where she'd left it. The one item he kept was the card that would gain him entry into her hotel room.

Before leaving his room, Judd made two calls. One was to room 1620, which got the answering service after four rings. The second was down to the front desk. The lovely Latino clerk whom he'd generously tipped during his check-in was happy to provide him with the information that his friend Kyle Warner had left the hotel twenty minutes ago, and his beautiful female friend, Lucy Weston, was at that very moment greeting another female friend in the lobby.

The way was clear.

"LUCY."

Lucy stopped abruptly. She'd have recognized that French accent anywhere. She turned to face her old nemesis, half expecting to find the woman still topless even though they were in the middle of the hotel lobby.

The raven-haired beauty wasn't topless, but she might as well have been for the skimpy halter top that barely covered her voluptuous breasts.

Lucy produced a smile as phony as the French bombshell's. "Hi, Danielle."

"It's so great to see you, Lucy." Danielle lied like a pro.

"I suppose you've already seen Kyle," she said in a chilled voice.

"Is Kyle here? How delightful."

Lucy eyed Danielle shrewdly. Now why would the woman bother to lie about having already had that little tête-à-tête with Kyle on the beach?

Just then, Lucy eyed her fiancé coming in from the front entry of the hotel. *Speak of the devil!*

Kyle didn't notice either woman at first, but they both noticed him.

"He still looks *magnifique*," Danielle murmured.

"We're engaged," Lucy said, her tone gone from chilly to frozen. "To be married," she added, in case there could be any misunderstanding in the translation.

Danielle merely curved her full ruby lips in a siren smile.

THIS CERTAINLY WASN'T the first room Judd had entered uninvited, but it was the first room occupied by someone for whom he had disturbingly serious feelings, not to mention that it was a room this *someone* was sharing with her fiancé. Judd tried to keep his eyes off the king-size bed that the engaged couple would be sleeping in together that night. But physically avoiding the bed didn't make a difference as his imagination was doing a number on him. And it wasn't Kyle and Lucy *sleeping* together that he was picturing. The image made him feel both sick and insanely jealous.

There was only one thing to do. Nail the bastard before the evening was out. Better that Lucy lay in the huge bed alone that night, crying her eyes out, than wrapped in the arms of a low-life crook. Buoyed by the image of Kyle Warner spending the night on a hard cot in a small cell, Judd headed straight for Warner's laptop computer that sat closed on the hotel room desk.

He flipped open the lid, turned the machine on and scanned the hard drive. One folder in particular seemed interesting. It was marked Private. Judd wasn't surprised that when he went to open it, all that came up on the screen was a request for the password.

Judd typed in "Lucy."

LUCY AND DANIELLE WATCHED Kyle head directly over to the check-in desk and have a brief word with the trim, attractive Latino woman behind the counter. She nodded and retrieved a package for him. Kyle moved a few steps away and ripped the parcel open. He peered inside, then looked nervously around the lobby.

That was when he spotted his fiancée standing next to his former girlfriend. A quick smile appeared on his lips, but it didn't fool either woman. They both knew there was no way he could be pleased to see the two of them together.

Lucy started for Kyle, but Danielle darted in front of her, getting to him first.

"Kyle, so great to see you. Lucy just told me you were here. And that you two are going to be married. Not that

I'm surprised. I always expected Lucy to get you in the end. My loss, her gain,'' Danielle cooed.

Lucy wasn't so sure. "So you haven't touched base yet with Danielle.'' She eyed her fiancé closely.

"No. No, but it's…great to see you, too, Danielle.'' He donned one of his endearingly boyish smiles. "Well, actually it's a bit…awkward.''

Lucy was irritated by his smile, but she was even more irritated by his bald-faced lie. It was one thing when it was Danielle, quite another when it was her own fiancé. But then she quickly rationalized that perhaps Kyle simply didn't want to give her any cause to feel jealous.

Did that mean there *was* cause?

"It's silly to feel awkward, Kyle. Isn't it, Lucy?'' Danielle was really laying it on thick as she zestfully linked arms with the pair. "In fact, let me buy you both a drink and we'll toast to your everlasting marital bliss.''

Danielle was assertively steering them all toward the Tango Room, but Lucy had had her fill of the French vixen. If Kyle was the man she hoped he was, he would quickly beg off once she did.

Disentangling herself from Danielle's overzealous grasp, Lucy said, "I really need to change out of my bathing suit and take a shower. Maybe some other time.'' *Like when hell freezes over.*

Lucy looked expectantly at Kyle. He, however, was focused on the cocktail lounge. "A nice frozen mango daiquiri would really hit the spot right about now.''

Lucy had a spot she wanted to hit.

"Come on, Luce,'' he coaxed. "You look like you could do with a drink.''

"No, I don't,'' she said irritably. "Besides, the bar doesn't open till five.''

Danielle shrugged as if that weren't much of a deterrent.

Lucy was almost to the elevator when she realized she'd left her tote bag in Judd's room and her room key was in her bag. Well, she really should stop in and check on him again anyway.

When she arrived at his room, she found a folded note tacked to the door.

Great. He was gone for an hour. Now she'd have to go back down to that cocktail lounge and get Kyle's key.

4

BEADS OF SWEAT DOTTED Judd's brow despite the cold blasts of air pouring out of the air-conditioning vents. He'd gone through about thirty password possibilities, but none of them had been the *open sesame* word that would give him access to the locked file. And he'd found nothing in Kyle's suitcase or in any of the bureau drawers to give him a hint of what that password might be.

He also noted that his quarry was definitely traveling light. Not even an appointment book. It was almost as if Kyle had anticipated his things might be searched. Could Kyle be on to him?

More likely, the embezzler was simply smart enough not to carry around any items that might be incriminating. Unless, of course, he could be quite sure they were well safe guarded behind a locked file.

He looked around the bedroom, as if the space itself might hold some clue. But all he saw was that damned king-size bed. Coupled with the sheer mint-green silk nightie he'd spied earlier in one of the bureau drawers and his imagination immediately went astray again. And it certainly wasn't Kyle Warner that Judd was picturing in that slinky negligee. Discovering that the creep was a cross-dresser as well as a crook would be too much to hope for.

He focused back on the computer screen. *Come on, Judd. Think. Think.*

As LUCY HEADED to the Tango Room, she fully expected to find Danielle fawning all over Kyle. And Kyle enjoying every minute of it. So she was taken aback, to say the least, to see the two of them sitting at a small table at the far end of the otherwise empty lounge, having what looked for all the world to be a heated argument.

Now what could they be fighting about?

Danielle caught sight of her first. Even from that distance, Lucy could see Danielle mouthing *Lucy* to Kyle. He quickly turned in her direction, smiling and waving her over. Danielle also made an effort to smile, but as Lucy approached their table, she could see that Danielle could not quite extinguish the fire still smoldering in her dark eyes.

No question the twosome were definitely uneasy. And not at all happy about the intrusion, even if Kyle covered up his discomfort by pulling over a chair for Lucy and Danielle waved to the bartender so that Lucy could get a drink.

Lucy glanced over at Derek and then looked above his head to the old-fashioned clock on the wall over the bar. It was only 2:35 p.m. If it were true that the bar didn't start serving until five, how come Kyle had been served that mango daiquiri and Danielle was halfway through a martini? Not likely, Lucy thought wryly, that her fiancé and his ex-girlfriend were also friends of Rico Morales. That would really be pushing things.

The only reasonable conclusion she could draw was that Derek bent the rules for other reasons, as well. Like a seductive smile from a voluptuous, beautiful woman with a sexy French accent. Or maybe it was Kyle's manly good looks that had done the trick.

Purely out of a rancorous desire to lengthen their discomfort, Lucy considered joining the pair for a drink. Not to mention she was curious to know what their argument had been about. But she knew both Kyle and Danielle were talented at concealment and she seriously doubted either of them would give away any clues as to the reason for their altercation.

"I just popped in for a key to our room," Lucy said stiffly. "I left mine in Judd's room and he's gone off for a stroll."

"How's he doing?" Kyle asked solicitously.

"Yes, how is Judd Turner?" Danielle asked.

Lucy found it odd that Danielle would ask after Judd. It was Lucy's impression that men like Judd didn't exist for women like Danielle. She was surprised Danielle even knew his name. But then she supposed Kyle must have told her about the mishap at the pool.

"Judd's great," she said succinctly. "The key, Kyle?"

"YOU WHAT?" Judd's grip on his cell phone intensified.

"I called your hotel room well over an hour ago, Judd," Roz snapped. "The maid was supposed—"

"Oh God, the telemarketer."

"What?"

"Roz, you didn't say who was calling?"

"Judd, how would I leave a message for you to call me back—ASAP, by the way—if I didn't leave my name."

"Your whole name?"

"No. Yes…I think I might have. Why—?"

"It was Lucy Weston who picked up the phone, Roz. And if you gave her your last name, she could have looked you up in the phone book and discovered you run an investigation agency. Lucy's a smart woman with a vivid imagination, and she's a journalist. She'd easily put two and two together and figure out I work for you." Which would mean she'd know he was a liar, and pretty soon realize he was also a first-class bastard.

"She probably didn't even remember my last name, Judd. Stop panicking. Are you getting anywhere with that file?"

"No. And the longer we chat on the phone, Roz, the less time I have to—" The rest of the sentence jammed in his throat as his eyes caught the little light on the hotel room door's inside lock switch from red to green. Someone was coming into the room.

"Judd? Judd, did I lose you? Judd—"

With one hand he clicked off his cell phone, with the other he snapped the lid down on the laptop. The front door of the hotel room was just opening as he dashed into the glistening white-marble-and-tile bathroom and shut the door.

He heard music. Singing. Sounded like Frank Sinatra. And then the occupant began to sing along with the radio. He couldn't make out most of the words but he heard the duo singing something about a "tender trap."

He was trapped, all right.

Judd doubted the soprano singing along with Frank belonged to Kyle. It had to be Lucy. He cautiously cracked the bathroom door open an inch.

Lucy, still singing, was lifting the sheer white cover-up over her head.

Even though her white swimsuit was now dry and no longer semitransparent, Judd was quick to note that it still gloriously showed off her exquisite figure. He couldn't pull his eyes away, nor could he control his immediate and intense physical response to the sight of her.

Lucy suddenly stopped singing.

Judd was afraid she'd heard heavy breathing coming from the direction of the bathroom.

Damn, she was turning her gaze his way. Judd darted from view.

He heard padded footsteps approaching. He looked

around in a panic. No windows. He dashed into the tub and quickly pulled the plastic-lined white terry-cloth curtain across the rod.

A thin slit at the showerhead end of the curtain gave Judd a sliver of a view. It was enough to see that Lucy was no longer wearing her bathing suit.

He felt light-headed. He also felt mightily aroused. He closed his eyes, leaning against the tile wall for support.

It was very quiet in the bathroom. What was Lucy doing? He opened his eyes again and peered out from the slit in the curtain.

She was at the sink, staring into the mirror. From his less than advantageous position, he could only make out the right side of her face in the mirror. But it was enough for him to surmise that she looked troubled.

He didn't know the cause of that look, although he could certainly make a few educated guesses. But whatever the reason, it hurt him to see her unhappy. It had always been hard to see her that way. He had longed to be the one able to put the joy back in her face. But it had always been Kyle. It still was Kyle.

"Luce? You here?"

Judd gasped. Fortunately, the sound was drowned out by Kyle's call from the bedroom.

Judd saw a flash of irritation cross the half of Lucy's face that was visible to him. Then she vanished from view.

"I'm just about to take a shower, Kyle."

And before Judd could think what to do next—her hand shot through the shower curtain. He barely managed to dodge her hand as she reached for the tap and turned it on.

A blast of icy water hit him. His second cold shower in less than an hour. Only this time he was fully dressed. Again he dodged her hand as she felt the temperature of the water, then adjusted it by turning the tap over to the side reading Hot.

Too hot!

He bit back a scream as he tried to edge away from the steaming spray. But there was no escaping it.

Fortunately, Lucy did a second test of the water and again adjusted it.

Just right!

At least it would be until she got into the tub and discovered him.

He was granted a temporary reprieve, though, for as Lucy started to part the shower curtain to step in, the bathroom door opened.

"Hey, beautiful, want me to scrub your back?" Kyle drawled.

Oh, great, Judd thought, bad enough to have Lucy join him under the shower much less make it a threesome.

"No, thanks." Lucy's tone was colder than that first blast of water Judd had felt from the shower. "Would you close the door, Kyle. You're letting in a draft."

"Lucy, if you're bent out of shape because of Danielle—"

"Please close the door."

"I swear to you, I have no romantic interest in her. If it makes you feel any better, she's in a serious relationship with a guy here in Miami Beach. Has been for over a year now. In fact, she wants me to meet him tomorrow night if he gets a chance to drop by. He's loaded and he's not happy with his current stockbroker. Could be a real gold mine for me. For us."

"Kyle, I'm thrilled for Danielle. I'm thrilled for you. Now will you please shut the door." Her voice was tight and emphatic. Kyle sighed deeply.

She stepped into the shower at precisely the same moment Kyle reluctantly shut the bathroom door. A nanosecond later, she saw that she wasn't alone. Her eyes widened in shock and her mouth opened in a scream that would surely bring Kyle bursting back into the room.

Acting on pure instinct—okay, maybe it wasn't so *pure*—Judd pulled her naked body to him, wrapped his arms around her, and captured her scream with his lips.

Judd flashed on those endless schoolboy fantasies he'd had of making love to Lucy in a steamy, hot shower. And now that fantasy had come true. Granted, he hadn't pictured himself clothed at the time. But even under these absurd, bordering on farcical, conditions, the reality went far beyond any fantasy he'd ever had.

Judd felt a rush of desire unlike any he'd ever experienced. The closest he'd come to the feeling was ten years ago. Ten years ago when his lips had first—and last—touched Lucy's lips. The kiss they'd shared then had been so rapturous, so intense, so incredibly passionate, he'd never forgotten it. Even if she had. And, despite his concerted efforts—he'd certainly kissed many beautiful women since that magical kiss—the magic had never returned.

Until now.

LUCY'S ALARM quickly turned to zeal as their kiss deepened. And deepened some more. Here she was, naked, in her shower, in the fervent embrace of a fully dressed man—who happened *not* to be her fiancé—who was, very possibly, a racketeer, a mobster and heaven only knows what else, since she couldn't, for all her vivid imagination, come up with a single rational explanation for his presence in her bathtub.

Her vivid imagination notwithstanding, here he was, here she was, here they were. Kissing. And damn him, Judd had gotten even better at it over the past ten years.

No one, not even Kyle, gave himself over to the task of kissing a woman like Judd did.

Did he kiss every woman this way?

The question quickly flitted out of her mind, as she, too, gave herself over to the task at hand. At this point she completely forgot what had sparked the kiss in the first place.

When Judd finally released her, she slumped breathlessly against the tiled wall of the tub.

"Are you okay? You look a little—"

"Blurry?" Lucy finished, removing his glasses.

"That's better."

Lucy didn't agree. There was Judd wearing a goofy, drunken smile. Here she was, stone-cold sober, wearing nothing! Acutely aware of her nakedness, she crossed her arms over her breasts, mortified by the hardness of her nipples. At the same time she fruitlessly attempted to arrange her legs and elbows so as to feel less exposed from the waist down.

"Are you crazy?" she gasped.

"Luce? Did you call me?" Kyle shouted from the bedroom.

Judd gave her a pleading look.

She hesitated. "No, I was just…singing to myself."

Judd smiled gratefully at her.

"Get out of this tub," she demanded sotto voce.

But just as he was about to comply with her harshly whispered order, the bathroom door opened. She grabbed onto his sodden Hawaiian shirt and pulled him back into the tub. He nearly lost his balance and had to cling to her to keep from falling.

"Lucy? You okay?" Kyle asked solicitously.

She quickly popped her head out from behind the curtain. "Fine. I'm fine. Just dropped the soap."

Judd quickly handed over a bar of soap.

She waved the bar at Kyle. "Oh, here it is. Got it."

"Well, be careful. You hear about all kinds of accidents happening to people in their bathtubs."

"I'll be careful." Her tone lacked conviction.

"Say Luce, you weren't using my laptop by any chance?"

Judd silently cursed himself for his carelessness.

"What? No. Why?"

Kyle shrugged. "I thought I'd shut down, but I guess I must have just put the thing to sleep. No problem. I'm just going to take a little siesta for about an hour and then go check on Judd. If he's feeling okay, I'd love to spend a little time catching up with him."

I'd love to catch up with you, too, Warner, Judd was thinking.

"Hey, beautiful, maybe when you finish your shower, you can snuggle under the covers with me."

Judd violently shook his head.

At first Lucy thought he was only responding to the idea of her joining Kyle in bed. But she quickly realized the broader problem. With Kyle in bed at all, how was Judd supposed to get out of the hotel room without being discovered? While she certainly wanted some explanations from Judd as to what he was doing in her bathroom, she wasn't particularly eager for Kyle to hear those explanations, as well. Of course, she could deliberately let Kyle discover Judd's presence and say "tit for tat." But that presumed there was any tit-for-tat going on between Kyle and Danielle. He'd sworn there wasn't. But he'd also sworn he hadn't seen Danielle on the beach earlier in the afternoon.

Anyway, even if there was any hanky-panky being hatched between Kyle and Danielle, Lucy was not the kind of person to stoop to spite as recourse for her fiancé's potential infidelity.

Which left only one solution.

"Kyle, do me a big favor, darling, and run down to the gift shop for me. I need some...tampons."

She saw Judd arch an eyebrow, obviously recalling that she had supposedly dashed down to the gift store *earlier* for female stuff.

"I thought your period wasn't due for a couple of weeks," Kyle called out, disappointment clear in his voice.

"I...I guess I'm...irregular," she muttered, turning away from Judd as she felt her face grow hot.

As soon as the hotel room door closed, Lucy practically leaped out of the tub. She was grabbing for a bath towel when she started to slip on the wet tile floor. A gasp escaped her lips a moment before Judd dodged for her. They went down together, the terry shower curtain that he had vainly tried to hold on to for balance coming down on top of them. The copper shower rod quickly followed, one end clipping his head in precisely the same spot that was already sporting a pebble-sized bump. No doubt it would be the size of a goose egg by that evening, he thought.

She righted herself first, taking some of the curtain with her and drawing it up in front of her body. What completely eluded her was that her back and, therefore her beautiful butt, was fully and gloriously reflected in the large mirror behind her.

"Okay," Lucy said breathlessly. "I'll start by telling you what I've figured out so far and you, Judd Turner, will then fill in the blanks."

"Kyle will be back in a few minutes, Lucy. What if we—?"

"If you keep interrupting me, you'll use up all those minutes."

He held up his hands up in surrender. Water dripped

down his arms. His soaking clothes stuck to his skin. His feet were swimming in a good inch of water that had gathered in his shoes. But the worst part was the damn padding he was wearing. The water had caused it to both inflate and grow leaden. He couldn't begin to imagine how misshapen he must look. Fortunately, Lucy seemed to be too caught up in her tirade to notice.

"Okay," she said again. "I'm going to start by giving you the benefit of the doubt and presume you never meant to get in over your head."

"That's certainly true," he agreed.

She pushed wet strands of hair away from her face. "But you got caught up in it, and when you realized you were in too deep you discovered you couldn't get out."

"Again, true," he said.

"And now there's Rico Morales."

His eyes widened.

"Don't look so surprised. I know all about Rico Morales. Even about the eleven o'clock p.m. meeting tomorrow night."

He felt sick. If she knew about Morales, even about the meet-up time, then she must be involved in Warner's embezzlement scheme.

"Look, Judd. I want to help."

A flicker of hope coursed through him. She wanted to go help him. She wanted to redeem herself. Even if it meant ratting out her fiancé. Things were looking up. "You do?"

"But first you need to come clean. I can't help you if you're determined to hold out on me."

"I've wanted to come clean from the start, Lucy. It was just I was afraid—"

"Of course you're afraid. He's a very dangerous man."

Was she referring to Morales or Kyle? Judd wasn't sure.

She narrowed her gaze. "Is there a girlfriend?"

He gave her a blank look.

"Roz number one," she said.

Hesitating, he shook his head. "No. No girlfriend." *Not yet...*

"So the only Roz you know is the private investigator, Roz Morrisey."

He'd told Roz that Lucy would figure that one out soon enough. He nodded sheepishly.

"So who was Roz number one?"

He sighed, not sure how to answer that question. Even if his cover was blown, he'd promised Gina he wouldn't reveal her involvement in this affair. It would destroy her friendship with Lucy. Bad enough Lucy was being betrayed by her fiancé. And by him.

"Well?" she asked impatiently.

"Just a woman who was...helping me. No one you know," he lied, and felt awful about it. He silently vowed, that when this whole mess was over, he'd never again lie to her. Then again, the opportunity would probably never arise, since she was bound not to ever speak to him again.

"You must be in some serious trouble to be needing so much help."

"In trouble?"

"I think the first thing you need to do is get out of Miami." She scowled. "No, Morales has probably got a network of goons who'd track you down." Her scowl deepened. "How tied in with Morales and his operation are you?"

"What do you know about Morales's operation?"

"I know enough."

Judd felt sick. That wasn't the answer he wanted to hear.

They both heard the hotel room door slam shut, quickly

followed by Kyle's voice. "I'm back, Luce. Got you a box of twelve."

She cracked open the bathroom door and peeked out. "Wrong kind."

"What?" Kyle sounded puzzled. "But this is the brand you always—"

"Yes, but the blue box not the white."

"I never saw a blue—"

"Kyle, don't argue with me. I need the blue box."

"Lucy, I didn't see a blue box in the gift shop."

"Well, then go to a drugstore. Is that such a big thing to ask the man who loves you to do? Take a meager little walk over to a drugstore? Is it so much to ask that you get me the...the right color box? Is it—?"

"Okay, okay," he soothed. "Just don't go all PMS on me, Luce. I'll go to the ends of the earth if that's what it takes to find the *blue* box."

A wicked smile curved Lucy's lips as Kyle turned and headed down the hallway. He'd have to go to the ends of the earth. There was no blue box.

Judd sneezed.

"You've got to get out of those wet clothes," Lucy said.

He sneezed again. "You're right." He started to exit the bathroom, his shoes squishing with each step on the tile floor.

"Hold it."

He looked nervously back at her.

"You haven't explained what you were doing in my bathtub."

He sneezed once more. "I really need to change—"

"You're not getting off that easy," she said.

"I...wanted to...see you."

Her brown eyes glinted. "You saw me, all right."

"I didn't mean—" A smile curved his lips. "You do

look beautiful, Lucy. I don't know what Kyle meant about you being bent out of shape because of Danielle Brunaud. I don't care what her *shape* is, I can tell you it couldn't begin to hold a candle to yours."

"So you're an expert."

She didn't say it as if she believed it. Even though it was relatively true.

"All I'm saying, Lucy—"

"It's what you're not saying that I want to know, Judd."

He shivered, probably because of his soaked clothing, the air-conditioning and her inquisition.

"Couldn't we talk after I get out these wet things?"

She gave him closer scrutiny. He didn't only look wet, he looked *different*. Funny, she hadn't noticed before how much of a gut he actually had. She supposed it had been better concealed when his shirt was dry and not clinging to him. If she was turned off by his appearance now, she certainly hadn't paid it any heed when he was kissing her with such devastating ardor in the shower.

Before she could say anything else, Judd faked a quick, emphatic series of sneezes and made a beeline for the door.

He'd gotten halfway across the bedroom when she called after him. "I'll be at your room in fifteen minutes. You better have some answers ready, Judd."

"My, my, my, what happened to you? Last I looked the sun was shining brightly. Don't tell me you took a dip in the ocean during your walk."

Danielle Brunaud was leaning languidly against his hotel room door, the note Judd had tacked on his door in her hand. She was the last person he expected to find waiting for him. Or had any desire to see, for that matter.

Ignoring both her question and her skimpy attire—a

sea-blue halter top and a pair of body-hugging black
stretch pants slung low enough to reveal a diamond stud
in her belly button—he slipped his card into his lock. The
card didn't work. He hastily remembered it wasn't the one
to his room, but to Kyle and Lucy's. Positioning himself
so that his back was to Danielle, thereby making it impossible for her to detect his sleight of hand, he quickly
reached into the pocket of his sodden pants and pulled
out the correct card. This time, when he inserted it, the
green entry light flashed on.

He sneezed as he opened his door.

"So, I gather I'm not going to get an explanation," she
said, slipping past him and stepping into his room, uninvited.

Standing at the open door, his hand still on the knob,
Judd gave her a less than welcome look. "I really need
to change."

"Go ahead," she said blithely, giving no indication of
taking the hint. More likely, she was simply choosing to
ignore it. If she was taking in his pathetically misshapen
appearance, she gave no sign of it. She had a way of
looking at him without noticing he was actually there.
Same way she'd looked at him back in college. Judd felt
a flash of irritation, betting that if he'd met her under
different circumstances, looking the way he really looked
now, she'd have noticed him plenty. And, for Lucy's sake
as well as his own, he'd have enjoyed snubbing her. Danielle Brunaud was a woman who could use a taste of her
own medicine.

All of his rumination, however, begged the question.
Since his present appearance was not going to ring any
of Danielle's bells, what was the reason for the social call?

His annoyance gave way to curiosity. Danielle impressed him as a woman who invariably had an ulterior

motive for everything she did. He'd have to wait her out until her purpose became clear.

She slinked across the room as he gathered some dry clothes from his closet—another equally loud multicolored Hawaiian shirt, this one sporting palm trees and flamingos instead of parrots, and another pair of pleated white slacks, two waistband sizes larger than his usual size—and headed for the bathroom to change. Not that he thought for an instant she would mind or probably even pay attention if he changed right there in the bedroom. Although, she'd be bound to sit up and take notice when she got a gander at his waterlogged stuffing.

Danielle was kneeling in front of his minibar, checking out the alcoholic offerings as he stepped into the bathroom and shut—and locked—the door. *Better safe than sorry.*

He quickly stripped down and dried off. The padding, lying in a sodden heap on the tile floor, would have to be abandoned for now. It would be hours before it all dried out. However, since a very sudden weight loss would be mighty hard to explain, he saw no alternative but to use some folded-up towels as a replacement. This assignment was doing *nothing* for his self-image!

After he wiped off his glasses and put them back on, he turned to check out his appearance in the mirror door of the medicine chest. That was when he saw the fake set of braces sitting on the glass shelf above the sink.

Damn. He'd forgotten to put them back on before heading up to Lucy's hotel room to snoop around. Had she noticed?

How could she have helped but notice? If her eyes hadn't spotted the change, her mouth had to have.

He'd need to make something up if she questioned him. More lies. Judd jammed the braces back in place.

When he returned to the bedroom, Danielle was stretched out on his queen-size bed, her lustrous long black hair fanned out on his propped-up pillows, a glass of Scotch in each hand.

She smiled seductively as she stretched out one hand in his direction, inviting him to join her in a drink. No question, there was something the French siren wanted from him. And it wasn't his body!

He took the glass from her hand.

She patted a spot on the bed, and he sat down beside her.

Clinking his glass with hers, she said, "Here's to good times."

He arched a brow.

She laughed. "Don't worry," she said, mistaking his expression for alarm. "I don't bite."

He downed his Scotch in one long swallow. "Good. I bruise easily."

She sipped her drink, eyeing him over the rim of her glass. Then she slowly lowered the glass, maintaining her gaze. "So, Judd, I hear you've become quite the entrepreneur since I last saw you."

The light was beginning to dawn. Danielle had two interests. Sex and money. In no particular order.

"I'm doing okay," he said, deliberately being vague.

Now she arched one of her exquisitely plucked dark eyebrows. "I bet you're doing more than okay."

Was she trying to hit him up for a handout?

Then he remembered what Kyle had told Lucy. According to him, Danielle had hooked up with a man with deep pockets here in Miami. A man she wanted Kyle to meet. A man in search of a new stockbroker. It didn't make sense to Judd that she'd be needing money from him.

Danielle smiled coquettishly. "Don't worry, darling. I'm doing more than okay, myself."

He pretended ignorance. "Oh, that's great, Danielle. What kind of business are you in?"

She laughed coyly. "A business that's both profitable and pleasurable. Isn't that the best kind?"

"I wouldn't know. I can't exactly say that owning Laundromats brings me a lot of pleasure."

"Maybe it could, if you give it a chance." She edged closer to him, her tone oozing simulated sexuality.

"What do you mean?"

"I have a very *close* friend who's always on the look-out for new ways to invest his considerable assets."

"A close friend?" Was she referring to her rich lover? Or had Kyle made up that story of Danielle's wealthy investor boyfriend to appease Lucy? Judd was beginning to think Kyle had sent Danielle over to his hotel room to do his bidding.

"I'd love for the two of you to meet. He lives right here in South Beach. A fantastic penthouse suite at the Roney. Of course, it's not his only residence. He's got an apartment in New York, a horse ranch in Argentina, a delightful villa in the South of France."

Judd scowled, barely listening to the property listings. She couldn't be referring to Kyle. They already knew each other. So clearly this other boyfriend existed.

"Don't look so worried, Judd. Rico doesn't bite, either."

Rico?

And suddenly Judd saw all the pieces fall into place. *Rico.* Rico Morales. He'd bet his bottom dollar on it.

This was too much to ask for. It was too perfect. Morales, Danielle, Kyle. The mobster, his moll and her old boyfriend, the embezzler. If Judd played his cards right, he might hit *three* birds with one stone before this weekend was over.

But he had to be careful not to give Danielle the

slightest glimpse of his hand. "I have been thinking about opening a few more Laundromats—"

"That's not the only way to increase your revenue, Judd." She let her hand fall provocatively on his thigh.

He produced a smile meant to radiate both arousal and awkwardness. "What...do you have in...mind, Danielle?"

"Dani. Call me Dani, Judd. All my close friends do."

"Is that what Rico calls you?"

Her hand traveled a few inches higher on his thigh. "Now don't start getting jealous, Judd. A girl can never have too many close friends." She leaned over to set her barely touched tumbler of Scotch on the bedside table. In the process, she made a point of positioning her chest across Judd's lap.

She was working awfully hard, no doubt hating every minute of this phony seduction. He could have told her she could save herself all the trouble since, if as he suspected, she was doing the bidding for Rico Morales, Judd wanted to meet Morales even more than *Dani* wanted the mobster to meet him. Of course, he wasn't about to say a word. Besides, he had to admit he was getting some perverse enjoyment out of watching her suffer through this charade.

She rolled over so that her head was now resting high on his lap. She smiled flirtatiously up at him, but he could see the pained look in her eyes. He wondered how far she'd be willing to go to get him in the program. He was pretty sure it was farther than he'd be willing to go. For all her lush beauty, Danielle Brunaud left his active libido cold.

"So when can I meet this friend of yours?" he asked casually, slipping a hand under her head and lifting it as he rose.

"Where are you going?" her tone was a mix of irritation and feigned disappointment. Or maybe the disappointment wasn't feigned. No doubt, she prided herself on her success at seduction.

He held up his empty glass. "A refill." Not that he'd wanted that first shot of booze, much less a second. But he needed some distance from her cloying come-on. He removed another tiny bottle of Scotch from the minibar.

Danielle stretched back out on the bed, resting her head on the pillows. "How about tomorrow afternoon? Say around five? That will give us plenty of time to get back for the gala banquet."

"I don't know, Danielle." He didn't want to sound too eager. "Why would someone like Rico be interested in doing business with a nobody like me? He lives in a penthouse. All I own is a little split-level house on the outskirts of Cincinnati."

She crooked her index finger at him. He pretended not to notice.

Not a woman who liked being ignored, she reached out and caught hold of his hand, tugging him back to the bed. "You don't belong in a dreary house in a dreary place like Cincinnati."

"I don't?"

She pulled him closer to her. Maintaining her firm grip on his hand, she lifted it to her breast, most of which was exposed thanks to the scant halter top. "With my help, and Rico's, you could be sitting pretty in a very short time."

He gave her a goofy, wide-eyed look. "Really?"

"Really."

"Gee…that sounds…great."

"Shall we shake on it?"

He glanced down at his right hand, which she was still holding captive against her breast. Winding her free hand around his neck, she smiled wantonly, then pressed her lips to his. Some handshake.

It was precisely at that moment that Lucy arrived at his door and found it slightly ajar. Thinking he'd deliberately left it that way for her entry, she strode purposefully into his room.

The truth was Judd had simply been too distracted by Danielle to shut the door firmly. Lucy's arrival was as much of a shock to him as it looked to be to Lucy. He knew that if she was looking for answers before, she'd be looking for a bunch more now.

5

As Judd pulled his mouth away from Danielle's, and when he sprang up from the bed, she emitted a sharp cry.

"Oh, *mon Dieu,* I'm bleeding," she gasped.

Lucy stood rigidly at the open door surveying the little love scene, as Judd turned from her and glanced distractedly over his shoulder at the French seductress. Blood was trickling from Danielle's mouth.

"It was your braces. They cut me," she whined, sprinting over to the mirror that hung above the low-slung white bureau to examine the damage.

That was when it hit Lucy. When he was kissing her not twenty minutes ago, he hadn't been wearing braces. She was certain of it. If she hadn't been so damn wrapped up in that intense kiss, she would have realized it at the time.

Hold it, she thought. Forget the braces for now. Concentrate on the fact that Judd Turner—nerdy, misshapen, Laundromat mogul—had gone from kissing her to kissing another woman—her arch rival no less—in a matter of minutes. What was it about this guy!

"I must get some ointment for this cut. I could be scarred. For life," Danielle gasped, her sham seductress voice replaced by self-absorbed agitation.

"I'm...sorry, Danielle," Judd muttered as she hurried for the door, her hand over her mouth. Although Lucy was standing right in her path, Danielle skirted around as though she didn't exist.

It was a different story when Danielle collided with Kyle, who was in the hallway just about to enter Judd's room.

"Dani, what's wrong?" Kyle asked solicitously.

Lucy's lips had tightened to a thin line. *Dani.* Lucy knew all too well that Danielle liked all her *close* friends to call her by her nickname.

"What are you doing here, Kyle?" Lucy demanded.

"I wanted to talk over some business ideas with Judd," Kyle retorted. "What are *you* doing here, Luce?"

"I am...wounded." Danielle broke in, with her hand still over her mouth.

"How did it happen?" Kyle asked, looking from Danielle to Lucy to Judd, then back to Danielle again.

Lucy laughed sharply, her eyes on Judd. "Who knew kissing could be so dangerous?"

Kyle gave his fiancée a befuddled look.

Danielle grasped hold of his arm. "Please...come with me to the pharmacist. I'm feeling a little...faint."

Lucy rolled her eyes.

Kyle wasn't sure what to do. His gaze once again fell on his fiancée. "Well...I..."

"Oh, go with her," she snapped. "Go get her a blood transfusion for all I care."

"Why are you angry at me, Luce?"

"I'm not angry," she said.

Judd knew she was lying. He was sure she was furious at the whole lot of them—Kyle, Danielle and himself.

He watched her step purposefully into his hotel room and shut the door firmly behind her. This time, unlike when he'd followed Danielle inside a short while before, he heard the lock click into place.

Lucy stood right in front of the closed door, her silence more of a demand for an explanation than any words. But as he looked at her, he couldn't think straight. Certainly not straight enough to come up with a story that she would conceivably buy.

She was so beautiful. All he could do was stare at her like a lovesick pup. Even though he admittedly preferred her naked and wet, she looked absolutely beguiling in her simple peach colored sleeveless shift, her auburn hair still damp from the shower. His gaze traveled downward. He took in the lush curve of her hips, the long, shapely legs. She was wearing a pair of cream sandals, her feet exposed, and he got lost in the exquisite perfection of all ten of her perfect toes.

But when his gaze returned to her face, he caught the shadow of hurt and betrayal reflected in her eyes.

He cleared his throat. "Lucy…I can…explain…about Danielle."

She bit her lower lip. "Oh, I'm sure you can come up with a good tale. But that's all it would be. A tale. A lie. Just like all your other lies."

"Lucy, that's not true. I—"

"Look Judd, you're a free agent. You can go around kissing every woman in Miami Beach if that's *your thing.* Just leave *me* out next time around."

"I wasn't kissing Danielle. She was kissing me."

"Is that what you told *Dani* about our kiss?"

His eyes locked on Lucy's. "I didn't tell *Danielle* about our kiss. And if I had, I would have said *I* kissed *you.* And I absolutely adored every moment of that kiss."

The look on her face said she didn't believe him.

"It's the truth, Lucy. And you know it is. You think this is easy for me? Well, it isn't. Seeing you again… All those old unrequited feelings…" He pressed his hand to his pounding heart. "All the fantasies, the longing… And then seeing you again after ten years…more beautiful… How is that possible? How could the most beautiful girl in the world get more beautiful?"

"You shouldn't be…flirting with me, Judd. I'm almost a married woman."

"That's like saying you're *almost* pregnant." The possibility that she was pregnant hit him hard. "You aren't, are you?" It would be bad enough to put her fiancé behind bars, but if Kyle also turned out to be the father of her unborn child—

"No, I'm not pregnant," she said, her face flushed.

"Good."

There was a dead silence between them for a minute.

"Why was Danielle kissing you?" she demanded.

He thought it best not to remind her that she'd already told him he didn't owe her an explanation. That she couldn't care less.

"She wasn't interested in my body, Lucy. She was interested in—"

She cut him off. "You know what? I'm up to here with your lies." She placed her hand beneath her chin. "I don't care why she was kissing you or why you were kissing her or why you got yourself into the mess you're in. It's none of my business. I was just…stupid. Stupid to think we were…friends. Stupid to…to want to help you. You obviously have plenty of other women ready to jump right in and…and rescue you." As she stammered her way through this speech, he was moving toward her. She backed up only to slam into the closed door after two steps.

"I don't want to be rescued by any other woman, Lucy."

He was inches from her. She could feel his breath on her face. Even though the air-conditioning in the room was on max, she could feel heat prickle the back of her neck. *Damn it, she wanted him to kiss her again. She wanted to kiss him back. She wanted—*

She pushed him away. "Kyle and I are getting married."

Judd held his ground, as well as her gaze. "Are you?"

She closed her eyes. "Yes. Of course we are."

"What about Danielle?"

Her eyes popped open. "Danielle is a—" She clamped her lips shut before some very unladylike profanities escaped through them.

"Kyle's not worthy of you, Lucy."

"There's nothing between Kyle and Danielle," she said. Now who was lying?

"Then why are you so upset?" he demanded.

"I am not...upset." She looked up defiantly into his eyes.

He stared her down.

Lucy could feel herself losing the battle. But she wasn't licked yet. "You don't know Kyle. You haven't seen or spoken to him in ten years. He's not the boy you remember, Judd. He's grown up. Matured. He's...changed."

"Has he?"

She poked him in the chest. "I know what you're doing, Judd Turner. You're trying to get the focus off yourself by turning the spotlight on me."

He reached out and wiped a tiny bead of sweat from her brow. "You're getting hot under the glare," he murmured.

She scowled, pushing his hand away. "When did you learn to...to talk like that?"

"Like what?"

"Like...like you're talking, that's what."

"Well, Lucy, I've grown up, too. I've matured. I've changed."

"You certainly have," she snapped. "You know something, Judd. I am sorely regretting having agreed to come down to this dumb reunion. And the festivities haven't even started yet.'' Well, they'd started, but not in the way she'd anticipated.

He smiled.

She held out for a minute, but then a smile broke across her cheeks, as well.

''I want to kiss you again, Lucy Weston.'' He leaned a little closer, capturing her with the full impact of his desire. ''And that's the truth. I swear to—''

She pressed her hands to his mouth, her smile fading. ''Don't do this to me, Judd. It isn't fair.''

''At least you believe me.''

She edged around him and moved into the center of the room, surreptitiously wiping more beads of perspiration from her forehead. She was desperately in need of some breathing space.

She looked across at him, grateful that he'd remained standing near the door. She didn't feel altogether safe, even from this distance. Only safer than she'd felt close up. ''How about if I ask some of the questions?''

''Okay. Shoot,'' he said, trying to pull off a nonchalant stance as he inwardly tried to prepare for the onslaught.

''Start with the braces.''

He smiled crookedly, revealing a mouth full of metal-work. ''Yeah…the braces. I had a feeling you might ask about them. They're…um…what you might call—''

''Bogus?''

He sighed. There was no point in making up some ludicrous story that she was not about to buy anyway. He held up his hands in surrender.

''It's obvious you're worried about being recognized by someone,'' she said.

He felt an all-too familiar wave of guilt cut through him. He couldn't meet her gaze.

''FBI?''

He looked her in the eye. ''What?''

"DEA?"

"Lucy—"

"IRS? CIA? Come on, Judd. I'm running out of letters here."

"It's just not something...I can talk about. At least not right now."

She felt a mix of disappointment, irritation and frustration. "So, you're saying you don't trust me."

Her remark triggered a lingering anxiety that she might be involved in some way in Kyle's criminal activities. But Judd erased the feeling. Or at least he altered it. If she did have anything to do with it, he decided it was strictly inadvertent. But even if she knew nothing about her fiancé's sticky fingers, Judd couldn't risk confiding in her. Out of some misguided loyalty to Kyle, she might feel compelled to tip him off. He closed his eyes, trying to wish his way out of this situation.

"Judd, there is a way out of this mess you've gotten yourself into."

He slowly opened his eyes. "There is?"

"Listen, I've covered enough stories like this. People, basically decent, well-meaning people who...got mixed up in something and then...realized they were trapped."

Truer words had never been spoken, he thought.

"But you're not trapped," she said emphatically. "You can cut a deal."

"Cut...a deal?"

"Turn state's evidence against Morales. Depending on how much you know... Well, maybe you won't get off scot-free...maybe you'd have to do some time, but it wouldn't be nearly as long—"

"Lucy, I'm not going to prison."

"They all say that, Judd."

"Look, I'll be able to explain everything to you later." He felt a sinking sensation in the pit of his stomach. If things went as he hoped with this assignment, she wouldn't need or want him to explain anything to her.

She was exasperated. "Oh, please, Judd. If you're going to stand there and lie to me—"

"I swear to you, this is one thing I'm not lying about."

Her gaze narrowed. "You mean everything else has been a lie?"

"Wanting to kiss you again wasn't a lie. The kiss we shared wasn't a lie. And while I take full responsibility for having started it—" He moved toward her again. It seemed to be the only direction that made any sense to him, even though he knew, logically, it didn't make any sense at all.

This time, when she backed up, she fell onto his bed.

He pointed his index finger at her. "You, Lucy Weston, contributed your full share—"

She straightened up just as he got to her. "You…you caught me…off guard."

"I'll grant you that. For the first few seconds," he added with a teasing smile. The feel of her lips on his, their tongues entwined, her wet, naked, svelte body pressed to his, was almost as vivid now as it had been during their hot shower. He knew this last kiss, even more than the first, would be an indelible memory. He also knew that Lucy could not have responded to him the way she had if she truly was in love with Kyle Warner. Nor would she be so willing to help him. Albeit, as it had turned out, she thought he was the one in trouble with the law, not Kyle. But somehow he'd set things right with her. He had to. Ten years ago, he'd kept his longing for her locked inside himself. He'd never even tried to win her affection, much less her love. He'd convinced himself he didn't stand a chance. Even with Kyle out of the picture.

Well, this time around, Kyle in the picture or not, Judd

was going for the gold. Because that's what Lucy was. Pure gold.

"Will you take those dumb braces off," she muttered as she again dodged by him.

Judd gladly complied, tossing the sham metalwork onto the bedside table. He offered a wide smile. "Better?"

Damn him, she thought. It was better. "I can't figure you out, Judd Turner. One minute you're this...this—"

"Nerd?"

"And next minute you're...Don Juan."

"I guess you could say I'm a man of many sides."

"And I'm not sure I care for any of them." But she was lying through her teeth.

He picked right up on it. "If you're not sure, that means you might care for at least one of them." He knew he was taking a dumb, not to mention dangerous, detour from his assignment. He should be putting all these intense feelings for Lucy on temporary hold. But he could not dismiss the high voltage between them any more than she could.

"Let's stop playing games, Judd. Either you're going to come clean or I'm washing my hands of you."

She waited, chin tilted up, toe tapping, arms folded across her chest.

He couldn't let her walk out. But he couldn't tell her the truth. And he couldn't bear to make up any more lies. He was left in a complete quandary.

Lucy sighed. Then, without another word, she turned away and started for the door.

"Did you know Danielle Brunaud was involved with your pal, Rico Morales?"

She spun back around to face him. "What?"

"The rich investor Kyle was telling you about when we were—"

She held up a hand to stop him from finishing the sentence.

"He was talking about Rico Morales."

"Why did you call Morales *my* pal?" she demanded. "If Morales is anyone's *pal,* he's yours."

"And Danielle's," he said, deciding not to get into a discussion of his relationship—or current lack thereof—with the mobster.

"You're sure about Danielle and Morales?" she clearly wasn't convinced.

"They're lovers. She told me herself."

"Before or after the kiss?" Again she held up her hand to indicate she didn't want an answer.

She started pacing. "So that's why Danielle latched onto Kyle the instant she laid eyes on him. She wants to introduce him to Morales so that hood can rope him into investing some of his ill-gotten gains."

For a second, Judd thought Lucy was owning up to her knowledge of her fiancé's criminal tendencies. But then he realized she was referring to Morales. Another disquieting thought hit him.

"How well do you know Rico Morales, Lucy?"

She rolled her eyes. "What's there to know? He's a mobster. He's been up the river. I'm sure he's got his hooks into a lot of people just like you, Judd."

He was wondering if the same thing had happened to her. Maybe she'd met him when she was covering his trial. Or before that. Maybe she'd covered the investigation. She might have done a story on him. Gotten an interview. Gotten to know him. Maybe she'd been misguided into believing she could help Morales go straight. Instead, he'd seduced her—

Was this the real reason she'd come to the reunion? Was Morales doubling his odds of getting Kyle Warner's cooperation in whatever new felonious schemes he had in mind, by using both Danielle and Lucy as pawns?

"Judd, you've got to keep Morales from getting his hooks into Kyle."

Hold everything, Judd thought, confused. Either he had it all wrong about Lucy setting Kyle up for her mobster lover or she was having second thoughts. Or...

Judd had another sickening thought. What if Lucy was afraid to cross the mobster, but she really didn't want her future husband tied in with the mob? She could be using him as her pawn. *She* wouldn't be the one keeping Kyle out of Morales's clutches. She'd get good old Judd to do it.

Great. She wanted him to protect her crooked fiancé from her crooked mobster lover.

"It's not that Kyle is...dishonest," she said. "It's just that he could be tempted...if a lot of money was involved...."

Maybe Kyle wasn't the only one tempted by money. Maybe, deep down, Lucy wasn't really all that different from Danielle Brunaud. Maybe Lucy was also driven by sex and money. Morales probably had both. Kyle certainly did. Judd was thrown by the whole idea.

"Oh, Kyle would convince himself there was nothing...wrong with what he was doing, but—"

"You mean he's good at lying to himself." *Not to mention lying to you, Lucy. Not to mention you lying to me....*

His mind was reeling. He couldn't make sense of any of it.

Lucy bristled. "You're the last person to be calling someone a liar, Judd Turner."

He wearily expelled a breath. She was right. Who was he to talk?

Her expression softened. "I know you don't...like Kyle, but...please look out for him...for my sake, Judd." Her eyes locked onto his, her expression so earnest it broke his heart.

He sighed heavily. How had it all gone so wrong?

6

"JUDD, IT'S SATURDAY afternoon. The reunion will be over by tomorrow morning. What have you got?"

Nothing but a headache and heartache, he thought.

"Today's been a total bust so far. Warner slept in until nearly noon, so I couldn't get near him or his room. Then we had this dumb boat ride around Miami harbor. Warner buzzed my room and asked me to join him. I was hoping he'd finally get down to talking business. I show on the boat and guess what?"

"He didn't," Roz said.

"You got it," Judd said, not adding that Lucy hadn't been on board, either. "I just got back. So there you have it. My progress report in a nutshell," he added dryly.

"Well, cheer up, I've got something for you. Gina Reed called me a few minutes ago. Found out something that might be important. She popped into the office this afternoon, thinking, since it was Saturday, no one would be around and she could do some more snooping. Only Warner's secretary was there. She got nervous when she saw Gina, and babbled something about finding a client folder that had been misfiled in another broker's file cabinet. She was all upset about it because Warner is *paranoid*—the secretary's word—about keeping all his client info under lock and key in his office."

"Why doesn't that surprise me?" he said sardonically.

"Maybe this will surprise you," Roz continued. "Warner's secretary refused to let Gina have a look at the folder, but Gina was able to catch a gander at the client's name—''

''Get to the point, Roz.'' His eyes were on his watch. It was almost five. He was expecting Danielle to show up any minute to escort him over to Morales's penthouse. Now more than ever, he was literally itching to meet this Romeo mobster. His hands clenched into tight fists.

''You're sounding awfully tense, Judd. It doesn't have anything to do with your reunion with Lucy Warner, does it?''

''Who's the client, Roz?''

''A mobster by the name of—''

''Rico Morales.''

''How the hell did you know?''

So Kyle was lying to Lucy—big surprise—about Danielle introducing him to Morales tonight. The mobster was already a client of his. Kyle was just covering his bases.

''Wait a second,'' he muttered. ''Then Lucy wasn't the one who set him up with Morales. Maybe I had it all wrong.'' A weight suddenly lifted. If he was wrong about that, maybe he had it all wrong. He laughed.

''Judd, are you all right? You're babbling.'' Roz was really bewildered now.

''Sorry. Just thinking out loud. This is getting damn complicated. I need to…I need to go, Roz. I'll fill you in…later.''

''How about a few hints, Judd? I think—''

He clicked off his cell phone, once again cutting his boss off midsentence.

BY FIVE-FIFTEEN, Danielle had not arrived, and Judd was getting antsy. Worried that she was having second thoughts about introducing him to Morales, he decided to go looking for her. He tried her room first, but there was no response to his knocks. Either she wasn't in there or—

He flashed on an image of Danielle and Kyle rolling around on her bed. He knocked again. Harder. And kept it up for almost a minute. If the pair was in there, at least Judd would have the satisfaction of disturbing their activities.

A middle-aged man occupying the room next door popped his head out and gave him an angry look.

"Do you mind?" the man said sharply. "I'm trying to take a nap."

"Sorry," he said. "It's...my sister. She's a little... deaf."

"She's also not in her room."

"She isn't?" For a second Judd thought Danielle might be in her next-door neighbor's hotel room.

"These damn walls are paper thin. I can hear every time your sister's door opens and closes. It closed over an hour ago. And it hasn't opened since."

"That doesn't necessarily mean she's out," Judd said. "She could have gone *into* her room an hour ago—"

"Like I said, pal, these walls are paper thin. Your sister's not the quietest person. No disrespect meant. Believe me, if she was in her room, I'd know it."

Judd believed him. He went down to the lobby, stopping at the front desk. His snitch, the pretty, young desk clerk, wasn't on duty so there was no way to find out if Danielle had left the hotel or not.

He surveyed the crowded space. While he didn't spot Danielle there, he saw a slew of old Florida State classmates, all of them wearing ID tags with their college yearbook photos attached, milling around, hugging, slapping backs, chattering away. A few people waved in his direction, but only a couple came over to greet him. He hadn't exactly been Mr. Popular back in college.

He started across the lobby to check out the Tango Room, but he was waylaid before he got there.

"How's the noggin?"

Judd didn't place the slight man at first, but then he realized it was Gary Burke, the biochem student from Florida State who'd become a gynecologist, and who had checked him out when he'd hit his head at the pool.

Judd's hand automatically went to the back of his head. As he'd predicted, thanks to that collision with the shower pole, the bump was, indeed, the size of a goose egg. Not that he had any intention of getting into this second mishap with Gary. "Oh, it's fine."

"No more stars in your eyes?" There was a twinkle in Gary's eyes.

"I'm seeing perfectly clearly now," Judd assured him. That might have been the biggest whopper he'd told all day!

"You looking for Lucy?" That twinkle was still present.

"No," he said. "As a matter of fact, I'm looking for another old classmate. Danielle Brunaud. Do you remember Danielle?"

Gary laughed heartily. "Man, who at Florida State doesn't remember Danielle? Not that she ever gave me the time of day." He squinted at Judd. "Don't tell me you two had a—?"

"No."

Gary nodded. "No. I didn't think so." He gave Judd's shoulder a sympathetic pat. "Guys like us never did get girls like Danielle." He winked. "Or Lucy Weston. Man, talk about a knockout. That guy Warner's one lucky bastard." His lips compressed. "You'd think he'd be satisfied with one out of two."

"What do you mean?"

Gary shrugged. "I probably shouldn't be telling tales out of school—"

"We're not in school anymore," Judd reminded him.

Gary glanced around the lobby, waving at a few old classmates. Only one of them waved back. Judd was surprised to see that the waver was a small but very attractive blonde. He didn't recognize her. And from this distance, she appeared younger than most of the other alums.

"When Bri and I were strolling down Lincoln Road Mall a short while ago—" He paused, waving again to the good-looking blonde who was now wending her way toward them. "That's Bri. We've been married almost four years." He nudged Judd. "We're not all in Kansas anymore," he said with both pride and adoration, his eyes following his lovely wife's progress.

Judd was pleased to see that Gary Burke had gotten the last laugh. But right now he wanted the doc to concentrate on his tale. "So you were strolling down Lincoln Road…"

Gary nodded. "Right. And we popped into one of those pricey designer boutiques because Bri spotted this really beautiful and—naturally—very expensive pair of Brazilian leather slacks in the window. You couldn't miss 'em. They were cranberry-red—wait. I'll let Bri tell it."

Gary's wife had made it to her husband's side by now and she kissed him lovingly on his cheek.

"Bri, darling, this is Judd Turner. Judd's one of the good guys," he said affably.

Bri shook Judd's hand. He saw that she was even better looking up close. And he doubted she was a day over twenty-five.

"I'm glad to hear that," she told Judd, then cast a bemused glance over at her husband. "Because the rest of your old classmates—" she made a sweeping gesture with her hand "—seem depressingly dull. Most of them must have majored in basket weaving back in college."

"Bri's a criminal attorney. The youngest partner at Carter, Rutenberg & Taylor.'' Gary winked. ''If you ever get into any trouble with the law—''

Judd felt a shiver run down his spine.

She poked her husband. ''Hey, we both promised—no business talk while we're down here.''

The pair kissed.

Judd cleared his throat. ''Gary was telling me about your visit to a boutique on Lincoln Road.''

She giggled. ''Did he get to the part about the dressing room?''

Gary laughed along with his wife. ''No, I thought I'd let you tell it since you were the eyewitness.''

''Eyewitness to what?'' Judd asked, narrowing his gaze.

''I was in my dressing room, trying on this divine pair of leather slacks, which, by the way, I bought—''

''Naturally,'' Gary said amiably, slipping an arm around his lawyer wife's narrow waist.

''And all of a sudden I hear these…moans coming from the dressing room next to mine. Well, naturally I thought someone must be ill—''

Gary smiled. ''Naturally.'' His eyes sparkled mischievously. ''What else would you think?''

She giggled again. ''Certainly not that the moans weren't the result of pain, but—''

Gary couldn't wait for his wife to get to the punch line. ''Bri walked in and caught them in the act. Kyle Warner and Danielle Brunaud.''

Judd couldn't say he was surprised. He'd just gotten the location wrong.

Bri was laughing harder. ''And here's the funniest part. The woman—she was French and well, you know the French—looked straight at me while the guy was hurriedly pulling up his trousers, and she nonchalantly asks me to get her a pair of slacks in a size four like the ones I was wearing.''

"She thought Bri was a salesgirl," Gary said, chuckling.

Judd had as good a sense of humor as the next guy. And if the story had involved any other pair of lovers, he would have gotten a few laughs out of it himself. But he was far from being amused. "How did you know it was Kyle and Danielle?" he asked her.

"I didn't. But I pointed them out to Gary as they were leaving the boutique."

Gary sobered up a bit. "Is it true Warner's engaged to Lucy Weston?"

Judd's gaze narrowed. "Not for long."

7

IT WAS AFTER five-thirty in the afternoon when Danielle swept into the lobby like a movie star arriving at her world premiere. And the swarm of alums still meeting and greeting among the potted palms, chalky columns and oversize ultramodern furnishings treated the French femme fatale as such. As soon as they spotted her—and in those cranberry-red leather formfitting pants, she was hard to miss—hordes of "fans" swarmed over to her, cooing, fawning, pecking air kisses in the vicinity of each cheek, giving the celebrity her due.

"Danielle, you look incredible."

"Danielle, how do you keep so trim?"

"I love your hair that way, Dani."

"Those slacks. My God, I couldn't wear leather slacks like that if I worked out five hours a day. And that color is divine."

Judd, who'd made his way through the crowd, eyed the red leather pants.

"Size four?" he queried dryly when he was an arm's length away from the star attraction.

Danielle couldn't hear him for all the compliments bombarding her. But she did see him. And the instant she did, she pulled him closer, throwing her arms around him. "Judd, there you are, darling."

As Danielle's gushing fan club watched this amorous greeting between the *beauty* and the *beast,* they were stunned into silence. A number of mouths literally gaped open. Judd laughed inwardly. This was the only speck of enjoyment he was likely to be getting out of Danielle Brunaud's Oscar-winning performance.

So he decided to milk it.

"Dani, you're late. I hate to be kept waiting," he scolded lightly, giving her Brazilian red-leather-clad butt an overzealous pinch.

She emitted a squeal of pain, but she wasn't about to be thrown off her performance. "I'm sorry, darling. But, truly, it couldn't be helped."

He bit back an acid remark. "Truly?"

She stroked his cheek. "I'm here now, darling. Shall we go?"

He caught a few more alums' mouths fall open.

But there was one person, standing apart from the others, whose mouth was shut tight.

Judd's fleeting speck of enjoyment flew the coop as he watched Lucy turn her back on him and stride purposefully into the cocktail lounge.

"A MARGARITA."

Derek leaned across the bar. "Didn't you tell me earlier today that you're allergic to tequila?"

"What if I did?" Lucy snapped.

"A margarita is made with tequila."

"Make it a double."

The bartender raised an eyebrow. "One of those days, huh?"

"Oh, no. I've never had another day remotely like this one."

"Well, then, are you sure you wouldn't rather have that tequila straight up? It'll fix what ails you a lot faster than a margarita."

She sighed. How could she get fixed when she couldn't even grasp what was wrong with her?

Derek set a shot glass, a bottle of tequila, a salt shaker and a few wedges of lemon on the copper bar in front of her. He poured her the first shot. She skipped the ritual of a lemon squeeze and salt, and downed the shot in one gulp. She gave a little shiver as it went down, then poured herself a second.

"You aren't planning to drive anywhere, are you?" he asked.

The second shot went down easier than the first. "I don't plan to move from this stool for the rest of the day. Or night. Or...whatever."

"Aren't you one of the alums? There's a gala bash being held for you guys in the Palm Room tonight. And a cocktail hour's going on on the terrace as we speak. That's why this place has been empty all weekend. Just about everybody staying at the hotel is down here for the reunion festivities."

"I'm not feeling...very sociable." She twisted her tongue around the word *sociable,* and she spilled a few drops pouring herself a third shot.

"You might want to slow down just a wee bit, Lucy."

"I might." She chugalugged the third shot. "But I don't."

Derek removed the bottle from the bar and replaced it with a dish of nuts. "Munch on some of these and tell me your troubles. I'm a real good listener."

She absently scooped up a few cashews and popped them into her mouth.

After munching for a couple of minutes, she squinted at the bartender. "Remember that couple that was in here yesterday? The pair that wanted to buy me—" she hic-cuped "—a drink."

He nodded. "Dynamite-looking twosome."

"One of who...whom..." She giggled. "Whom...is... my fiancé."

"Oh, so that's why you're bummed out. Hey, I wouldn't worry if I were you—"

But before he could finish, she said, "I kissed a man in my shower. Yesterday."

Derek cocked his head. "I take it this man wasn't—"

"My fiancé? Nope. Nope, he wasn't. And he's fat."

He looked as if he didn't know what to say. "Well, looks aren't…everything."

"But he doesn't kiss like a fat man." She went to lean her elbows on the bar, but missed the mark. "Oops."

"You doing okay?"

"Great. Where's the tequila?"

Derek seemed to think that distracting her was the best response. "So tell me some more about this fat guy, Lucy."

She looked conspiratorially around the lounge. It was still empty. "He doesn't really wear braces." She pressed her fingers to her lips. "This can't go any further."

He smiled, holding up his right hand. "Scout's honor."

"He actually has *exceptionally* nice teeth."

"Well, there you go."

"And those glasses?"

His smile broadened. "He doesn't really wear—"

"Shh."

"Sorry."

"He's really a very good kisser."

"So, you like him."

"No. No, no, no, no."

"That many nos. Hmm."

"Was it that many?" Lucy popped a few more nuts into her mouth, then leaned closer to the bartender.

"He's in some kind of trouble. And I want to help him. But will he let me?"

"No?"

"Nooo."

"Well, maybe he's just trying to keep you out of trouble."

She gave Derek a lopsided smile. "You're right. You're absolutely right. He's not a bad guy. He's a..."

"Fat guy?"

She giggled again. "No. A good guy. He's a good guy. I know it. I am a very good judge of people." She poked her own chest, losing her balance and almost slipping off the stool. "I'm fine. I'm fine. Don't worry about a thing."

"I say neither of us should worry about a thing."

"You know what I've decided, Derek?"

"I hope it's that you've had enough to drink."

She stepped down from the bar stool, gripping the edge until she got her sea legs. "I'm going to help him whether he likes it or not. Because...because that's what people do. They help each other."

"I thought you didn't like him."

"I didn't say that." She swayed slightly. "Did I?"

Derek smiled. "Maybe I just didn't hear you right."

"I need a favor. A really *big* favor."

"Sure, Lucy. What can I do for you?"

"Could you help me up to my room? I'm not feeling...too well."

"Um, sure. Let me get someone to cover the bar and I'll zip you up there."

A minute later, a substitute at the bar, Derek guided her out of the cocktail lounge, through the lobby and into the elevator. "What floor?"

"Fourteen. I'm in 1405."

When they arrived at the door, Lucy stuck her hands into the pockets of her shift. "Darn it. Where did I put my key?" She slumped against the door. "Ooh, I really need to...lie down."

He patted her back. "Hold on for just a sec. I'll find one of the maids on the floor and get her to let you in."

"That is so sweet of you, Derek. You are definitely one of the good guys. If you ever need any help—"

He patted her shoulder, then took off down the hall. With a faint nod of satisfaction, she watched him go. In no time at all he was back with one of the hotel maids, who unlocked the door to Judd Turner's room and even offered to come inside with her to turn down her bed.

"That won't be necessary. I really appreciate your help. Both of you." Lucy slipped some bills out of her pocket. The maid took a twenty, but Derek refused to take a dime.

Lucy smiled to herself as she stepped into Judd's room and shut the door firmly. Her drunk trick, which she'd used on a few previous occasions when she was tracking down a story and needed access to someplace she wasn't supposed to have access to, had once again worked like a charm.

Not that it had been entirely an act. The three shots of booze had left her feeling a bit light-headed. But she was sober enough to search Judd's room and, hopefully, dig up some clues that would help her figure out just how much trouble he was in.

RICO MORALES, wearing white trunks, sunglasses and nothing else, was stretched out on a lounge chair on the enormous terrace of his penthouse apartment. The view of the ocean was breathtaking, but neither Morales nor his two *associates,* as they were introduced to Judd, seemed to be paying any attention to the spectacular sight. Morales appeared to have his eyes closed beneath the sunglasses and his associates had their eyes glued on Judd. Tweedledee and Tweedledum were big, brawny and, Judd guessed by the bulges beneath their jackets—packing. Despite the fact that it was almost six o'clock in the afternoon, the temperature was still in the eighties and the infamous Florida humidity had to have hit the one-hundred percent mark. The two thugs were not exactly dressed for the weather. They were all in black. Black suits, black shirts, black ties, spit-shined black-tasseled loafers. Two more men, also in uniform, remained inside the lavish living room, which was done up in gilt and leather and wall-to-wall mirrors. Judd noticed that one of the curved leather sofas nearly matched the color of Danielle's pants. She blended in perfectly.

Morales, a small, slender man with a pockmarked complexion and jet-black hair slicked back from his narrow face, was sipping a frozen cocktail through one of those flexible kid's straws. He didn't offer either his girlfriend or his visitor a drink. He didn't even invite them to sit down.

"So, Dani tells me you're in the laundry business." Morales, who spoke with a thick Brooklyn accent, didn't so much as turn his head in Judd's direction.

"Well...yes," he said, after a quick sideways glance at Danielle. "I do have a number of...Laundromats. Started with a couple. Right in my home town of Cincinnati—"

"You know Gus Santorelli?"

"Um...no. Is he a *friend* of yours?"

Morales's lips curved in more of a smirk than a smile. "Not anymore, he ain't."

The two goons mirrored their boss's smirk.

Judd glanced at Danielle again. She was trying her best to smile brightly, but was starting to perspire. He guessed that it was more than the weather that was getting to her.

"Mind if I go inside and get myself a drink, Rico?" Danielle's French accent did not conceal the placating note in her voice. She shifted from one spiked heel to the other, but she didn't make a move. It was clear to Judd she was waiting for permission to leave. She didn't get it. She didn't get so much as a nod.

She stayed put, fabricating another smile for Judd. But this smile looked about as legit as the last one. Plus, she was perspiring some more.

Judd was perspiring plenty, as well. And while the thick wad of terry towels he was using for bulk was soaking up some of his sweat, it was making the improvised padding soggy and lumpy. It was no understatement to say he was feeling the heat. Not to mention the tension. He deliberately let it show. Even if Morales didn't appear to be looking his way, he was certain the mobster was taking everything in.

The foursome stood around as Morales finished his drink, making slurping sounds with the straw as he got to the bottom of the glass. It was the only sound on the terrace. When he was done, the mobster stuck his hand out, and Tweedledee quickly took the glass from his boss. The goon held the glass up in the direction of the living room. In less than a minute, Judd caught sight of a svelte brunette, dressed in a skimpy maid's uniform that could have doubled as a stripper's stage costume, come bustling across the vast living room and out the sliding door onto the terrace. She was expertly balancing a second frozen cocktail on a gilt tray. Another flexible straw was sticking out of the drink.

Tweedledum removed the new drink from the tray and handed it to Morales. The two goons clearly each had their own assignments.

Judd observed Danielle eyeing the chilled drink longingly as Morales put the straw between his thin lips. He also caught the mobster's sadistic smile. Morales was taking everything in, all right.

"I told Dani I got enough business acquaintances, but she seems to think you might be hungry. Is she right?"

Judd knew he was being tested. If he came off sounding either too dumb or too smart, it would make Morales suspicious. "I guess you're not talking food here." Judd chuckled at his own joke. No one else so much as cracked a smile. He stuck his hands into the pockets of his slacks. "I suppose I'm as hungry as the next guy."

"Which next guy is that?" Morales asked. Now this line got chuckles from both the goons and Danielle. Judd let a couple of beats pass and then he joined in.

"So?" The instant Morales spoke, his audience stopped laughing. Judd made sure he was the last to stop. Too bad, he thought, no one there could appreciate his performance. Then again, if any of them did appreciate it, he was well aware it would be *too bad* for him.

He cleared his throat. "The guy with the BMW and a cool pad overlooking the ocean."

Danielle beamed at him, then at her mobster boyfriend. This time there was no question that the smile was authentic. "See, Rico," she cooed. "Didn't I tell you?"

A GASP OF ALARM ESCAPED Lucy's lips. Then she edged a little closer to what had, at first sight, appeared to be a dead animal in the corner of Judd's bathroom floor. On closer inspection, she saw that the object was neither deceased nor animate.

There, in a heap, lay a damp pillowlike thing fitted with Velcro straps. And beneath that was an equally wet foam cushion that looked markedly like—

It didn't take long for her to go from revulsion to bewilderment to a sharp awareness. Her gaze fell on his leather shaving kit. She snapped it open. Inside, along with all his shaving gear, she unearthed a small container holding a pair of contact lenses.

Returning to the bedroom, she checked out his bureau drawers and closet. His entire wardrobe, save for the crumpled outfit he'd worn when she'd caught him in her shower yesterday, and was now hanging over the shower curtain in his bathroom, still bore price tags. What was even more illuminating was the name of the store on the tags. Karlins. Karlins was a chain of department stores. But the chain was strictly a Florida operation. There were no Karlins Department Stores anywhere in the vicinity of Cincinnati, Ohio.

She sat down on the edge of his bed. No wonder he'd been acting strangely. He wasn't fat. He didn't wear glasses anymore. Or braces. And it was exceedingly unlikely he lived in Cincinnati. A short while earlier, her suspicions already mounting, Lucy had put a call through to Cincinnati Information. The operator had no phone listing for any Judd Turners. She'd wanted to give him the benefit of the doubt, telling herself he simply had an unlisted number. But all her doubts were now used up.

She sighed. Okay, so now she'd confirmed what she'd already suspected. Judd was carrying out an elaborate charade. Far more elaborate than she'd surmised. What she still didn't have the answer to was, *why?*

She rose from the bed, crossed the room and checked out his desk again. There'd been no clues there when she'd gone through it a few minutes earlier, and no new clues magically materialized on second inspection. She glanced once more down at the chrome wastebasket beneath the desk. Empty. She kicked it in frustration. It tipped over and rolled a few inches. That was when she spotted a crumpled piece of paper that had inadvertently missed its designated target.

She knelt and snatched up the paper. As she was about to smooth it out, she heard a clicking sound. Her eyes shot to the door, and she caught the handle turning. Any second now, Judd was going to walk in there and catch her.

She raced across the room and dove under the bed just as the door opened. She held her breath as she lifted the bed skirt a fraction of an inch and saw a pair of men's cordovan boat shoes crossing the room.

A disturbing sensation hit her. She lifted the cloth a bit higher. Now she could see the bottom few inches of a pair of trousers. They were pale gray.

When Judd had left the hotel with Danielle, the trousers he'd been wearing were white. And Lucy remembered the three shoe boxes in his closet. One was a Nike box, the newly purchased sneakers it'd previously contained now drying out on the bathroom floor. A second box held a pair of shiny black patent-leather dress shoes that he was, no doubt, planning to wear with the recently purchased tacky pale blue tux. The third box, empty like the first, was another Nike box. It didn't take a detective or a reporter to figure out he was wearing those sneakers now.

So who belonged to the boat shoes and the pale gray slacks? She knew one man who owned both. Her fiancé, Kyle Warner.

How had he managed to gain entry to Judd's room? The answer was forthcoming. So were a second pair of shoes. Sensible, low-heeled black pumps.

"Thanks so much… Is it Betsy?" Kyle asked, putting on his Cary Grant accent.

"That's right, Mr. Turner. Betsy Riley. Head Housekeeper."

"Please, call me Judd."

Lucy scowled. *Why that sneaky little devil. Kyle was pulling almost the same con she'd just pulled. And all he'd had to do was turn on that Warner charm.*

"Well, Judd, happy to oblige. You're not the first guest to leave his key in his room." Betsy hesitated. "By the way, I'm off duty at midnight."

"I'll definitely make a note of that, Betsy."

"You do that."

Lucy saw the pumps pivot and disappear from the room. Kyle's shoes remained put. The door shut.

Okay, so now she knew how he'd gained entry into Judd's room. Next came a more puzzling question. Why? She doubted she'd get the answer to that one as easily as she had to the first.

She felt a tickle in her throat. There was dust under the bed; the maid service left something to be desired.

Lucy was allergic to dust mites. She kept swallowing fitfully, trying to keep herself from breaking into a coughing attack. If Kyle discovered her under Judd's bed, he'd certainly want to know why as much as she wanted to know what Kyle was doing there. But her desire not to be discovered outweighed her curiosity.

Kyle's feet were no longer in view, but she could hear drawers opening followed by riffling sounds, then drawers slamming shut. His shoes came into view again when he headed for Judd's closet. He, too, examined the garments and the shoe boxes.

He made for the desk next, giving it a thorough search. She clutched the crumpled slip of paper in her hand. For all she knew, it was blank or there was some innocuous note scribbled on it. But, somehow, she thought it might be important. Again the big *why?*

He was crossing the room, heading for the bathroom. Lucy held her breath. Any moment now, he'd discover the damp heap on the bathroom floor. He'd put two and two together.

And then what?

The mounting tension made the tickle in her throat worse. She didn't think she could swallow down her urge to cough much longer.

She heard Kyle start to open the bathroom door. *Oh, no...*

Then she heard voices coming from right outside the

hotel room door. One of the voices had a French accent. The other voice was male.

Lucy saw the boat shoes dash back across the bedroom. Now Kyle was trapped. For a terrifying moment, she was afraid her fiancé was going to hide under the bed, too. She breathed a sigh of relief when she saw him head for the closet.

The closet door shut, the door to the hotel room opened, and Lucy coughed all at the same time. Each sound managed to mask the others.

"I'm bushed, Danielle—"

"Dani. Now that we're going to be more than friends, Judd—"

Lucy's lips compressed. She told herself she couldn't care less if Judd and Danielle were becoming an item. In fact, she should be thrilled. If Danielle were otherwise occupied, she'd keep her fangs off Kyle.

So why *wasn't* she thrilled?

"I don't know, Danielle…Dani. Are you sure your boyfriend's scheme is—?"

Lucy's brows knit together. Finally, some answers.

But, instead there was silence. Well, not quite silence. She risked a peek. All she could see were two pair of shoes. Spiked heels and Nike sneakers. Facing each other. Tips touching.

"See, I'm living dangerously," Danielle cooed.

"Well, I guess Rico wouldn't be too happy if he caught you kissing me," Judd muttered.

Danielle laughed. "I wasn't referring to Rico, silly. I meant your braces. When do they come off, by the way?"

"Oh…oh, well…"

"Never mind, darling. Listen, I'm parched. Let's catch the last few minutes of the alum cocktail party before we change for the banquet."

"No, I really don't think—"

"I agree. Who cares about the dumb reunion. I say we skip the whole affair and...have one of our own right here."

Lucy saw the spiked heels turn gracefully and head over to the bed. Then she felt the mattress sag above her. "Do you want to call room service or shall I?"

"On second thought, I wouldn't mind touching base with some old friends," Judd blurted. "Besides, I'd really love to see a few more eyes pop out when I walk in there with the most beautiful alum to have ever graced Florida State on my arm."

Lucy groaned. Then realizing with alarm that the sound might be overheard, she clamped her hand over her mouth. Luckily, the creaking of the springs as Danielle rose from the bed kept the groan from giving her away.

She was about to expel a sigh of relief when Judd and Danielle exited the room. Then she remembered that she still wasn't alone.

Not for long, though.

She heard the closet door open, and Kyle's feet scampered over to the front door. She heard him crack it open, pause there for several protracted seconds—no doubt checking for an all clear—before he hurriedly slipped out of the room.

Her relief at her fiancé's departure was accompanied by a coughing fit as she crawled out from under the bed. Rising to her feet, she felt a wave of dizziness. Those three shots of tequila, combined with the stress of the past few minutes, had finally gotten to her. She sat back down on the edge of the bed, dropping her head in her hands.

8

LUCY'S HEAD POPPED UP, her eyes shooting toward the hotel room door. The handle was turning. *Oh, no, not again...*

She dropped to her knees and scrambled under the bed as the door opened. *Who was it this time? Judd? Kyle returning? The maid come to turn down the bed?*

Three guesses and all of them wrong.

For one thing, there were two of them. They were both wearing black Italian leather loafers with tassels. And they both had big feet. She also got a glimpse at the cuffs of the trousers. Black.

The two men stood near the door.

Lucy lifted the bed skirt an inch and risked a fuller glimpse. She saw two grim-faced hulks dressed in black suits, black shirts and black ties. They looked like undertakers or mobsters. She quickly let the bed skirt drop, thinking with a shiver that maybe they were both!

"These little passkey cards are a cinch. We gotta go into business—"

"What? Like you invented 'em, Arnie? I don't think the boss would be too happy with you taking credit—"

"Okay, okay. Just a thought, Joey. So, what are we looking for?"

"We'll know that when we find it."

"How exactly are we gonna know it?"

"Don't start with me, Arnie."

"Who's starting? What? I can't ask a simple question?"

"How about you start asking some smart questions for a change?"

"Very funny. You're a barrelful of laughs, Joey."

"Come on. We ain't got all day. You do the bathroom, Arnie. I'll take the bedroom."

"How come I always get the bathroom?"

"You don't always get the bathroom."

"Yeah? Name one time I didn't get the bathroom."

"Will you give it a rest, Arnie?"

"See, I told ya—"

"Mendez."

"Mendez? No, no. I distinctly remember—"

"Oh, yeah. Okay. Okay, give me a sec."

"You can't come up with a single name."

"So, big deal. I can always count on you to make a mountain out of a rat hill."

"Mouse hill."

"Huh?"

"You're not so smart, Joey."

"I don't think I'm so smart, Arnie. I just think I'm a hell of a lot smarter than you."

"Oh, yeah?"

"Yeah."

"Well, I'm not taking the bathroom this time."

"Don't start with me, Arnie."

Lucy closed her eyes. *Start with him, Arnie. Stay out of the bathroom.* She may not have known who these two bozos were, but she knew one thing for sure. If they discovered the pile of stuffing in the bathtub, Judd's cover would be blown.

And then what?

She was convinced, whatever it was, it wouldn't be good.

"Did you hear that?"

She held her breath. Had he heard her breathing? What if they found her under the bed? She was equally convinced nothing good would come of that, either.

She heard a clicking sound.

"What? I don't hear nothing, Arnie. Would you put that piece away?"

Panic caught in her throat.

"You gotta get your hearing checked, Joey."

"I got twenty-twenty hearing. And I don't hear— Hold it."

"See. See."

"Shut up, Arnie. Someone's just walking down the hall."

"Yeah? So how come that someone's footsteps just stopped? And how come that green light just—"

"Shut your trap already and get in the closet."

"Man, I always get the closet—"

Lucy began to tremble. If Arnie always got the closet, where did Joey usually hide? She didn't need three guesses....

Panic ricocheted through her entire body as she tried to prepare herself for discovery. Did Joey have a piece, too? As if she needed to ask!

She squeezed her eyes shut, silently praying.

And, miraculously, her prayers were answered.

Joey didn't dive under the bed. Even as she questioned where he'd gone, she heard the door to the terrace slide open.

The door from the hallway opened and shut. Judd's hotel room was busier than Grand Central Station.

A new pair of shoes entered. These shoes were practical white oxfords. The kind of shoes worn by the maids at the hotel.

Lucy heard a tut-tut sound as the maid crossed over to the open door of the terrace.

"Don't these people know you don't keep doors open when you got the air-conditioning on?" the maid muttered.

Lucy heard the door slide shut, then a click. The maid had not only closed the slider, she'd locked it. Now if only Lucy could send some mental telepathy the maid's way and get her to lock the closet door as well.

No such luck.

She saw the tips of the white shoes by the bed. First on the right side, then they moved around to the left. The maid, humming to herself, was removing the stark-white spread and turning down the equally stark-white blanket.

Then the feet disappeared. Lucy thought at first the maid was going to leave, but then she heard a faint *tut* sound coming from the direction of the bathroom.

"Now what is all this? I declare some of the guests at this hotel are into the weirdest things. And don't they know if you leave wet things lying about, you attract water bugs?"

Lucy heard a rustling sound like a plastic bag being shaken open. This was followed by faint thudding sounds like sodden stuffing being dumped into the plastic bag. She prayed her hearing was twenty-twenty and that the maid was removing the evidence.

As soon as she left, Arnie stepped out of the closet.

"Joey? Joey, where are you?"

Lucy saw the black loafers heading toward the bed. Her panic returned tenfold. Any second now, Arnie was going to peer under the bed, looking for his partner. Only it wasn't Joey he was going to find....

She didn't know if she could take much more of this. Then again, the alternative wasn't terribly comforting.

"Arnie. Hey…" Joey's muffled shout was followed by several raps on the glass slider.

"Hey, what're ya doing out there?"

"What do you mean what am I doing? What do you think I'm doing? Let me in there."

Lucy exhaled her fast-held breath as Arnie's shoes headed for the slider. She heard the door open and then slide open.

"How'd you lock yourself out?"

"I didn't lock myself out, you idiot."

"I don't like being called an idiot, Joey. Do I go around calling you an idiot?"

"You've called me an idiot."

"Yeah? When? You tell me one time—"

"You know what? This is just plain dumb. I'm gonna take the bathroom. You, Arnie, can do this room. What do you say about that?"

"You mean it?"

"I mean it."

"That's real decent of ya, Joey."

"Well, Arnie, that's me. Decent."

Yeah, right, Lucy thought sardonically.

"And just to show ya I can be as decent as you, Joey, I'm gonna take the bathroom."

"No…"

"Yeah. I want to. I mean it."

"Okay, Arnie. If that's what you want."

"That's what I want, Joey."

LUCY HAD BEEN UNDER the bed for almost an hour, and was sweltering, the air-conditioning cut off by the heavy bed skirt. So far the men in black hadn't yet checked under the bed. But she was terrified of her luck running out.

"So, now what?" Arnie asked.

"What do you mean, now what?"

"We didn't find nothin', Joey."

"Idiot. I know we didn't find nothin'."

"It really gets me sore, ya always calling me an idiot, Joey."

"Don't start with me, Arnie."

"I'm just saying—"

"Listen to what I'm saying," Joey said.

"I don't hear ya saying nothin'."

"That's because you won't shut up long enough to let me talk."

"Okay, so talk."

"We go back to the boss and tell him his new boy's looking good."

"What about the boss's feelin' that there was something fishy?"

"Hey, did we find anything here, Arnie?"

"You know we didn't, Joey. What are ya asking me for?"

"It was rhetoric."

"Huh?"

"You know, when you ask a question, only you already know the answer."

"Now, that's dumb."

"It ain't dumb, Arnie. It's—"

"Yeah, what is it, Joey?"

"Will you stop asking so many dumb questions? Come on. Let's get out of here before someone else walks in."

"Hey, ya think I wanna hang around?"

Go already, Lucy urged silently. She was starting to feel light-headed and queasy.

She felt a fraction better when she heard the front door open.

"Hey, what do you got there, Arnie?"

"Huh? Oh, just some stuff from the bathroom."

"Soap? Mouthwash? Shampoo?"

"I left the sewing kit. Those needles, man. You couldn't find the hole in a haystack."

"You really are an idiot, Arnie."

"I'm warnin' ya, Joey. You keep calling me an idiot—"

"What's the guy gonna think, Arnie? He goes into his bathroom, looking for his stuff and it's gone. Huh, what's he gonna think?"

"I wasn't thinking. Oh, that's one of those rhetorical questions, right?"

"Go put the stuff back, Arnie."

"You think, just the soap, Joey? There's another bar—"

"Put everything back, you idiot. Exactly where you found it all."

"Okay, okay... Next time, you get the bathroom, Joey. That's all I gotta say."

LUCY DRAGGED HERSELF out from under the bed, hoping the cool air in the room would quell some of her nausea. But it had the opposite effect. She barely made it to the bathroom.

A couple of minutes later, feeling a good deal better, she washed her face and rinsed her mouth. She silently thanked Joey for making Arnie put back the complimentary mouthwash. She was turning off the tap when she remembered the crumpled piece of paper she'd found behind the wastebasket—still under the bed. In all the commotion, she'd completely forgotten about it.

The last thing she wanted to do was crawl under that bed again. But the newshound in her was more determined than ever to get to the bottom of all these goings-on. She would snatch the paper and make a beeline out of Judd's room. Kyle was probably looking all over the hotel for her. Little did he know he'd almost found her not twenty minutes ago. Which reminded her that she had another mystery on her hands. The mystery of what Kyle was looking for in Judd's room. And why.

She stepped out of the bathroom and was halfway to the bed when she was brought up short by a sharp rap on the hotel room door. She froze in place.

"Judd? Are you in there?"

The woman's voice sounded vaguely familiar.

"Judd? It's Roz. Open up."

Roz. The private detective.

Lucy watched in horror as the red light on the lock once again turned green. No. No. This wasn't happening. This couldn't be happening again.

Lucy had to make a split-second decision. Make a bee-line for the bathroom or do a racing dive under the bed? She opted for the bathroom. At least it was cool in there.

"Judd? You in here?" Roz entered the bedroom just as Lucy made it to the bathroom.

Lucy flattened herself against the bathroom door. *Don't look in here. Please don't look in here....*

She bit back a gasp as Roz rapped on the closed bathroom door. "You in there, Judd?"

The door handle started to turn. She dashed over to the tub, jumped in and drew the white terry curtain halfway across the shower bar. Roz would be able to see he wasn't in there and, hopefully, go away.

The bathroom door opened. Lucy held her breath. Moments later, it shut again. Her legs were so rubbery she sank down to the bottom of the tub.

"Oh, there you are," she heard Roz exclaim. A moment later she heard the hotel room door close.

Lucy cautiously got back to her feet, climbed out of the tub and tiptoed over to the bathroom door so she could hear the conversation more clearly.

"What are you doing here?" Judd asked.

"I started to get worried about you. Thought I'd pop down and make sure things were going okay."

"They're going okay," he said.

"What about Warner?"

Lucy scowled. Why was the detective questioning him about Kyle? His answer might explain why Kyle had been searching Judd's room.

"Warner? Don't ask."

Ask, Lucy urged. *Ask.*

"Are you getting anywhere with him?"

"Not as far as Danielle Brunaud is."

Her scowl deepened. *What does that mean?*

What does that mean?" Roz echoed her thoughts.

"The wife of one of the alums was trying on some slacks in a boutique over on Lincoln Road and heard moans coming from the next dressing room. She went to see if someone was sick only to catch Kyle and Danielle having an intimate little *reunion* of their own."

Lucy gasped.

"What was that?" Roz asked.

Tears of rage and hurt spiking her eyes, Lucy clamped her hand over her mouth.

"I didn't hear anything. Look, Roz, I've got to get dressed for the banquet. Warner waylaid me in the lobby a couple of minutes ago and made his first pitch. The bastard," he muttered. "He's lucky I didn't lay him out right on the spot."

"That wouldn't be in character, Judd. Which means it wouldn't be a smart move."

"I know. But it sure would make me feel better. Can you believe that jerk? When he's engaged to the most incredible woman on this planet?"

He's not going to be engaged to her for long, Lucy thought bitterly. *I should have listened to Gina. And to*

Judd. And to my own heart, she admitted. Deep down, she'd known all along there was something lacking. Wasn't that the real reason she kept putting off setting a date for the wedding? It wasn't only that she could never get herself to fully trust Kyle. There was something missing between them. All the bells and whistles you were supposed to feel when you were truly in love. That magical spark.

Like the spark she'd felt when she and Judd had kissed.

Had he just called her the most incredible woman on this planet?

She stared down at the sparkling two-carat diamond engagement ring on her finger. She yanked it off and, without even a moment's hesitation, tossed it into the toilet.

"You need to stay focused, Judd," Roz was saying firmly. "You want to get back at Warner, you know the way to do it."

"Oh, I know the way, all right," he responded vehemently.

"Any closer on the password?"

Lucy frowned. Password?

"Actually, I have a couple of ideas," he said. "Once I see that Warner's settled in at the reunion banquet, I'll pay another visit to his room."

"And Morales?"

"Keep your fingers crossed, Roz. If everything goes according to my plan, I'll have Morales and Warner nailed. And I'll toss in Danielle Brunaud for good measure."

"Sounds great," Roz said. "Only, I get the feeling things haven't exactly gone according to plan so far."

AFTER ROZ LEFT, Judd stripped off the repugnant Hawaiian shirt and baggy white pants, tossing them onto a chair.

The towels he'd used as substitute stuffing lay on the floor. Kicking them aside, he moved over to the closet and pulled out the repellent blue tux he'd picked up at Karlins. It was the worst-looking suit in the store. When Kyle had ambushed him in the lobby a few minutes ago, he'd tried to drag him over to the men's boutique next door to buy him a black tux. Judd had forced himself to stay in character.

"That's really nice of you, Kyle. But I just wouldn't feel comfortable in some fancy tux."

"Judd, you sell yourself way short. You're not a bad-looking guy. You get yourself in shape, stay away from the barber for a while, switch to contact lenses, and work on your wardrobe and you could have plenty of dynamite dames eating out of your hand."

"Even a *dame* like Lucy?" Judd asked before he could stop himself.

Kyle chuckled. "Hey, man, there is no other dame like Lucy."

Judd felt his hands clench into fists. *I know that, you jerk. Far better than you know it.*

"So what size are you?" Kyle asked, oblivious to the subtext.

"No, I couldn't. Besides, these boutiques are way overpriced. A designer tux could go for...I don't know...a few hundred bucks anyway."

"Try a grand." Kyle slapped his back. He had to stick his clenched fists in his pockets. "But it's my treat. And believe me, a grand's a drop in the bucket for me."

"So you're doing well."

Kyle smirked. "Very well. In fact, I've got a bit of money to burn."

"Burn?"

Another slap on the back. He grit his teeth.

"How'd you like a partner, buddy?"

"A...partner?"

"A *silent* partner, of course."

"You want to be a part owner of a string of Laundro-mats?"

"What's wrong with that? I've been on the lookout for some good investments. And investing with a good friend—hey, what could be better than that?"

Judd forced a smile. He knew Kyle was handing him a line about the good friends, but maybe Roz was right that the creep was so shallow this was as good as his friendships ever got.

Kyle wrapped a meaty arm around his shoulder and gave him a little squeeze. "I could put a good chunk of change into the business. Enough to open quite a few more laundries. Maybe we'd even spread into dry cleaning. The only thing is...well, I wouldn't necessarily want all this dough to show up on the books at one time."

"Why not? There isn't anything...questionable...?"

"Come on, Judd. Would your old buddy, Kyle, get in-volved in anything that wasn't strictly on the up-and-up?"

That's exactly what my old buddy *would do,* Judd thought.

"No, it's just that I don't want the IRS hitting me up all at once. I'd give the money to you in one lump sum and then you could spread it out over time—"

Their conversation was interrupted by a couple of mod-erately drunk alums. They were ex-football pals of Kyle's who insisted on dragging him off for some reunion toasts. Judd thought they'd be lucky if they could remember their way to the bar.

The alums didn't invite him to join them. He doubted they'd even *seen* him. But Kyle tried to tug him along.

"No, that's okay. I really need to get upstairs and—"

Kyle didn't bother to wait for him to finish his excuse. He gave his *good friend* a final slap on the back and a promise that they would "work on our business plans later."

"You bet we will," he muttered acerbically as he stepped into the elevator and hit the button for the four-teenth floor.

Now, as he laid the tacky blue tux on his bed, he flashed on the elegant black Armani tux hanging in the huge walk-in closet of his Fort Lauderdale beachfront condo. It had cost him well over a thousand bucks. And if he had to say it himself, he looked like a million bucks in that suit.

He stripped off his underwear and laid the glasses and braces on the bedside table. Then he did some stretching exercises for a few minutes. They didn't help to ease his taut muscles, for he was still all keyed up. And sweaty.

A quick, cool shower would hit the spot!

LUCY GASPED as pellets of ice-cold water rained down on her. She gasped again, this time more audibly, when Judd stepped into the tub. He joined in on the second gasp. His was even louder than hers.

"Is this your idea of a joke, Lucy?"

She couldn't respond. She couldn't do anything but stare at his gorgeous, muscular body, a stab of sudden, overpowering desire nearly making her lose her balance.

"Satisfied?"

A flush of heat rose in her face and she quickly dropped her gaze to the floor of the tub. Her dress was soaked through and she was shivering.

He reached around her and adjusted the temperature so that it was lukewarm.

"Better?"

She grimaced. "This isn't very funny, Judd." She pulled the curtain aside and stepped out of the tub.

Stepping out after her, he grabbed a towel from the

towel bar and wrapped it around his waist. "Am I laughing?"

"Am I?" she shot back.

"How long have you been in here?" he demanded.

"Long enough."

Tears smarted in her eyes, but since she was already dripping wet, there was no way for him to tell she was crying.

He cupped her chin, tilting her head up, and held her gaze. "I'm sorry, Lucy."

"No you're not." She swiped his hand. "You've always hated Kyle."

"You're wrong. About my not being sorry," he said, pressing his lips to her wet hair. "I hate the bastard for hurting you."

She shut her eyes, the tears slipping past her closed lids and rolling down her cheeks. "I feel so...stupid."

He turned her around to face him, a lopsided smile on his lips. "How do you think I feel?"

Tremors coursed under her skin, but she quirked a smile. "I don't know how you feel, but you look damn good, Judd."

"So do you," he murmured. "You look more than good."

She swiped at her cheeks.

"My dress is...ruined," she mumbled.

"No, it isn't. It'll dry out. Turn around."

Turn around. Was it only yesterday afternoon he'd said those same words to her at the pool? Then, it had been a gruff order. Now, it was a murmured appeal.

She pivoted so that her back was to him. He lowered the zipper of her sodden shift and eased it off her shoulders. The garment slipped down her body into a wet puddle on the floor.

"Water bugs," Lucy said hoarsely.

"What?"

"Nothing."

He released the clasp on her bra, then guided her around to face him as he removed the undergarment. Her nipples were hard little pebbles.

"Tell me this isn't a dream, Lucy."

She gasped as his lips caressed her right nipple and then her left. "If it is a dream, I don't think I want to wake up," she whispered, arching her back as his tongue flicked across her nipples.

He smoothed her wet hair from her face, and she clutched his shoulders to keep her balance. Her legs felt rubbery again and her heart was hammering wildly in her chest.

This is crazy, Lucy told herself even as waves of yearning coursed through her body. Twenty minutes ago, she was engaged to be married to another man. Twenty minutes ago, she hadn't known that her fiancé had cheated on her.

Was that what this was? Payback? Tit for tat? Was she just using Judd to settle the score?

She wasn't aware she'd drawn away from him until she felt him release his hold on her. She met his gaze. His expression revealed both disappointment and understanding.

"I was hoping we wouldn't wake up this quickly," he murmured.

"I want to know what's going on, Judd."

"He smiled. "I would have thought that was obvious."

"That's not what I'm talking about. What is Kyle up to? And how do Morales and Danielle fit in? And what is everyone under the sun looking for in your room?"

He scowled. "Who's everyone?"

"You tell me."

"How am I supposed to tell you when I don't know

what you're talking about? You're not making any sense, Lucy.''

''Well, that makes two of us, Judd Turner.''

He stood there, baffled. She wagged a finger at him.

''I know what it is,'' she said. ''You don't trust me. And I know why.''

''Great. Tell me,'' he said.

''It's because I'm a TV news reporter. You're worried I'll leak the story.''

''What story?''

She narrowed her eyes. ''Exactly.'' She started to reach for her clothes.

''Lucy—'' As he went to stop her, his fingers accidentally skimmed her breast.

Her nipples were still hard. ''Damn you, Judd.''

''I'm sorry.'' He immediately dropped his hands to his sides.

''This is ridiculous.'' Lust warred with her anger and a myriad of other feelings as she stood facing him in the bathroom, the two of them naked, wanting each other.

But they both knew there were too many complications, even if the specific issues were different for each of them.

''I've waited ten years, Lucy. I can wait a while longer,'' he said with dispirited resignation as he reached past her for another bath towel. He wrapped it around her damp, glistening, glorious body.

She could see goose bumps rising on his bare chest. She felt an almost overpowering impulse to reach out and stroke them away. She wanted to warm him from head to toe. She wanted to press her body against all those beautiful, well-defined muscles—

He lifted a wet strand of her hair from her eyes. His touch was like an electric shock, zapping all her feelings except one. Desire. Desire for Judd.

JUDD WATCHED, awestruck, as Lucy let her towel drop. It puddled at her feet. "What if I don't want to wait?" Her voice was a tremorous whisper.

He felt as if he were standing at the edge of a precipice. One misstep and he could go careening right over the cliff. Here she was, Lucy Weston, the girl of his dreams, standing before him in all her naked glory, offering herself to him. Tears literally burned the insides of his eyelids. He had never wanted her more than he wanted her at that moment. Longing rang in his ears like a constant hum.

He could have broken down and cried from lust. And if that's all it was, he'd have flung off his towel, scooped her up in his arms, carried her off to his bed and made wild, passionate love to her.

But it wasn't just lust. And if he had sex with her now, he knew that the afterglow would fade very quickly. She would feel embarrassment, confusion, shame, remorse. Then the anger caused by his holding out on her would return. Worst of all, she'd pull away from him. Possibly forever.

Needing to call up every ounce of resolve, he stooped and picked up the towel, resolutely wrapping it once again around her exquisite body.

Lucy sighed. In that sigh, he could hear embarrassment, rejection, frustration and anger. He, on the other hand, felt only loss.

"I think this is my cue to leave." Her gaze shifted to her wet clothing on the tile floor. She shrugged. "I guess I can go like this. If I run into anybody, I'll just pretend I've got a bathing suit on under the towel and I'm wet from a dip in the pool." She shrugged again. "I don't really care what anyone thinks." As she spoke, she edged around him, opened the bathroom door and then came to an abrupt stop.

He knew that if she dropped that towel again, all the

resolve in the world wouldn't be able to stop him from having her.

But she didn't drop the towel. All she did was reach over to the chrome handle of the toilet and flush it.

When she glanced back at him, Judd could see the smile of satisfaction on her face.

"Lucy?"

She didn't respond. Instead, she walked over to the bed, knelt down and retrieved that errant slip of paper from under the bed. Judd, a puzzled expression on his face, stood at the open bathroom door clad in a terry bathrobe, watching her.

She smoothed open the paper and laughed dryly. It was blank.

"All that for nothing," she muttered, tossing it into the trash bin and retrieving her tote bag, which she'd left behind earlier that day.

Her hand was on the doorknob and she was about to make her exit when he called out to her once again.

"It's okay, Judd. You don't have to say anything." She turned the knob, and started to open it.

"Lucy, Kyle is—"

"Right here, good buddy," Kyle announced as he popped his head around the door, his eyes on Judd. "I just came up to apologize for those jocks—" He was all smiles until he got a look at his fiancée. Then his eyes popped open.

"Lucy? What the—? What are you—? Tell me you're wearing something under that towel." Kyle's gaze then shot to Judd, also in a bath towel. Also damp. "Say, what's been going on between you two?" His question rang with suspicion and betrayal.

She glared at Kyle. "You want to know what's under my towel, you two-timing bastard?" She opened it and flashed him. Then she shoved her stunned *ex*-fiancé aside as she wrapped the towel back around her naked body and strode purposefully down the hall to the elevator, an extra little bounce in her step.

9

"WHAT DO YOU MEAN there are no other rooms?" Lucy demanded.

"I'm sorry, Ms. Weston, but the hotel is full because of the reunion festivities."

She hung up the phone. Well, there was no way she was going to share this room with Kyle tonight.

"Lucy, let me in." Kyle's card had allowed him to open the door, but the bolt she had thrown prevented him from opening it more than a few inches.

She ignored his plea.

"You'll have to find someplace else to stay tonight," she snapped. "I'm sure *Dani* would love to share her bed with you. Or do the two of you just do it in public places?"

"Lucy, I don't know what you heard, but it isn't true. I swear."

"Go away, Kyle."

"Will you at least give me a chance to explain—"

"Explain? You mean *lie*."

"I love you, Lucy. That's no lie."

"Save your breath, Kyle." She sank down on the king-size bed. Kyle's black silk pajamas were neatly folded on top of his pillow. She snatched them up, rose, strode out to the terrace and tossed them over the railing.

He was still at the cracked open door.

"First of all, you're wrong about me and Dani... Danielle. Second of all, if anyone should be feeling betrayed, it's me. And to come on to Judd Turner of all people. Why'd you pick him, Lucy? Because he's a good friend of mine? I know you couldn't be attracted to that geek—''

"You call all your good friends geeks?" she retorted.

"You know what I mean, Luce.''

She did. She also knew that if Kyle had gotten as close a look at Judd as she had in his shower, he wouldn't still be calling him a geek.

"The poor guy was so scared I'd take a swing at him he bolted for the bathroom and locked himself in.''

She smiled. She was sorely tempted to tell her ex that if anyone was going to get in the first swing, her money would be on Judd. And after the punch landed, she doubted Kyle would be in any shape to swing back.

She headed over to the closet and retrieved the pale gray satin cocktail dress she was going to wear to the banquet. She'd debated going to the reunion bash at all. She could fly out to L.A. that night instead of the next morning. She'd even gotten so far as to put a call through to her travel agent, but she'd hung up before anyone answered the phone.

There were still too many questions she wanted answers to. If Kyle hadn't shown up in Judd's room at just the wrong moment, she believed Judd would have spilled the beans. Now that he'd had time to rethink his impulsivity, he would very likely change his mind. If that was the case, she was determined to change Judd's mind again.

"What if we both put our little mistakes behind us, Luce?" Kyle's voice was an unappealing whine.

What had she been thinking all this time? How could she have ever been in love with Kyle Warner? How could she ever have found this vain, shallow man desirable?

When she said, "The only mistake I made was getting involved with you in the first place," she meant it with every fiber of her being. Whatever happened from this point on, one thing she was certain of was that she would never again let Kyle Warner back into her life. She was well and truly over him. For good.

For the first time in months, she felt a burden lifting off her. She felt free. And with that sense of freedom came the realization that she wasn't even all that angry at Kyle. He was, after all, what he'd always been. A liar, a cheat, a womanizer. She'd been looking at him through rose-colored glasses. Now that she'd taken the glasses off, she could see him with crystal clarity. And what she saw wasn't an attractive picture.

There was silence on the other side of the door. She waited for him to give up and leave. No such luck.

"Would you at least let me get my things out of the room?"

"I'll see they're delivered to Dani's room for you."

"I'm not going to stay with Danielle, Lucy. I told you, she's got a boyfriend. And it's pretty serious between them."

"You mean Rico wouldn't be any too happy with her— or you—if he found out about your little *reunion* in that dressing room this afternoon?"

"Lucy, don't even joke about that," Kyle whispered.

"Who's joking?" The truth was, she had no intention of ratting out Kyle. But she did get a modicum of satisfaction from making him sweat a little.

"You don't know who you're messing with, Luce. Rico Morales is a…powerful man down here."

"You mean he's a mobster."

"Damn it, Lucy. Don't be stupid. You could get me into some serious trouble—"

"I think I'm a little too late for that." Her gaze fell on Kyle's computer. And then she recalled the question he'd asked her when she was in the shower—with Judd. "Say Luce, you weren't using my laptop by any chance?"

A snippet of another conversation between Judd and Roz clicked in her mind.

"Any closer on the password?"

And Judd's answer.

"Actually, I have a couple of ideas. Once I see that Warner's settled in at the reunion banquet, I'll pay another visit to his room."

That explained why Judd had been up in the room earlier. He'd been after something on Kyle's laptop. When he'd heard her come in, he must have ducked into the bathroom just as she'd done when she was down in his room a short while ago.

And something else was now clear to her. Judd hadn't hired Roz Morrisey. He worked for her. He was a private investigator. Investigating Kyle.

Investigating him for what?

"Lucy, believe me," Kyle said hoarsely at the door. "You don't want to get involved with Morales. He knows you're a TV news reporter. And if he thinks you're knowledgeable about...anything...he might just have to..." There was a brief pause, then he lowered his voice to a harsh whisper. "*Take care of you.* Do you understand what I'm saying, Luce? Don't mess with the man. For your sake." Sounding like the afterthought she was sure it wasn't, he quickly added, "And mine."

"Go away, Kyle." She walked over to the desk and lifted the lid of her ex-fiancé's laptop.

She didn't want to risk him hearing her turn it on. She'd have to wait until she got rid of him.

"I need my tux, Luce." There was another brief pause. "And my laptop."

"You're not going to work during the banquet. I'll send the laptop along with the rest of your stuff to Danielle's room. But you can have your tux.'' She strode over to the closet and pulled it out. She even grabbed the shoe box containing his dress shoes. Then she headed to the terrace.

''You'll find them in the same place as your pajamas,'' she announced as she pulled open the door.

LUCY TRIED every password possibility she could think of, but none of them gained her access to Kyle's locked file. She stared in abject frustration at the screen. Whatever nefarious activities her ex-fiancé was up to, she was convinced the answers lay within that file. She felt certain of two things. One, that Judd Turner had more of a clue as to what was in that file than she did, and, two, that Rico Morales and Danielle Brunaud fit into the picture in some way.

She made up her mind. Two heads were better than one. Closing the computer, she quickly dressed for the reunion even though the banquet didn't start for another hour. She didn't plan to head straight down to it. Her first stop was going to be Judd's room. She tucked the laptop into her tote bag and started to leave.

She was closing her door, paying little attention to anything else, when she heard a disquietingly familiar voice around the corner.

''Arnie. What did I say? I said left. Not right. Left.''

''You said *right*, Joey.''

''I said right, when you said it was left.''

''Exactly. You said right.''

''Arnie, you idiot. I meant *correct*. Correct, it's left.''

''So why didn't you just say *correct*? Anyway, how many times I gotta tell ya, don't call me an idiot?''

''Look at the numbers right in front of you. What do they say?''

''What, now you're testing to see if I can read? It's not

bad enough I gotta put on a monkey suit so's we fit in, I also gotta take a reading test."

"Rooms 1600 to 1640, then an arrow pointing *left*. And what room are we looking for, Arnie?"

"You know what room we're lookin' for, Joey."

So did Lucy. She managed to slip back into her room while the two goons were doing another of their Abott and Costello-esque routines.

She could hear their less than delicate footsteps heading in her direction down the hall. She already knew they could easily break into the room. She'd already seen them get into Judd's with expert ease. She figured they had some kind of passkey; they probably had them for most of the hotels in town.

They were still arguing outside the door.

"I'm telling you, the boss said 1630."

"And I'm tellin' ya, Joey, he said 1620."

"You gotta get your hearing checked, Arnie."

"Oh, yeah? Who heard the maid coming when we were in that nerd's room a coupla hours ago? Huh? Huh? You didn't hear nothin', Joey."

She knew they'd get around to checking her place before long. She debated throwing the bolt on the door. That would buy her a little time. It would also broadcast that someone was in the room.

A shiver of alarm coursed through her. What if Kyle had contacted Morales to warn him that his ex-fiancé was getting very suspicious? What if these hoods had been sent over by Morales to take care of the nosy TV news reporter?

"Okay, Arnie, I'm gonna prove it to you. You stay put and I'm gonna walk back over by the elevator where there's a hotel phone. I'm gonna call down to the desk and confirm that Warner's in 1630. And after I prove I'm right, I'm gonna call you *idiot* whenever I feel like it and you ain't gonna make so much as a peep of a complaint. You hear that, Arnie?''

"Yeah, Joey, I hear it just fine."

Lucy felt a flicker of curiosity about what was going to happen when Joey discovered Arnie was right after all. But she wasn't curious enough to stand around and find out. Nor did she feel confident that they wouldn't find her if she hid somewhere in the room. She'd been lucky in Judd's room, but she wasn't about to count on that luck holding.

She had to get out of there.

With Arnie standing guard right outside her door, she wasn't escaping that way.

There was only one alternative.

Earlier, when she'd been out on her terrace bidding Kyle's pajamas and tux fond farewells, she'd noticed that the terraces throughout the hotel, while shielded by solid concrete privacy walls, were otherwise attached. All she'd have to do was climb over her railing, edge around the wall and climb over onto one of the adjoining terraces.

It was the second part of the plan that had her more than a bit nervous. While edging around the wall, she'd be hanging sixteen stories above the ground. She was a little queasy when it came to heights.

She was a lot more queasy when it came to guns. Especially when they were being held by dumb goons and being pointed right at her.

She slipped open the sliding door and stepped out on her terrace. She was still carrying her tote bag containing Kyle's computer, almost leaving it behind because it would certainly be an added encumbrance while doing her vaults. But she couldn't risk letting the laptop fall into the wrong hands. Morales's hands would definitely fit that description. And it was possible the goons had been sent to snatch the computer.

With the straps of the tote bag slung across her shoulders, she started to lift herself over the side of the railing.

Just don't look down. Don't look down. Don't look...

She didn't heed her own advice. A compulsion overtook her when she was halfway over. A gasp of alarm escaped her lips as she stared down the sixteen stories to the poolside area. From that height, the pool itself bore an unnervingly close resemblance to a bucket.

She clung to the railing, one foot still on the terrace floor, the other dangling in thin air. It didn't help matters that her cocktail dress had a slim skirt and she'd had to hike it up to the tops of her thighs in order to do her gymnastic maneuvers.

Voices from inside her hotel room startled her just as she was making the daring move of swinging her other leg over the railing in anticipation of edging around the concrete wall to relative safety.

"You know what this means, don'tcha, Joey?"

"Yeah, yeah... I still say the boss said 1630."

"So now what? Ya gonna call the boss an idiot? Yeah, big shot, go ahead. Call the boss an idiot. That I'd like to see."

"Will you shut your trap already? Take the bathroom."

"Oh, no..."

Lucy was desperately trying to find a foothold between the bars of the railing. Unfortunately, they were spaced only a few inches apart. Her square-toed dress shoes weren't helping the situation. Nothing for it but to jiggle her feet out of them. She almost unthinkingly followed their fall, but came to her senses before she did.

If she had seen her shoes land, she might have been able to make out that one of them had struck a tray of champagne glasses a waitress was passing around to alums still gathered poolside for the pre-banquet cocktail party. She might then have seen the tray drop, glasses crashing on the patio. She surely would have noticed first the waitress, followed in short order by the guests, all looking upward toward the terrace where she was now precariously hanging over the railing.

"OH MY GOD, she's going to jump."

"Somebody do something. Call the police."

"No, the fire department. That's who you call when there's a jumper."

"Who is it? Can anybody tell who it is?"

Judd, who'd been on the poolside patio making small talk with Gary and his wife, Bri, was almost certain he knew who it was. Which was why he was making a mad dash through the lobby for the elevator.

Don't do it, Lucy. He isn't worth it. No man is worth it.

The elevator doors opened and Judd, dressed in his blue tux, braces and glasses once more in place, rushed in, keeping other guests from entering behind him. "Emergency," he shouted, pounding on the button that closed the doors. He had to make it up to the sixteenth floor with as few stops as possible.

Hold on, Lucy. Please, hold on until I get there.

It felt to him as if the elevator were creeping upward an inch an hour. Guilt suffused him. Was he partly responsible for literally sending her over the edge? If he hadn't rejected her, would she have felt driven to take such desperate measures?

If only he'd followed his heart. If only he'd made love to her as he'd wanted to do. If only he'd told her how much he loved her. If only he'd been able to explain everything to her.

Now it might be too late. He pounded on the button imprinted with the number sixteen as if somehow that would get him there faster.

LUCY WAS TOO HIGH UP to hear the commotion below, but then the hotel's fire alarm system went off. The sudden, unexpected eruption of the shrill siren startled her and caused her to almost lose her footing. *Perfect,* she thought. *On top of everything else, the hotel is on fire.* She even considered for a moment the possibility that Kyle had set it.

When she made another attempt to get her footing, she saw Morales's boys were also surprised by the fire alarm. Despite the noise, she could hear them arguing.

Arnie popped his head out of the bathroom. "What's goin' on, Joey?"

"I told you you were deaf. What's it sound like, you idiot?"

"Joey, I'm warnin' ya—"

"It's a fire alarm."

"Fire alarm? You mean there's a fire?"

"You know any other reasons for fire alarms, you idiot?" He glared at Joey.

"So now what?"

"I don't know about you, Arnie, but me, I'm gonna get my ass outta here on the double. You wanna be part of a barn fire, be my guest."

Lucy saw Joey make a beeline for the door. Arnie, however, remained put.

"This ain't a barn fire, Joey. It's only a *barn* fire if it's a *barn.* What we got here is a hotel fire, pure and simple."

"What we got here is a total idiot. You comin' or not?"

"What do we tell the boss, Joey?"

"What do we tell the boss? We tell him—"

"Hey, Joey. Who's that?"

Uh-oh, Lucy thought, realizing Arnie had seen her.

"Who's what?" Joey was already at the front door.

"The dame. You blind as well as deaf, Joey? There's

a dame out there. On the terrace. Well, she's not exactly *on* the terrace.''

Joey looked out, his eyes locking with Lucy's. "What the—?"

She panicked, almost losing her grip. The straps of the tote bag shifted, somehow managing to end up around her neck, the bag behind her back. The weight of the laptop inside exerted unwanted pressure on the straps. She gagged.

"Whaddaya think, Joey?"

Desperate to elude them, she managed to readjust her tote and get a toehold first between two rails of her terrace and then, by swinging her left leg out, make toe contact between two rails of the terrace next door. Both hands were still gripping her railing. Now she had to let go with her left hand and reach past the two-foot-thick concrete barrier, and blindly grab onto her neighbor's railing. Then she'd have to release her right foot and her right hand—

"Just some dumb broad freaked by the fire, taking the quick route out," Joey concluded.

"It may be quick, but it ain't gonna be pretty," Arnie said. "Ya think maybe we should give her a hand?"

"You think maybe we wanna get trapped up here and die of smoke inhalation, Arnie?"

"No, but—"

"You wanna play Kid Galahad, be my guest, Arnie. I'm making a beeline for the fire stairs."

"Hey, Joey, ain't Kid Galahad a wrestler or somethin'? Joey? Hey, Joey, wait for me."

Relief surged past Lucy's panic as she saw Tweedledee and Tweedledum beat it out of the hotel room.

But her panic returned when she realized getting herself back on solid ground was going to be no easy feat.

Thinking through the execution of the entire series of dangerous maneuvers proved overwhelming. She told herself to take it one step at a time. As she was trying to execute the first move, she heard a second round of sirens that grew steadily louder.

Fire engines.

Until now, she hadn't been convinced there was an actual fire in the hotel. The arrival of the fire department convinced her. And froze her in place. Which way should she go? The way that was farthest from the fire.

She risked checking to both sides of her and then she looked up. There were only two floors above hers. And there was no sign of flames or even wisps of smoke emanating from any of the rooms. The fire must be below her. Holding on with every ounce of strength she had, she looked down to see where the fire was brewing.

She didn't see any flames or smoke. What she did see was a huge gathering of people on the poolside patio who were all looking up at her. Some were waving wildly, others had their hands clasped around their mouths making makeshift megaphones. They were shouting up at her, but she couldn't make out what they were saying over the ever increasing noise of the sirens.

She felt dizzy.

"Lucy, don't. Please—"

She heard that. Her gaze shot to the sliding door of her terrace, which he was yanking open as he cried out to her.

She smiled anxiously. "Judd."

He edged cautiously onto the terrace. "I know you feel terrible right now, Lucy, but it'll pass. I promise you. Kyle isn't worth it."

"You don't have to tell me that, Judd."

"Then...is it because of me, Lucy?" He edged closer to her. He was dressed for the banquet. Baby-blue tux, braces and glasses in place, dry padding concealing what she now knew to be a magnificently flat stomach.

"I guess it is. In a way," she said, seeing past the disguise to the man that set her heart racing.

"Oh, Lucy, don't you know how I feel about you?"

"Well...not exactly."

"I love you. I've been in love with you since the very first time I set eyes on you back in our freshman psych class."

"You hid it pretty well. You still do," she added. "I practically threw myself at you, Judd Turner, and you—"

"Oh, Lucy, don't you know how much I wanted you? But I was afraid..." He hesitated.

And, finally, she got it. "Afraid I was mixed up in whatever Kyle's got himself into."

"No." He was at the railing now, his hand cautiously reaching out toward hers. "You aren't, are you?"

"Of course not. Do you think I'd be hanging out here sixteen stories up, if I were involved?"

Guilt colored his face. "Oh Lucy, this is all my fault."

"It isn't *all* your fault, Judd," she said, even though she was sore at him for suspecting her of being a crook. "Kyle certainly contributed his fair share. And so did Morales."

"Morales?"

"He sent those goons here. I think they came looking for the computer. But—"

"Goons?"

But before she could explain, two firemen burst onto the terrace. "Okay, miss, we're here to help you," one of the firemen said in a pseudo-soothing voice.

"You don't have to do that," she said, as it finally dawned on her that everyone, including Judd, had utterly misconstrued the reason she was hanging over the terrace. They thought she was contemplating suicide!

"My name is Fred. And my partner here is George. We're going to take this nice and slow, Miss..."

"Lucy. Her name is Lucy," Judd said. "And she's the woman I love with every fiber of my being."

The firemen both smiled. "You hear that, Lucy?" Fred said brightly. "This guy here is nuts about you."

"If he's so nuts about me, how could he possibly think I was up to no good? Why didn't he trust me? Why hasn't he told me the truth?" she demanded.

Fred and George gave Judd the evil eye. "You keeping secrets from the woman you love?"

"It's not that simple," he said.

"Oh, yes it is," she countered. "And...and I'm staying right where I am until he...comes clean."

The firemen continued to glower at Judd.

"Lucy, couldn't we please talk *after* you climb back onto the terrace?" he pleaded.

"I don't think so, Judd. I do what you want and you'll just wheedle your way out same as before."

"No, I won't do that, Lucy."

"Not if we have anything to say about it," George said emphatically.

Judd nervously shifted his weight from one foot to the other.

"If it changes anything," she said, focusing her full attention on Judd, "you might like to know I've broken off my engagement to Kyle."

The two firemen shifted their gazes from Judd to Lucy, and both of them now looked perplexed. "You've got a fiancé?"

"I *had* a fiancé," she corrected. Her hands were getting sweaty as they gripped the railing. She desperately wanted to be yanked back to safety. But she knew she wouldn't be able to exert nearly the same pressure on Judd after she had both feet back on the ground.

"You mean it, Lucy? You and Kyle are...?"

She smiled at him. "History. And I promise you, this

time history is not going to repeat itself. Now, will you tell me what's going on?" *And do it fast before I lose my grip...*

Judd looked at the firemen. "Could you let me have a few words in private with Lucy?"

Fred and George weren't so sure.

"Please," she pressed. "I promise not to jump—" *and hopefully not fall* "—if Judd tells me the truth."

"We'll be right inside the room there, Lucy," Fred said. George pointed his index finger at Judd. "You tell the lady what she wants to know."

He nodded.

"Okay, Judd. Shoot," she said as soon as the firemen made their exit.

"I don't own any Laundromats."

"Go on," she hurried him along, eager to be helped back to safety.

"I don't live in Cincinnati."

"I know all that. You're a private eye. You work for Morrisey Associates in Fort Lauderdale. You're after Kyle. And he's involved with a mobster and his moll. And I don't think his involvement with *Dani* is solely biblical."

He smiled. "You know a lot."

"I also know there's a locked file on Kyle's computer that we both want access to. The only difference is, you have a pretty good idea what's in it."

"Records," he said. "Gina Reed believes Kyle's been skimming large sums of money off of clients' investments, but she has no proof. She hired me to get that proof."

Lucy's eyes narrowed. "So that was Gina on the phone."

"Yes," he admitted with a sigh. "Okay, so now you

know everything. Will you please let me help you climb back over now?''

Lucy wanted nothing better. But she held out for one more minute. ''Did you mean it, Judd? You've always been in love with me?''

''I'll prove it to you once you're safely in my arms again.''

DISASTER STRUCK just as Judd was reaching for Lucy to help her back over the railing. He didn't have a clue what was happening until after he heard her scream. And by then it was too late.

The next thing he knew, the two firemen were blasting back onto the terrace. George got him in a viselike stranglehold, yanked him away from the railing and threw him to the ground. For the third time that weekend, Judd's head made contact with a hard surface.

Before he blacked out, he heard Lucy scream once more.

10

JUDD CAME TO with a start, Lucy's scream still thundering in his head.

"No, no. Oh, God, no...." He tried to sit up, but two firm hands held him down.

The hands belonged to Dr. Gary Burke. "Take it easy, Judd. It's going to be okay."

But it wouldn't be okay. It would never be okay again. Lucy was gone. And he'd let it happen. He'd let her fall. But how?

"Sorry there, son. I didn't understand what was happening. I heard her scream and I saw you and...I guess I thought you were trying to push her..."

Judd tried to bring the fireman into focus. "What?"

"A misunderstanding," George said, his fire helmet in his hand.

Judd pressed his hands to his face as tears started streaming down his cheeks.

"I know it hurts," Gary soothed. "But I've given you a shot and the pain should ease in a little while. You're really a pretty lucky guy, considering, Judd."

A rage washed over Judd's anguish. His hands shot away from his face. "Lucky? Is that what I am? I've lost Lucy forever and you tell me I'm lucky, *considering?*"

"Who says you've lost me?"

He gasped. "Lucy?" He couldn't believe his eyes. She was standing right there. Right next to Fireman Fred.

"I was afraid I'd lost *you,* Judd," she said, kneeling beside him.

"Tell me this isn't a fantasy, Lucy. Tell me you're really here. That you're alive."

She pressed her lips to his and kissed him. He wrapped his arms around her and deepened the kiss.

"I guess he's gonna be okay," George said with relief.

"All I can say is," Gary concluded, "the guy has a heck of a hard head."

When their lips finally parted, she and Judd found themselves alone in her hotel room.

He stared at her in amazement. "I heard you scream. I thought—"

"It was the computer."

"What?"

"My strap broke."

He rubbed his sore head. Nothing she was saying was making any sense.

"Judd, I'm sorry. I'm so sorry. I probably should have left it where it was."

"Left what?"

"The laptop. Kyle's computer."

He remained baffled. "So, where is it?"

Lucy bit her lower lip. "In the pool."

He grinned. "Taking a swim?"

She didn't so much as crack a smile. "I'm serious, Judd. And now you'll never be able to find out what's in that locked file. All your efforts and—" She shook her head woefully.

"How did the computer get in the pool?"

"It fell from the terrace. Along with my tote bag. The strap broke just as you were about to grab me. That's why I screamed. The next thing I knew, Fred was heaving me back onto the terrace and you were out cold on the ground."

"That's why you screamed? Because of the laptop?"

"Oh, Judd, now we'll never nail Kyle."

"Yes we will, Lucy." *Wait a minute. What was he saying?*

He sat up, ignoring the sharp pain that zigzagged down the back of his scalp. So much for the pain medication. "Listen, Lucy, *you* are not nailing Kyle. *You* are staying out of this ugly business."

"No, I'm not," she said adamantly.

"If this is all about landing a breaking story—"

"It *was* about wanting to help you."

"I don't need your help."

"Don't you?"

"And I don't want it," he added, desperate to keep her out of harm's way. Now that she was no longer in the dark, not to mention no longer Kyle's fiancée, she presented a serious danger to the whole money-laundering scheme. While Kyle might be squeamish about taking physical action to protect the operation, Judd knew that Morales would have no such qualms. And now that Lucy had come back from the dead, he was not about to risk losing her ever again.

She rose and smoothed down her cocktail dress, which was, remarkably, still intact. The same could not be said for his blue tux.

"Have it your own way, Judd," she said coolly.

"Lucy, let me explain—"

She held her hand up. "You've already explained everything that needs explaining."

He started after her, but a wave of dizziness overtook him and he sank back down onto the bed. Between that conk on the head and the painkiller Gary had shot him up with, he was in no condition to go anywhere at the moment. Besides, he told himself, better that she be furious with him than he end up truly being the cause of her demise.

ROZ MORRISEY WAS PLEASED as punch that Lucy was still alive, but she did not take well the news of the computer's demise. "Now what are you going to do?"

That was the million-dollar question. Judd wished he had the answer.

"I'll figure something out," was all he could come up with.

When he clicked off his cell phone, he remained put on Lucy's bed. His head was still throbbing, but it wasn't as bad as it had been. However, the medication Gary had administered was really kicking in, making him incredibly drowsy. He could feel his eyes starting to close. He tried to fight it.

But, for all his effort, he lost the battle. Once again, he was out like a light.

"WHAT THE BLAZES is he doing here?"

"Could you not use the word *blazes*, Arnie?"

"Hey, ya should be happy it was a false alarm, Joey."

"I am happy. Don't I look happy?"

"No. Ya don't look happy. Come to think of it, I don't ever remember you looking happy."

"I've looked happy plenty." Joey glared at his partner in crime.

Arnie glared back. "Yeah, name one time."

It was turning into a full-blown contest. "Don't start with me, Arnie."

Arnie's brown eyes narrowed into slits, grimacing for all he was worth. But Joey had this way of clenching his jaw so the veins popped in his temples. No question, Joey had the glare thing down to perfection.

Arnie, knowing when he was beat, sauntered over to the bed. "Ya think he's a goner?"

"He's snoring, you idiot. Do dead men snore?"

"It could be a death rattle. Ya ever think of that, Joey?"

"Search him."

"Why do I have to search him?"

"Okay, fine, Arnie. I'll tell the boss you were too spooked—"

"Who says I'm spooked? I think maybe you're spooked."

"Fine, I'll search him."

Arnie blocked Joey's way. "What am I looking for?"

"I'll tell you when you find it."

Arnie went to work, frisking Judd from head to toe. Judd didn't so much as move a muscle.

"He ain't packing," Arnie said. "This is it." He held up a cell phone and a narrow billfold.

Joey swiped both from Arnie's hand.

"Hey, I get whatever dough—"

Joey gave his partner a look of sheer disgust. "We ain't petty thieves no more, Arnie."

Joey pocketed the phone and flipped open the wallet. Arnie spotted the top bill in the money clip. "Nothing petty about a hundred smackers."

Joey wasn't paying any attention. He was slipping a driver's license out of the hidden pocket of the billfold. He grinned broadly as he examined Judd Turner's photo and real address. With his smile fixed in place, he looked over at Arnie. "So, tell me. Do I look happy now?"

"I SHOULD BE very angry at you, Lucy."

"*You* should be angry at *me?*" she said, trying to keep her voice down.

"Forget the tux and the pajamas. That laptop was worth over three grand."

It wasn't until that moment, standing there at the banquet, that Lucy realized Kyle thought she'd deliberately tossed the computer over the terrace. So he still had no idea she was on to him. She might just be able to use that to her advantage.

"I guess I went a little too far, Kyle. But you hurt me," she said, looking aggrieved.

"Were you really contemplating suicide, Luce?"

She glanced away. He cupped her chin, drawing her back to face him. "Oh, Luce. No woman has ever gone that far for me."

The bastard. He took her supposed suicide attempt as a point of pride. How proud of himself would he have been if she'd jumped?

"I felt so betrayed, Kyle." What she really felt was disgusted.

"I never meant to hurt you."

"Well, I'm sorry about the computer."

He stroked her cheek. "Don't worry about it. It's insured."

"I know, but all your files...I mean everything on it's lost now."

"Hey, I'm not a jerk, Lucy. You think I didn't back everything up on my zip drive?"

She tried to contain her flurry of excitement. "You did?"

"Of course." He patted his chest. "I always keep a copy on me. Just in case."

She beamed up at him. "Shall we dance, Kyle?"

"THE BOSS SAYS bring him over to the Roney." Joey clicked off his cell phone.

Arnie motioned to Judd with the barrel of his gun.

"Guess we're goin' for a little ride, Mr. Private Investigator."

Judd wasn't in any position to argue. But he was trying to weigh his options as the two goons nudged him out of Lucy's hotel room. Hard to weigh thin air, though.

As he was being involuntarily guided down the corridor to the elevator, he saw his first opportunity to make a break for it. A few doors ahead of them, a hotel waiter was stepping out of one of the rooms, wheeling a cart full of the remains of a guest's room-service dinner. Judd kept a slow, steady pace, Arnie and Joey right behind him, as they approached the waiter.

"Don't try anything funny," Joey whispered in his ear, pressing the gun into his back for emphasis.

"Yeah," Arnie echoed menacingly.

Judd didn't plan to try anything funny. With his cover blown, Morales wasn't having him escorted back to his apartment to perform a comedy routine for him. No, nothing funny about his plan. It was deadly serious.

He put his plan into motion as he started to skirt past the waiter and his cart.

"Evening, gentlemen," the waiter said politely.

Arnie and Joey both backed off Judd a few steps so they wouldn't raise any suspicions. He had counted on this. With a sudden surge of speed, he sprang in front of the cart and shoved it with all his might into the waiter and Morales's goons.

He heard the cart crash into the men, but didn't wait around to inspect the results. Hoping Arnie and Joey weren't dumb enough to start shooting in front of a witness, he bolted down the hall, past the elevator and headed for the door marked Fire Exit.

He'd made it down to the fifteenth-floor landing when he heard pounding footsteps above him. Too close for comfort, Judd picked up his pace.

"Turner, give it up," Joey shouted, his order reverberating off the concrete walls of the stairwell.

"You ain't making it any easier on yerself," Arnie added. Both men already sounded out of breath.

Judd flew down the stairs, grateful for all his years of fitness training. If he could just make it to the lobby—

A shot rang out when he hit the landing on the fifth floor. It ricocheted off the metal fire door, missing him by a matter of inches. He sprinted over the railing onto the stairs half a flight down.

He felt cold comfort when he heard Joey chastising Arnie. "Idiot, I told you not to shoot. Ya wanna bring the cops on us?"

"Don't call me an idiot, Joey. Anyways, I'd rather deal with cops than the boss if we show without Turner," Arnie retorted, gasping for breath.

LUCY WAS NUZZLING her lips into Kyle's neck as they did a slow fox-trot in the banquet hall.

"Oh, Luce, you're driving me crazy," Kyle groaned.

"That's the idea," she said, her fingers surreptitiously slipping inside his tuxedo jacket.

"Hey, what're you doing?"

She scowled. Not surreptitious enough. She playfully nibbled the tip of his earlobe. "Feeling your big, strong pecs," she murmured, trying to capture just the right note of awe in her voice.

And Kyle, being the narcissistic jerk that he was, flexed his muscles for her.

"Ooh, they're sooo big," she cooed, her lips moving from his earlobe to his mouth. She kissed him zealously as her fingers made contact with the disk tucked into his inside jacket pocket.

Precisely at that moment, Judd burst into the crowded ball room, the lights brightened, the music stopped abruptly and a drumroll went off. One of the alums was on the stage at the mike asking for attention.

Judd's attention, however, was focused on Lucy and Kyle playing kissy-face. So much for their broken engagement, he thought miserably.

Lucy caught his eye and she beamed a smile of victory his way.

But he didn't smile back. That kiss instantly knocked all the joy out of him. Kyle had won again. *How could you go back to him, Lucy?* And then a deeply disquieting thought assailed him. Had she been playing him for a sucker this whole time? Had she deliberately tossed that computer over the terrace so there'd be no incriminating evidence with which to charge her ex-fiancé? *Ex*-fiancé? Not very likely. If he weren't feeling so devastated, he would have been good and mad.

"Okay, boys and girls, it's that time," the alum was announcing, his voice reverberating over the loud speakers.

Arnie and Joey, panting and gasping for breath, barreled into the ballroom. Judd spotted their entrance and quickly ducked behind a thick white alabaster pillar.

"The time we've all been waiting for—"

He nearly jumped out of his skin when he felt a hand on his shoulder. "You aren't trying to dodge me, are you?"

He spun around to face Danielle Brunaud, dressed in a very low-cut red sequined cocktail dress that fit her like a second skin.

"You look upset, darling." She stroked his sweaty cheek.

"The announcement of our king and queen—"

"Upset? Me? No." Judd looked past her shoulder. He saw Tweedledee and Tweedledum separate, casing the guests. The goons might have attracted notice if everyone's attention weren't eagerly focused on the stage, their anticipation palpable. He didn't give two hoots about the announcement. His only goal at the moment was to make it out of the hotel in one piece. Which wasn't going to be very likely if the Tweedle boys nabbed him.

"Now I hope everyone's cast their votes—"

"And since I believe in ladies first, we'll start with the announcement of the queen of our ten-year college reunion."

Judd saw Lucy and Arnie starting to converge on him from opposite sides of the room.

"Ten years ago she was the class beauty and now, she's even more beautiful. And still as smart and classy as all get-out."

Danielle slipped a small mirror out of her sequined evening purse, did a quick check of her makeup and practiced her acceptance smile. Judd was busy trying to decide in which direction to bolt.

Lucy, who'd started out closer to him than Arnie, called to him when she was a few feet away. "Judd, I need to speak to you. It's important—"

He caught a glimpse of Arnie slipping his hand inside his jacket. He was sure he was reaching for his gun.

Another drumroll resonated throughout the room. Arnie could pull off a shot and no one would even hear the pop above the din.

"Judd—" Lucy stopped, her eyes widening in alarm as her gaze fell on Arnie, who was only a few yards away from him.

Danielle, too busy preparing for her coronation, didn't notice anyone but herself... Until Lucy charged into her and sent Danielle flying into the goon.

Arnie fell back into a waiter carrying a tray of champagne goblets. His head met the tray and champagne rained down on him as he hit the ground. Danielle got some of the spray as she toppled down over the mobster, sequins scattering over the pair as the seams of her form-fitting dress gave way.

The end of the drumroll drowned out Danielle's string of French curse words.

"The queen of the ten-year Florida State reunion gala…"

Lucy clutched his arm. "I've got it, Judd—"

Suddenly spotlights danced down on the two of them.

"Lucy Weston. Come on down, Lucy, and receive your golden crown."

With insult, not to mention humiliation, added to injury, Danielle struggled to her feet, her disheveled appearance also captured in the glittering spot lights.

Mortified, she fled. But Lucy stood frozen, looking like a deer caught in a car's headlights. Her fingers were still gripping his jacket as applause broke out and all eyes fell on her. All eyes, that is, save those of Tweedledee, picking himself up off the floor, and Tweedledum, who was sprinting toward him. Pulling her hand, Judd quickly tugged her toward the stage.

"Judd. Judd, wait. I need to tell you—"

He couldn't hear her entreaty over the music, the band having started a tune that bore an unsettlingly close resemblance to the "Wedding March."

As they wended their way toward the stage, alums gathered behind Judd and his reluctant queen, bestowing congratulations on her. And effectively preventing Joey from getting to his target.

The alum who'd made the announcement reached down and pulled Lucy up onto the stage with one hand, his other hand clutching a golden crown and scepter.

Another alum, a female this time, now stood in front of the microphone. "And now," she announced, "for the king of the night. I bet none of you need three guesses."

She slipped a piece of paper from an envelope, then looked over to the band. "Drumroll please."

Joey placed a firm hand on Judd's shoulder as the musical introduction began. "I could finish you off right now and no one would hear a thing," the goon hissed into his ear.

"King of the reunion and Lucy Weston's king for all eternity, the dreamboat of all dreamboats, our own football hero, Kyle Alexander Warner. Come on up, Kyle, and join your beautiful queen."

Judd stiffened as the barrel of Joey's gun poked into his rib cage. Off to his right, Kyle was sprinting through the crowd toward the stage. He came to a perplexed halt when he spotted Joey, whose free arm was now slung across Judd's shoulder. Then he saw Arnie coming up behind Judd. Kyle looked from one goon to the other. "What are you—?"

Kyle didn't get to finish the rest of his question. Two of his college football buddies hoisted him up and, between them, carried their king onto the stage.

Judd missed seeing the king and queen being crowned. He was being escorted out of the ballroom by Joey and his wet, disgruntled sidekick.

LUCY, GOLDEN TIARA ASKEW on her head, scepter clutched in her hand, was standing beside her beaming king when she spotted Judd, wedged between Joey and Arnie, heading for the exit. She gasped in alarm, instantly surmising that he was not leaving willingly. She flew off the stage, her crown crashing to the ground.

"Luce. Luce, what are you doing?" Kyle called out to her, one hand holding on to his crown. "Where are you going?"

"Get out of my way," she pleaded as she broke through the crowd of baffled alums on the dance floor.

"Please, please…" Her scepter was a lot more effective in clearing her path than her words.

Kyle, looking mortified at the abrupt desertion of his queen, leaped from the stage and took off after her.

He tossed out various excuses for her flight as he threaded his way through the crowd. Everything from "stage fright" to "a bad case of cramps from a bad shrimp."

She finally made it out to the lobby just in time to see the two goons muscling Judd through the double glass doors to the street.

"Stop! Thieves!" Lucy screamed at the top of her lungs, pointing to the threesome. One of the bellhops, a bodybuilder in white shorts and a pale blue jersey, who was standing nearby, managed to get his hands on the scruff of Arnie's neck.

Arnie was brought to a jolting halt. Since he was holding firmly onto Judd, that brought Judd to an abrupt stop beside him. Joey, oblivious to what was happening, and presuming that his partner and their hostage were right in step with him, was making a beeline for his black sedan, which was parked right out in front of the hotel.

It wasn't until he heard the scuffle that Joey turned back to see Arnie and the bellhop wrestling each other. What he didn't see was Judd.

Neither did Lucy.

By the time she made it across the lobby to the hotel entrance, he had vanished.

"This one of the thieves?" the brawny bellhop asked her, having successfully wrestled Arnie to the ground. Arnie was a big guy, but the bellhop was bigger and heavier. He was using his considerable weight to keep Arnie down.

"Get off me, ya big ape," Arnie huffed.

She scowled as she looked down at the struggling goon. "Where is he?" she demanded. "Where's Judd?"

By now a small crowd had gathered. Another bellhop, equally buff and also dressed in the shorts and jersey uniform, was already on his cell phone to the police.

"The cops are on their way. What'd he steal from you, miss?" the bellhop asked as he stuck his cell phone back into its hip holster.

Kyle was elbowing his way through the crowd. He was still wearing his crown. "Luce, what's going on?" Then he looked down at the ground and saw Arnie. His nose scrunched, and he started to quickly back off. Kyle could smell trouble. And he didn't want the stink anywhere near him.

Lucy was looking frantically around, hoping to spot a sign of Judd. But she still didn't see him, nor did she see Arnie's partner in crime.

She started to move out toward the road, but the bellhop who'd called for the police, caught hold of her arm. "You better wait here so you can give the cops a statement, miss."

JUDD SAW HIS CHANCE when Arnie released him to take a swing at the bellhop. For a change, luck was with him. A new guest was just stepping out of a cab as he made his break. Judd dove past the new arrival into the back seat and told the taxi driver to "Step on it."

A block from the hotel, he pulled himself up to a sitting position and glanced out the back window.

A black sedan was hot on his tail. It was close enough that he recognized Joey behind the wheel.

"Where to, mister?" the cabby asked in a lilting Spanish accent. He smirked when he saw Judd's ghastly tux.

"Anywhere. Just as long as you lose that car behind us. There's a hundred-dollar bonus in it for you." It was only after he made the offer that he remembered that

Tweedledee had his wallet, which contained his ID and all his cash. Well, he'd make it up to the taxi driver.

Unless Joey caught up with him. Then he knew there'd be no making it up to the cabby, or to anyone else for that matter.

"I GUESS I WAS…mistaken," Lucy muttered. "I thought he stole my purse." So much for that lie. Dr. Gary Burke's wife, Bri, upon learning of the suspected robbery, had retrieved Lucy's small silver clutch bag where it had rested on one of the tables inside the banquet hall the entire evening. After presenting it to Lucy, Bri had been rather disappointed at the lackluster response she'd received. As she complained to her husband afterward, "Just a touch of gratitude *would* have been appreciated. And I thought you said she was the nice one."

Robbery Detective James Rodriquez, a middle-aged man with dark hair and a mustache, wasn't looking happy. He was sitting behind the hotel manager's large steel-and-glass desk. The manager, who was quite distraught thanks to a near suicide and an alleged robbery at the hotel, both in the matter of a few hours—and both involving the same woman—had vacated the office so that the detective could take Lucy's statement in private. She sat in an ultramodern and ultrauncomfortable canvas-and-leather chair across from the detective.

Rodriquez scanned his notes briefly, then returned his gaze to her. He didn't say anything right away, which only contributed to her nervousness. Which she supposed was the point. She tried to appear calm and unruffled. Even if she was far from either.

After combing his fingers through his dark hair, then rubbing his five-o'clock shadow with the palm of his hand, the detective finally addressed her. "The bellhop said there were three of them."

She didn't respond. After all, the detective hadn't actually posed a question. She was working on the assumption, the less said the better. At least until she knew that Judd was safe and sound.

Rodriquez scowled. "So, was he right?"

"Right? About...?"

The detective splayed his fingers on the manager's exceptionally tidy desk. "Three crooks, Miss Weston."

"Three? Well...actually, two. The other fellow, the one in the powder blue tux, wasn't...involved."

"Involved in what, precisely?"

She'd walked smack into that one, all right. If only Judd were here. He was the pro. He'd know exactly what to do. Of course, if he were here, she wouldn't be getting the third degree.

"I'm not exactly sure what they're involved in, Detective Rodriquez." That much was true enough.

The cop tapped his pencil in a steady tattoo on his notepad. "You don't know what they were involved in, but whatever it was, the one in the blue tux wasn't involved."

She knew how lame that sounded, but she merely nodded.

"And how do you know that, Miss Weston?"

"He's...one of the...alums. A good...friend of mine."

"And his name is—?"

Lucy hesitated.

"You do know the name of your *good friend*," he pressed.

"Judd. Judd Turner. From...from Cincinnati." She looked away. She was a terrible liar and she was sure the cop would see the lie in her eyes.

"And where is Mr. Turner now?"

She gave the detective a wan look. "I wish I knew."

"You're saying you don't know where Judd Turner is?"

"He...disappeared."

"And the other guy? The *bad* guy?"

She shrugged. "He...disappeared as well."

"So they disappeared together," Rodriquez postulated.

"Oh, I hope not," she said earnestly.

"And why is that?"

"Really, Detective, I think that should be obvious."

He exhaled loudly, then rapped his hand on the desk a few times. "We seem to be going around in circles. Let's start over."

Lucy groaned inwardly. All she wanted to do was leave and go try to track down Judd. And, once she knew he was safe, gloat a little when she presented him with the disk she'd pilfered from Kyle. If Kyle did, indeed, have a complete record of his files on that disk, that would include the all-important locked file. She even had a good idea about the password that would gain them access into the file.

If only Judd were all right.

JUDD WAS SURE THAT in another life the taxi driver had been an Indy 500 racer. Unfortunately, the streets of Miami Beach weren't a racetrack. Traffic clogged the narrow streets, and even with all the driver's expert maneuverings, zigzagging a series of right and left turns in no discernible order, Joey, in his black sedan, continued to breathe down their necks.

Judd knew it was only a matter of time before the taxi driver would hit a traffic snarl that would stop his cab long enough for Joey to pop out of his car and make a grab for him. Considering that Joey was armed and he wasn't, Judd was well aware his chances of escape were slim.

He leaned forward in the back seat of the cab. "Make your next left up ahead and just slow down a little bit as soon as you make the turn. I'm going to pop out."

The driver glanced back, smiled and gave a little salute. He was having a great time. That made one of them.

Judd hesitated, checking out the ID name and photo posted on the dashboard. "Listen, Mr. Sanchez...about that hundred bucks...I'm afraid the guy behind us has got my wallet. But I'm good for it, I swear. I'll get the money to your cab company within the next few days."

The driver's cheery disposition vanished in a flash. He slowed the cab. A half block before the left turn. Judd's heart caught to his throat. This was not the spot where he wanted to exit. This particular street was deserted, whereas once they turned the corner onto busy Collins Avenue, he stood a fair chance of making a run into one of the shops lining the street and ducking out a back exit. Hopefully accomplishing that before Joey even realized he was no longer in the cab.

Judd caught the driver's eye through the rearview mirror. Whatever it was the driver saw reflected in his gaze, it settled his mind. His foot hit the gas pedal and they jerked forward.

Judd's heart returned to its proper place.

"DID YOU EVER SEE Arnold Kelby before?" Rodriquez asked Lucy.

She gave him a blank look. "Who?"

"The man you accused of robbing you, Miss Weston." The detective's tone was clipped, and he was now rubbing the knuckles of one hand across the palm of his other hand.

"Oh. Oh, Arnie."

The policeman leaned forward in his seat, his eyes narrowing suspiciously. "So you do know him."

"No...not, exactly."

"How about *inexactly?*" he pressed.

She shifted in her poor excuse for a chair. Not that she would have felt comfortable in any chair at the moment.

"I've seen them."

"Them?"

"Arnie and...Joey."

"Joey?"

"I think they're...partners."

"And Joey is—?"

"The one that got away. The one in the black tux, not the—"

"Baby-blue tux," Rodriquez finished for her.

She nodded.

"And Joey's last name is—?"

"I have no idea. I told you, I don't really know either of them. But I do know—"

"Yes?"

She had boxed herself in. Now she was at a loss as to what to say next.

After a tense pause, she finally said, "I think they've broken into a few rooms here at the hotel."

"And you think that because—?"

She felt a bead of sweat trickle down her back. "Because they...broke into my room."

"You were in your room at the time?"

She looked away again. "Not...exactly."

The detective scowled, clearly growing impatient.

"I was...sort of...on the terrace."

Rodriquez set his pen and paper on the desk, then folded his arms across his chest. "To be exact, Miss Weston, according to the hotel manager, you were hanging over the terrace, sixteen floors up, contemplating suicide."

Lucy flushed scarlet. "It was a...misunderstanding."

"There seems to be a lot of that going on."

"That's because it's...complicated."

"As I understand it, you had an argument with your fiancé and became very depressed—"

"I wasn't depressed. I was angry. He had sex with another woman. In a ladies' dressing room. Besides, he's a...jerk. And...I wouldn't so much as stub a toe over him much less kill myself."

Rodriquez leaned back in his chair, staring contemplatively out the window, then shifted his gaze back to her. "So maybe this is about Judd Turner."

She swallowed hard.

"Are you involved with Turner?"

Not as involved as she wanted to be. "Not—"

He lifted a hand. "I know. Not *exactly.*"

She smiled. "Exactly."

"Okay, let's try this one. Are you here covering a story for your news show?"

"I'm here for my tenth college reunion, Detective. I've already explained that."

"You may have explained a lot of things, Miss Weston, but somehow the more you explain, the more confused I get."

Lucy gave him a sympathetic smile. "That can happen to the best of us."

He cracked his knuckles. "Let's get back to Arnie and Joey. Why did they break into your room?"

"Because they're crooks. Why else?"

Jimmy Rodriquez rubbed his face, as if to erase the ever-mounting frustration he was feeling. "That's *exactly* what I want to know."

Her smile vanished.

"Tell me, Miss Weston. How well do you know Rico Morales?"

She could feel the color drain from her face. She looked

sharply across at the cop. "I never met him in my life. But..."

"Spit it out, Lucy." He had not only moved to calling her by her first name, he'd softened his tone considerably, sounding like a kindly uncle.

And she needed someone on her side. Someone she could trust. Someone who could help her find Judd and see if he was safe. Someone who could do something about it if he wasn't.

"I don't know all of it," she began.

11

AN AGITATED ROZ MORRISEY arrived at the hotel a little past nine o'clock that evening. Lucy and Detective Rodriquez hustled her into the manager's office. The hotel manager wasn't very happy at having his eviction extended.

"You haven't heard from him?" Lucy asked Roz anxiously.

"He hasn't called in and I couldn't risk calling his cell in case the phone's gotten into the wrong hands." Roz looked over at the detective. "Did you get anything out of Arnie Kelby?"

Rodriquez's expression was glum. "We had to let him go. Morales sent over his high-priced shyster lawyer and—" He shrugged.

"I don't see why we can't go pay a little visit to Morales," Lucy said.

"You think he's going to just invite us in, maybe offer us drinks, shoot the breeze?" he said sardonically.

"You'd need a search warrant," Roz said. "And you'd have to have just cause in order to get a judge to issue one."

"I think kidnapping Judd Turner is a pretty just cause," Lucy countered.

"We've got no proof Morales is holding Turner," Rodriquez said wearily. He'd been over this with Lucy a dozen times already.

She popped up from her chair, a look of fierce determination on her face. "Well, *I* don't need a search warrant."

He lifted his eyes to the ceiling. "You won't get past that mobster's door. And if you did, I'd say your chances are slim that you'd get back out again."

"I'll take my chances," she said adamantly.

Roz blocked her path. She was taller and bigger than Lucy. And equally determined. "You can't go off half-cocked, Lucy. We need a plan. So, sit down and let's figure one out."

Lucy stood stubbornly in place.

Roz smiled sympathetically. "You love him, right?"

Tears brimmed in her eyes. "I...think so."

Roz nodded. "Sit down."

Dabbing at the tears, she relented.

JUDD FLEW OUT of the slow-moving cab, nearly losing his balance, and only barely made it to the curb as he spotted Joey's sedan squealing around the corner. He crouched behind a parked van. At least, he thought it was parked.

Unfortunately, the driver had stepped back into the van moments before Judd had leaped out onto the street. Not only did the driver pick that inopportune moment to pull out—leaving Judd fully exposed, he pulled out right in front of Joey's car. To make matters worse, the sedan stalled.

On the plus side, Joey was so angry at being cut off—demonstrated by his blasting horn and torrent of curses—that he didn't take his eyes off the cab that he still thought was getting away with his quarry.

Keeping low, Judd turned away from Joey, who was trying to get his car started up again, and made a dash for a small bodega a few feet away. He was starting to push open the door to the grocery store when he heard a car door slam shut behind him. In the reflection of the store's glass door, he spotted Joey getting out of his car and heading for the hood.

Hoping the goon would be occupied with his car troubles, Judd pushed open the door and hurried into the bodega, praying there was a back entrance. To buy himself a bit more time in case Joey did catch sight of him, as soon as he stepped into the store, he turned and threw the bolt on the door, leaving the storekeeper and the three customers inside greatly agitated.

One of the customers, a heavyset young man, dropped to the floor. A late-middle-aged woman clutched her purse to her chest. The third customer, a teenage girl, began to cry.

It quickly dawned on him that they all thought this was a stickup. He held his hands out to quell their anxieties. ''This isn't what you think.''

There was a sharp rap on the locked glass door. The teenager screamed. Judd glanced behind him and saw Joey standing there, a menacing grin on his face, a gun in his hand.

''Everyone. Down,'' Judd shouted, hastily obeying his own order. The girl collapsed onto the floor. The older woman threw her bag at him.

''Take it. Take it all. Only please…don't hurt me. I'm a grandmother…''

He scrambled on his belly over to her and yanked her to the ground seconds before a bullet whizzed over them.

But the shot had come from the wrong direction. This was confirmed when he heard the glass door to the store shatter.

The shopkeeper, smoking weapon in hand, had taken a shot at Joey.

He'd missed, but Joey didn't stick around to test the shopkeeper's aim a second time round.

Judd caught a rearview glimpse of the scared-off goon running like a bat out of hell down the street.

The older woman was sobbing. The teenager was out cold. The young man had wedged himself under a shelving unit and seemed to have gotten stuck there.

"It's okay now, everybody. You can get up," he said as he started to get to his feet.

"You're not going anyplace, buddy," the shopkeeper warned. "I may have missed your partner, but I promise I won't miss you."

Judd felt the poke of yet another gun barrel in his ribs.

"YOU'RE WHERE?"

Lucy hovered over Roz. Rodriquez, who'd jumped to his feet when her cell phone rang, stood anxiously waiting by the desk.

"Where is he?" she asked impatiently. "Is he okay?"

"Just a sec, Judd." Roz looked from Lucy to the cop. "He's in jail."

"In…jail?" She was stunned. "Why?"

"What are they charging you with?" Roz asked Judd.

Her brows lifted into perfect arches as she listened for close to a minute.

"What? What?" she badgered.

"Hold…hold on, Judd." Roz again looked from her to Rodriquez. "He says…armed robbery."

"Huh?" She was completely flummoxed.

"It seems he and his *partner* tried to hold up a grocery store."

"Partner?" Lucy echoed.

Roz returned her attention to her frantic operative on the other end of the line. "Yes, Judd, I'm here. Yes, of course it's a terrible misunderstanding. Yes, yes, of course we'll get you out. Just sit tight. Yes, yes I know there's not much else you can do." She clicked off.

"Roz, what's going on? This doesn't make any sense," Lucy said.

"I'll explain it to you both on our way over to the police station."

IT TOOK A GOOD HALF HOUR of wrangling down at the precinct house to get things cleared up. At a few minutes past ten Judd was finally released. He was not a happy camper. Seeing Lucy out in the station's lobby anxiously waiting for him did not buoy his spirits. When he looked at her now, all he could picture was the image of her and Kyle kissing on the ballroom floor. It felt like having a hole blown in his chest.

He focused on Roz. "This whole assignment has been a disaster from start to finish." He ripped off his glasses, spit out the braces, then tugged his shirt free from the bright pink cummerbund that accessorized his hideous blue tux and yanked out the wad of toweling. "That's it. I've had it. We're washed up anyway without Warner's computer."

Lucy was baffled and hurt by the cold shoulder she was getting from him. Hard to believe that only a few hours ago this very same guy was professing his everlasting love for her.

Men.

"We're not washed up," Roz contradicted him. Then beaming at Lucy, she said, "Thanks to your girlfriend."

Judd raised an eyebrow. "You've got that wrong, Roz. Lucy's not *my* girlfriend. And now that she conveniently drowned Warner's laptop, he's going to get away with his crimes and the two of them can live happily and *richly* ever after. Was that your wedding present to your future husband, *Luce?*"

She was too angry to speak. So she did the only thing she could think to do. She took a swing at him, catching him square in the jaw. He staggered back into Detective Rodriquez, who was coming over to join them. She turned on her heels and stalked off.

Rodriquez righted Judd, who stood rubbing his sore jaw. "What's she got to be angry about?"

Roz sighed. "Plenty, Judd."

"WHY DIDN'T SHE say anything?" Judd said dolefully.

"You didn't exactly give her a chance," Roz countered.

"You could have stopped me."

"That's like saying I could have stopped a speeding bullet."

Rodriquez cleared his throat. "Lucy was dead-on about the password. I ran the disk on one of our computers upstairs and got into the file."

Both Roz and Judd instantly shifted their attention to the detective. He was smiling. "I've already put in a call to the Feds. We're going to be able to nail Warner for embezzlement and, even better, Morales and his crew, including his right-hand man—or in this case woman— Danielle Brunaud, for drug trafficking, extortion, money laundering, you name it. Warner's been working with Morales for close to five years now. He's kept records of every interaction, as well as an extemporaneous chronicle of illegal activities. It's more than we could have hoped for."

"What was the password?" Judd asked.

Rodriquez smiled. "Big Boy."

"Big Boy? I don't get it."

The detective looked over at Roz. The corners of her mouth twitched.

"Is someone going to let me in on the joke?" Judd said peevishly.

Rodriquez gestured to Roz to tell him.

"Lucy figured it out. She told me it's...um...what Kyle affectionately calls his...member." She could barely get the words out before both she and Rodriquez broke into a peal of laughter.

A DOZEN MALE AND FEMALE Federal agents and a handful of plainclothes Miami Beach policemen, led by Detective Jimmy Rodriquez, converged on the Regale Hotel at 10:45 p.m. They entered the Tango Room and had a few brief words with the bartender, Derek Marshall, who proceeded to clear the room of guests. The agents and cops then scattered about the bar, taking the place of the evacuees. Derek got them drinks and raised the volume on the sound system.

At precisely eleven o'clock Kyle Warner and Danielle Brunaud sauntered into the cocktail lounge from the lobby. Three minutes later, Morales's two hoods, Arnold Kelby and Joseph Spolsky, stepped into the lounge from the ocean-side entrance. They gave surreptitious nods to Warner and Brunaud, who'd taken seats at a corner table for four, then spent the next couple of minutes casing the joint. When they felt confident they'd spotted no one they recognized, namely Judd Turner and Lucy Weston, they exited. A minute later they returned with Rico Morales.

The Feds and the cops moved in quickly and quietly. Guests in other parts of the hotel would know nothing about the arrests until they read their newspapers the following morning.

Well, two of the guests would know about it beforehand—Judd Turner and Lucy Weston. They not only knew what was going down, they would both be spending much of the night at the precinct house giving statements.

"LUCY, YOU'VE GOT TO TALK to me sometime," Judd entreated.

He stood in front of the door leading out of the precinct, blocking Lucy's exit.

"I'm very tired, Judd. It's nearly four in the morning. I have to get back to the hotel and pack. I'm catching a seven a.m. flight to L.A." She'd switched her flight from Monday to the first one out Sunday morning. She'd had her fill of South Beach, Kyle Warner and, especially Judd Turner.

"I'm so sorry, Lucy. I...didn't...understand."

She glared at him. "No, you didn't."

"When I saw the two of you kissing on the dance floor—"

She lifted a hand. "I know, Judd. You've already explained."

"And you won't forgive me."

"I really have to go." Her stony voice belied her anguish and confusion.

"When will I see you again?" He was careful to word it that way. Making it clear that this wasn't going to mark the end of their relationship. In his mind, he and Lucy had hardly begun.

"I don't know. I can't think straight. It's all been...too much." She gave him a plaintive look. "Please, Judd. I need time. We both need time."

"If you need time, I can accept that. But I don't need any more time. I've wasted too much time as it is. I love you."

She made no response. He tried to tell himself that her silence was better than if she'd told him she didn't love him back. This way she left a door open, if only a fraction of an inch.

"Can I call you?"

She shook her head.

"Will you call me?"

"I...don't know." She fought back tears. Walking

away from him now had to be one of the toughest things she'd ever had to do. But she'd meant it when she'd said it had all been too much. She really did need time. She'd already come dangerously close to making one big mistake. Had she not come to her senses in the nick of time—in no small part thanks to Judd—she might very well have ended up not only marrying Kyle, but spending her honeymoon visiting her husband in the state penitentiary.

She swallowed hard. "Goodbye, Judd."

"Don't say goodbye. It sounds so final. Couldn't we just say...see you later?"

She looked away.

He stepped aside and she walked out the door, not looking back.

He watched her go. "See you later, Lucy," he whispered.

12

"HOW'D YOUR TESTIMONY GO?" Gina asked.

Lucy shrugged. "It wasn't as rough as I'd expected."
She shook her head. "Kyle had the gall to sit there looking betrayed. He even managed a few crocodile tears. And
wait, this is the best part. He had his lawyer ask me for
his engagement ring back. To help pay for his defense."

Gina raised her eyes to the ceiling. "That man is too
much."

Lucy kicked off her shoes and put her feet up on her
couch. "I'm bushed. I can't wait for this trial to be over."

Gina watched her friend closely. "Judd Turner's due
in tomorrow to give testimony."

Lucy knew Gina wanted to observe her reaction, so she
deliberately donned a nonchalant expression. She hadn't
seen or spoken to Judd since their encounter at the Miami
Beach precinct house two months ago. But there hadn't
been a day during those two months that she hadn't been
tempted to pick up the phone and call him. A few times
she'd got as far as dialing his number. Once, she'd let his
phone ring two times. But she hung up before he answered, afraid that if she heard his voice, she'd be done
for.

Her attempt at nonchalance didn't fool Gina. "Why are
you being so darn stubborn?"

"I'm not the only stubborn one," she said petulantly.

"You told him not to call you."

She made no response.

"Didn't you?" Gina pressed.

"That shouldn't have stopped him from trying." Even as she said it, she knew she was being unfair to Judd. He was honoring her wishes. Giving her time. Letting her sort out her feelings.

The problem was she couldn't sort them out being apart from him. And yet she was scared to make the first move. How much of what he had professed to feel for her back in Florida had been fueled by the danger and heightened excitement of the moment? Their contact had been so intense, so brief.

Tears spiked her eyes. Gina sat down on the sofa beside her friend. "Oh, Lucy, you love him. Admit it."

"That's the crazy thing," she sniffed. "I do love him. And I didn't tell him when I had the chance."

"Don't be so hard on yourself. If you want to talk about crazy, what you went through down in Miami Beach was crazy. How could you think straight?"

"That's exactly what I told him."

"And he understood."

She looked anxiously at Gina. "Did he really? I'm afraid I hurt him, Gina. Maybe enough so that he had some second thoughts."

"My guess is Judd's only thoughts these past two months have been about seeing you again. Which he's going to do tomorrow."

"I'm finished testifying in the morning. He won't be on the witness stand until the middle of the afternoon."

"So, hang around the courthouse."

Lucy sighed. "I don't know, Gina. I don't think I could bear it if I saw him and he...he no longer felt the same way about me. I'd be able to tell in a flash. His eyes can't lie." She swiped a few tears off her cheek. "Have I ever told you about Judd's eyes, Gina? They are the most incredible shade of blue."

"I know. Paul Newman eyes," she said, teasing her friend affectionately.

"More incredible." Lucy sniffed again. Gina dug out a tissue from her purse.

"Here. Blow."

She obeyed the order, then stuck the tissue in the pocket of her slacks.

Her phone rang. Her heart jumped. "Please...get it, Gina."

Gina rolled her eyes but reached for the phone. "Hello?" A short pause. "Oh hi, Roz."

Lucy bit down on her lower lip.

"Did you fly in with Judd?" she asked.

Lucy held her breath.

"Oh. Oh, I see."

"What?" she asked.

"Right," Gina said slowly, responding not to her, but to something Roz was saying on the other end of the line.

"Sure. Sure, we'd love to meet you for a drink," she said, even though Lucy was shaking her head.

Gina glanced at her watch. "Eight o'clock? No problem. Where?"

Lucy tugged on her sleeve. "Count me out," she whispered.

"See you," she said, hanging up.

"Judd isn't with her?"

Gina shook her head. "He's on some assignment. It must be pretty important because the D.A.'s agreed to reschedule his court appearance until Friday. Roz will give her testimony tomorrow."

"Friday?" Friday was three days away. An eternity. And in the back of her mind, Lucy couldn't help thinking that if Judd really loved her, no assignment would have kept him from seeing her as soon as he possibly could.

Gina gave her shoulder a little shake. "Come on. Powder your nose and we'll go meet Roz."

"I'm really not up to it," she said despondently.

"That's exactly the reason you're going."

She sighed, but she knew better than to argue with Gina once her friend had made up her mind.

JUDD LOOKED LIKE a million dollars. He was wearing his favorite Armani double-breasted navy suit with thin cream pinstripes, and a paisley blue-silk tie. His hair had grown back. He'd developed the habit over the past month of running his fingers through the thick, dark strands as if to confirm that the awful crew cut he'd sported down in Miami Beach was truly no more.

His hand slid absently over his jacket across his absolutely flat stomach, confirming that there wasn't so much as a hint of a paunch. Another habit since Miami Beach.

Those weren't the only two habits he'd developed thanks to that wild weekend....

The doorman nodded solicitously when he gave his name. A faint smile curved Judd's lips. He wondered what the doorman's reaction would have been if he'd been in his nerd disguise. Oh, he'd have gained access—that had been arranged ahead of time for him—but Judd doubted the doorman would have been quite so ingratiating.

His footsteps echoed on the marble floor as he crossed the lobby. He paused for a moment, feeling an unaccustomed rush of nervousness. Doubt. Worry.

This assignment was riskier than any of the others he'd taken on.

He squared his shoulders and began walking again toward the elevator, his stride quick, purposeful. He pressed the up button. To the right of the elevator was an elaborately carved mahogany hall table, above which was a large, ornate gilt-framed mirror.

Judd glanced in the mirror as he waited for the elevator, giving himself a critical assessment. He noted the dark strands of hair curling at the back of his collar—he hadn't been to a hair stylist in two months. He noticed that, despite his Florida tan, his complexion bore a faint pallor from several nights of not sleeping well. The tension he was feeling showed in his eyes.

He adjusted his already perfectly adjusted tie. *Get a grip,* he ordered his reflection. *You've come through every other assignment in one piece, more or less. You'll come through this one, too.*

But would he?

The elevator door slid open. An elderly woman, holding a miniature schnauzer to her breast, stepped out. She smiled at Judd. The dog, however, growled.

An omen of things to come?

He stepped into the elevator, telling himself he wasn't a superstitious man.

"WHAT KIND OF AN ASSIGNMENT?" Lucy asked Roz as the three women nursed martinis in a fashionable bar on Manhattan's Upper West Side.

Roz fidgeted with her cocktail napkin. "I'm really not at liberty to say."

She picked up on Roz's nervousness.

"But it's dangerous," she pressed.

Gina took a sip of her drink, watching the two women over the rim of her glass.

"Every assignment has its...risks." Roz picked up her drink and took a hefty swallow.

"You're worried about him," she said.

"Lucy," Gina broke in, setting down her drink, "I'm sure it'll all work out fine."

She scowled. "Roz isn't so sure." She eyeballed Judd's boss. "Are you?"

"Judd's the best there is. If anyone can pull this off, he can," Roz mumbled evasively.

Lucy caught what looked to her like a knowing glance between Roz and Gina. Had Roz shared something with Gina in that phone conversation and asked her not to share it with her? What did her best friend know that she didn't? What was Gina keeping from her? And why?

She felt angry at being kept in the dark. But even more than that, she felt afraid. What if something happened to Judd? What if she was never going to get the chance to—

She sprang up so quickly from her chair, it toppled over. "I love him." She made this intimate revelation in such a loud, earnest voice, every eye in the bar fell on her. Several customers started to applaud.

SLIGHTLY TIPSY and more than slightly on edge, Lucy stepped into her apartment and flicked on the light switch. Despite her entreaties to both women, she'd gotten no other information out of either of them.

She walked into her bedroom, aware that she wasn't quite steady on her feet. She sank down on the edge of her bed and put her head in her hands.

After a few moments, she looked up, a new resolve in her heart. She picked up her phone and dialed Judd's cell phone number. She had to tell him how she felt. Before it was too late.

He answered on the third ring. His voice was low and tense.

"Yes?"

"Judd, it's me. Lucy. Can you...talk?"

"Lucy? Is it really you?"

"I know you're in the middle of a dangerous assignment. I saw Roz tonight here in Manhattan."

"Lucy, I really can't..."

"Judd, don't speak. Just…just listen. I love you. I knew I loved you down in Miami. But I was…"

"Angry," he finished her sentence.

"No," she said. "Scared. I was afraid to trust…"

"Me?"

"No. Me."

"And now?" he asked in a whisper.

"And now I…I want to spend the rest of my life showing you how much I care. Only…"

"Only what?"

"Only I'm terrified that the rest of *your* life is going to be…very brief." Tears ran down her cheeks.

"Lucy, are you crying? Don't cry."

"I'm not crying."

"Where are you right now?"

"Right now? Here…in my bedroom." Her eyes still glistening, she stood up. "I'm…getting undressed." She began undoing the buttons of her blouse.

"Mmm. I like imagining that," he murmured.

"I'm slipping off my blouse." She shrugged out of the sleeves.

"Are you wearing one of those lacy white bras like you wore that day?" he asked.

She smiled. "This one's mint-green. It matches my lace panties," she said, sliding down the zipper of her trousers. She felt a little embarrassed. And far more than a little aroused.

"I've…never had…phone sex…before," she admitted, her cheeks flushing. "But, if you can't be with me, I at least want you to know what…you're missing, Judd. That way you'll be very careful. You won't take any dumb risks like…like you did down in Miami."

"They weren't dumb, Lucy." His voice had lowered a notch, sounding huskier. Sexier.

Her heart raced. "I'm stepping out of my slacks."

"I can picture your exquisite body so perfectly. But it's not the same as the real thing."

"Oh, Judd, we should have made love that day in your hotel room."

"I wanted to, Lucy. I never wanted anything so badly. Until this minute."

"I...wish you were in my arms right now."

"I do, too. You can't imagine how much."

"I'm unfastening my bra," she whispered provocatively. "Now my panties. I'm naked now, Judd."

"Lucy, I'm dying here."

"Don't say that. Please don't say that."

"Don't worry. I'm going to be fine. No, I'm going to be great."

"Is that a promise?" She crossed her bedroom and stepped into her bathroom.

"Judd? Judd, are you still there?" She pulled the phone away from her ear, checking to see if it was still on. It was.

"Judd, please say something. Are you there? Are you okay? Is it that you can't talk right now? Has somebody come in? Are you in danger? Oh, Judd, if you're still there...if you're listening, please remember that, whatever happens, I love you with all my heart. And I'll be waiting for you, darling. No matter how long it takes...."

She continued to clutch the phone for several minutes, hoping he'd come back on the line. Instead it went dead.

Reluctantly she pressed the off button on the phone and set it down on the sink. Maybe he would call her back.

She shivered. Sticking her arm past her shower curtain, she turned on the tap. While the water was warming up, she slipped the pins out of her hair and shook it free.

She had one leg inside the tub when she saw him. Her heart almost stopped.

"You? You...all this time...? And you let me...?" She

was fighting for breath as he stood there under the spray of the shower, still decked out in his double-breasted suit.

"*This* is your...assignment?" She didn't know whether to throw a punch at him or throw herself into his arms.

Judd helped her make the decision. He drew her to him. "You said you love me, Lucy. And that you'd wait. No matter how long it took."

"That was before I realized—"

He stopped the rest of her words with a soul-searing kiss.

Her fingers found their way to the buttons of his sodden jacket.

"You better get out of these fancy duds. I hope they're drip-dry," she said breathlessly.

Judd smiled as he slipped out of his jacket. "I hope they take forever to dry."

He smoothed back her hair and looked lovingly, longingly into her eyes. "You're right. We should have made love that day," he murmured. "But better late than never."

She pulled his loosened tie over his neck, eager to rid him of all his clothes, eager to finally press her naked body to his. "Much better," she whispered back.

He began stripping quickly with her help. Finally he was naked. He pulled her to him, but she held him off.

"Promise me one thing, Judd."

"Anything," he rasped.

"That you'll never again wear a Hawaiian shirt."

They both laughed.

Then Lucy found Judd's lips again.

Bells and whistles filled the tiny room.

The Husband Hotel

Darlene Gardner

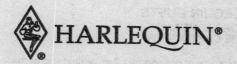

HARLEQUIN®

TORONTO • NEW YORK • LONDON
AMSTERDAM • PARIS • SYDNEY • HAMBURG
STOCKHOLM • ATHENS • TOKYO • MILAN • MADRID
PRAGUE • WARSAW • BUDAPEST • AUCKLAND

Dear Reader,

Story ideas can pop up in the most unexpected ways. My sister Lynette's family was staying in a hotel because of space constraints while we were all visiting our parents. She kept telling me about the hardworking, professional hotel manager who was temporarily living at the hotel while she whipped it into shape. I took one look at Zineb Outnouna, an exotic beauty from Morocco, and knew I had to write a story featuring a hotel manager.

The Husband Hotel is that story. Although the heroine doesn't have much in common with Zineb—I'm sure Zineb didn't have a cat hiding in her room or an undercover maintenance man spying on her—I hope I've conveyed a little of what it's like to work at a hotel.

So thanks to my sister for pointing out a job with fun story possibilities and thanks to Zineb for telling me about that job.

Hope you enjoy!

Darlene Gardner

Other books by Darlene Gardner

HARLEQUIN DUETS
39—FORGET ME? *NOT*
51—THE CUPID CAPER

Don't miss any of our special offers. Write to us at the following address for information on our newest releases.

Harlequin Reader Service
U.S.: 3010 Walden Ave., P.O. Box 1325, Buffalo, NY 14269
Canadian: P.O. Box 609, Fort Erie, Ont. L2A 5X3

To my dad,
who could teach the father in this book a thing or two.
You're the greatest!

1

DARKNESS seemed to creep up from the river, surrounding Jay Overman in a kind of inky weirdness as he stood on the deserted pier. He scuffed his Dock-Siders against the weathered wood, wondering why Cliff Patterson had suggested this as a meeting place.

Jay would have refused to meet just about anyone else at the Occoquan River at dusk on the grounds that mosquitoes might chomp them to death, but Cliff wasn't just anyone.

He was the savior who'd once rescued Jay's father's business from the brink of bankruptcy. Cliff had made the save with a personal, no-interest loan in the name of friendship. Even though Jay's father paid back the money within a year, he'd never stopped talking about how he owed Cliff Patterson.

When Jay's father died, the debt of his gratitude had transferred to Jay. Now Cliff needed a favor, and Jay wasn't about to deny him.

Still, Cliff's insistence on an assignation at this short pier adjacent to an abandoned boat dock was weird.

The place was so deserted Jay wouldn't have been surprised had a pair of sunglasses bearing an audiovisual message been dropped into his hands from a hovering helicopter.

He gazed at the late-summer sky but saw nothing but gray-black clouds and all-pervading darkness. The river wasn't even a mile from I-95, but Jay couldn't hear traffic noise. It seemed incredible that Washington, D.C., was only twenty miles north of where he stood.

A mosquito the size of a small bird buzzed not-so-sweet nothings in his ear. Jay had once stared down a black bear until it fled into the forest, but mosquitoes he couldn't take. He slapped at it.

"Ow," he said when his hand connected with his ear. As he shook his smarting hand, the mosquito buzzed on.

He glanced at his watch. The appointed time was now, which meant Cliff should be arriving shortly. He wasn't the kind of man who showed up fashionably late.

No sooner had Jay had the thought than he heard the crunch of twigs and leaves, signaling the other man's arrival. He squinted until a figure materialized out of the darkness, crossing the space between them with ground-eating steps.

If Jay hadn't spent a lifetime finely honing his masculine tendencies, he might have taken a running dive off the deck. Cliff was dressed entirely in black, but he'd left his shock of short white hair uncovered. For a moment, his disembodied head seemed to be floating toward Jay.

He resembled the headless horseman plus the head minus the body and without the horse.

Actually, Cliff had a powerful presence even without

the black garb. He was a large man in his late fifties with intense dark eyes and a low, husky voice. Though fair-minded, he had a way of getting what he wanted. The employees who worked for him in nearby Prince Edward County, where Cliff held the lofty position of county manager, had undoubtedly learned that simple truth long ago.

He stuck out a callused hand and clasped Jay's.

"Good to see you, Conner James," he said heartily, using the name Jay shared with his late father, the name nobody called him besides Cliff. His handshake was so enthusiastic it was as though they'd come upon each other by chance instead of arranging to meet in the twilight.

"Cliff," Jay said.

Cliff had moved away from northern Virginia twenty years before, so Jay had known little about him until Cliff relocated to the area six months ago and looked him up.

They'd had lunch together a few times since, mainly to reminisce about Jay's father. A splash sounded in the darkness, which Jay readily identified as a fish leaping from the water.

"You back at your real job yet or are you still fooling around with that bra nonsense?"

Jay felt his face color, the way it used to when the boys at school called his father the Panty King. He'd played high school football, rebuilt car engines and become a civil engineer to distance himself from the family business and still he was known as the reigning Bra Prince of Lace Foundations.

"I've got another month or so to go," he said.

"What do you call that bra your sister talked you into designing again? Impeccable?"

"Impecca*bra*," Jay corrected, scuffing his feet and again clearing his throat. "But I'm sure you didn't call me out here to Mosquitoville to talk bras." He made yet another unsuccessful slap at yet another gargantuan mosquito and muttered under his breath, "Although that one was big enough to wear a bra."

"No, no, my boy. This isn't about bras." Cliff's eyes scanned the darkness, and he lowered his voice to a whisper. "I know I've been secretive, but it can't be helped. I couldn't take a chance we'd be overheard."

"Not much chance of that out here." Jay didn't think mosquitoes had ears. Did fish?

"Asking you to come to the house was too risky. Sometimes she stops by unexpectedly."

"She?"

"Tara."

"Your daughter?" Jay had never met her, but Tara was one of Cliff's favorite subjects. He claimed she'd inherited her father's drive to succeed and her late mother's beauty, a combination Jay would have liked to see for himself. "This favor involves your daughter?"

"Yes." Cliff gave a decisive nod. "It's a volatile situation. Extremely sensitive. Top secret, in fact."

A little while ago, when Jay had imagined helicopters looming overhead and assignments that self-destructed after ten seconds, he'd thought his imagination was careening out of control. But maybe he hadn't been so far off the mark, after all. Maybe there was danger involved in the favor Cliff had to ask.

Jay was barely breathing as he waited to find out what it was.

"I want you to stop my daughter from getting married."

Jay's breath whooshed out of his lungs. He tapped one ear, trying to convince himself he hadn't heard correctly. But it wasn't as though there were acoustic problems out here. He could hear the slap of waves against the pier and the song of the crickets just fine.

Forget about fighting crime. His mission was to fight matrimony.

"Please say you don't want me to be the guy who stands up when the preacher says the bit about speaking now or forever holding his peace."

"No, no, no." Cliff slapped his thigh with every negative he uttered. Jay could only hope a couple of mosquitoes got caught between his hand and leg. "She doesn't have a fiancé. Not yet. I want you to prevent her from finding one."

Jay rubbed his brow. A part of him was relieved the favor didn't involve danger, but a bigger part would rather stamp out injustice than fend off fiancés.

"Aw, c'mon, Cliff. Think about what you're saying. Don't you want your daughter to marry a man who'll provide for her? Don't you want her to give you grandchildren?"

"Of course I want those things." Cliff set his lips in a stubborn line. "But not right now."

"Why not?"

"Tara's only twenty-four."

Despite himself, Jay could understand Cliff's point. At twenty-six, Jay didn't intend to marry for a very long time. Certainly not before he extricated himself from the bra business, reestablished his engineering career and found a woman who didn't mind waiting for a ring.

But that didn't mean everyone else felt the same way. Tara had been legally an adult for six years. Heck, he'd gone to high school with a woman who had two husbands and four kids by her age.

"Did I tell you that last month the hotel chain she works for made her a resident manager?" Cliff asked.

Jay nodded. He had. Several times. In fact, Tara's job was the reason Cliff had resettled in Virginia. He couldn't bear to be where his daughter wasn't.

"The hotel is small, hardly worthy of her. But it's a stepping-stone to the big time. If she makes a good impression, she moves up to one of their bigger properties. In a few years' time, she'll be running the show at a five-star resort."

"Maybe she doesn't want to run the show."

Cliff snorted. "Are you kidding? This is my daughter we're talking about. She could teach Barnum and Bailey a thing or two."

"Say again?"

"Barnum and Bailey, the circus people. She was raised to run the show. That's what us Pattersons do.

Take those high-wire artists. They don't need some man holding them up when they walk across the rope. Or those women who do the handstands on horseback. Do you see a man sitting in the saddle so they don't fall?''

"What about the woman that the magician saws in half? If he didn't put her back together again, she'd get double takes for the rest of her life.''

"That's just it.'' Cliff shook a fist, ignoring Jay's attempt at humor. "I want Tara to be the magician who saws the *man* in half. Being self-sufficient is the name of the game, my boy, you mark my words.''

Despite the mad gleam in his eyes, Cliff made sense. A career woman was in a position to want a man but not need one. But this was the twenty-first century. Women had been successfully juggling marriage, career and children for decades.

"Okay, I see your point. But why can't she have a marriage *and* a career?''

Cliff shook his head, clearly exasperated. "Because she won't be thirty for six years.''

"Thirty? What's so special about thirty?'' Jay had a flash of insight. "Oh, I get it. That's how old you were when you married.''

"Exactly, my boy. And I'd recommend you wait at least that long, too,'' Cliff said. Jay didn't tell him he planned to do exactly that, because it would only add more ammunition to Cliff's argument. "There's plenty of time for love and romance after you establish a career. In your twenties, your head should be full of getting ahead in the world.''

"If Tara's been promoted, sounds like her head's in the right place to me."

Cliff paced from one side of the pier to the other. The space was so narrow that Jay feared he might fall into the drink. "I *thought* her head was in the right place." He scratched his chin. "Although I can't quite figure out how she came out of college with a degree in hotel management when I thought she was majoring in public administration."

"Hotel management's probably full of opportunities to get ahead."

"I'm sure it is." Cliff's strong face crumbled. "Except Tara claims she went into the field to find a husband."

"You're joking," Jay said.

"I wish I were." Cliff grabbed Jay by the shoulders. A passing cloud uncovered a silvery moon, which reflected the glint in his eyes. "The girl's gone mad. Mad, I tell you. She's working at a hotel in Reston that's full of single businessmen. She calls it husband-hunting ground."

Jay gulped. Talking his way out of fighting matrimony was proving to be quite a battle.

"Maybe she'll weed out the bad and pick out the good," Jay said slowly. "Maybe she'll find a son-in-law you can approve of."

"She's not going to be choosy." Cliff squeezed harder. If Jay wasn't such a sturdy man, he'd have bruises. "She's too busy to date, so she says she's going to pick one who looks good."

Jay frowned. No wonder Cliff was in such a lather. He'd heard of women so desperate to get married that love didn't play into the equation. It sounded like Cliff had spawned one.

"I don't know what's come over her," Cliff said, his expression miserable. "She's never given me a whit of trouble."

"Maybe career isn't enough for her."

"But Tara is the consummate career woman, always has been. She's never been interested in weddings, babies or anything like that."

Jay raised his eyebrows. "You're sure about that?"

"Positive. It must be temporary insanity. Give her two more weeks on the job, and she'll see how rewarding a career can be. Then she'll stop this nonsense about finding a husband."

Cliff finally released Jay's shoulders. Jay resisted rubbing them, figuring a real man wouldn't, but hoped he didn't say anything that led Cliff to latch on again. He dreaded his next question even more than his next mosquito bite, but it had to be asked.

"Where do I come in?"

Cliff jabbed his finger at him. "You're the one who can get her over the hump."

"Me? How?"

"The maintenance man at her hotel just quit."

"That's too bad." Jay suspected that good maintenance help was hard to find. Cliff was silent, watching him, and Jay's brain went to work. He didn't like the conclusion it reached.

"You can't be suggesting I find a maintenance man to spy on her so she doesn't get herself a husband."

"Of course not," Cliff said.

Whew! That was a relief. Dishonesty wasn't Jay's style, but neither was failing to fulfill his obligations. He'd loved his father far too much to refuse to pay back the favor he owed Cliff, no matter what it was.

The older man took a deep breath and smiled. Here it comes, Jay thought. Here comes the reason he was standing on a lonely pier at dusk with the mosquitoes, the fish and Cliff Patterson.

"I don't want you to find someone else to spy on her," Cliff said. "You're going to be the maintenance man so that *you* can spy on her."

2

TARA PATTERSON fought to keep her hands at her sides so they wouldn't shove the pushy businessman through the open doors of the elevator.

She felt caged inside the contraption. He had a foot wedged against the side of the car, rendering it immobile as he extended his business card as though he were Adam offering Eve an apple. Only the temptation was missing.

He was handsome enough, in a buttoned-down sort of way, but his cologne was strong enough to fell a moose.

"Call me anytime. Morning, noon or night," he said, raising coal-black brows that shadowed his eyes and made them look predatory. He took a step backward and, finally, the doors started to close. "I especially prefer nights."

She took the card, gave him a bland smile, then ripped it into tiny pieces when she was alone in the elevator. Her impulse was to throw the pieces into the air and watch them fall like confetti, but she liked to keep the hotel neat and tidy.

The Reston branch of the Excursion Inn, located about twenty miles outside Washington, D.C., in northern Virginia, was known in the business as an express hotel. To keep costs down, the hotel didn't employ bellboys or a concierge. A continental breakfast came with the price of one of its seventy rooms, and guests were welcome to use the communal pool, hot tub and fitness room.

Tara's goal was to continue to transform the sterile environment into a home away from home for her guests, and she wasn't going to let anything deter her from that mission. Even her annoyance at the Mr. Colognes of the business world wouldn't dissuade her.

To think her father actually believed she was setting a trap to lure one of those guys into marrying her.

Tara leaned her head against the back wall of the descending elevator and groaned. She'd lived with her father long enough to know the best way to handle him was with a smile and a nod. That way, he never realized she planned to do exactly as she pleased instead of what he commanded her to do.

Isn't that how she'd managed to get a degree in hotel management instead of doing his bidding and majoring in public administration? By the time he realized something was up, she'd graduated.

How could she have lost her cool and told him she was husband hunting? How could she have agreed when he pointed out she was too busy to date? How could she have shrugged and told him she was into random selection?

Could it be because she didn't see anything wrong with getting married before age thirty? She had plenty of friends who'd married young, and they seemed content. They had husbands to love them and children to hug them, not an overbearing father so out of touch he didn't realize his daughter was too professional to date hotel guests.

She stepped off the elevator into the lobby and almost fell over. Sadie Mae Monroe, a high school friend she'd hired last week because nobody else would, plowed into her.

"There you are, T.P.! Come quick!"

Panic flowed off the petite, freckled redhead like rain. Sadie Mae was usually in a state, most often because she'd spilled orange juice over the paperwork or assigned a guest to an occupied room, but panic wasn't one of her typical emotions. Regret and remorse, yes, but not panic.

Thoughts of her father flew from Tara's head as Sadie Mae clasped her hands. "Sadie Mae, what's wrong?"

"Bu-bu-bubbles. Bubbles everywhere."

"Bubbles? Isn't that the name of your dog?" Tara loved animals, truly she did, but Sadie Mae was a struggling single mother who could barely take care of her toddler. The dog was too much for her. "You brought him to work, didn't you? He's loose here in the hotel, isn't he?"

"Bubba's not loose." Sadie Mae's eyes were wild as she swung her head in a vigorous denial. "Bubbles loose."

Tara fought to keep her balance as Sadie Mae dragged her down the hallway that led to the fitness room and indoor pool. When she wrenched open the door, Tara saw bubbles—the foaming, frothing kind that children blew at birthday parties. Only these bubbles weren't coming from plastic wands. They were overflowing from the hot tub in great boiling masses that covered half the pool deck.

"Oh, my gosh." Tara let go of Sadie Mae's grip and slip-slided toward the hot tub. "There are bubbles everywhere!"

"That's what I said," Sadie Mae added. "Bubbles."

Even if Tara could see the hot tub, she wasn't certain how the controls operated, and someone had to turn the blasted thing off. The maintenance man. He knew how to do it.

"Quick, go get Wilbur," she instructed as one of her legs slid forward in a semi-split that tore a rip up the side of her skirt. Bubbles instantly covered the length of leg the rip exposed.

"Wilbur quit two days ago," Sadie Mae reminded her. "Remember, he said there wasn't room enough in the hotel for both me and him."

Tara groaned, moving forward through the froth of bubbles on her hands and knees. How could she have forgotten the way Sadie Mae had knocked over Wilbur's bucket of paint and kicked over the ladder he was standing on? It turned out Wilbur didn't have any patience for incompetence even if Sadie Mae was only trying to help.

Who would have guessed it would be so hard to find another maintenance man? Tara's classified ad had produced no viable candidate, but she hoped to have better luck that afternoon when she interviewed the poor jobless soul her father had recommended. Too bad she hadn't already hired him.

The bad news about being a manager in a hotel that got by with the sparest of staffs is that she was the backup in every emergency.

What she wouldn't give right about now for a man wearing a tool belt.

"Can I help?"

A deep-pitched male voice called from across the pool deck, and Tara looked toward the source. A particularly large bubble floated in front of her eyes, and she squinted, the better to see through it.

A blurred Adonis strode in her direction on long, jeans-clad legs. He had thick, dark hair and a face so compelling her mouth dropped open and she tasted foam. His forehead was high and broad, his cheekbones slashing, his jaw strong.

He confidently moved past Sadie Mae and entered the sea of foam with a determined set to his mouth. His body in motion was a lovely thing to behold, his broad shoulders rolling and his muscles bunching as he closed in on the hot tub.

Was that a tool belt dangling from his narrow hips? Oh, she hoped she wasn't seeing things because of the bubbles in her eyes.

"T.P., do something!" Sadie Mae yelled, and Tara realized the bubbles were spreading.

Panicked, she turned away from the man and moved her hand forward, expecting to brace it on more deck. Instead she hit water.

"Help," she called to the advancing savior before she disappeared into the water. She had barely enough time to draw in a breath before the whole of her body was submerged.

It hardly registered that she'd gone and fallen in the hot tub before strong hands gripped her under the arms and yanked her to the surface. Then he was hauling her out of the tub as though she weighed nothing and setting her in front of him on the deck.

"Towels. I'll go get towels," Sadie Mae said and dashed off.

"Are you all right?" the man asked. The French twist she usually wore had come loose, and he brushed her dripping hair from her face as his beautiful eyes examined her. They were a light brown that reminded her of cream soda, her favorite soft drink.

Was she all right? She'd just been rescued by a man with cream-soda eyes who'd braved danger for her. Well, okay, pseudo danger. If that didn't make a woman go weak in the knees, what would? Perhaps, the sane part of her brain replied, a man who knew how to operate a hot tub.

"The bubbles," she sputtered. "Can you turn them off?"

"Well, yeah," he said, reaching into the water. He located the power switch with unerring accuracy, and Tara heard the slight whine of the hydrojet propellers decrease as the water in the tub stopped churning.

He straightened, and she raised her eyes to meet his. She'd lost her shoes during the ordeal, which subtracted

the extra inches her high heels provided to make up for
the fact that she was five feet four. He was much taller,
easily two or three inches over six feet, and so sexy a
pulse pounded in the base of her throat.

With hair that nearly brushed his collar, a brawny
build and workman's clothes, he was a refreshing change
from the businessmen who crammed the hotel. One of
his dark, arching brows had a thin white line of scar
tissue through it, making him look a little dangerous. The
water in the spa had been hot, but wherever he touched
her, she was hotter.

"Who are you?" she breathed.

A CORNER of Jay's mouth kicked up as he regarded the
dripping-wet beauty before him. He'd been dreading the
moment of walking into the hotel and spinning his web
of lies, but nobody had been at the front desk. He'd
thought he heard a shriek and had followed the sound to
the pool. Now, with Aphrodite in his arms, the feeling
humming through his body definitely wasn't dread.

She had the prettiest olive skin he'd ever seen, with
huge chocolate-brown eyes, a high forehead and a nose
that was slightly crooked and more charming because of
it. Her lips were so lush and full they formed a siren's
mouth in her heart-shaped face. Straight, dark hair cas-
caded wetly down her back.

"The name's Jay Overman." His eyes dipped lower,
to the saturated material of her blouse, and he forgot to
ask her name.

Even as the male in him reacted to the loveliness of

her breasts, something about them struck a wrong note. They should have been perfect. They were high, round and exactly the right size.

It took him only seconds to figure it out. Her bra. It didn't quite fit. She was between a B and C cup, and she'd gone with a bra too big instead of one too small.

The Impeccabra, the custom-made garment he'd designed on a dare from his sister, Sherry, would eliminate the tiny folds of material marring those perfect breasts.

"I can fix that," he said, raising his eyes to hers.

"Do you really think there's been damage?"

Damage? Was she serious? Granted, her bra was all wrong, but her breasts were still beautiful enough to get him all worked up. He frowned. "I don't think a bra can damage them."

"A bra?" She looked confused. "But that wouldn't cause all those bubbles, even if it got stuck in the controls. I figured the hot tub overflowed because some kind of bubble mixture was dumped into it."

As if on cue, giggles sounded from the entrance to the pool area. Jay had a glimpse of two laughing preteen boys before they disappeared down the hall. He'd had a clear view of an empty bubble container.

"I'd say those are your bubble boys," Jay told her, hoping she'd forget his slip about the bra. Hell, he hoped he'd forget it. Sure, he'd designed the Impeccabra, but he'd done it for his sister. He certainly didn't have bras on the brain or anything as horrifying as that. He was an engineer, not an underwear fashion consultant.

"Pete and Sean," she said, her eyes narrowing. "Wait till I get my hands on those two."

She was too young to be their mother. But from the way she'd been wading through the bubbles, trying to right their wrong, he figured she was either related to them or... The thought was enough to make him speechless. She took a step backward and held out her hand.

"I'm Tara Patterson," she said. "The manager of Excursion Inn."

Tara Patterson, the husband hunter.

Jay made it a point to avoid giving attractive women the up-and-down, but he couldn't help noticing the rip in Tara's skirt and the wet, shapely thigh it exposed.

An image of her father's anxious face was imprinted on his mind. No wonder Cliff needed someone on the scene. A woman like Tara probably had a legion of male admirers, not all of whom could be avoiding the altar.

"I got the towels." The petite woman with the wild red curls hurried across the deck and skidded on the wet floor, stopping just short of them.

Jay grabbed one of the towels she held out and handed it to Tara. Then he shook her wet hand, reminding himself she was husband hunting.

"Great," he said. "You're the woman I'm here to see. Your father sent me over about the maintenance job."

"Huh?" Tara blinked and dropped his hand.

"You sure don't look like any maintenance man I've ever seen," the redhead added.

Jay didn't know why not. He jiggled the tool belt he'd fastened around his hips to make the deception seem more real and uttered what he feared wasn't going to be his last lie.

"Yep, that's me. The maintenance man."

The second lie came on the heels of the first when he told himself he hadn't felt the charge of electricity that shot through him when he'd been holding Tara in his arms. Even if he wasn't here to stop her from getting involved in a relationship, he'd hardly start one with a woman with marriage on her mind.

Still, she did look good soaking wet. Damn good.

The redhead's gasp of dismay was so loud he thought she'd read his thoughts.

"Look at your blouse, T.P.," she exclaimed. "You can see right through it."

He watched Tara look at her blouse and pull the towel tighter around herself. "Just give me a couple minutes to change," she told him, blushing adorably, "and I'll meet you in my office."

She swiped her dripping hair and gave him a smile that reached all the way to her dark, liquid eyes.

Then she turned, affording him such a clear view of the outline of her shapely body that he had to clamp his lips shut. Either that or call her back and tell her not to change out of her clinging clothes for him.

Or maybe he'd offer to help her out of those clothes. While he was at it, he could personally measure her for an Impeccabra.

He watched her until she disappeared from sight. No longer thinking about bras, now he had breasts on the brain. Naked ones, at that.

TARA SHIFTED in her seat and tried very hard not to dwell on the bubbling lust the man across the desk had inspired when he'd pulled her out of the hot tub.

Her office was so small that he filled it with his presence. The oxygen supply seemed low, probably because he was using it all up. She drew a deep breath. Without oxygen, she wouldn't be able to think. And she was pretty sure something was wrong with his application.

She'd changed into a dry blouse and skirt, and her long hair was once again arranged in a twist. She breathed deeply, reminding herself that she was a businesswoman interviewing a potential employee. She'd keep the conversation strictly professional.

"Is that a naked man on your desk?" he asked.

The blood drained from her face as she spotted the four-inch plastic figurine beside her pencil sharpener.

"No," she said, snatching the figurine from her desk. Unfortunately, she picked him up by the extended part of his anatomy. Red-faced horror replaced white-faced horror.

She pulled open a desk drawer and dropped the figurine inside, where she'd thought it was in the first place. Bare Bob landed on his back, and there was nothing little about his disproportionately sized appendage. She slammed the drawer.

"He's not mine. Well, he is mine. But only because Sadie Mae won't take him back." She chewed her bottom lip, dreading the day she'd confessed to Sadie Mae that she didn't date much. "She claims he's a good-luck charm."

"How so?" He put his forearms on his thighs and leaned forward. A lock of dark hair fell across his brow. She breathed in, caught his scent and almost swooned.

"She said…" Tara's voice trailed off. She couldn't very well tell him that Sadie Mae said if Tara kept a naked man in her office, she might soon have one in her bed. Especially while she was wondering what Jay would be like in bed. She needed to get their conversation back to business. And fast. "He's supposed to help me make the right hiring decisions."

A slow, devastating grin spread across his face. "You mean he helps you strip away the unimportant details and focus on the bare facts?"

"Exactly." She looked at his application, desperately trying not to picture what Jay would look like stripped naked. He'd look perfect. Pulse-pounding perfect.

She stared at the application, deciding it wouldn't hurt to send Bare Bob a silent plea to help her figure out what was wrong with it. After a moment, she had it.

"You left the work history section on the application blank. I can't hire you until I talk to a former employer."

There was a significant pause before he answered. "I don't have a former employer."

Puzzled, she examined the application. It listed his age as twenty-six, which meant this couldn't be the first job he'd applied for.

"I do work for hire. I'm a…" He seemed to be searching for a word. When she lifted her head, her gaze fell on his mouth. His lips were full for a man's, as though they'd been made for kissing. "…handyman."

Her eyes dropped to his hands. They were square, with long fingers, broad palms and blunt nails. She wouldn't mind if Jay got handy with her.

"Yep, I'm a handyman," he repeated a little too loudly. "You break it, I fix it."

She blinked, dispelling the image of his hands on her body. He meant he handled odd jobs, not women. Then why did he sound as though he was trying to convince himself of that fact? Was he lying about being a handyman?

"So you don't have references?"

"Oh, no. I have references." He shifted his powerful body so he had access to his back pocket and withdrew a piece of paper. He unfolded it and handed it to her.

The paper felt warm to her touch, so it took her a moment to focus on the words in front of her instead of the buns in back of him. *Act professional,* she reminded herself. She didn't suppose she could call on Bare Bob to help her with that.

"All these people work for Prince Edward County," she said slowly as she examined the list, "the same as my father."

"You know how it goes. One customer refers you to another, then another and another. That's what happens when you're a good handyman. You know what they say. A good handyman is hard to find." He was talking too much, she thought. Suspiciously too much. Abruptly, he stopped. "So, do I pass? Is Bare Bob telling you to hire me?"

Forget about Bare Bob. Her instincts were telling her

there was more to Jay Overman than he was letting on. That wasn't the only thing that was talking to her. Her libido was urging her to send him off to work for someone else so she wouldn't be bound by professional ethics to keep her hands off him.

But she needed a maintenance man and he needed a job. She didn't doubt he'd be good at it. He'd solved the Bubbling Hot Tub Crisis, swabbed the deck clean while she'd changed her clothes and came highly recommended by her father.

He was almost too good to be true.

"I'm going to call a couple of your references, but I don't foresee a problem." She quoted the distressingly low hourly wage that was the hotel chain's going rate for maintenance staff. He readily agreed to it. "Can you start tomorrow morning?"

"Sure thing." The warmth from his smile seemed to travel across the desk and seep inside her. He unfolded his long length from the seat at the same instant Sadie Mae opened the door and poked her head through it.

"You got a minute, T.P.?" Sadie Mae redirected her attention to Jay and smiled. "You might think we call her that on account of her initials, but it's because she used to toilet paper trees when we were in high school."

Tara felt her face grow hot. "Tree. One tree. Not trees."

"T.P.'s a sweetheart," Sadie Mae said. "But woo, wee, you better not cross her. Coach Arrington found that out the hard way. Didn't he, T.P.?"

"Only because he was such a jerk that he wouldn't

allow the girls' sports teams to use the bathrooms in the locker room after school." She huffed, still angry about it after all these years. "As though sports facilities were for his football players only."

"Nobody said you weren't right, T.P. It was because of you the girls got their own locker room. You should be proud of the nickname."

"Yeah, there's nothing more glamorous than being associated with toilet paper day in and day out."

"I'm sure Sadie Mae means it in the best possible way," Jay said, winking at her.

Tara sent him a grateful look, thankful for the wink. It seemed as though he was commiserating with her. Since she'd hired her old high school friend after discovering she'd moved from Pennsylvania and was living mere miles from the hotel, there was a lot of commiserating to do. "How can I help you, Sadie Mae?"

"Mr. Merrimack is out here, and he won't go away until he talks to you. He's quite insistent."

Jay scowled. "Sounds like this Mr. Merrimack is pretty upset. Want me to come with you to help sort it out?"

"There won't be any need for that," Tara said, stepping in front of Jay. A part of her appreciated the way he was ready to leap to her defense, but she didn't need protection from George Merrimack. "We're finished here, so I'll talk to him."

Tara stepped out of her office, holding her breath while she maneuvered around Jay so she wouldn't overdose on how good he smelled.

She spotted George leaning against the front desk, both elbows on the counter. George was a computer salesman who had invited her to have a drink with him every one of the five days he'd been staying at the Excursion Inn. No matter how many times she said it, he didn't take no for an answer.

"Tara, sweetheart," he called when he saw her. "How's my favorite lady?"

Despite herself, Tara smiled. With his prematurely balding hair and perennial five-o'clock shadow, George wasn't much to look at, but he had an infectious personality that made him hard to dislike.

"Hello, George." She'd stopped calling him Mr. Merrimack days ago, because he wouldn't hear of it. "What can I do for you?"

"You know what you do for me, sweetheart, but you can't do it tonight," George said so loudly that Tara wanted to shush him. She was acutely aware that Jay was lingering outside her office, probably making sure that George wasn't dangerous. "I'm meeting clients for dinner, so I won't be back until late. I can't ask you to stay up and wait for me."

As though she would. Still, George was such a cheerfully optimistic suitor that Tara felt a rush of affection for him and a twinge of envy for the woman he'd eventually marry. His intended wouldn't suffer from a lack of attention.

"Have a good time then," she said. "This place won't be the same without you."

He reached across the counter, took her hand and gave

it a gallant kiss. "I'll miss you while I'm gone, sweetheart. Save some time for me tomorrow. I have an offer you won't be able to refuse."

She laughed when he waggled his eyebrows. She even pretended to catch the kiss he threw her when he got to the double doors in front of the hotel. George was due to check out the day after tomorrow, and she'd miss him when he was gone.

She was still laughing when she turned to Jay, but the laugh died on her lips. He was leaning against the door frame, examining her with lazy interest. She felt his examination clear to her bone marrow.

If he'd thrown her a kiss, she wouldn't catch it. She'd probably run across the room for one of the up-close-and-personal variety.

"So we're all set for tomorrow," she said, once again adopting her all-business voice. "You'll be starting earlier once you settle into the job, but why don't you come in at nine o'clock?"

"I'll be here, boss." He saluted her and straightened to his full height. She watched him walk out of the hotel, wondering what he was hiding and admiring the way his slight hip roll jostled his tool belt.

She forgot about Sadie Mae until the clerk bumped into her. Tara's hand shot out, steadying herself against the desk. Meanwhile, Sadie Mae continued toward the computer as though nothing untoward had happened.

"Did you get a load of those buns of steel?" Sadie Mae grinned. "I bet he has better tools than any of the ones on his belt."

"Get those ideas out of your head. The workplace is not the place for a romance," Tara snapped, then clamped her lips shut. She'd sounded jealous, which wouldn't do at all.

"Oh, don't get into a snit, T.P." Sadie Mae put an arm around Tara and gave her a smacking kiss on the cheek. "I was just joshing you. The last thing I'm in the market for is a romance, but I can admire the scenery, can't I? You sure were."

"I was not," Tara protested.

Sadie Mae laughed. "Then why were you humming the tune to 'Gimme Gimme Good Lovin'?'"

"I was not," Tara retorted, then colored as she realized that was exactly the song that had been running through her mind. She bit her lower lip. "You don't think he heard, do you?"

"Don't worry, hon. That song was an oldie even back when we were in high school. I don't think anybody knows the tune to it anymore. But oh, baby, I bet our new maintenance man knows how to give good lovin'."

"Sadie Mae, stop that," Tara admonished, but she was blushing.

"You started it. Jeez, put a naked man in your office and look what happens."

JAY OPENED the door to his town house, letting in the early morning sun and his sister, Sherry.

"I know you said you weren't going to be available all week, but this can't wait," she said, shouldering past him into the town house before he could issue an invitation.

He shut the door behind her, knowing there was no way to stop her when the subject was business. When their father had died a few years back, their mother had retired to Florida and put Sherry in charge of Lace Foundations.

Since then, she'd been devising ways to bulk up the business's steady but unremarkable profits. She'd hit on a winner when she challenged a reluctant Jay to use his engineering training to design a bra with an impeccable fit.

The prototype, which relied on a series of precise measurements individual to each customer, showed so much promise that she'd decided the company should deal exclusively in bras.

She'd persuaded Jay to take a leave of absence from engineering to help her deal with everything from patents to marketing to setting up a Web site.

She hadn't looked back once.

"Good morning to you, too, Sherry." He trailed her into his kitchen. She'd gone straight to his coffeepot and was helping herself to a cup. She took three scoops of sugar out of the jar and added them to the brew.

"Ugh." She made a face after she'd had a gulp. "How can you drink it this strong? It tastes like mud."

"You sure it doesn't taste like coffee-flavored sugar?"

"Very funny," Sherry said, setting down the cup. Jay didn't think his sister needed the caffeine anyway. She was a dynamo on sturdy, stocking-clad legs. Her shoulder-length dark-blond hair was cut in a no-nonsense style and, as usual, she wore a tailored suit that screamed businesswoman. "But I don't have time for jokes. I need to know what droppage is, and I need to know now."

"Why?" Jay asked, instantly alert. "Has there been a problem with lift and thrust?"

Sherry shook her head. "Nothing like that. A major retailer is interested in carrying the Impeccabra, but he wants his questions answered first."

Jay was as confident of his design as a man who built suspension bridges could be, but he'd go back to the drawing board if the customers weren't happy. "Women have to account for droppage when they're measuring the distance between the top of the shoulder to the center of the breast."

"What do you mean?"

"You measure from where you want the center of your breast to be, not from where it actually is. That way, you get good lift."

"Maybe *you* should tell him this. I might be able to explain droppage, but what if he asks about circumference and molding?"

"Okay," Jay said. "Write down his number, and I'll call him later. I'm sure I can take a couple of breaks during the day."

"Exactly where is it that you're going?" His sister crossed her arms over her chest as she looked him over. "What's with the work clothes? And why are you wearing a tool belt?"

"I already told you. I'm doing a favor for Cliff Patterson."

"You didn't tell me the favor involved wearing a tool belt. Who are you going to be? Mr. Gadget?"

"Nothing that exciting," he said, figuring he might as well explain. He and Sherry didn't make a practice of keeping secrets from one another. "I'm going to be a hotel maintenance man."

Briefly, he told her about his meeting with Cliff Patterson at the abandoned pier and how he'd promised to spend the next two weeks keeping potential husbands away from Tara. He left out his impression that Cliff didn't have any qualms about asking for his time because he didn't think bras were worthy of serious attention.

"How awful." Sherry shuddered while Jay absently scratched at one of the welts the ravenous mosquitoes had left on his skin. "No wonder the poor man's worried. I should have been his daughter. I'm not getting married until I'm at least thirty-five. I've got bras to sell."

"What about having children?"

She walked across the room and patted his cheek. "You're the one who wants children, Jay. And everyone knows men can propagate as long as there's magic left in the wand."

Jay cleared his throat. "Can we not talk about magic wands?"

"It's so cute when you go shy on me," Sherry said, then laughed. Dating back from childhood, it rankled Jay when she said he was cute. It rankled him even more that she knew it. "What's this Tara like, anyway? Does she have that lean, hungry, predatory look?"

Jay shook his head. "She's beautiful." He thought about the way she'd quizzed him about his job history as though she knew something was wrong but couldn't quite put her finger on it. "Smart, too."

"She can't be all that smart if she's looking for a husband before she establishes her career."

"She *does* have a degree in hotel management."

"Sounds to me like she wants the MRS degree. Just make sure she doesn't look in your direction. There's something about you that makes women get that nesting instinct. Look at what happened with Evie."

Jay had broken a long-term relationship with Evie a year ago precisely because she wanted to get married and he didn't. But that had as much to do with Jay not wanting Evie as it did with him not wanting marriage.

"Tara's not like Evie," Jay said, not sure why he thought so. Considering that she already seemed to have lined up a matrimonial candidate, she was acting exactly like Evie. "Besides, you know there's no way I'm looking for a bride. I'm there to stop her from getting married, not to marry her myself."

Sherry's face creased in a grin. "And exactly how are you going to do that, little brother?"

Jay had a mental image of George Merrimack kissing the back of Tara's hand. Too bad he wouldn't be able to bring himself to pick the smaller man up and toss him out on the street. "I'll think of something."

"You will?" Sherry arched a perfectly shaped eyebrow. "You've always been analytical, darling, but I've never thought of you as devious."

"I can be as devious as the next guy," Jay retorted.

Sherry laughed. "If you say so. Far be it from me to argue with a devious mastermind."

"Now you're making fun of me," he said tightly. No way was he telling her about the difficulty he'd had spinning lies while Tara interviewed him.

"I don't mean to, Jay. Truly I don't. But I can't imagine you doing anything underhanded. You don't lie. You don't cheat on your taxes. You don't even jaywalk." She paused. "Scratch that. Considering your name, I guess you do jaywalk, but you know what I mean."

"Just because I'm not usually underhanded doesn't mean I can't be. Besides, how hard can it be to stop men from flocking around a beautiful, intelligent woman?"

Sherry tapped her bottom lip with a forefinger, suddenly serious. "That's the second time you've complimented Tara Patterson. I have a piece of advice for you, little brother. No matter how beautiful and smart this Tara is, your loyalty has to be to her father. We owe him big for what he did for Dad."

"I know that," he said irritably.

"In that case," Sherry said as her grin returned, "go get 'em, Mr. Gadget."

3

THE THEME SONG from *Mission: Impossible* was running through Jay's mind later that morning as he approached the Excursion Inn, making his head pound along with the beat.

He'd had no choice but to accept his mission, but he was no secret agent. When he assured Sherry he was devious enough to dream up a plan to keep men away from Tara, he'd been blowing smoke.

Sherry was right. He wasn't devious at all. He certainly wasn't devious enough to successfully play the part of an undercover maintenance man.

Where was Tom Cruise when you needed him?

He took a deep breath and pushed open the door to the hotel, and an impression of warmth immediately struck him. Guests were dining on a continental breakfast that was being served in a portion of the lobby, and the scents of coffee and cinnamon rolls filled the air. Every table was graced with an arrangement of fresh flowers.

He'd been distracted yesterday by a sense that something was wrong and hadn't noticed that the lobby was decorated in warm shades of orange, green and gold. Nor had he spotted the framed needlepoint on the walls with sayings such as "It takes heart to make a hotel a home" and "There's no place like hotel." The story of the three little piggies was there, too, except the last one built a hotel of bricks.

He turned left, then right, searching the place for George Merrimack. Immediately, he spotted Tara, who was working the front desk. Her dark hair, which had looked so sexy long and loose, was pulled back in a simple twist. Her skin had a healthy glow, as though she'd spent time outdoors this summer. Her dress was made of a buttery yellow material that looked like it would be soft to his touch. And, oh, he wanted to touch her.

Not that he would, considering she was searching for a husband and he wasn't looking for a wife.

With great difficulty, he dragged his gaze from her and continued canvassing the place for his quarry. Merrimack was nowhere in sight, but Jay didn't consider that to be a bad thing.

He shook his head. There was no use delaying the inevitable. He'd given Cliff Patterson his word that he would drive men away from Tara and, by George, that's what he was going to do.

"What do you mean, my bill's six hundred ninety-eight dollars? I've only been here one night."

A booming, irate, masculine voice rose above the murmur of conversation and the hum of the coffeemaker. Wondering why he hadn't noticed a hulking behemoth with an attitude seconds ago, Jay turned once again toward the front desk.

Instead of a behemoth, he saw a small, gray-haired,

bespectacled man fuming at Sadie Mae, who was holding her wild red hair by the roots and grimacing.

"Where do you think we are? The Ritz Carlton?" the diminutive man shouted. Jay couldn't see his face, but the bald spot on the back of his head was turning red.

Jay automatically moved toward the front desk, but he needn't have bothered. Tara was instantly at Sadie Mae's side, smiling at the man and punching keys on her employee's computer.

"Good morning to you, Mr. Wentzel. It seems Sadie Mae forgot to tabulate your auto-club discount. She meant to say the room was ninety-eight dollars. Didn't you, Sadie Mae?"

"Y-y-yes," Sadie Mae stammered. If it hadn't been for her freckles, her face would have been devoid of color.

"See? It was an honest mistake." Tara continued to work her charm so that by the time Mr. Wentzel left the front desk, she'd transformed him from a grizzly to a teddy bear.

"I'll be with you in just a moment." Tara glanced at Jay and smiled when he approached the desk a moment later, and he felt his lips curl in an answering grin.

Something about the tilt of her head reminded him of her father, and he remembered that she was hell-bent on getting married. He tried to stop the smile but he felt air hit his teeth all the same.

A moment later, she pushed aside her paperwork and gave him her full attention. "Good morning. You'll be pleased to know your references checked out fine."

They should, he thought, considering that her father had gotten his friends to lie and say he'd worked for them.

She leaned forward slightly, and he breathed in the scent of strawberry shampoo. "You should have told me about the difficulties you've been having," she whispered.

"What difficulties?" he whispered back, bringing his head closer to hers. He imagined he could feel the heat of her skin and had an irrational urge to run his finger over the slight imperfection of her nose.

She lowered her voice even further. "Going back to school to get your degree. My father told me all about it."

"Your father told you I was taking college classes?"

"No, of course not. GED classes. It's okay. I know you didn't finish high school."

"But I graduated from the University of Virginia!" he blurted.

Her eyebrows lifted and her mouth fell open. "How could you have after you dropped out of high school to help your poor auntie Em keep her farm going? That's why you've had a problem finding a steady job, isn't it?"

Too late, Jay realized his mistake. Cliff must have concocted the cockamamie story to explain his nonexistent job history. But Auntie Em? Had he also told Tara his sister's name was Dorothy, the farm was in Kansas and they had a dog named Toto?

"Being a handyman *is* a regular job," he mumbled, straightening from the counter.

"But why—"

"I'd like to get started," he interrupted. He wanted to tell her he hadn't spent the last five years jobless, but he couldn't without further blowing his cover. "Just tell me what to do, and I'll do it."

He saw a flash of hurt in her eyes at his brusque tone and he damned himself for putting it there. She squared her shoulders but still didn't look as businesslike as his power-suited sister.

"There's a storage room at the end of the hall. You'll find a box of light bulbs there. I'd like all the bulbs in the exterior hallways replaced."

"T.P. thinks the hallways are too dark." Sadie Mae, who had finished with a customer, launched herself into the conversation. "She thinks brighter bulbs will make the place more cheery."

"It probably will," he said, putting more distance between them so Tara wouldn't ask any more questions about Auntie Em and Kansas. He was nearly out of hearing range when Sadie Mae let out a cry of dismay. He slowed his steps.

"Oh, T.P., I can't believe I forgot to tell you this." The redhead's voice carried across the lobby. "The night clerk asked me to pass on a message from George. He didn't make it back until three in the morning, but he said you're welcome to come up there and wake him any time you like."

"That's George for you," Tara said, chuckling. The chuckle, more than anything, irked Jay.

He continued toward the storage room, wondering what to do about George Merrimack. What he wanted to do was forbid Tara from going to his room and waking him, but he doubted that was the wisest course of action.

Waking Merrimack himself and ordering him to get the hell out of town wasn't much wiser, but Jay didn't have a better idea. Neither did he have Merrimack's room number, and he doubted Tara would give it to him.

But what about Sadie Mae? Now that was a different matter.

FIFTEEN MINUTES later, after he'd replaced a grand total of two light bulbs, Jay took the back stairs to the lobby and stuck his head around the corner to get a view of the front desk.

The coast was clear. Sadie Mae was alone behind the counter. As he approached her, the scent of nail polish assailed him.

"Hey, Sadie Mae."

She started, and her elbow bumped the container of dark red polish, spilling it over the desk.

"Oh, no." Sadie Mae grabbed a piece of yellow cloth off the back of the chair to mop up the polish. When she was finished, the desk was still smeared scarlet. So was the cloth. Only it wasn't a cloth.

"Did you just ruin your sweater?"

"It's T.P.'s sweater," Sadie Mae wailed. "She's

gonna kill me. I'm not supposed to paint my nails on the job."

"Then why were you?"

She held up one of her hands, revealing imperfectly covered fingernails. "The chipping. I couldn't stand the chipping."

"She's not going to kill you." If Tara was predisposed to violence, Sadie Mae would be long dead. "You couldn't have kept it from her anyway. She'd have smelled the polish."

Sadie Mae's face fell even further. "I'm gonna have to show her the sweater, aren't I?"

Before Jay agreed to go undercover, that's what he would have done. But he couldn't let his innate honesty get in the way of repaying the favor his father owed Cliff. He needed information from Sadie Mae, and helping her out of a jam might smooth the way.

"Not if you throw the sweater in the trash can. Then maybe she'll think she lost it."

Sadie Mae's face brightened. She stuffed the ruined garment in the trash. The smeared red polish still marred the desk, but he had done what he could.

"Will you help me out with something?"

She nodded. "Anything."

"There was a guy in the lobby yesterday I think I might have gone to school with. George Something-or-other."

"George Merrimack? You went to school with George Merrimack?"

"That doesn't ring a bell." Jay affected a frown. "The

guy I knew had a thing for the number three. He'd have insisted on being put on the third floor.''

"George Merrimack's in room two-oh-nine."

"Must not be the same guy then," Jay said, moving away from the desk. Take that, Sherry. He was, too, getting the hang of being duplicitous.

In a matter of minutes, Jay was staring at the Do Not Disturb sign that hung from the doorknob of George Merrimack's room. Great. That meant Merrimack was still inside, no doubt asleep because of his late night.

The Excursion Inn probably fit his needs perfectly. It provided a comfortable environment where he could get a good night's sleep. However, if circumstances changed, Merrimack might pack up and leave.

That would be one bachelor down and Jay hoped, not too many more to go.

Jay took his hammer from his tool belt and frowned while he surveyed the hall. Pounding would surely roust Merrimack from sleep, but there was nothing to pound. The only nails he noticed were the tiny ones holding the room-number plate in place. But tiny nails were better than no nails.

"Here goes," he said, drawing back his hammer and pounding. He hadn't taken three good swings when he heard a loud, shrill, unmistakably female voice.

"Stop that pounding! Don't you see the sign? Why, I oughta—" The woman's voice trailed off when the door flew open. Jay couldn't tell how old she was or what she looked like because her face was slathered in night cream, but she definitely wasn't George Merrimack. The tiny pink curlers that covered her head were the real tip-off.

"Aaiee." She screamed, covering her face with her hands. They came away caked with white goop. "Uh, don't go away. Stay right there."

The door slammed in his face. He rocked back on his heels, wondering where he'd gone wrong. It was possible that Merrimack and the lady had shared a night of passion. But, in his experience, face cream and curlers weren't aphrodisiacs.

More likely, Sadie Mae had given him the wrong room number.

He hadn't yet replaced all the light bulbs on the second floor, but he figured he'd come back to them later. It wouldn't be wise to stick around.

He'd no sooner replaced his hammer in his tool belt than the door was flung open again. His eyes almost popped out of their sockets. This time, he could tell what the woman looked like way too clearly.

Without the curlers, her fair hair fell in tight ringlets about a round face she'd wiped clean of night cream. He judged her to be ten years his senior and, from the leg sticking out of the front slit of her dressing gown, not at all concerned about the age difference.

"Helloo, there." Her voice was no longer shrill but so low-pitched he feared she had something stuck in her throat.

"Sorry about the pounding." Jay backed up a step. "I was making sure the room-number plate was firmly attached to the door."

It was a pathetically flimsy excuse, but she bought it.

"So you fix things, do you?" She batted her eyelashes and stepped to the side of the door. "Come on in, and I'll find something else for you to fix."

"Actually, I was on my way downstairs. I'm needed in the game room."

She frowned. "This hotel doesn't have a game room."

"That's odd," he said, backing away. "Then I'll have to figure out why they need me there."

He hurried down the hall, relieved he'd gotten away with the shirt still on his back, while he contemplated his next move.

His gut instinct was that Merrimack was in either Room 109 or Room 309. Sadie Mae, he remembered, had been adamant that Merrimack wasn't staying on the third floor. Jay thought about that for a moment, then headed for floor number three.

The pounding hadn't worked out so great, he thought when he was standing outside Room 309, so he wasn't keen on trying it again. Especially because this, too, could be the wrong room.

He rubbed his chin, wishing he could come up with a plan. But this cloak-and-dagger stuff wasn't his style. Earlier, when he'd dodged Tara's questions about his college degree, he'd had to bite his tongue to keep from apologizing. Figuring he'd have to wing it, he knocked on the door.

A bleary-eyed George Merrimack answered his knock after a few moments, and Jay gave a silent thanks to Sadie Mae. What hair Merrimack had was wet, and he was wearing a plain white undershirt with dress pants. His feet were bare.

"Maintenance," Jay announced gruffly.

The other man, who was a good seven or eight inches shorter than Jay, backed up a step. For some crazy reason, he looked intimidated. "I didn't report a problem."

"One of the maids did." Jay thought fast. Merrimack had obviously just stepped out of the shower, so Jay couldn't claim a problem with the plumbing. "Seems one of the feet on your bed frame collapsed."

"I don't think so," Merrimack protested, but Jay ignored him. He stepped into the room, past the smaller man, and headed directly for the bed.

"It'll just take a minute to fix," he called over his shoulder as he located the intact bed frame.

He waited a beat for Merrimack to close the door, using the sound to muffle the swift kick he gave the frame with his steel-toed work boot. It buckled but didn't break. Quickly, before Merrimack walked into his line of vision, he kicked the foot of the bed frame a second time.

A corner of the bed crashed to the floor.

"What was that sound?" Merrimack asked as he came into view.

"I didn't hear anything." Jay crouched to examine the broken foot. He'd cracked it clean in two. He looked at Merrimack and shook his head. "Don't know how you slept on this bed last night. The way it's sloping, I would've thought you'd have fallen off."

Merrimack scratched the side of his mouth as he examined the bed, one corner of which made a sharp angle with the floor. "The bed wasn't like that a minute ago."

"Sure was." Jay narrowed his eyes. "You weren't drunk last night, were you?"

"Well, maybe a little, but—"

"So what do you think of the Excursion Inn?" Jay figured he should take the opportunity to find out a little more about his target. Maybe then he could figure out Merrimack's Achilles' heel and devise a workable plan of action.

"I didn't have any problem with the hotel until a moment ago." The man's voice changed, grew smaller, higher. "You broke the bed, didn't you?"

Jay ignored him, making a grand show of turning part of the broken foot over in his hand and examining it. Finally, he sighed. "Can't do much about this now. I'll have to come back later after I get a new part."

Jay raised himself to his full height. Merrimack backed up again, irritating Jay. The guy actually seemed to be afraid of him. Sure, he was tall. And, yeah, he worked out at the gym regularly. But he'd never hurt anybody.

Merrimack was so nervous it was making Jay uneasy. He longed to leave the room, but he needed to feel Merrimack out about Tara. "How about the hotel manager? What do you think of her?"

"Oh, no. That's why you came in here and broke my bed, isn't it?" The smaller man's face blanched. He backed up another couple of steps, which brought him flush against an armchair. He promptly tumbled into it.

"I don't break things." Jay strode across the room toward Merrimack. "I fix 'em."

"Don't touch me." Merrimack pressed himself against the back of the chair and raised his palms. Jay frowned. He'd intended to offer Merrimack a hand to help him out of the chair.

"I didn't touch her," Merrimack continued. "I swear I didn't."

Jay blew out a breath, wondering what kind of person Tara had gotten herself mixed up with. Did Merrimack have an aversion to flesh-to-flesh contact?

"Touch who?" Jay asked.

"Tara." Merrimack whispered the name as though afraid to say it out loud. "You're her boyfriend, aren't you? That's why you're pulling this tough-guy act. You came to threaten me."

Jay screwed up his face, staring at the other man in wonder. He wasn't threatening anybody. He believed in settling disagreements with words instead of violence.

He started to tell Merrimack that, but the other man didn't give him a chance.

"Please let me live!" he cried.

Jay rolled his eyes. Oh, brother. Was this guy for real?

"I swear I'll stay away from her. Honest, I will."

That got Jay's attention. He loathed being thought of as a bully, but it was for the greater good. What would it hurt if he pretended Tara was his woman? It wasn't as though he had a better plan to keep men away from her, and she'd never have to know what was going on.

He surveyed Merrimack, who was squirming in the

chair, his hands still protecting his face. He actually felt a little sorry for him. But, in the undercover business, he couldn't afford sympathy. Not if he was going to accomplish his mission.

"You do that," he said gruffly. "I don't want other guys around my woman."

IT TOOK TARA a few minutes to realize she was no longer focusing on the rows of occupancy rates in front of her on the computer screen.

Her mind kept wandering to Jay and what he'd blurted out. Why had he chosen not to use his college education and how had he managed to get one in the first place? Come to think of it, what had led her father to believe he didn't have a high school diploma?

Jay had probably mentioned that he was taking night classes, and her father assumed he was working toward his GED. No way could her father know about the University of Virginia. She wanted to ask Jay how he'd finagled it when Auntie Em had all those problems on the farm, but she didn't have the right.

She got up and stretched her shoulders, deciding to finish her report to the home office later. It wasn't as though she didn't have a hundred other things to do.

Since she'd finished the hotel's management trainee program and been given a hotel of her own to manage six weeks ago, she'd learned that a resident manager's job was never done. She shivered a bit and decided that before she did any more work, she needed her sweater.

The strong scent of nail polish hit her nostrils when

she opened her office door, which meant Sadie Mae had been at it again. She wondered if it would do any good to repeat that personal grooming was best done on personal time. She doubted it. Once she got off work, Sadie Mae had time only to tend to her toddler.

"Sadie Mae," she called as she walked out of her office, but no one was manning the front desk. Where had she gone off to now?

She'd no sooner stepped in front of the computer than George Merrimack approached the desk, dragging his suitcase. His shirttail was hanging out of the waistband of his slacks, his socks didn't match and he'd forgotten to do his comb over.

"Good morning, George." She smiled at him. "Looks like I didn't have to go upstairs and wake you after all."

"No!" he shouted, looking over his shoulder. "Don't even joke about something like that."

Tara frowned. George didn't seem himself this morning, but she didn't know him very well. Maybe he wasn't a morning person.

"Whatever you say." She spoke calmly because of the strange, nervous light in his eyes. "Why don't you tell me how I can help you?"

"I'm checking out."

"Checking out? But I thought you were staying with us another night." She knew George lived in Memphis, because he'd tried to lure her there with promises of a visit to Graceland. "Didn't you say your plane wasn't leaving until tomorrow?"

"The airline said I could fly standby later tonight.

Planes aren't too crowded after midnight.'' He looked down, around, then finally at Tara. "Can that redheaded clerk check me out?''

His request stung. She'd had an understanding with George since he'd arrived at the hotel. He flirted outrageously with her. She smiled and didn't take him seriously. Now the arrangement had changed, and she didn't know why.

"I'm not sure where Sadie Mae is,'' she said.

"Yoo-hoo. Here I am, T.P.'' Sadie Mae, cradling a steaming mug, rushed across the lobby and slipped into position behind the desk. She set the mug down with a thump, sending hot coffee sloshing over her hand.

Sadie Mae yelped. "I knew drinking this much caffeine would burn me sooner or later,'' she said as she cradled her hand.

"I better get some cream for that,'' Tara said, regarding her worriedly. "I'm pretty sure there's some in the first-aid kit.''

"Really, I'm fine,'' Sadie Mae said, but Tara rushed to the supply room anyway. When she stepped out of the supply room, the kit in hand, she stopped short. Jay was half a hallway ahead of her, his tool belt jiggling as he moved in that sexy, confident way of his.

A boy running full tilt charged around the corner from the direction of the lobby and plowed into Jay, who reached out strong arms to steady him.

"Whoa, buddy. Where's the fire?'' she heard him ask.

The boy, she saw, was one of the culprits from yesterday's bubbling hot tub incident. Jay treated him like a friend, ruffling his hair, grinning at him, even picking up his slingshot and examining it.

Slingshot?

Tara raced down the hall, visions of maimed guests dancing in her head. The kid disappeared in the opposite direction before she reached Jay.

"Stop that boy," she called, drawing Jay's attention. He gave her a lazy, confused smile.

"Can't. He's already gone."

"But he has a slingshot! Do you know what kind of damage a kid like that can do with a slingshot?"

"Relax. He doesn't know how to use it," he said as he shifted his weight from one foot to the other. Before she could relax, he added, "That's why I'm going to show him how later."

"Swell."

"Anybody ever tell you that you worry too much?"

"I'm a hotel manager. I'm supposed to worry."

"Are you also supposed to carry around a first-aid kit in case of an accident?"

She looked at the kit in her hands. Oh, no. Sadie Mae. She'd taken one look at Jay Overman and forgot about her friend. "Sadie Mae burned herself."

"Burned herself?" Concern and a palpable urgency replaced the amusement on his face. "Then let's go."

He grabbed her hand and took off. She was rushing, but still had to take two steps to his one. As they approached the front desk, Tara noticed the pallor of George's face clear across the lobby.

"Hurry," George entreated Sadie Mae, casting panicked glances at them over his shoulder.

"This is hurrying," Sadie Mae said, but George was no longer paying attention to her. He was hefting his bag and dashing for the exit.

"Mr. Merrimack, wait!" Sadie Mae called after him. "You forgot your receipt."

"Mail it to me," he yelled and disappeared through the doors.

"That was strange," Tara mused as Jay pulled her the rest of the way to the front desk. Not only hadn't George blown her a kiss, he hadn't told her goodbye.

"Where are you burned?" Jay asked Sadie Mae, anxiety making his voice thick.

Sadie Mae held out her hand, which appeared perfectly normal aside from a faint reddish area of about a square inch. "See? It's this little blotch right here," she said cheerfully.

Tara saw the tension seep out of Jay's shoulders before she opened the first-aid kit and removed the antiseptic. She slathered it on the back of Sadie Mae's hand. "There. That should make it feel better."

"Thanks, hon. You worry about me more than my own mother." Sadie Mae smiled at her. "I'm worried about Mr. Merrimack, though. What do you think got into him?"

"He seemed like he was afraid of something," Tara mused.

"He was in a hurry. That's all," Jay said.

"But—"

"I was hoping one of you ladies could help me," Jay interrupted. Tara wondered if there was some reason he didn't want to talk about George. "Where do we keep our spare feet?"

"Spare feet?" Sadie Mae's eyes widened comically. She patted Jay's hand. "I hate to break it to you, but people don't have extra feet."

Jay let out a rich, sonorous laugh that reverberated inside Tara. The man had one gorgeous laugh.

"I don't mean human feet," he said. "I mean the feet on a bed frame. The ones holding up the bed."

"We don't keep spare parts for bed frames," Tara said. "We've never needed them before."

"We do now," Jay said as a telephone rang. Tara looked around but couldn't pinpoint where the sound was coming from. Then she noticed Jay had a cell phone clipped to his tool belt. A cell phone?

"You're ringing," Sadie Mae told Jay.

Jay turned his back, unclipped the phone and brought it to his ear. Tara strained to hear what he was saying.

"I'll have to call you back on that, Sherry," he whispered into the phone. "I'm busy."

Apparently, the person on the other end of the line wasn't taking no for an answer. Jay listened for another moment, sighed audibly and said, "I don't have time to talk about droppage right now."

Then he hung up. Tara bit her lip. Droppage? What was droppage? And who was Sherry? He wasn't wearing a wedding ring, so was she his fiancée? His girlfriend? Neither thought was palatable.

"We need to order a new foot for the bed in room three-oh-nine," he said as though they hadn't been interrupted.

Room 309? Tara immediately recognized the room as the one George Merrimack had occupied. Was Jay the reason for George's premature departure? Was he what George feared?

Another phone rang, but this time it was the one on the counter. Sadie Mae picked up the receiver as Tara looked Jay up and down, from his sable-brown hair to his steel-toed work boots. He was brawny, certainly, but he had an innate gentleness that had come out when he dealt with Sean, the bubble boy.

It was ridiculous to think that George was afraid of him. He was nothing more than a sexy man wearing a tool belt.

Wasn't he?

She noticed his eyes on her and no longer felt the chill in the air. She no longer needed her sweater, no longer cared if someone named Sherry already had a claim on him. Moments ago, when he'd hurried with her through the hotel, he'd proved once again that he was the ultimate hero, the kind of man who unwaveringly offered his assistance to anyone who needed it.

What she needed was another dunking in the hot tub, but only if someone lowered the temperature of the water to freezing.

"The lady in room two-oh-nine says she needs a maintenance man pronto," Sadie Mae announced, and

Jay broke eye contact. "Something about a motor needing revving."

"Oh, brother," Jay said, rolling his eyes.

Tara tipped her head. "What does she mean by that?"

"You don't want to know," Jay said, but she did.

She had more questions about Jay Overman than answers, not the least of which was what was she going to do about the way he made her own motor rev.

4

JAY STRAIGHTENED from behind the pillar where he'd been keeping an eye on the front desk and stealthily trailed a young, clean-cut businessman to the elevator.

The man looked a little like Michael J. Fox: short, compact and so boyishly cute he probably still got his cheeks pinched. He had an air of innocence about him that had most likely gotten him out of trouble his whole life long, but it didn't fool Jay.

He'd seen the way the boyish businessman had smiled and flirted with Tara. He'd seen it, and he had to stop it.

Not because he wanted to smile and flirt with her himself, of course, but to fulfill his promise to Cliff Patterson.

Jay hovered behind the Boyish One, waiting for the elevator car to descend while he thought about how to defuse this latest threat to Tara's single status.

As though sensing someone was behind him, the man turned his head without moving his body. For an instant, before his shoulders shifted with the movement, he resembled Linda Blair in *The Exorcist*. His sky-blue eyes were at the level of Jay's neck. Slowly, they rose and focused on Jay's face.

Jay knew he should scowl. His mission was to make

sure that the guy considered Tara off-limits, but he was having a hard time with intimidation tactics.

Four days had gone by since George Merrimack begged Jay to spare his life, and he could still picture the smaller man hunched in the chair. None of the other eight or nine men he'd warned off since then had reacted quite so severely, but how was he supposed to glower when that image still haunted him?

He smiled. Then, to make sure the other man didn't feel threatened, winked.

The man's forehead creased in obvious agitation, and he turned around, his shoulders stiffening. He picked up his bag as the elevator car arrived but walked swiftly in another direction.

So much for expecting his fellow man to appreciate a friendly gesture.

Jay braced his hand against one of the open doors of the elevator and called, "Hey, buddy, want to ride up with me?"

The boyish businessman kept his eyes straight ahead and walked faster. Shrugging, Jay let the elevator doors shut and followed, barely turning the corner of the hall in time to see the other man yank open the door to the stairwell.

By the time Jay reached the steps, the businessman was half a flight ahead of him. Jay picked up his pace, the tools on his belt jostling against each other and producing a metallic clanging.

The businessman went faster. Jay took the steps two at a time while he wondered at the man's curious behavior. He was acting as though the hounds of hell were chasing him when all Jay wanted to do was talk.

The Boyish One was undoubtedly the nervous type, which meant he might not be receptive to a frontal assault. Jay thought it best to use a little small talk before he let it be known that he and Tara were an item.

The man was fumbling with his key card at the door to his room when Jay caught up to him.

"So do you come here on business often?" Jay asked. The man shot him a pinched look before returning his attention to his key card. Jay frowned. Could he be wondering how Jay knew he was in town on business? "A guy like you in a good-looking suit like that, you've got to be here on business, right?"

The green light that was supposed to flash when the key card was inserted correctly wasn't shining, prompting the man to press the card deeper and harder into the slot. Jay immediately identified the problem. He reached across the man and removed the card from his fingers.

"Here, let me. You're putting it in the slot upside down."

His arm brushed the sleeve of the man's suit jacket. The man sprang away as though he'd touched an inferno. Jay inserted the card properly, and the green light came on, allowing him to push open the door.

He held it open wide and turned to the man in triumph, expecting a thank-you.

The boyish businessman squared his shoulders. Jay saw his chest expand as he drew in a slow, deep breath.

"I don't know how you got the wrong impression, but I'm not interested."

Jay absently rubbed his chin. "You're not? You sure *seemed* interested."

"Listen, no offense, but I don't lean that way."

"You don't?" Jay couldn't believe he had read the signals wrong. He could have sworn the man was salivating while he talked to Tara. Hadn't the guy noticed the way that green dress hugged her figure or how her skin looked like it would be sleek to the touch? What red-blooded man wouldn't salivate?

"So I'm sure you'll understand when I don't invite you in. Not that I'm not flattered by the attention, but I prefer women."

Women? What was he talking about? Jay thought over the last ten minutes, beginning with the wink at the elevator, and grimaced. Oh, no. It looked like he should have gone against his instincts and scowled.

"It's you who doesn't understand." Jay took a step forward. The Boyish One took a step backward. "You know the hotel manager you were talking to downstairs?"

The man nodded, but he still looked nervous, as though he expected Jay to pounce. Oh, brother.

"She and I have a thing going."

The man's blue eyes got big and wide. With a sudden movement, he darted around Jay, nearly executing a back bend in his determination not to touch him. When he was in front of the door, he snatched the key card out of Jay's fingers and backed inside the room.

"Whatever kind of sick proposal you're making, the answer's no. Ménages à trois aren't my bag. Especially when one of the trois is a man."

Before Jay could protest, the door slammed shut in his face. He stared at it in shock, debating whether he should knock and explain. But what if the guy was the competitive type? What if explaining that Tara wasn't into threesomes sent him chasing after her for a twosome?

The sigh Jay released was heavy with resignation. He figured any trick that kept men away from Tara had to be considered a success.

Jay looked up and down the hallway, thinking this wasn't a strategy he cared to repeat. Maybe intimidation tactics were the way to go, after all.

TARA COULDN'T believe she'd let the time get away from her. She should have done her payroll, ordered new towels for the pool area and helped Sadie Mae figure out how to scrub crayon marks off her son's bedroom wall, but first things were first.

Alley needed her, and she was late.

She hurried down the hall to her suite, almost groaning aloud when she spotted Fred Cromwell coming the opposite way.

She'd mentally dubbed him the Extremely Happy Guest until she'd realized his normal expression was more dour than the Grinch's before he stole Christmas.

That's when she'd reached the conclusion she'd mistaken extreme flirtatiousness for extreme happiness. Fred Cromwell, it seemed, was only merry around her.

She pasted on a smile and tried to think of a gracious way to rebuff him without offending should he ask her out.

"Hi, Fred," she said, bracing for his megawatt smile.

His Grinchlike expression didn't change. Neither did he slow his pace. As he passed, she thought she heard him mutter, "Keep away. Keep far away."

Tara's relief was tempered with confusion. Dating from the time George Merrimack had made an all-out dash from the lobby to the street, the hotel guests had been treating her oddly. No, that wasn't quite right. The *male* hotel guests had been treating her oddly.

They were friendly enough when she first made their acquaintance but backed off soon afterward. Just last night, the silver-haired businessman who had suggested she join him for after-dinner drinks in his room had suddenly announced he was going on the wagon.

She hadn't intended to take him up on the invitation, but she could smell whiskey on his breath as he'd announced his sobriety.

She frowned. She prided herself on treating the guests with courtesy and friendliness. Was she going about it the wrong way?

She was so lost in thought she didn't notice that Jay was in the hall until she reached her room, which was quite a feat because usually she couldn't help noticing him. Neither, probably, could all the women she noticed noticing him.

If she had the power to fashion a man, she couldn't come up with a better prototype than Jay. He had so much lean muscle molded over his six-foot-plus frame that she felt the need for an oxygen machine every time she looked at him. All that male beauty simply made it hard to breathe.

If it hadn't been for the scar crisscrossing his eyebrow, his face might have been too perfect. She'd read somewhere that humans considered symmetrical faces most appealing, and his was in perfect harmony from his high forehead to his cream-soda eyes to his square chin.

But the most attractive thing about Jay Overman was that he didn't seem to know he was handsome.

She'd been watching him for days, admiring his easy charm and the way the other hotel employees gravitated toward him. He paid as much attention to the elderly woman who ran the breakfast room as he did the pretty teenager who cleaned the rooms. He didn't seem to notice the way female guests flirted with him, and he chatted with the young boys who gravitated toward him.

He was easily the most likable person she'd ever met, except George Merrimack certainly didn't seem to like him. Come to think of it, she'd seldom seen an adult male guest get within ten feet of him.

"Hey, Tara." Jay gave her the grin that lit up his face and made her feel like she was bathed in light. "Where's the fire?"

"Fire?" Her hotel radar detector went on alert. "There's a fire?"

He laughed. "Relax, Miss Worrywart. Nothing's burning. I was just wondering why you're in such a hurry."

"I'm not in a hurry," she denied, a few seconds before a meow sounded behind her door. She closed her eyes. Oh, no. Alley must have heard her voice.

"What was that?" Jay asked.

"Nothing."

Alley emitted another meow.

"I heard a noise," Jay said.

Tiny claws scratched at the door in a good imitation of a claw-brandishing killer in a teen horror flick. To cover the sound of the scratching, Tara raised her voice. "I didn't hear anything."

Jay tipped his head and narrowed his cream-soda eyes. "You've got a cat in there."

"I do not." Tara rose to her full height and lifted her chin imperiously. "Now, if you'll excuse me, I'm in a hurry."

"You said you weren't in a hurry."

She clamped her lips shut, thinking furiously. She wanted to confide in Jay about Alley, but they hadn't progressed to the point where they shared confidences. She'd come across him talking on the cell phone he kept clipped to his tool belt numerous times in the past few days, and she was still no closer to finding out what droppage was. Or who Sherry was.

Neither had she solved the mystery of how he'd managed to obtain a college degree while helping out his auntie Em. She'd quizzed her father about it, but it seemed Jay was as much a mystery to him as he was to Tara.

"This is embarrassing, but I think I might have left

my stove on." She touched her nose, self-consciously afraid it might be growing.

"So check." Jay was leaning against the wall, smiling at her, obviously with no intention of going anywhere.

She edged the door open, intending to quickly slip through the narrow opening, but Alley rushed out and rubbed against her legs.

"I knew it," Jay said. "I knew you had a cat in there."

"Shh." Tara picked up Alley with one hand while she reached out and yanked Jay inside her suite with the other. She shut the door and leaned against it.

He cocked an eyebrow. "Let me guess. The stove's off, but the cat's out of the bag."

Tara cradled Alley protectively, afraid Jay might comment on her appearance. She was scrawny and of an indiscriminate breed with healed claw marks cutting through her tawny fur as though she were a veteran street fighter. She wasn't beautiful, but Tara loved her anyway.

Instead of commenting, Jay put out his hand toward the cat as though he meant to stroke her.

"Don't," she warned. "Alley doesn't like strangers. She…"

Her voice trailed off as Alley leaned into Jay's hand, purring as he rubbed behind her neck. "That's funny. I fed her for a week before she let me touch her."

Jay shrugged. "What can I say? Cats like me. My sister Sherry's cat always comes to me, too."

Relief poured over her like a waterfall, so heavily that she realized she'd been obsessing about Sherry's identity. But Sherry wasn't his girlfriend. She was his sister. Jay continued stroking the cat, making Tara wonder what it would feel like if his broad hand stroked her. Merely watching him handle the cat was enough to make her skin grow hot.

"You like this, don't you?" he asked, and it took her a moment to realize he was talking to Alley. When he focused on Tara, the strong planes of his face had gentled and a half smile curved his lips. "Where'd you find her?"

Tara swallowed, telling herself his tender expression was for her cat, not her. "Out back behind the hotel," she said. "She was so skinny I could see her ribs. It about broke my heart, so I started putting cat food out for her. Anybody could see she needed a home."

Jay took his hand away and focused on Tara as her words registered upon him. "That sounds like you're going to keep her."

Tara gathered the cat closer to her chest and buried her lips in the animal's fur as though Alley were the Ms. Universe of the cat world. Lucky cat.

"Of course I'm going to keep her. Take a good look at her. Alley's an alley cat. Who else would take her?"

"But doesn't this hotel have a no-pets policy?"

She nodded. "I could lose my job if the wrong person found out about her, but I refuse to take her to the pound. You know as well as I do what happens to the cats people don't adopt."

Something inside him softened at her declaration and

the fierce way she was holding the skinny cat, as though nothing was going to take Alley away from her.

She was the same way with Sadie Mae, who was the human embodiment of a stray cat. The clerk was so muddled Jay couldn't imagine anybody else hiring her, but Tara kept her on and even defended her.

Tara, it seemed, had a soft spot for strays. And, despite her husband-hunting tendencies, Jay was rapidly developing a soft spot for Tara.

"I won't tell anybody," he said. "I promise."

Their eyes met and held, the moment lengthening. She had bedroom eyes, he thought. The dark, fathomless kind that hinted at great passion. The kind that belonged to a woman who would fight for the underdog, whether it was a stray cat or a group of girls banned from the locker room bathroom. He moved forward, compelled by her gaze, wondering if he were crazy.

"Cuckoo."

Semantics, semantics. Cuckoo. Crazy. What was the difference? Tara started, and the cat leaped out of her arms, causing Jay to jerk backward and wonder if Tara and Alley had heard that little voice in his head, too.

"Cuckoo."

This time, Jay realized it wasn't an internal warning voice but Tara's cuckoo clock chiming the hour. He spotted the clock just in time to see a comical caricature of a rooster darting inside.

"I, um, should get Alley some food," she said. Her face was slightly flushed, contributing greatly to the possibility that she'd wanted him to kiss her.

He raked a hand through his hair. Darn it. He knew better than to want to kiss her in return. Even if he hadn't been busy keeping men away from her to fulfill his promise to Cliff, he knew enough to steer clear of her.

She wanted to get married, for Pete's sake. So desperately that she'd turned her inn into the husband hotel.

Even as he had the thought, Jay's mind wanted to dismiss it. Tara was a competent professional who could take care of herself, just as her father had claimed. He was having an increasingly hard time believing she had matrimony on her mind.

While Tara filled the cat's dish and poured water into her bowl, he examined his surroundings.

He'd been in a number of rooms in the hotel, but hers was nothing like the rest. Colorful curtains graced the windows, and braided throw rugs spruced up the carpeting. Framed needlepoint sayings, similar to the ones he'd seen downstairs, dotted her walls.

Her tiny kitchen was a testament to domesticity. Artfully arranged pot holders and dish towels lent it a sunny touch of yellow. Copper pots hung from hooks above the stove. And, of course, there was the cuckoo clock. He could imagine her bustling about a tastefully decorated home of her own in domestic bliss. In domestic *married* bliss.

Even her refrigerator looked like it belonged to a married person. She'd attached colorful, childish drawings to it with small magnets. He squinted, taking a closer look, because two of the magnets had nothing whatsoever to do with domesticity.

"These are Bare Bob magnets, aren't they?" He grinned at the likenesses of the naked figurine she kept in her office.

"Oh, my gosh." She covered her face with her hands, but he could still see the skin peeking through her fingers. It was a telltale red. "I knew I should have thrown them out. I shouldn't have listened to Sadie Mae when she pointed out no one ever comes up here."

"Hey, don't be embarrassed," he said, absurdly glad her hunt for a husband hadn't progressed so far that she was inviting men to her room.

He came across the room to remove her hands from her face. The minute he touched her, he knew it was a mistake. She was warm and soft, and a subtle, enticing scent clung to her skin. Her face was flushed, making her look even more becoming, but he wanted to put her at ease. "I like nudity."

It was the wrong thing to say. Immediately, his mind stripped her of her clingy green dress and he imagined her as naked as the magnets on her refrigerator. She stared at him, her mouth slightly parted, as though she knew what kind of erotic pictures were moving sinuously through his mind. He was still holding her lightly by the wrists and he felt her pulse rate accelerate. His heart thumped in response.

Remember Cliff, the sane part of his brain screamed. *Remember the promise. Remember this is a woman who wants nothing more than to be married.* He cleared his throat.

"What I meant to say is that there's nothing wrong

with nudity,'' he clarified. ''I didn't mean I want to see you naked.''

''You don't?'' Her brows drew together and she looked...insulted.

''No, no. I didn't mean that,'' he denied quickly, then blurted the truth. ''I do want to see you naked.''

The look she gave him was so skeptical he realized she thought he reversed his position because he'd hurt her feelings. He let go of her wrists and put his hands on her shoulders, leaning closer as he made his point.

''I'm *dying* to see you naked. When I pulled you out of the hot tub, I had to chomp down on my tongue so I wouldn't ask if I could help strip you out of your wet clothes.''

Her eyes widened, her mouth dropped open, and he realized he'd gone too far. Way too far. Even though he wasn't really a maintenance man, for the time being she was his boss. And it wasn't kosher to let your boss in on the fact that you wanted to see her naked.

Next thing he knew he'd be telling her all the things he wanted to do to her while she was naked. She was looking at him with such heat in her gaze it nearly scorched his eyeballs.

His cell phone rang. Darn that Sherry. She was always calling at the most inappropriate times. A few hours ago, she'd phoned while he was running water to test the effectiveness of one of the four new faucets he'd installed on the third floor. As usual, her problem couldn't wait. Either he explained the intricacies of the Impeccabra's design to a major retailer pronto or they could forget about that particular retail market.

Jay had to rush out to his car, dig up the paperwork and spend fifteen minutes on the phone convincing the retailer of the bra's viability.

"I better answer this," Jay said, reluctantly drawing away from her. He unclipped his phone, flipped it open and got ready to listen to Sherry's latest problem.

Instead, Cliff Patterson's booming voice came over the line.

"How goes it, my son? Any developments to report?"

I'm inside your daughter's suite where I just got finished telling her I wanted to see her naked.

"No, no, nothing." Jay walked a few paces from Tara and cupped his hand over the phone so her father's voice wouldn't carry. "Everything's going according to plan."

"No snags?"

"Not since you told her about my auntie Em," Jay whispered, but he and Cliff had already had that conversation. "Listen, now's not a good time to talk."

Cliff lowered his voice. "She's there, isn't she?"

"Affirmative." Jay closed his eyes. *Affirmative?* Had he actually said affirmative?

"I'll hang up then," Cliff said. When he did, Jay had the insane urge to say, "Over and out."

"Was that my father?" Tara asked as he reclipped the phone.

Jay's impulse was to nod, but he squelched it because he doubted he could explain why Cliff was phoning him.

Somehow, he didn't think she'd buy a maintenance emergency. "No. Not your father. No, sirree."

"But I could have sworn—"

"Can't talk now. Gotta go," he interrupted. "I've been so busy replacing bathroom faucets on the third floor I haven't gotten around to fixing that broken lock on the door by the parking lot."

That stopped whatever she'd been about to say. "I didn't know we had replacement faucets."

"Yep. I found them in the supply room. The old faucets are so worn it made more sense to replace them than fix them. I did four today."

"Great," Tara said, smiling at him.

The smile was so luminous that an answering one automatically crossed his face. "I need to get to that lock before quitting time. So I'll be on my way."

A moment passed. Then two. The only sounds in the room were the ticking of the cuckoo clock and Alley's purrs as she rubbed against his leg.

"Jay?" Tara's soft voice broke into the silence. She had a great voice. Low and melodious. Sexy.

"Yeah?"

"You're still here."

She was right. He was still there, about a dozen feet from where he wanted to be, which was in her bed. With her. Oh, brother.

"I'm going," he said.

She stepped aside so he could move around her, but the space was so narrow that his body brushed against hers. Desire, hot and instant, flared through him.

He tamped it down and walked out the door.

"Stupid, stupid, stupid," he muttered as he walked down the hall, away from the temptation she presented.

But the self-recriminations didn't help. He still wanted to see her naked.

5

"IT'S RAINING UPSTAIRS."

Tara cradled the cup of coffee she'd picked up at the continental breakfast counter and regarded Sadie Mae and her peculiar announcement through bleary eyes.

She'd been up half the night, alternately fantasizing about how sleek and powerful Jay Overman would look naked and berating herself for the fantasies.

An employee deserved more from a boss than to be the object of her wild sexual fantasies, even if he'd started them by being so understanding about her cat and then making that remark about wanting to strip her out of her wet clothes.

She was the boss. She was supposed to let him know that cracks about how much he wanted to see her naked were way out of line. Instead she'd nearly told him that she'd show him hers if he showed her his. Her fingers had itched to strip off his clothes. Her only saving grace was that she'd managed to keep her hands to herself.

She wasn't sure she could summon the patience to deal with Sadie Mae on four hours of sleep, but she had to try. She took a deep breath and smiled at her friend.

"Good morning, Sadie Mae." Tara gestured expansively toward the glass doors of the lobby, through which the sun shined radiantly. "As you can see, it's a beautiful day. Not a raindrop in sight."

Sadie Mae shook her red curls so they bounced like living springs. "I didn't say it was raining outside. I said it was raining *upstairs*. I've had three calls this morning from guests who say their ceilings are dripping." She pushed a pad across the counter to Tara. "I wrote down the room numbers."

Tara set down her coffee cup and examined the list. All of the rooms were on the second floor, which struck her as significant. After a moment, the reason occurred to her. Yesterday Jay had replaced bathroom faucets on the third floor.

"Are the leaks in the bathrooms?"

Sadie Mae nodded while Tara processed the information. If Jay had installed the faucets incorrectly in the third-floor bathrooms, that could account for the leaks on the second floor. But Jay had replaced four faucets, not three.

"Did you page Jay?"

"I was supposed to page Jay?"

"He *is* the maintenance department."

As if on cue, the front doors swung open and the maintenance department strode through. Jay greeted Mrs. Burnside, the white-haired senior citizen in charge of the continental breakfast, and she giggled so uproariously she sounded like she'd taken a hit of laughing gas. *A sincere smile, a hard-muscled body and a jingling tool belt will do that to a woman,* Tara thought.

Stop it! Tara shut her eyes so they'd stop stripping off

his clothes. What kind of resident manager was she? Her hotel had sprung a leak and she was fixated on how Jay would look nude. Better than Bare Bob, she guessed.

"There's Jay now." Sadie Mae waved her arms wildly, like a runway worker directing a plane. "Yoo-hoo, Jay. Over here. We've got an emergency."

An emergency, Tara reminded herself, that must be handled with the participants fully clothed.

As Jay got nearer, her gaze traveled up his body to the surprising fullness of his mouth, and she wondered if she could convince him the emergency required mouth-to-mouth resuscitation.

Stop it! She shut her eyes again, tighter this time, vowing not to open them until she got control of herself.

"Tara, are you okay?" She heard Jay's anxious voice, felt his strong hands on her chin. A shiver of awareness coursed through her. "Open your eyes, sweetheart. If there's something in your eye, it won't come out until you open up."

IF HE DIDN'T clench his teeth to keep his tongue from betraying him, he could very well blow his cover.

The thought thundered through Jay's mind ten minutes later as he walked down the third-floor hallway with Tara at his side.

He was glad nothing was wrong with her eye, but he was irked that she thought he'd installed the faucets incorrectly.

True, he hadn't consulted directions before undertaking the project, but he knew how to install something as simple as a bathroom faucet.

He was a civil engineer, after all. He knew how things worked. He'd designed Impeccabra, hadn't he?

The notion to tell her that was so overwhelming he clamped his teeth. It was either keep quiet or prepare to explain what an engineer with a college degree was doing posing as a maintenance man.

"We should check room three-one-one first," Tara told him. "The other three rooms are occupied. I hope the guests will do as Sadie Mae asks and not run the water until we can make the repairs."

Her voice was brisk and professional, and he wondered if she was trying to put distance between them because of that crack he'd made yesterday about longing to see her naked.

He still didn't know why she'd been closing her eyes so tightly as Sadie Mae proclaimed an emergency, but since she'd opened them she'd looked at him with cool detachment.

Good. He couldn't deny that he wanted the woman from yesterday back, the softhearted one whose mouth had parted invitingly while he'd prattled on about nudity. But getting involved with Tara would be insane.

He was there to drive away matrimonial candidates, not to become one himself.

So what if she smuggled stray cats into her room, gave jobs to her klutzy friends and exuded a soft sweetness completely at odds with the picture of a grasping professional woman her father had painted?

Jay happened to agree with Cliff Patterson about **not** getting married until being firmly established in a career. His own father hadn't wed until he was in his mid-thirties, when he was already financially stable and established as the Panty King.

Jay had yet to establish himself in the engineering industry, where he was one of dozens of engineers employed by a construction company to work on transportation projects. He supposed some people would consider designing the Impeccabra verification that he was moving up in the world, but that didn't count.

It wasn't as though he was going to make a career out of fashioning ladies' underthings. He was not the Bra Prince. Not really. He was a civil engineer and the man Tara's father had deputized to stop her from getting married.

"I'm sure it's only a minor problem, nothing that'll take long to fix," he said as she stopped in front of Room 311 and inserted her key card.

He followed her inside the room and paused in the entrance, patiently waiting for her apology, because he was sure he'd installed the faucet exactly the way it was supposed to be installed.

"Oh, my heavens."

As apologies go, it wasn't what he expected.

Neither did he expect his work boots to make squishing noises as they sank into the wet carpet of the alcove leading to the bathroom. Or the inch or so of standing water on the bathroom floor. Or the fact that he'd evidently left the water running all night.

"Oh, no," Tara exclaimed as she rushed into the bathroom and shut off the tap. "How could this have happened?"

"Gremlins?" Jay suggested, but she wasn't buying it.

He sighed, hardly believing he was immersed in a faucet fiasco that could flush him into the open and blow his cover. But there was little point in denying something that was obviously his fault.

"I must have forgotten to turn off the tap after I checked to see if the water was draining properly," Jay mused, wondering how that was possible. A flash of insight gave him the answer.

The faucet in Room 311 had been the fourth and final one he'd replaced the day before, and he remembered standing back to admire his handiwork. As he had in the other three instances, he turned on the tap to check the drainage.

That's when Sherry had rung him with her plea for help, and he'd needed to consult the design work he kept in his car. He remembered leaning over to shut off the tap as he talked, but he must not have cut off the flow completely, causing the water to fill the sink and spill over.

Once again, he'd had bras on the brain.

He didn't think it would help his cause any if he told Tara that.

"Maybe it's not as bad as it looks," he said, splashing through the water to join her in the bathroom. He expected the sink to be brimming with water, but it was only about a quarter full.

That was strange. That must mean there was a problem with the building's pipes, unless she was right and he had bungled the job. He scrunched down and opened the cabinet door. The bottom of the cabinet was filled with water. He stuck his head underneath the sink to get a closer look and felt his head hit a hard pipe. Water gushed over him, making him jerk backward.

"It looks pretty bad to me," Tara said as water streamed down his face.

"Let me try that again," he said, bracing one hand on the cabinet floor to support his weight while he ducked his head under the cabinet one more time.

By the time he felt the floor move, it was too late. His hand crashed through the dampened floor, setting off a chain reaction. He heard what he feared was plaster loosening from the ceiling of the bathroom below and falling with a thud onto whatever was in its way.

He also heard a shocked masculine scream.

His arm had sunk past his elbow into the floor. Gingerly, he removed it and sent a horrified-looking Tara a hopeful look.

"I don't suppose you told Sadie Mae to ask the guest in room two eleven to stay out of the bathroom till we checked this out?"

Wordlessly, she shook her head. Then they were both up and dashing out of the room, through the hotel and down the stairway, intent on finding out what had happened to the screeching guest in Room 211.

Something about the room number nudged at Jay's

mind, but he didn't realize why until they reached the second floor.

The same boyish businessman Jay had chased through the hotel the day before was in the hallway outside the damaged room. He was barefoot, his only clothing a pair of bright blue boxers decorated with miniature Humpty-Dumpties.

"The bathroom's collapsing," he announced. He was jumping up and down as though the sky was falling.

"We had a minor problem with the upstairs plumbing, Robby," Tara said calmly, coming forward and taking the Boyish One by the arm. "The plaster on the ceiling must have loosened and fell."

Her words didn't ease boyish Robby's panic, so Jay stepped forward and clasped him by the other arm.

"Calm down, buddy," Jay said, making his voice low and soothing. He hoped he wasn't dripping on the other man. "This is all my fault. I left the water running in the upstairs bathroom."

The man's eyes swung to Jay and widened in recognition. "You!" he cried.

Robby yelped and sprang away from them, shaking both Tara and Jay's hands off his arms.

"You're crazy, man. Crazy." His voice was so high-pitched it sounded as though he'd sucked the helium from a balloon. "You're not going to intimidate me into saying yes."

Oh, brother. The Boyish One still thought Jay was trying to get him to be part of a threesome. Jay moved forward, intending to calm him down.

"Don't come any closer. Three's a crowd," he yelled before disappearing inside the damaged room and slamming the door behind him.

For a moment, neither Tara nor Jay said a word. Jay could feel his cover slipping and knew he had to do something to put it back in place. Unfortunately, only one idea occurred to him. *Bluff.*

"I think that went rather well," he said, wiping moisture from his forehead while he gave her his most winning smile.

AN HOUR LATER, Jay pinched the bridge of his nose as he examined his leaky handiwork and tried to figure out what he'd done wrong.

Tara had cordoned off Rooms 311 and 211, deciding it made sense for him to tackle the small problems first to prevent another impending disaster.

That made sense to Jay, but he'd spent the last fifteen minutes unable to figure out the puzzle. Replacing a faucet should have been a simple matter.

Not only was he an engineer, but he was a guy. He could replace a leaky faucet. He went over the steps in his mind as he peered under the cabinet at the plumbing fixtures. He'd closed the shutoff valve supplying water to the fixture. Loosened the nuts connecting water lines to the faucet. Removed...

"Jay."

The voice startled him so much he jerked and hit his head on the underside of the cabinet.

"Oh, my gosh, are you all right?"

He ducked his head so he wouldn't hit it again and looked up to find Sadie Mae peering at him. Her shirt was so tight it was possible to tell that, unlike Tara, she was wearing an extremely well-fitting bra. Jay was curious as to the brand, but he wasn't particularly interested in what was underneath the bra. Not in the same way that he wanted to get a peek at Tara's skin. He frowned.

"I'm fine," he said, refraining from rubbing the spot even though it hurt like the devil. "You surprised me, that's all."

"The door was open so I walked in. I came up here to see if you needed any help."

"Help? Why would I need help?" He tried to give her a smile, but his lips wouldn't quite curve.

She bit her lip and narrowed her eyes. "You can't figure out why your faucets are leaking, can you? I wouldn't mind taking a look, if you want."

He was about to ask her what good that would do when it struck him that Sadie Mae couldn't make the problem any worse. What the heck.

"Sure," he said. "Why not?"

He let her take his position on the floor next to the sink. He watched her riot of red curls disappear under the cabinet while he stood back with his arms crossed over his chest, waiting for the inevitable. Less than a minute later, she reappeared, her green eyes shining with intelligence.

"You forgot the washer. When you do that, splash. You get leaks. If you take apart the water-line connection and put it back together using the washer, it'll work fine."

She moved out of the way and Jay took a look for himself. Man, she was right. He'd left out the washer. Not only that, he'd done the other three faucets the same way. And all because the boxes containing the new faucets had been missing them, a fact he should have realized way before now.

"How'd you know that?" he asked her when he'd stood up.

"Aw, it's nothing. My dad's a plumber. It's amazing the things you pick up when the dinner table conversation revolves around valves and pipe wrenches."

They smiled at each other, and Jay understood why Tara was going to such lengths to help her. Sadie Mae had a good heart, the kind that drove her to help a man she hardly knew. He'd be honored to call her a friend.

She shifted, and her hip knocked against a pair of pliers on the counter, causing it to tumble to the floor. She jumped and crashed into Jay, whose back slammed into the wall.

For a moment, before they both got their equilibrium again, she was plastered against his chest.

She jumped back, putting five feet between them. "Good thing T.P. didn't see that. She wouldn't like it. Not that she'd ever admit it."

"What wouldn't she like?"

Her face colored. "Nothing. Forget it. Forget I said anything. I'm sure she doesn't want you to know."

"Know what?"

She stared at him for a moment, then blurted, "That she wants to see you in her office."

"She doesn't want me to know that she wants to see me in her office?"

"Of course she does. That's why I came up here. To tell you that."

"I thought you came up here to help me with the plumbing."

"Don't listen to me. You can't believe a word I say," Sadie Mae said breezily before she rushed out of the room with Jay following hot on her heels.

Considering what Sadie Mae had intimated, he was very much looking forward to what Tara wanted to say to him.

SHE HAD TO fire him.

Tara sat in her office, her elbows on her desk, her head in her hands, as she arrived at the awful, inescapable conclusion. Jay's plumbing mistake had resulted in thousands of dollars of damage, and it was her duty to report it to the home office.

Excursion Inns Limited had liability insurance, but the powers that be would still want a full accounting of the incident, complete with the name of the guilty. She couldn't keep Jay out of it. No matter how much she wanted to.

She lifted her head only to meet Bare Bob's hard plastic glare.

"Don't look at me like that," she told the figurine. "It's not like I want to fire him."

Bare Bob's expression didn't change. Funny that she'd never noticed the glare on the figurine's face before, but she supposed his other body parts demanded more attention.

"How'd you get out of the drawer, anyway?"

She picked him up, yanked open her drawer and unceremoniously dropped him inside. Sadie Mae was undoubtedly the culprit responsible for his reappearing acts. She should either have a talk with her friend or find the figurine a better hiding place.

She knew she should just throw Bare Bob out with the garbage, but she wouldn't. Was it because she believed, as Sadie Mae did, that a naked figurine in her office would get the live article in her bed? Or was it because she wanted that naked man to be Jay Overman?

She let out a disgusted breath. Fat chance of that happening after she fired him. She could hear the conversation now. "I have to send you packing. Wanna be my Bare Jay?"

Or maybe she should call him Jaybird. Weren't people always talking about how naked they were?

She thumped herself once on the forehead, trying to get her mind off her maintenance man's anatomy. She had more pressing things to think about.

Such as how she was going to fire him.

Three quick raps sounded on the office door. Jay stuck his head into her office, looking impossibly handsome.

"Hey, Tara." She felt the warmth of his smile clear across the room, making her feel worse for what she was about to do. "Sadie Mae said you wanted to see me."

That was odd. Even though she needed to see him, she hadn't asked Sadie Mae to fetch him. But he was here now, and to send him away would be cowardly. And if Cliff Patterson had taught her anything, it was not to be a coward.

"Come in." She sat up as straight as she could so he wouldn't guess she was nervous. "I do need to talk to you."

He moved into the room with an ease she envied, stopping beside her desk and reaching into his back pocket.

"Before I forget, I couldn't resist getting these yesterday when I was at the grocery store."

Her mouth gaped open when he stretched out a hand full of foil packages. Her breath snagged in her throat.

"Why..." She stopped before she finished the question, because she knew why. He must have noticed the lascivious way she'd been looking at him yesterday. She only hoped her tongue hadn't been hanging out. Instead, she said, "I didn't know they sold them in the grocery store."

"They're giving out samples of Kitty Kittles everywhere."

"Kitty Kittles?"

He lowered his voice. "They're a new treat for cats. I got the tuna-flavored crackers, but they also come in fish flavors."

"Oh."

"They're for Alley." He paused and screwed up his mouth. "Not that I'm a cat lover. No, it's dogs for me.

Enormous, massive dogs. Great Danes, Saint Bernards, malamutes.''

The way he was carrying on about colossal canines, Tara wouldn't have been surprised had he gone for broke and mentioned Clifford the Big Red Dog. But he stopped abruptly and changed the subject.

"I know why the sinks were leaking. I should have realized the boxes with the new faucets were missing washers, but I didn't. Without them, the pipes leaked."

"So that's why the ceiling fell down on room two eleven?"

"Yep." A corner of his mouth hiked up in a self-deprecating smile. "I tried to find Robby to apologize, but I didn't have any luck."

"That's because he checked out a little while ago," Tara said. "I tried to give him some free hotel vouchers to make up for his trouble, but he couldn't get out of here fast enough."

"I'll apologize the next time he stays here, then."

"He says he's never coming back." Simply relaying that fact caused Tara's stomach to clench. "To tell you the truth, that hurt. I'm trying to attract guests to the hotel, not to drive them away."

"*You* didn't drive him away."

"I don't know about that. I certainly couldn't calm him down. He was looking at me in the strangest way."

Jay winced. "Did he mention me?"

She shook her head while she regarded him curiously. "Any reason he should have?"

"No," he said quickly. Too quickly? "It's just that,

considering he was outside the bathroom when the plaster fell, bolting like that's a pretty extreme reaction.''

''I have a feeling Robby Fairchild's the master of the extreme reaction,'' Tara said on a sigh.

''Tell me about it,'' Jay muttered.

Tara hardly paid attention to his last comment because they'd come to the part of the conversation she'd been dreading. She drew in a breath and made herself proceed. Her heart felt so heavy that it seemed to be weighing her down in the chair.

''Unfortunately, as you've probably guessed, I can't ignore an incident of this magnitude. The hotel has experienced significant damage that I'm required to report to the home office.''

''I'll pay for it.''

''You'll what?''

''Give me a bill, and I'll pay for the repairs.''

Pay for the repairs? How could he do that when he wasn't earning much over minimum wage and her father had confided that he really needed this job?

''I can't let you do that,'' she said slowly, watching him closely for a reaction. He shrugged like a man who was used to taking responsibility for his mistakes. Like a man who not only had a college degree but the money that often went with it.

''Why not?''

''Because...'' She faltered. She couldn't very well quiz him about how he could afford the repairs. Besides, it was entirely possible he didn't have any concept of how much those repairs would be. "Because the hotel has liability insurance."

"Then I'll pay the deductible."

"No. No," Tara said, but she wasn't quite convinced that she was saving him from himself. Something very strange was going on with Jay Overman, but unfortunately he wasn't going to be around long enough for her to find out what it was. This was it. This was where she told him he was going to pay for his mistake with his job, not his wallet. She drew in a deep breath. "I didn't want to see you to talk about those faucets."

She wasn't sure if she was more surprised by her declaration or if he was. Her money was on herself. She was supposed to be firing him precisely because of those faucets, not disavowing any connection with them.

He'd remained standing while she talked to him, and now he shifted all his glorious weight from one foot to the other. The muscles in his thighs bulged through his jeans. He cocked a dark, perfectly shaped eyebrow.

"Then why did you want to see me?"

Because I want to uncover your secrets and solve the mystery of who the real Jay Overman is, Tara thought. Not to mention that she couldn't stop fantasizing about what he looked like naked. For one heart-stopping moment when he'd offered her the Kitty Kittles, she'd wished he were handing her condoms.

"Because...I need you to fix the showerhead in my bathroom."

What had come over her? What she needed was to fire him. Except she found that she couldn't. Not when he was so willing to take responsibility for his mistake. Not when he was looking at her with those dreamy cream-soda eyes. Not when his mere presence made her pulse jump with wild abandon.

"Sure thing. I'll get to it after I finish reinstalling those faucets. Say about six o'clock."

"But you get off work before then."

"Not today. After what happened with the faucets, I need to stay on the boss's good side."

He winked at her and sauntered out of the office while she took in the width of his shoulders, the play of muscles in his back and the fabulous way those jeans molded his rear end.

She picked up some papers from her desktop and fanned herself while she thought about how to leave Jay's name out of the report to the home office. If she blamed worn pipes, nobody would be the wiser. The hotel would pay for the repairs, no questions asked, and Jay could keep his job. A job that didn't require a college education.

She rubbed her chin while she thought. Jay was coming by to fix her broken showerhead at dinnertime, which afforded her the perfect opportunity to invite him to share a meal with her while she interrogated—er, got to know him better.

She glanced at her watch. Show time was less than two hours away. She hurried out of the office, going over menu choices in her head while she scoured every flat surface she passed for a weapon of destruction.

She had a dinner for two to cook and a showerhead to bust.

6

THE SHOWERHEAD in Tara's bathroom looked as if it had lost a battle with a sledgehammer.

It wasn't just broken. It was busted, one half of it smashed almost beyond recognition. Jay had figured the showerhead had sprung a leak when Tara had asked him to fix it. He'd even double-checked with Sadie Mae on the proper way to make one stop leaking before coming upstairs. He'd expected drips, not near destruction.

He let the shower curtain fall shut, noticing that it was pale pink and dotted with tiny white flowers instead of stark white like the curtains in the other Excursion Inn bathrooms. He started to reach for a towel but thought better of it and wiped his hands on his jeans. The towel, which matched the shower curtain, looked too pretty to soil.

Following his nose to the kitchen, he found Tara with her back to him, stirring some delectable-smelling dish. He propped an elbow against the wall and watched her efficient movements as she hummed a soft tune to herself.

Alley rubbed against one of his legs, and he bent to stroke the cat, never taking his eyes from her owner. He hardly noticed when Alley grew tired of his stroking and quietly retreated to the far corner of the room.

Tara's long, luxurious hair was up in that infernal bun again, but he found consolation in the graceful line of her neck. He longed to press his lips to the delicate-looking skin where her neck met the slope of her jaw, longed to hear whether he could make her sigh in pleasure and turn to meet his mouth with hers.

When his mouth watered, he tried to believe it was because it had been months since he'd had a home-cooked meal. But he knew deep down that he was lying to himself. His reaction had much more to do with the lovely cook than the food she was preparing.

Annoyed at the direction of his thoughts, he straightened and cleared his throat. "How'd you say that showerhead got busted again?"

She whipped her head around, obviously surprised to find him standing there watching her. Her face was flushed from the heat of the stove, but for a crazy moment he wished he were the cause of the flush.

"Um, it fell."

"But it screws into a fixture attached to the wall. How could it fall?"

She bit her lush lower lip, making him ache. He concentrated on trying to read her expression to take his mind away from the ache and realized she looked puzzled. "It must've come loose."

He scratched his chin and tried very hard to focus on showerheads but instead conjured up a mental image of Tara underneath one, her head tilted toward the spray, her body... Jeez. He had to stop this.

He cleared his throat again. "A fall couldn't have done that kind of damage."

"It was a *very* hard fall."

He was about to protest again but let the subject drop. She obviously didn't have any more insight into how the showerhead had gotten damaged than he did.

"I'll need to replace it with a new one from the supply room," he said. "Shouldn't take more than a few minutes. I'll be out of your way by the time dinner's on the table."

The tip of her tongue peeked out of her mouth to wet her lips, sending his equilibrium into a crazy spin. She smoothed an errant piece of dark hair from her face and smiled. "Actually, I was wondering if you'd like to join me for dinner."

Even though he'd been hoping for her to say exactly that, the safe thing would be to refuse, fix her shower-head and be on his way. Tara Patterson was working a crazy kind of magic on him that could only complicate the reason he was at the Excursion Inn in the first place.

"I'm making a marinated beef roast with baked potatoes and Caribbean-style vegetables," she said, as though he needed any more incentive. "You're welcome to join me."

No. Say no.

"I'd love to," Jay heard himself say.

"Good," she said, and he watched undisguised pleasure spread across her features. Something that felt suspiciously like happiness built inside him as he anticipated spending an evening in her company until he realized he was standing there grinning like a lottery winner.

He jerked a thumb at the door. "I'll go get the showerhead."

"I'll get dinner on the table," she said, but instead she stood there watching him.

It was so difficult to make himself leave her and walk out the door that he wondered if he were insane to agree to sit down to dinner with her. The way his hormones were raging, he doubted he'd be able to get through the night without touching her.

By the time he was on his way to her suite with the new showerhead, he'd decided he couldn't be trusted.

The only logical course of action—the only *right* course—was to dream up an emergency, extend his apologies and leave.

He gathered his resolve as he neared Tara's suite, slowing slightly to get around a man carrying his luggage into the room next to Tara's. The man nodded at Jay, a half smile on his handsome, chiseled features.

Jay's eyes flew to the ring finger of the man's left hand. Empty. His relationship-wrecking radar went on full alert. The man screamed eligible bachelor, and all that separated him from Tara was a thin wall.

He returned the man's nod but didn't smile.

"Just going to have dinner with my woman," he said gruffly. "She's the manager of this here hotel. Yes, sirree. She's my woman."

He nearly added, "You stay away from here, ya hear?" but thought that might be laying it on too thick.

The half smile on the man's face faded, and he disappeared into his room, pulling the door shut. Jay heard the dead bolt turn.

Jay paused, then gave Tara's door a quick rap to let her know he was back. All thoughts of inventing an emergency so he could escape with her virtue intact had vanished.

It was his duty to have dinner with Tara.

That way, he could be sure she wasn't wandering the halls, bumping into men who even to Jay looked like prime marriage material. Not, of course, that Jay noticed things like that. He had his manly reputation to protect. And his women to keep other men away from.

JAY POLISHED OFF the last of the vegetables Tara had dribbled with some sort of delectable sauce, sat back in his chair and sipped his wine.

He hadn't had a home-cooked meal since he and Sherry had visited their mother in Florida over Christmas. Usually he preferred chicken and rice to meat and potatoes, but Tara had done wonderful things with standard fare.

She'd also created the perfect dining experience with a beautifully set table complete with china and cloth napkins, classical music playing softly in the background and an exquisitely chosen bottle of French burgundy.

The candle burning in the middle of the table sent light flickering over her heart-shaped face, softening her features and making her look even more beautiful.

Jay thought he was in danger of sensory overload.

"Wow. That was great," he said. "Where'd you learn to cook like that?"

She shrugged but he could tell by the way her lips

curved that his praise pleased her. "It's something I picked up around the house growing up."

The answer was so unexpected that he let out a short laugh. "Don't tell me Cliff taught you, because that's one single father I'd bet my life can't cook."

She tilted her head, regarding him curiously. Suspiciously. "I hadn't realized you knew my father so well."

He shifted in his seat, barely refraining from grimacing. He'd not only called her father by his first name but revealed he was aware that she'd grown up without a mother.

"I don't," he denied, which, after all, was true. "I got an impression of him from a couple of things he said. And, uh, he must've mentioned that his wife died when you were a baby."

"That's surprising. We hardly ever talk about that."

She rose abruptly, busying herself with clearing the dishes, making him wish he could take back the comment about her mother. He picked up his plate and silently followed her to the sink. When she pulled open the door to the dishwasher, he turned on the tap to rinse his plate, handing it to her as though they'd worked this way dozens of times.

"I imagine growing up without a mother must've been rough," he said, but she didn't reply.

The whoosh of water and the clack of the dishes when she set them in the dishwasher were the only sounds in the kitchen for a full minute. Then, finally, she broke the silence.

"I grew up with a succession of housekeepers who were supposed to keep an eye on me when Dad was at work," Tara said softly. She had such a faraway look in her eyes that he suspected she was seeing the past. "My favorite was a woman named Maxie. She could do everything—cook, clean, sew, knit. I used to follow her around the house like a puppy, watching everything she did, drinking it all in."

"What happened to her?"

Tara lifted her shoulders in a casual gesture at odds with the tightness in her voice. "She left after a couple of years. They all did."

The bits and pieces that he found puzzling about her snapped into place. No wonder she was hunting for a husband. She probably wanted to create the kind of household she'd missed out on, the kind with a husband and wife who loved each other, the kind he'd grown up in and taken for granted.

"I understand," he said softly.

"Understand what?"

Too late, he realized he wasn't supposed to know that she was searching for a husband. And he certainly wasn't about to let her in on the little secret that his sole purpose at the Excursion Inn was to keep men away from her.

"I understand, considering how domestic you are, why you went into hotel management."

TARA DIDN'T process the rest of his sentence. "*Domestic?* I'm not domestic," she denied.

He pointedly looked around her suite and fingered a pot holder she'd embroidered with a dainty daffodil. "Could've fooled me."

She put her hands on her hips, amazed by his perception of her. She was Cliff Patterson's daughter, taught from a young age that succeeding at a career was more important than breathing. He hadn't instructed her in the fine points of domesticity.

"Enjoying embroidery, cooking and decorating doesn't make me domestic."

"So you don't want a husband, a home and a family?"

Tara frowned, because she was becoming increasingly aware that was exactly what she wanted. Her father might preach that she should wait until age thirty to marry, but she didn't see the point. Not that she intended to randomly select a mate and rush to the altar. For Tara, love and marriage really did go together.

"That still doesn't make me domestic," she said.

"Why did you go into hotel management then?"

"I fail to see how working at a hotel makes me domestic."

"Oh, come on, Tara. You call your guests by their first names, hang framed needlepoint and stock the place with fresh flowers. What is a hotel, after all, besides a home away from home?"

Her mouth gaped as she considered what he said. Was he right? Had hotel management attracted her because it afforded the opportunity to practice domesticity on a grand scale? Did she enjoy managing the Excursion Inn because it was like running a household in a really big house?

"Heavens to Hildegarde, I think you're right," she said, staring at him in awe. He touched her cheek, a curiously indulgent smile on his face.

"Who's Hildegarde?"

The way his touch warmed her was so unexpected that her brain waves went on momentary hiatus. "Pardon?"

"Hildegarde?" His hand moved from her cheek and lightly brushed the errant strands of hair from her face. "The more common phrase is 'Heavens to Betsy,' but you said 'Heavens to Hildegarde.'"

"Oh, that. It's just an expression my father and I use. My mother's name was Hildegarde."

He made a face that was so comical she laughed.

"My father says she went by Hilda most of the time."

"Heavens to Hildegarde, I can see why."

She smiled at him, aware that his broad but gentle hand was still in her hair. She'd wondered days ago what it would feel like to be touched by Jay Overman. Now she knew. It was heavenly.

Their eyes met and held, and their smiles faded. They were standing beside the refrigerator, but the air heated all the same. Desire crackled between them, as tangible as the meal they'd just eaten.

Desire? The realization caused Tara to step back and break the invisible connection. She turned to the dishwasher, calling herself all kinds of a fool. Jay Overman was her employee, for Pete's sake. She'd convinced herself that by feeding him a meal she'd have the opportunity to figure out what he was hiding, but now she realized that wasn't the real motivation behind her invitation.

The bald truth was that she'd asked him to dinner because she was attracted to him.

"Anything wrong, Tara?" Jay asked.

"No. Nothing," she said brightly. Too brightly. She should dream up an emergency and send him away before she did something she'd regret.

Send him away, she told herself. *Send him away. Send him away.*

"Would you like to stay?" she asked, then pressed her lips together before she tacked "overnight" onto the end of the question.

He nodded, and minutes later they retreated to the sitting room she'd spruced up with a colorful, Oriental-style rug and a pretty textured throw she'd paired with the sofa.

The room wasn't much more than an alcove equipped with a television and a stereo. It wasn't large enough to accommodate a chair, so Tara sat next to him on the sofa, bringing up the possibility that she'd suggested moving to the sitting room precisely because she wanted to be close to him.

Alley, who had been secluded in Tara's bedroom, suddenly appeared, hopped on the sofa and snuggled next to Jay.

Tara could smell the clean male scent of him, feel the heat that seemed to come off him and invade her. She wanted to nestle against him, the same as her cat. But, perhaps even more, she wanted to delve into the reasons a college graduate was working as a maintenance man.

"I've been meaning to talk to you about what you said the other day," she began.

The hand stroking Alley stilled, and he turned to her with a contrite expression. "I shouldn't have said that."

"Don't apologize," she said. "It's perfectly all right."

She couldn't read all the expressions that crossed his face but thought she recognized delight before he asked, "So you don't mind that I want to see you naked?"

She brought her hands up to cover the flames she felt spreading across her cheeks. "I meant what you said about graduating from college."

His mouth formed an O before he uttered the word. He resumed stroking her cat, not looking at her as the silence between them lengthened. Some interrogator she was. Not only couldn't she get him to answer a simple question, she doubted she had the right to ask it.

"I'm sorry I pried," she said finally. "I understand that you don't want to talk about it."

"It's not that. It's...complicated." He stopped, blew out a breath, ran a hand over his face.

"I'm a good listener." She had a sudden flash of insight. "This has something to do with your sister and the reason she's always calling you, doesn't it?"

Jay considered the question, wondering how much he could tell her without lying. Because he couldn't explain about his engineering degree, he focused on Sherry. "She calls me for business advice," he said slowly.

"Let me guess," she said before he could expand. "Your family has a business and you've resisted going into it."

His face must have mirrored his shock at the conclusion she reached because she pressed her hands together. "I'm right, aren't I?"

"Yeah, you are." His college degree wasn't in business, as she no doubt assumed, but his resistance was real enough.

She positioned her body at an angle to his and leaned slightly forward. "So why don't you want to go into the family business?"

"The family business deals in lingerie," he said flatly.

Her brows drew together. "What's wrong with lingerie?"

He let out a short laugh. Alley must've picked up on his sudden tension because she jumped from the sofa and left the room. "You wouldn't ask if you'd grown up with the Panty King for a father."

"I don't follow."

He took a breath and resurrected the painful memories. "The kids at school, that's what they used to call my dad. But Dad said he didn't care what they called him as long as his underwear kept selling."

"I think being proud of what you do is admirable."

"Then he should have put himself in that commercial instead of me and Sherry."

"What commercial?" she asked. Then her eyes widened. "Don't tell me he made you prance around in your underwear?"

Jay felt a reluctant smile curve his lips. "He sold ladies' underwear, remember? He wouldn't have gotten much mileage out of a cross-dressing son. Even if I was only six."

"So what did he make you do?"

"It wasn't what he made us do. It's what he made us say." Jay shuddered at the memory, remembering how the words had come back to haunt him. "We looked straight into the camera, smiled our brightest smiles and said…"

"Go on."

"Listen to the Overmans when we say it's what's underneath that counts."

She grimaced. "That's pretty bad."

"It gets worse. The commercial was rerun for years. It's one thing to be advertising lingerie when you're six. It's another when you're a preteen. They used to call me the Panty Prince."

"Ouch. So what did you do?"

"Hung out with my uncle when he was rebuilding car engines. Learned to shoot a hunting rifle. Played for the football team."

"Is that how you got this?" she asked, reaching out to trace the thin scar that ran through his left eyebrow. Only her forefinger was touching him, but his entire body was on alert.

"Yeah. I lost my helmet on a play but made the tackle anyway."

"It sounds to me like you rebelled against your father's business with all things male."

"I guess I did," he said, surprised he was confiding in her. He'd never talked about this before, not even with Sherry, who hadn't been teased about the commercial as unmercifully as he had. But this was dangerous territory, considering all he was hiding from her.

"What about you?" he asked to change the subject. He lightly touched the crooked place on her nose. "Unless I'm mistaken, this has been broken."

"Oh, that. Sammy Baumgartner, the school bully, punched me in the nose when we were in the third grade."

"He did? Didn't Sammy's mother tell him not to beat up girls?"

"Sammy was short for Samantha, and she was an equal-opportunity bully. I got in the way of her fist and little Mikey McGillicutty's face. I was so mad at her for being such a bully, I swung back. It was the first and last time I ever resorted to physical violence."

"So you broke her nose, too?"

She smiled sheepishly. "No. I missed. But I did tattle on her and she was suspended from school for three days."

"Remind me not to cross you," he said, uncomfortably aware that he was doing exactly that. From the way she smiled, he could tell she didn't think that was likely. And that she didn't intend to be sidetracked.

"We're getting off the subject, which is you and your college degree," she said. "I was wondering why you don't use it to go into another kind of business? Why become a maintenance man?"

Good question, Jay thought as he scrambled to come up with an answer that made sense. Why? Think, think, think.

"It's man's work," he said gruffly. Oh, brother. He sounded like a chest-pounding idiot.

"It sounds like this Panty Prince stuff has really gotten into your head. You should tell your family once and for all that you don't want to go into lingerie. Maybe then they'd stop bothering you."

He let out a heavy breath. "It's not that easy. My father died a couple years ago, and my mother retired to

Florida, leaving Sherry to run the business. It's my responsibility to help her."

"Wouldn't she discharge you of the responsibility if she knew how much you hated it?"

"I don't exactly hate it." The statement surprised Jay because it was the first time he'd voiced the sentiment. How best to explain this to her? "Lately I can't seem to stop looking at women's chests."

He saw Tara swallow. "That's not surprising. You *are* a man."

"You don't understand. I don't mean I'm looking at their breasts. I'm looking at their bras."

"There's a difference?"

"Not if they're wearing the right kind of bra. Ideally, a bra should fit so well that nobody should be able to tell you're wearing one." Jay's eyes dipped to the ill-fitting bra Tara wore under her shirt. The Impeccabra would do wonders for her. "It's staggering how many women wear bras that don't fit properly."

She gazed at her shirt as though examining what was underneath for flaws. "It's hard to find the right bra. The last time I went bra shopping, I must've tried on a dozen kinds."

"And that's the one you chose?" He couldn't hide his grimace.

"Don't you like the fit?"

"Well, no. The perfect bra should hug the chest so snugly the material is at one with the skin. Your bra has unsightly puckers that are ruining the lovely line of your breasts."

She ran her hands over her bra for flaws, and he tried

his best not to react. He was attempting to be clinical here. "I don't feel any puckers," she said.

"The excess material isn't on the top where you're touching. It's on the sides." He stopped, realizing that his hands were hovering above her chest and that he'd been about to give a hands-on demonstration. But how was he going to get his point across if he didn't? "Will you let me show you?"

"Sure. If you think it will help," she said, still worriedly examining her chest.

His hands expertly stroked the sides of her breasts while he tried to ignore the heat that immediately coursed through his bloodstream. He was a professional bra designer, and she was in dire need of his assistance.

He pinched the excess material at the sides of her bra between his thumbs and index fingers. "See what I mean?" His voice came out thick, husky and without a hint of professional detachment. He cleared his throat. "This bra is doing your beautiful breasts a disservice."

He lifted his gaze from the marred beauty of her breasts to her eyes, which had darkened to an even richer shade of chocolate. He'd made his point about her bra, but his palms were still flat against the sides of her breasts. Obviously, the removal signal his brain was sending hadn't reached his hands.

"So what do you think I should do about it?" Her voice was soft, her breath warm against his face.

He relaxed his thumbs and forefingers but still didn't take his hands away from the warm softness of her breasts. He wet his lips. "My family's business has a new bra out called Impeccabra."

Jay wasn't sure whether he moved forward or she did, but her face was suddenly closer to his. He saw tiny laugh lines around her eyes. He saw her swallow. "Impeccable?"

His control snapped, and he moved his hands from her breasts to cup the sides of her face. "Are you ever," he growled and brought his lips down on hers.

At the first touch of their mouths, it felt like the blood flowing through his veins had turned to lava. She tasted of wine and sweetness and heat, and her response was as generous as the woman herself.

He'd wanted to kiss her since he hauled her out of the hot tub and she looked at him with huge, grateful eyes, but he couldn't have imagined that together they'd generate this swirling, fiery heat.

He stabbed his fingers through her hair, feeling the pins come loose as the long strands swept over his hands like heated silk. He cradled the back of her head and slanted his mouth over hers so he could deepen the kiss.

She moaned deep in her throat and their tongues mated, fueling the desire. His brain tried to signal that he should stop the madness of the kiss, that it flew in the face of the very mission her father had sent him to accomplish, but no part of him was listening.

His body grew hard, and an emotion he couldn't identify clogged his chest, filling him with an almost unbearable tenderness. He'd known on some level that kissing her would be like this, which was why he'd tried so hard to resist her. But she was irresistible. Utterly and completely.

He moved his mouth to the side of hers to trail kisses

down her neck and felt her moan reverberate inside him. Her shirt had three little buttons that trailed from the neckline and he undid them, planting kisses on the soft skin he uncovered.

When he loosened the shirt from the waistband of her skirt and ran his hands over the firmness of her stomach, she raised her arms and he reverently pulled off her shirt. The ill-fitting bra went next, more than proving his assertion about the loveliness of her breasts. Her skin was creamy, her taut nipples rosy. Her eyes were dewy as she watched him look at her.

"It's a crime to cover any part of you up," he said before he brought his mouth to her breasts to taste her, laving the nipples with his tongue. She moaned, arching her back as he gave her pleasure.

"No fair," she said after a moment, the words barely intelligible. "You still have your shirt on."

Jay made quick work of his shirt, unfastening the buttons and shrugging out of the garment before she could ask him to take it off a second time. Her eyes stayed locked on his as he worked, but her hands ran through the rough hairs on his chest, down the planes of his stomach and stilled.

"Jay?" Her voice was soft, breathless. "I feel something."

"Me, too, honey," he said as he nuzzled the soft skin where her jaw met her neck. "Me, too."

"No," she said, and he felt her shake her head. "I mean I feel something on your chest. Something bumpy."

He had a sudden impulse to scratch, but he ignored it

and went back to nuzzling her neck. "I'm sure it's nothing."

She gave him a gentle push backward, forcing his lips to break the connection with her skin, and lowered her gaze. Her eyes widened, and she brought her hands to her mouth. He hoped she was gaping at the size of his arousal, but he feared that wasn't the case.

"I knew it was something. Look at your chest, Jay. And your arms. And—oh, my gosh—your face."

It only took a glance to understand what she meant. Irregularly shaped patches of raised red skin, surrounded by paler areas, covered his arms. No sooner had he spotted them than they began to itch.

Hives. He had hives.

He closed his eyes, cursing his rotten luck. This hadn't happened in years, mainly because he made it a point to steer clear of peanuts and their byproducts. But he hadn't eaten anything like that tonight. Tara had served meat, potatoes and that delicious vegetable dish with the unusual sauce.

Oh, no. The sauce.

"By any chance, was that peanut sauce on the vegetables?"

She nodded, then understanding seemed to dawn on her. "You're allergic to peanuts, aren't you?"

"Yep," he said.

She pulled on her shirt, covering her lovely breasts, and almost tripped in her haste to get off the sofa and to a phone. He wasn't sure what bothered him more, his hives or her retreat. "I'll call a doctor."

"There's no need. If I take an oral antihistamine, they'll go away in a few hours."

"Are you sure that's all you need?"

What he needed was her, but he probably looked like hell, and his body was suddenly so itchy he would have dived into a vat of calamine lotion if one were handy.

There was nothing like hives to kill the mood.

7

BY THE TIME Jay reached the Excursion Inn the following day, his hives were gone and so was his guilt over what had almost happened with Tara the night before.

After she'd insisted on running out to the drugstore to buy the antihistamine, he'd left her, not sure which itch was worse—the one from the hives or the one he had for Tara.

He'd spent the next few miserable hours trying not to scratch and berating himself for betraying Cliff Patterson's trust.

His thinking had cleared at about the same time as his hives as a remarkable thought had occurred to him.

He'd promised Cliff to keep potential fiancés away from Tara, but Jay himself didn't fit into that category. He had no plans to take a bride and no intention of becoming a husband. Not for years yet, anyway.

What was the danger of getting to know Tara and exploring the heated chemistry that sizzled between them? No matter what her plans were, he knew *he* wasn't headed for the altar. By becoming involved with Tara, he'd make sure she didn't walk down the aisle, either.

He'd had impressive success keeping her admirers at

bay by telling them she was his woman. Just think how much more successful he could be if it were true.

It was a foolproof way of discharging his family's obligation to Cliff. The method might not be conventional, but the result would be the same. And in Cliff Patterson's world, Jay thought, results were all that mattered.

Since it was Friday morning, the timing was perfect. He needed to devote some time to Lace Foundations this weekend, but he meant to spend the bulk of it getting to know Tara better.

Sadie Mae was at the front desk, holding the phone to her ear with one hand while she clutched a cup of coffee in the other. She must have liked what she heard because she let out a joyful little shriek. Unfortunately, she punctuated it with a joyful little jump that caused some of the coffee to slosh out of her cup and onto the computer keyboard.

He made a detour to the men's bathroom for paper towels, which he handed to her when she hung up the phone.

"You're a sweetheart," she said, giving him a grateful smile as she mopped up her spill. "I don't usually spill things—" She stopped abruptly and slanted him a sheepish look. "Okay, I do spill things, but I have an excuse this time. My neighbor is coming over to watch Cargo."

"Cargo?"

She looked up briefly from the scene of the spill. "Yeah. He's in the office with T.P. Would you do me a favor and tell her that my neighbor will be here in about a half hour?''

''Sure,'' he said, because in the office with Tara was exactly where he wanted to be. Maybe he could reciprocate for the meal she'd served him last night by taking her out to dinner. A peanut-free dinner.

The door was ajar so he rounded the corner, intending to announce his presence. The words stuck in his throat. Another male with a mop of bright red hair had his arms around Tara and his lips pressed to her cheek.

Judging by his size and the fact that he was sitting on her lap, Jay pegged him to be about two years old.

''What a sweet kiss that was, Cargo,'' she said, gazing into the little boy's face as she smoothed the hair from his brow. Her hair was down, exactly the way he liked it. ''Your mommy's lucky to have a sweet boy like you.''

Her smile had such a wistful quality that Jay was certain one of her fondest dreams was to be a mother. It wasn't difficult to imagine her cradling his child in that same loving way, but of course that wasn't going to happen.

She looked up then, her smile growing when she spotted him in the doorway. His pulse kicked up a few beats, and he smiled back. ''Good morning.''

The little boy turned in Tara's arms and peered at him. ''Whozat?''

''That's Jay. Your mother calls him Tool Man,'' she said. Jay's eyebrows rose, and she shrugged apologetically. ''Sadie Mae has a nickname for everyone. She hasn't realized we could all rebel and start calling her S and M. This little guy here is Cargo."

"Why Cargo?"

In answer, she smiled and gently pried open the little boy's hand. She pulled out a miniature replica of a flame-red car and set it on her desk. The redhead rolled the car across a notebook and over a tape dispenser.

"Car go beep beep," he said.

Jay laughed. Cargo was still distracted by the toy, so he whispered an aside to Tara. "That's a terrible name for a kid."

"Tell me about it," Tara whispered back. "I'm hoping he grows out of it, but knowing Sadie Mae she'll call him something equally awful. Like Zit Face or Big Feet."

"She wanted me to tell you that her neighbor will be here in a little while to baby-sit."

"Oh, good," Tara said. "There was a problem at the day-care center this morning, so Sadie Mae brought this little guy to work. I'll let them hang out in my suite."

Jay lowered his voice. "With Alley?"

"Cargo won't tell anybody." She bussed the boy on the cheek. "Will you, honey?"

Sadie Mae breezed into the office, crossed the room to Tara's desk and picked up her son. "Mrs. Burnside found some Cheerios for you, darling." She grinned at Tara. "Thank Tara for watching you."

The little boy put his chubby hand to his mouth and blew a sloppy kiss to Tara, which she pretended to catch and blow back.

"Car go honk honk," he said, running his car over the top of his mother's hair.

"You're a good boss," Jay said when he and Tara were alone.

Tara grimaced because she was a bad boss, a very bad boss. And she would have been worse if he hadn't broken out in hives. Forget about being saved by the bell. She'd been saved by the hives.

"I hardly think letting Sadie Mae bring Cargo to work for an hour qualifies me for some kind of award."

"That's not what I meant. I've been here for almost a week and I see how you treat your employees. Everyone likes and respects you."

A bolt of guilt sliced through her at the mention of the respect she'd worked so hard to earn. How much would her employees respect her if they knew she had a thing going with the maintenance man? Even if it was a very good thing. A thing that was so all-powerful it was consuming her dreams. A thing she was afraid might start with the letter L.

"Listen, Jay—"

"You're off tonight, right?"

"Yes, but—"

"I'd like to take you to dinner." He closed the door behind him with a soft thud and walked purposefully across the room. Oh, Lord, he was gorgeous. If he looked like this in a work shirt and jeans, what would he look like in date clothes? Or in nothing at all. "I know this great place in Olde Towne Alexandria overlooking the Potomac."

He sat on the edge of the desk, looking at her in that intense, impossibly sexy way he had. *Say no,* her conscience screamed, but she couldn't get the words out.

"If you're worried about the hives, I promise I won't order anything with peanuts."

"It's not that," she said, pressing her lips together. On him, even hives looked sexy. "It's—"

"Don't you dare say last night never should have happened."

She gave him a pained look, because that was the last thing she wanted to say. *Don't say it,* she told herself. *Don't say it.*

"Last night should never have happened." She winced as the truth of the statement stabbed at her. "You work for me, Jay. Surely you can see that I can't get involved with an employee."

"But I'm not..." He trailed off and grew silent.

"Not what? Not a career maintenance man? I know that, but the fact is you're working at my hotel. So you're off-limits."

"What if I didn't work here?" he asked softly, and the words blew through her like a soft wind.

"The point's moot, Jay," she said just as softly. "You do work here. I know how much you need this job. As much as I want to, I can't go out with you."

"You want to go out with me?" The hope that bloomed in his eyes was unmistakable. "Now you're talking. That's the only thing you've said that I wanted to hear."

She got up from her desk and moved across the room

to get away from him. "I'm not going to deny that I'm attracted to you. After last night, you wouldn't believe me anyway. But whatever we started last night has to stop right now."

He straightened and walked across the room. Too late, she realized she shouldn't have abandoned the protective cover of the desk. He didn't stop until he was so close that she could feel the heat of his body.

"What if we can't stop it?" he asked, leaning closer to her. She told herself to back away, but she didn't. Not even when he softly grasped her shoulders. "What if I don't want to stop it?"

His face was only inches from hers. Her heart pounded and she wanted desperately to lean into his heat, to again feel the thrill of his mouth against hers. She'd been telling the truth when she said last night was a mistake, because getting to know him better had only made him more compelling, more sexy. Like a man she could tumble into love with. He moved closer, and she felt her resistance melt, felt herself start to tumble.

His hands were in the hair she hadn't been able to bring herself to pin up that morning, his heated breath on her face. *How can something that feels so right,* she asked herself, *be so wrong?* Her brain screamed the answer. *Because he works for you.*

"Don't do this, Jay," she managed to plead when he was a millimeter away from claiming her lips. "Don't make me compromise my ethics."

He stared at her a moment more, and there was no

way he could miss the desire in her eyes, not when she saw that same passion in his.

"Aw, hell." He bit the words out, abruptly letting her go. He reached out, as though he couldn't help himself, and brushed the pad of his thumb against her parted lips. Strain pulled at his features, tautening them, until he suddenly jerked away and walked to the door.

She fought against the need to call him back and stopped herself from doing so. He put his hand on the doorknob, then paused and turned toward her. His eyes were bright with desire, his face tight with it.

"This isn't the end, Tara," he whispered.

He left the room, closing the door behind him. She leaned against the wall, needing the support so she wouldn't sink to the floor. Her chest felt constricted, as though her breath were lodged there. She'd wanted him to kiss her more than she wanted to live, but he'd gathered the composure to stop. Just because she'd asked him to.

Her heart swelled with something that felt suspiciously like love, but she wasn't up to examining the feeling. Not when her body felt boneless and her mind like mush. She stayed slumped against the wall for long moments until her brain began to work again.

She didn't want her refusal to be the final word but she didn't see how it couldn't be when they were employer and employee. What had Jay meant by that parting comment? Did he intend to quit the maintenance job and go into the family business?

Tara wasn't entirely sure why he was resisting. Her

breasts tingled as she remembered the way his hands had felt yesterday on her chest. The man obviously had a thing for bras. Not only that, but with that kind of enthusiasm the family business would be lucky to have him.

What had he said the name of the business was?

She thought hard, replaying their conversation of a night ago, and realized that he hadn't said. Something had bothered her about the entire exchange. Even though he'd been sharing something heartfelt and emotional, she'd felt like he was holding back...something.

She'd had the same feeling on numerous other occasions, such as the time she'd felt sure her father was calling on his cell phone but Jay had denied it.

She frowned as something nudged at her brain. Something about the lingerie business. Her father had sometimes talked of a friend who owned a lingerie company, but she'd never met the man. She tried to remember his name but thought her father had only referred to him by his first name. Was it Conrad? No, not Conrad. Conner.

Conner? The name resonated so loudly that she hurried to the file cabinet and pulled out Jay's application. Jay was short for James, but James was his middle name. His first name was Conner.

She refiled the application and shut the cabinet drawer, puzzling over the discovery. Except she hadn't discovered anything yet. She knew Jay shared the first name of her father's friend and that they were both connected to lingerie, but that was all.

Unless...

She walked out of her office and found Sadie Mae behind the front counter tapping keys on the computer and looking confused.

"Sadie Mae, have you ever heard of a bra called Impeccable?"

Her friend glanced up from the computer almost as though she was grateful for the interruption.

'Not Impeccable, Impecca*bra*." She moved back from the computer and thrust out her considerable attributes. "What do you think these babies are wearing?"

"Impeccabra?"

"Right on. It's only the best bra ever made. Look at this." She smoothed her hands over her chest, and Tara hoped no one male was watching. Especially not Jay. "No more unsightly bra lines for me."

Tara was impressed but refrained from showing it. "Do you know what company makes this bra?"

Sadie Mae bit her lip while she thought. "I don't remember, but it's probably on the tag."

"Could you check?"

"Sure. I'll let you know tomorrow."

"I meant could you check now? In my office."

Sadie Mae gave her a sidelong look as she passed on the way to the office. "Good thing I love you so much, T.P., because I wouldn't do this for just anybody."

While she was gone, Tara reached into her memories for the name of her father's friend's company. The full name eluded her but after a moment she thought she remembered part of it. Lace something or other.

"Lace Foundations," Sadie Mae said when she came out of the office.

Bingo. That was it. Lace Foundations wasn't just her father's friend's business. It was Jay's family business, which meant something weird was going on. Why else hadn't he told her about the connection between their fathers?

Sadie Mae put a hand on her waist and cocked her hip. "Now do you mind telling me why you had me read my underwear?"

Tara's lower lip trembled as she considered that the heartfelt conversation she'd had with Jay the night before had been heartfelt on her side only.

"Come on, honey. You can tell me." Her eyes narrowed. "Is this about that thing you have going on with Tool Man?"

"Jay and I don't have anything going on," Tara denied hotly.

"Oh, pshaw. There are so many sparks flying off you two I'm surprised the hotel hasn't burned down. Don't try telling me he's not the man in your life."

"He's more like the man in my doghouse," Tara said dryly, figuring there was no use keeping the cause of her unhappiness from Sadie Mae. There never was. "He's been lying to me about his relationship with my father, and I don't know why."

Her friend made a face. A guilty face.

"Sadie Mae, is there something you're not telling me?"

"I'm sure it's nothing. Tool Man's such a nice guy. I'm sure there must be a reason—"

"Spill it," Tara demanded.

She fidgeted, then sighed in surrender. "It's just that I overheard him a little while ago on his cell phone leaving a message for somebody he called Cliff. That's your dad's name, isn't it?"

Tara's heart lurched. "What did you hear?" she asked sharply.

"That he wanted to meet him tonight at eight o'clock."

"Did he say where?"

Sadie Mae shook her head. "Just the usual place."

"There's only one thing to do then."

"What's that?"

"Follow him," Tara said decisively.

"Oh, no," Sadie Mae retorted. "If you think I'm going to let you take it upon yourself to follow that man, you're nuts."

Tara's lips thinned and her eyes hardened. "You can't stop me, Sadie Mae."

"Who said anything about stopping you? If I can find a baby-sitter for Cargo, I'm with you."

TARA PLASTERED her back against a large oak tree and tried to keep very still, hoping the dark clothes Sadie Mae had insisted they wear helped hide them from Jay's sight.

Not that he'd have any reason to suspect that two

women dressed in black were stalking him through the dark trying to unmask him for the lying dog he was.

The lying part was no longer in question, because Jay had made a quick stop in a pricey part of Alexandria before driving to this strip of parkland along the Occoquan River. In Tara's experience, men who were hurting for maintenance jobs didn't live in stately brick town houses. Jay did.

Unless, of course, he'd had a key to that town house for another reason. Could he have been town house sitting?

Stop it, Tara told herself. She must stop giving him the benefit of the doubt. So what if he'd given her a new meat thermometer this morning because she'd mentioned last night that hers was broken? So what if he'd picked up a special brand of cream for Alley?

Jay Overman was still a lying dog.

She thanked the heavens that Sadie Mae had lined up a baby-sitter or else Tara might have called off the tail and never found that out. When her lip trembled and tears threatened, she told herself she was better off knowing that the man she'd fallen for was a no-good, lying son of a gun.

A loud clap resounded in the night air, and Tara realized it had come from Sadie Mae.

"Shhh," she whispered.

"How did I miss that bugger?" Sadie Mae whispered back as she gazed at her hand. "The mosquitoes out here are as big as helicopters."

"With these long sleeves and pants on, there's hardly any exposed skin left for a mosquito to bite."

"I must have yummy hands, then, because they're chewing on them." Sadie Mae's comment was followed by another loud smack. "And a scrumptious neck."

"Do you have to slap so hard? If you keep that up, you'll be able to charge yourself with assault."

"Only a tremendous blow will kill one of these things," Sadie Mae said. "Uh-oh. Those nasty buggers distracted me. I didn't see which way Tool Man went."

"He went that way." Tara pointed east through a thicket of trees and undergrowth. "Now try to be quiet. We don't want him to know he's being followed."

Tara thought they were lucky he hadn't figured it out already. They'd been waiting in Sadie Mae's car in the hotel parking lot when Jay had finally left the hotel about an hour ago and gotten into an expensive-looking sports utility vehicle. The plan would have been flawless had Sadie Mae's elbow not hit the horn when they'd hunkered down to hide.

Thankfully, Jay hadn't come to investigate, and the chase was on. They'd trailed him first to Alexandria and then to the Occoquan, careful to keep off his bumper so he didn't know he was being followed.

Tara had thought they were on a wild-goose chase until he'd pulled to the shoulder of a two-lane road and parked behind a sleek sedan. A sleek, *familiar* sedan that belonged to her father.

As Jay had disappeared through the brush, she'd been so steamed and so hurt that she wasn't aware that Sadie

Mae had parked until her friend yanked open the passenger door and hauled her out of the car.

The steam was still there, but it had been tempered by curiosity as to why in tarnation Jay Overman was conducting a clandestine meeting with her father.

"There he is," Sadie Mae whispered loudly enough that Jay paused and turned. Quickly, before he saw them, they each dropped to their knees and hid behind some brush.

"My heart just about burst out of my chest when he stopped like that," Sadie Mae said when he'd resumed walking. "Do you think cops get this nervous on a stake-out?"

"I don't think cops talk this much," Tara said. "We have to be quieter."

"Can do, boss," Sadie Mae said, saluting her and giving her a grin. They started after Jay again, but hadn't gotten ten steps when Sadie Mae asked, "Did you know my cousin Lester on my father's side is a cop? You remember Lester? He was always smoking in the rest rooms when we were in school. My aunt Irene on my mother's side says the reason he became a cop is it was the only way to make sure he didn't get arrested."

"Sadie Mae!" Tara chastised.

"It's true. Irene is a mean gossip. Why, you should hear what she says about Uncle Fred and his secretary."

"I meant *be quiet.*"

Sadie Mae's hand flew to her mouth. "Oh, sorry. I forgot."

They resumed their tail, this time in silence. Tara tried

to come up with a reason Jay could be meeting her father that didn't have anything to do with her. By the time she caught sight of her white-haired father waiting for her would-be lover on a short pier overhanging the river, the best she could come up with was that they were both secretly employed by the CIA.

They weren't that far from Washington, D.C., and the CIA theory would go a long way toward explaining why Jay hadn't been up-front about who he was. Tara had a friend who hadn't known her father was employed by the agency until he'd retired. It was a long shot, sure. But a girl could hope, couldn't she?

Sadie Mae silently beckoned her over to a hiding place behind a conveniently fat tree, and she held her breath, praying that Jay and her father would speak in code names about secret missions.

"Are you making sure my daughter doesn't go through with that fool notion of hers to marry the first man who looks good?" her father asked in that booming voice of his.

Tara punched the tree with her fist, which hurt so much she cried out.

"WHAT WAS THAT?" Jay asked, turning and surveying the night. Logically he knew nocturnal animals that were heard but not seen were making the leaves rustle and twigs break, but he couldn't shake the feeling that he was being watched.

"Probably just a squirrel," Cliff said, obviously unconcerned.

"Squirrels aren't nocturnal," Jay said.

"What is it, Conner James? Don't tell me a big, old civil engineer like you is afraid of the dark."

"Of course not," Jay said quickly, drawing to his full height. This he-man act was a real pain sometimes. So was his conscience.

Why did he have to be born so honest that he felt guilty for deceiving Tara even when it was for her own good? Dread over being caught had driven him to take the extreme precaution of arranging to meet Cliff here, in the dark, at Mosquito Central.

He absently slapped at the titanic insect buzzing near his ear, cursing himself for being so paranoid. And all because Tara had almost figured out it was her father on the cell phone that night in her suite.

"Well? Give me a report." Cliff was looking at him expectantly. "Are there any prospects on the horizon or have you managed to run them off?"

Leaves rustled, almost as though something was kicking them, and Jay peered into the night once more. "I know I heard something that time."

"All sorts of creatures come out at night, my boy," Cliff said, putting his arm around Jay and turning him toward the river. "Now tell me if our plan is working."

More leaves rustled and twigs broke behind him, almost as though whatever was lurking in the brush was beating a hasty retreat, but Jay couldn't very well voice his suspicion to Cliff that whatever was out there had to be awfully large to be making so much noise.

"The plan worked so well it's time to abandon it. I

think I should quit. You don't need me at the hotel anymore."

"You're talking nonsense, son. You can't quit! Especially not when the plan's working so well."

Jay shored up his determination, because he'd expected Cliff to resist. He wanted to tell Cliff that his best chance of keeping men away from Tara was to abandon the job so he could date her himself, but he didn't think the older man would understand.

Cliff might view Jay as one of those potential fiancés he wanted Jay to drive off, which of course was ridiculous. But it would stop Jay's new plan dead. No. He had to convince Cliff without revealing his nonmatrimonial interest in Tara.

"She's over the hump," Jay said, using the words Cliff had uttered to him less than a week ago. "She's focused on her career, just like you said."

Cliff shook his head. "How can you be sure she's not still searching for a husband?"

Because, Jay answered silently, *I'm going to shower her with so much attention she won't be able to look at another man, let alone plot to marry one.*

"She has a good head on her shoulders," he said, trying not to let himself get sidetracked by remembering how soft and creamy those shoulders were. "This marriage thing was a temporary whim, an aberration. She's thinking straight now."

Cliff shook his head. "This doesn't sound like a good idea to me."

"Come on, Cliff. You didn't expect me to work there indefinitely, did you?"

"Is this about the bra business? Are you wanting to quit so you can make frilly lingerie?"

Jay's impulse was to automatically deny it, but he couldn't. Not only did Cliff's comment have a grain of truth, but it served Jay's purpose to let Cliff think it did.

"Sherry needs my help," Jay said. "The Impeccabra is making a bigger and better impression than we thought. Marketing it is taking an awful lot of time."

Cliff pursed his lips. "How can you think a bra is more important than my daughter?"

"I don't," Jay denied. "You said Tara would be over the hump in two weeks. Why is it so hard to believe it only took one?"

"I don't want my daughter to make a mistake she'll regret the rest of her life, and marriage before age thirty is a mistake."

"She won't make a mistake," Jay said quickly. He planned to personally see to it that the only man in Tara's romantic life was himself. "You know how much I loved my father and how indebted we were to you. I wouldn't make this promise if I didn't truly believe Tara was going to stay away from the altar."

Cliff stared at him for a long moment, his hair glowing white against the night sky, then finally clasped his shoulder. "In that case, my boy, you have my permission to quit."

Jay smiled while he mentally reviewed his new plan. Tara had already stated she wouldn't get involved with an employee, and his conscience wouldn't let him quit until he could provide Tara with some leads on a new maintenance man.

With any luck, he could track down a replacement over the weekend and hand in his resignation Monday morning.

If by some remote chance Cliff was right about Tara hunting husbands, surely she couldn't line up one by then.

8

TARA OPENED the door of her suite early Monday morning to find Sadie Mae in the hall, her fist poised to knock. Considering the barrage of calls she'd dodged from her friend over the weekend, it was nothing less than Tara had expected.

"Good morning, Sadie Mae," Tara said as she deliberately walked into the hall and closed the door.

Her friend tossed her head of red curls, open dismay on her pretty, freckled face. "Are you okay, hon? You didn't return my last three calls."

Tara sighed and took her friend's hands. "Please don't take this the wrong way. I know you're worried about me, and I appreciate it. I really do. But if I listened to you tell me I was making a mistake one more time, I was afraid I'd scream."

Either that or cry because of what she had to do.

"What am I supposed to say?" Sadie Mae asked. "That I don't think you're overreacting? That I think it's a grand idea you got my brother to agree to pretend to be your fiancé?"

"That would be nice," Tara replied and walked swiftly down the hall away from her friend. Sadie Mae cursed and trailed after her.

"It's a bad plan, T.P. Do you really think Tool Man will believe you're marrying Billy when he doesn't even arrive until this afternoon? What are you going to do? Say you got engaged at first sight?"

Ignoring Sadie Mae and the fact that her eyes started to water every time she thought about Jay, Tara took the flight of stairs to the second floor. She absolutely, positively could not let herself be swayed into changing her mind because she wanted with all her heart for Jay to be the upstanding kind of man she'd thought he was.

With Sadie Mae in tow behind her, she stopped in front of one of the rooms and rapped on the door. After a few seconds, the door swung open to reveal a burly, smiling young man with half his face covered in shaving cream. He had a startling resemblance to Sadie Mae, right down to his curly red hair.

"Spud!" Sadie Mae exclaimed. "You're not supposed to get here until this afternoon."

"Hiya, Sis." He winked at Tara as he swept past her to take Sadie Mae in his arms, swinging her around until she was giggling helplessly.

"Stop," she said, batting his face away. "You're getting shaving cream on me."

"What's a little shaving cream between siblings?" he asked, but set her down. "Roxie sends her love."

At the mention of his wife, he glanced at the wedding ring on his left hand. "I almost forgot. I can't be wearing this."

"You didn't answer me, Spud," Sadie Mae said as he

yanked off his ring and pocketed it. "Why are you here early?"

Billy gave a deep bow. "A damsel put out a distress signal, and I answered it."

"You said yourself that we couldn't expect Jay to believe we got engaged at first sight," Tara told Sadie Mae, ignoring the way her heart lurched when she said Jay's name. "This way, we'll tell him we had the weekend to make the decision."

"It's madness. It won't work."

"Though this be madness," Billy said, "yet there's no method in it."

"Isn't that from Hamlet?" Sadie Mae said. "Don't you mean there *is* method in it?"

"See, I told you I knew what I was doing," Tara said, taking advantage of Sadie Mae's momentary speechlessness to move between the siblings. "You have the plan straight, right, Billy?" she asked, leaning her head close to his. "Convince Jay Overman there's nothing you want more than to marry me."

"You're talking to a Shakespearean-trained thespian, my lady. Don't forget that I would have been a professional actor had I not gone to work for Micro Chips."

"Microchips?" Tara said in surprise. "I didn't know you'd gone into computers. I thought Sadie Mae called you Spud because you sold potato chips."

"I do," Billy said. "For Micro Chips. We deal in those little fun-size bags. Wanna see? I have some in the room."

"Maybe later," Tara said, patting his cheek. Her palm

came away covered in shaving cream. She held it up. "Don't you want to finish shaving?"

"Not really, considering it's not much fun at all. But it's a chore I must complete." He gave another deep bow. "I take my leave of thou, my lady."

"Thee," Sadie Mae corrected. "You take your leave of *thee*."

"Thou, too," Billy said and shut the door behind him.

Tara turned to Sadie Mae with a satisfied smirk. She wouldn't let her friend see that it hurt to make one. "See? It's all taken care of."

"You wouldn't say that if you'd seen him act. Last year, he lost the part of Romeo to a grandfather," Sadie Mae said.

Tara lifted her chin imperiously. "Grandfathers can be hot. Just look at Paul Newman."

"This one kept missing rehearsals because he couldn't get his dentures to fit. They fell out during the dance scene opening night. Plunk. It's a wonder Juliet didn't trip over them."

Tara walked down the hall with Sadie Mae still shadowing her from behind. Tara walked faster, the better to get away from Sadie Mae and the frightening things she was saying. But Sadie Mae followed her into the elevator.

"I don't understand why you're doing this, T.P. What if Tool Man really cares about you?"

Tara wanted that to be true so much that her heart swelled, but she knew it was a pipe dream.

"Get a grip," she said roughly to cover up the pain.

"All he cares about is fulfilling that ridiculous promise he made to my father. I told you I called George Merrimack and Robby Fairchild, didn't I? Jay told George I was his woman and gave Robby the impression I was a nymphomaniac in the hunt for a threesome."

"I don't know, T.P. I like the Toolster. I admit his methods are questionable, but he seems like the sincere sort to me."

"A sincere man does not pretend to be something he's not so he can pull one over on an unsuspecting woman. You heard my father. He's not a maintenance man. He's an engineer."

Sadie Mae frowned. "I'm worried about you, T.P. You know how you get when somebody crosses you. You don't think straight. Remember the toilet paper?"

"I thought you agreed with me about the toilet paper!"

"I did. I do. I'm just pointing out that you'll stop at nothing to put things right."

Tara crossed her arms over her chest. "Then Jay should never have entered that unholy agreement with my father."

"Just like you never should have entered your unholy agreement with my brother," she muttered.

Tara took her smaller friend by the shoulders. "Promise me you won't tell Jay what we're doing, Sadie Mae."

Sadie Mae sighed. "I don't like it, T.P., but of course I'll go along. I'm your friend, remember. Through thick and thin. Even though I think the thickest thing about this situation is your head."

MONDAY MORNING had been a long time in coming even though Jay had been immersed in bra business.

He and Sherry had spent much of Saturday successfully persuading five more retailers to carry the Impeccabra and nearly all of Sunday going through the e-mail generated by the Web page on the Internet.

Jay's favorite had been a reader comment that they should change the name of Lace Foundations to the more Internet-friendly ecups2go, but Sherry had rejected it because the original name had a loyal clientele.

The only action they'd taken was to offer to mail potential customers free measuring tapes to better assess their breasts.

All that activity should have monopolized Jay, but he hadn't been able to get Tara off his mind. He was so focused on seeing her again that he immediately spotted her when he walked through the door of the Excursion Inn.

She was standing at the breakfast bar helping a small, angelic-looking girl fill a glass of milk. She'd left her hair loose again, making his gut tighten with longing. When the girl's glass was full, Tara smiled at her and gently patted her on the head. The little girl smiled back, and something softened inside Jay.

If it hadn't been inappropriate to offer his resignation right then and there, he might have yelled it to the room.

But he knew he had to wait.

He patted his pocket to make sure the list of people looking for maintenance jobs that he'd gotten from the employment agency was still there.

"Good morning, Tara," he said when he was beside her.

"Good morning, Jay," she said, but her smile was cool. His disappeared. Instantly he knew that something had changed between Friday and today, but he didn't know what.

"When you have a minute, can I see you in your office?"

"Certainly," she said. "You don't mind if we finish breakfast first, do you?"

"We?"

"Billy and I."

"Billy?"

"Would you like to meet him?" Tara didn't wait for an answer but wove through the sea of tables until she reached one occupied by a good-looking, redheaded man who seemed vaguely familiar. He was smiling so widely Jay could see his teeth from fifty feet away.

"Darling," he drawled when they approached. For a moment, Jay wondered if Robby Fairchild was spreading rumors but then realized the endearment was directed at Tara. "I missed you when you were gone."

"I only went to get pastries," Tara said, producing a plate filled with cinnamon sticky buns.

"I know that, my lady, but parting was such sad sorrow."

Jay looked from the strange red-haired man to Tara and back again. What was he talking about? Parting was sweet sorrow, not sad sorrow. Sad and sorrow meant the same thing, for Pete's sake. And Tara wasn't *his* lady.

She was Jay's. Or at least she was going to be whenever he tendered his resignation.

"Who is this guy, Tara?" he asked.

"Jay Overman, this is Billy Trotter." She looked Jay straight in the eyes. "My fiancé."

Jay shook his head because none of this computed. Tara wasn't the sort of woman who'd get married just for the sake of getting married. Her father had overreacted by sending Jay undercover to stop her from finding a husband. Jay knew that in his gut.

"I must not have heard right," he said. "I thought you said he was your fiancé."

"I am her fiancé," Billy said, taking Tara's hand and pulling her into the chair beside him. When she was seated, he planted a monster kiss on the back of her hand. "We're fiancéd."

"I don't understand." Jay remained standing, his attention directed at Tara. Her face looked pinched and unhappy. "You weren't fiancéd Friday. Or," he added meaningfully, "Thursday night."

"We were betrothed over the weekend." Billy cut in. "We wooed in haste and mean to wed at leisure."

"No, no," Jay refuted. "If you wed in haste, you repent in leisure."

Billy seemed to consider that. "No, I'm pretty sure I got that one right. I don't think the two gentlemen of Verona said anything about repentance."

"I don't care what they said. It's crazy to get engaged to someone you just met."

"Since that's exactly what we've done, I beg to differ," Tara said. Frostily, he thought. "Now if you'll excuse us, we'd like to finish our breakfast."

Billy smiled widely. "If we do meet again, why, then, we should smile. Or is that we should frown?"

"Huh?" Jay asked. Billy started to speak, but Jay waved off his explanation and walked away from the table. He felt as though the Excursion Inn had just filled with a heavy, impenetrable fog. His brain refused to process the information he'd been given. It didn't seem possible that he'd left Tara alone for the weekend and now she was engaged. To a beefcake who misquoted Shakespeare, no less.

He hovered around the edges of the lobby, spying as the woman he wanted ate sticky buns with a man he hadn't known existed until minutes ago.

He'd scare him off, that's what he'd do. Maybe he'd resurrect the broken bed trick that had worked so well with George Merrimack. He was already sort of a master of the intimidating stare. Then, when Billy was gone, he'd talk some sense into Tara.

Billy half rose from the table, and every muscle in Jay's body got ready to pursue him, but then the other man bent and gave Tara a showy kiss on the lips.

The kiss hit Jay like a punch to the gut, immobilizing him. By the time he could function again, Billy had left the hotel and Jay concluded Tara must be in the small room adjacent to the breakfast area where Mrs. Burnside worked.

He didn't hesitate. Within seconds, he spotted Tara working alongside Mrs. Burnside at the counter, unpacking boxes of plastic silverware. The older woman turned first.

"Hello, Mrs. Burnside," Jay said, smiling because he genuinely liked her. "Is that a new hairdo? I like that shade of silver."

She self-consciously put her wrinkled hands to her head but flushed with pleasure. "You are such a dear man to notice."

Jay noticed that Tara was glaring at him, which didn't make any more sense than Tara getting engaged over the weekend. As far as he knew, Jay hadn't done anything objectionable.

"It's hard not to notice someone as nice as you, Mrs. Burnside."

She smiled wider then hurried toward him and clasped his hands. "Oh, my gracious, Jay. I can't thank you enough for recommending that Web site." She lowered her voice. "My bra came in Saturday and it fits like plastic wrap."

He leaned back, examining the fit with a satisfied smile. He resisted looking past the older woman for Tara's reaction. The subject of bras had come up innocently enough when Mrs. Burnside had asked about his family, but not all women would understand why he was offering lingerie advice to inquiring females.

"I'm glad, Mrs. Burnside. Spread the word, okay?"

"I'll be sure to do that. Oh, yes, I will," she gushed, giving a little giggle.

"Would you do me a favor, Mrs. Burnside, and give me a minute alone with Tara?"

"He doesn't need to be alone…" Tara began, but Mrs. Burnside was already walking out the door.

"Anything for you, Jay. Anything at all," she called over her shoulder.

Tara focused on the boxes she was unpacking, pointedly ignoring him. He watched her for a minute, his eyes falling on that soft place just under her chin, the place that made her moan when he kissed it.

"You mind telling me what's going on?" he asked.

"I already told you," she said, still not looking at him. "I got engaged over the weekend."

"To someone you just met?"

She shrugged. "I want to get married. Billy's as good a choice as any. Why do you think I went into hotel management if it wasn't to find a husband?"

Even though Cliff had claimed Tara told him exactly that, Jay hadn't believed it until this minute. Tara was much too levelheaded to hitch herself to the first man who would make a tolerable husband.

"That's insane."

She shook her head. "There's nothing insane about wanting to settle down and get married."

"There is if you pick any old guy to settle down with."

She was silent, and he could hear the plink of plastic as she unpacked the utensils. "What I do isn't any of your business."

"It is so my business." He was standing close enough that he could smell the fresh scent of her strawberry shampoo. He leaned next to her, capturing her hand so she couldn't unpack any more plasticware, and turned her to face him. He couldn't read her dark eyes, but the set of her full mouth was mutinous. "What about what happened between us Thursday night? Are you going to ignore that?"

A muscle worked in her jaw, and for a moment he had hope. "Yes," she said, dashing it. "I already told you, Jay. I had to eliminate you from my husband hunt because you work for me."

He felt his jaw drop. "I didn't realize you were considering me."

"Of course I was. I consider every single man who comes through the door. What kind of half-baked husband hunter would I be if I didn't? But you won't do."

"Why not? I'm as marriageable as the next guy," Jay refuted, then wondered why he'd said that. The entire reason he was perfect for a relationship with her was that he didn't want to get married.

"Maybe you are, but I've already lined up the next guy. Now, haven't I?"

"That's crazy. You can't marry some stranger just for the sake of getting married. I won't—"

"T.P.?" Sadie Mae appeared at the door, interrupting him. Jay swore under his breath when Tara pulled away from him. "Oops. I didn't mean to interrupt, but one of the guests is asking to speak to the manager." She looked from Jay to Tara and must have picked up on the tension in the room. "But I can put him off if you're busy."

"I'm not busy," Tara denied emphatically. "We're done here."

Sadie Mae gave him a sympathetic look as Tara breezed out of the room without another glance at Jay. But she was wrong. They weren't done. Not by a long shot.

He could no more give up his maintenance job now than he could his mission to make sure Tara didn't marry the wrong man.

JAY SPENT the rest of the day in a daze of disbelief, alternately keeping an eye out for Billy Trotter and wondering how he'd read Tara so wrong.

Lots of people with thick domestic streaks led perfectly sane lives, content with their single status until they met somebody they not only wanted to touch physically but somebody who touched their hearts and minds.

The way he and Tara had touched each other. Surely she'd been able to tell their touches went beyond the physical.

So why was she acting so loony? How could she possibly believe that she and this Billy character could have a fraction of what she already had with Jay?

He simply wouldn't believe that marriage was so important to her that it didn't matter who she married. Not when it was Jay she wanted, darn it. He could feel it in his very pores, not to mention points beyond.

An hour ago, he'd stopped by her office intent on demonstrating their mutual attraction, but Sadie Mae had informed him that Tara was spending the rest of the day in a meeting at the home office.

The redhead had relayed precious little else, even when Jay had pressed her about what was going on with Tara. All he'd gotten out of her was a request to service the hot tub.

He was so lost in his thoughts that he'd passed the exercise room before he spotted the very man responsible for muddying those thoughts.

Billy Trotter. The fiancé he'd yet to fend off. Well, he'd see about that.

He retraced his steps and peered through the glass doors of the room at his redheaded rival. Again he had a sense of familiarity but Jay would swear he'd never laid eyes on him before that morning. With his freckles and prominent nose, he had a face that was hard to forget. He also had this confounded likability thing going.

He was a smiler. Even when he was lifting weights.

Jay refused to let himself like the man. That'd make it all the more difficult to intimidate him, and intimidation was the key to saving Tara from her insane plan of getting married.

He pushed through the doors, but the man intent on ruining his life didn't look up. As Jay got nearer, he realized that Billy wasn't smiling. He was grimacing. And no wonder.

He was sitting on a padded seat, his back to the universal weight machine as he pulled down on an overhead bar connected to a thick cable weighed down with more plates than Jay had ever lifted.

"Wow," Jay said when Billy let the weights settle down. "I've never seen anyone lift that much. How'd you manage that?"

Billy's green eyes lifted to Jay, as though he hadn't noticed he was there until he spoke. He gave him one of his irritating smiles. "Lots of practice. I figured I had to do something because of the potato chips."

"Potato chips?"

"I can't stop eating them. But what do you expect from a chap who sells chips for a living? They keep coming out with new varieties. Salt-and-vinegar chips, red-hot chips, honey-barbecue chips. Even ketchup chips. How's a guy supposed to resist?"

"I suppose you have to sample them to be knowledgeable about what you're selling," Jay said, then almost smacked himself. He was supposed to be intimidating Billy, not discussing the merits of eating piles of potato chips.

"Exactly. But all those chips are taking their toll. I gained five pounds last month." He patted a stomach that seemed rock hard to Jay. "Look at this. My six-pack has turned into a spud pack."

"You look pretty good to..." Jay stopped himself in mid-sentence before he could bolster Billy's confidence. This was the enemy. The man who'd taken Tara from him. He made himself glower. "I didn't come in here to talk about potato chips. I came in here to talk about Tara."

"Oh, yes, Tara." Billy put a hand over his heart.

"What light through your old window breaks? It is the east, and Tara is the sun."

"Isn't that what light through *yonder* window breaks?"

"I don't think so. Shakespeare wrote *Romeo and Juliet* in the sixteenth century. Those windows had to be pretty darn old."

"But they weren't old in the sixteenth century."

"Well, no. But they're old now."

"I don't think..." Jay stopped himself before he got further drawn into the ludicrous vein of conversation. He didn't care about sixteenth-century windows. He cared about Tara. And frightening away this man who had swooped on the scene and ruined all Jay's plans. "We were talking about Tara."

"Yes, Tara," Billy agreed and grinned at him. What was it with this infernal grinning? Didn't he realize Jay was trying to strike terror in his heart? Billy got up, walked around the universal weight machine and added yet another plate to the stack. He didn't speak until he sat down and got his hands in position on the bar. "To think that I might not have met her if Micro Chips hadn't sent me on this sales trip."

"I thought you sold potato chips."

"I do. We deal in those little fun-size bags. Get it? Micro Chips?"

He gave Jay another smile, then his powerful biceps started straining again. Slowly, the bar ascended as the weights began to rise. Jay tried not to be impressed.

"How much longer are you staying?"

"Until the end of the week at least." Billy groaned as he pulled on the bar. "Then my love and I will figure the rest out. I'm already thinking Stratford-on-Avon for a honeymoon."

Hearing the other man speak of love, marriage and all that came with it was more than Jay could bear. "Come up with an excuse and leave now," he growled.

Billy looked momentarily confused, then his expression cleared and he let the bar down. The plates settled on the stack with a loud clack. He was breathing heavily. "That's the best idea I've heard all day. Okay, my excuse is that I'm tired of lifting weights."

Billy ducked his head and maneuvered around Jay, who didn't realize Billy meant to leave until he was at the door.

"Thanks for telling me to leave, bud," Billy called. "I really was sick of hoisting those suckers. They sure are heavy."

Then he was gone, leaving Jay staring after him with his mouth hanging open. What had gone wrong here? Had he lost his edge in the intimidation department? Or was it pointless to try to intimidate somebody who had the strength of Hercules?

Jay tapped his work boot against the linoleum floor while he thought how best to tackle the problem. It came to him like an epiphany. His problem wasn't with Billy Trotter, who Tara seemed to view as nothing more than interchangeable husband fodder.

No. His problem was with Tara herself and the way

she was deliberately turning away from the passion that sparked so easily between them.

"If at first you don't succeed, try and try again," he said aloud.

It wasn't Shakespeare, he thought as he went off in search of Tara, but at least it was accurate.

9

THE HIGHER-WATT bulbs she'd had Jay put in the fixtures brightened the hallway but couldn't lighten Tara's dark mood as she unlocked the housekeeping supply closet on the third floor Tuesday morning.

It had taken an extreme act of willpower to make herself smile at the guest who had asked for extra towels and more restraint not to stomp down the hall while tears streamed down her face when she went to get them.

Nearly four days had passed since she'd followed Jay to that pier on the Occoquan and overheard the plan he'd wrought with her father, and her anger and heartache remained.

Her father was so pigheaded and domineering that she might have expected him to pull something like this, but she'd never foreseen it from Jay.

She'd have sworn that he was earnest and trustworthy, traits that had made her open her heart to him. To think that he'd been playing her for a fool. To think that the only reason he spent time with her was so that other men couldn't.

She stepped into the closet and flipped on the light switch while her anger and misery warred with each other. For the moment, the anger got the upper hand.

Why, the man was such a cad that he'd not only lied about being a career handyman but he hadn't owned up to what he really did for a living.

Bra salesman, my breast. He was a gosh-darned engineer who, judging by his fancy digs, made wads of money. He'd fed her such a load of bull that she bet his Auntie Em didn't even have a farm. Heck, there probably wasn't an Auntie Em.

Her anger surged again, but she reined it in. Sure, she could have confronted Jay with what she'd learned, but that seemed far too tame considering the feelings he'd stirred up in her before she'd learned of his deception.

When he'd taken her unresisting body into his arms in her office the morning after they'd almost made love, she'd thought she was falling in love with him.

And for one brief moment, after he gallantly let her go when she asked him not to make her compromise her ethics, she actually believed she was in love.

In love. With a lying dog.

The upshot of it all was that it didn't seem to matter to her heart that he was a lying dog. She angrily wiped away a tear. Revenge might not be sweet, but by God she was going to get it.

"Tara."

As if her thoughts had conjured him up, the lying dog stood in the doorway of the closet, one hand on either side of the door frame as though he were afraid she'd rush by him and vanish. If only she could.

"Jay," she said simply, blinking to dry her eyes. She

didn't want him to know she was on to him, not when she had revenge to extract.

A smile tugged at the corners of his mouth, but she refused to label it irresistible. She could, too, resist Jay Overman, especially when she reminded herself that a deceitful heart beat inside that sexy body.

"I was starting to think you were going to avoid me forever," he said in a soft, low voice.

"I wasn't avoiding you," she denied, although she most certainly had been. After the meeting at the home office the day before, she'd arranged to meet Billy for dinner and drinks away from the hotel and hadn't returned home until late. Today, she'd had Sadie Mae on lookout so she could retreat when she heard he was advancing.

"Good," he said and stepped into the closet with her.

"What are you doing?" She gasped and retreated, desperately trying to get away from all that tall, brawny male. The retreat didn't work because there was nowhere to go. Her back came up flush against a hard, cool wall. To the left and right of her were floor-to-ceiling shelves filled with linens, soaps and toilet paper.

"Joining you in the closet."

A closet that was barely big enough for one person, let alone two. She cast a frantic look around while her breath came faster and her heart pounded harder. She was still determined to resist him, but it was maddening to realize that being angry at him didn't make her any less attracted to him.

He pulled the door shut behind him, and the tools on

his belt clinked faintly as they jostled against each other. She did her best not to hyperventilate. Darn him for wearing the tool belt even though it was nothing more than a deceitful prop.

"I have a few things I need to say to you in private," he said. He was wearing his usual sexy-as-sin uniform of jeans and a buff-colored short-sleeved shirt. He put his hands on either side of her, and his biceps bulged. So did her eyes as she took in the toned musculature of his upper body.

"But this is a closet." Her voice sounded strangled, so she cleared her throat. She drew in a breath and smelled a clean, masculine scent that made her heart beat even faster. "We can go to my office and talk."

"I like the view in here better." He smiled at her, long and slow, his heated gaze traveling over her face before dipping to the clinging red fabric of her shirt. His brows drew together.

"Hey, the puckers are gone," he said. "Your chest looks fantastic. Better than fantastic. Delectable." He wet his lips, sending a shimmer of heat through her, then understanding dawned in his eyes. "You're wearing an Impeccabra, aren't you?"

She tried to ignore the heat, tried to think about the betrayal, but she still felt like she was standing too close to a furnace. "So what if I am? It's a good product."

"I'm glad you think so." He seemed inordinately...pleased. More so than was warranted by a reluctant admission from a woman wearing a product designed by a company he professed not to care about. He was acting more like he'd designed the product. No, exactly like he'd designed the product.

"You designed the Impeccabra, didn't you?" she accused.

He broke eye contact, took his arms down and scratched his head. He closed his cream-soda eyes, and for a minute she thought he'd deny it. Then his eyes snapped open, and she read resignation in them.

"Yeah," he said flatly. "Want to make something of it?"

He asked the last question like a challenge, as though he expected her to subscribe to the silly notion that men who dealt in women's lingerie pranced around in silk and lace teddies.

She felt like railing at him for working as a maintenance man—no, as an engineer—when he could design something as extraordinary as the Impeccabra. She'd been there when he was admiring his handiwork on Mrs. Burnside's chest. Any fool could see he loved bras, but she was darned if she was going to point that out. Not when she was so blasted angry at him. Still, her soft heart couldn't let him think she was making fun of him.

"It was a compliment," she said tightly. "You're like an artist. The Michelangelo of brassieres."

"Well, it's, um, not something I, um, actually enjoy."

"Whatever," Tara said, not believing him for a second. He didn't answer, and the silence between them grew. So did the awareness. Just like that, it was back, along with Tara's realization that she was trapped inside a very small closet with a man who made her blood race.

Defiantly, she grabbed a couple of towels off a shelf. "I have work to do. Would you let me pass?"

He didn't move, not a drool-inducing muscle. "I haven't said what I need to say yet."

"Then say it." She tried to sound stern but came off sounding breathless. How was she supposed to get enough air when breathing meant subjecting herself to how intoxicatingly good he smelled?

"Don't marry Billy."

She'd been looking at a point somewhere along his chin—which was a very nice chin, by the way—but now her head snapped up. He looked so serious that she longed to tell him that of course she wasn't going to marry Billy. Then she remembered his liaison with her father and his assignment to keep her from the altar. She made herself sound flippant.

"Objection noted and rejected. End of conversation. Now will you let me pass?"

"Let me put it another way. I don't want you to marry Billy."

Of course he didn't. How else could he fulfill the mission he was carrying out for her father? She knew that was the reason, but something hopeful in her stirred and she heard herself ask, "Why?"

His hand reached out and glided through her hair, his fingers moving sensuously to her cheekbone and then over the planes of her face until they rested lightly against her lips. She felt her mouth quiver as he rubbed the soft pads of his fingers against her lips. The heat in his gaze was scorching.

"I think you know why," he whispered.

Then he was moving forward, slowly, deliberately. The towels she was holding dropped to the floor, and she reached out to stop him, placing her palms against his upper chest.

Push, she told herself. *Push. Push.*

The heat of his muscled body seeped into the flesh of her palms, making her long to explore if the rest of him felt this gloriously good. Her hands traveled upward, over his shoulders, around his neck, her fingers tangling in the short, soft hairs at his nape.

He gave a throaty groan and then his arms were around her, his mouth slanting over hers. She opened her mouth to give him greater access, and their passion ignited as though lit with a blowtorch.

He swiftly deepened the kiss, tangling his tongue with hers as their bodies strained to get closer. She rubbed restlessly against his arousal as the heat spun through her, pooling in her body's core.

When one of his hands cupped her breast, she thrust herself against it, hating the shirt that kept her flesh from being naked against his, hating even the Impeccabra.

This is what it felt like to love a man, she thought dazedly. Because there was no use denying it any longer.

She loved Jay Overman.

"Tara," he groaned against her mouth. "Say it. Say you won't marry Billy."

She loved no-good, rotten, I'm-going-to-get-my-way-at-any-cost Jay Overman.

The hands that hadn't been able to push him away

before untangled from his thick, soft hair, moved to his chest and gave a mighty shove.

Taken unaware, Jay went sprawling backward and landed with a thud against the closet door. It burst open, and he skidded into the hall on his rear end. He looked at her with a dazed expression as she pushed her hair from her face, shakily rearranged her clothes and picked up the towels from the floor.

"What did you do that for?" he asked in an injured voice.

She stopped herself from flinging her body on the floor with him and cleared her throat, willing her voice to sound harsh. "I'm engaged to be married."

He let out a short, incredulous laugh. "You can't possibly mean you're still going to marry the guy after the way you responded to me."

"I most certainly am," she said and pulled a date out of midair. "On Saturday."

She steeled herself against the hurt she saw in his face by remembering that he was putting on an act. Then she slipped out of the closet and skirted around him, walking quickly down the hall, trying desperately not to cry.

She hadn't gotten far when she almost careened into a small, white-haired lady, who stood gaping at her.

"In my day," the lady said in a shaky voice, "when I had a hotty like that inside a closet with me, I was smart enough to keep him there."

JAY POUNDED on the door to the room he'd watched Billy Trotter disappear inside moments ago.

It was Billy's bad luck that Jay had spotted him enter the hotel less than an hour after Tara had dropped the bomb about getting married Saturday, which was just four days away.

Jay pounded harder. He couldn't let it happen, not when Tara belonged with him. He needed time to make her realize that, which was why he had to get rid of Billy. Right here, right now.

"Maintenance," he yelled, and the door swung open.

Billy stood there, a mini bag of Cheddar and sour cream potato chips in his hand. He gave Jay a guilty grin.

"Caught me," he said, then held out the bag. "Want some?"

The scent of Cheddar cheese flowed from the bag, reminding Jay that he hadn't had lunch. "Don't mind if I…" He stopped himself before he could say "do." What was he thinking? This was the enemy. The man who was trying to marry the woman who belonged with Jay.

"No," Jay said forcefully. "I don't want any chips. I want to come in and fix what's broken."

"I didn't report anything broken, but you're welcome to come in and take a look." Billy stepped aside trustingly, still munching on a chip.

Jay closed the door and positioned himself less than a foot from Billy. "Tara tells me you're getting married Saturday."

"Saturday?" Billy repeated, then proceeded to gag and point to his throat.

Oh, brother. Jay wanted Billy out of the picture, but not by him choking to death on a potato chip. He whacked the other man a few times on the back, and the gags turned to coughs. A piece of half-chewed potato chip flew out on the floor.

"Thanks, man," Billy sputtered. "That chip must've gone down the wrong way. I gotta get a glass of water."

Jay quickly moved into the main room, searching for something to break. His eyes alighted on the television but he couldn't bring himself to smash it. The same went with the alarm clock. Unless he wanted to brand himself a liar, the only thing left was a lamp on the dresser. Before he could talk himself out of destroying hotel property, he took the hammer from his tool belt and swung.

"Wow. There *was* something broken." Billy walked into the room, a glass of water in one hand, the potato chips in the other. "You better get away from those pieces before you cut yourself."

Jay rolled his eyes. Why did Tara have to hook up with a nice guy?

"You didn't answer my question about Saturday," Jay said, trying to make his voice dangerously soft. He thought he pulled it off. Sort of.

"Saturday," Billy said, munching happily. He swallowed the rest of the chip and did a dramatic flourish with his arm. "I must dance with my feet on her wedding day."

Jay recognized the passage from the play *Kiss Me Kate,* which he'd gotten a kick out of when his English lit class had studied the original Shakespeare play in college. Not that he'd admitted that to anybody.

"Barefoot," he corrected. "You must dance barefoot on her wedding day."

"Now why would I want to do that?" Billy asked.

"Never mind," Jay said, annoyed that he'd let himself get sidetracked. He resurrected his dangerous-voice mode. "I wouldn't get married if I were you."

Jay looked around the room, desperate to break something else so he could reinforce his comment. His eyes alighted on the foot of the bed. Hey, it had worked before. There was no reason it couldn't work again. He swung out with his work boot—and caught the foot of the bed with the side of his boot instead of the steel-reinforced toe.

"Ow," he cried, hopping on one foot while hot pain shot through him.

Billy grimaced and patted him on the shoulder sympathetically.

"Now I see what you mean about not getting married on Saturday if you were me. With the bruise you're going to have, you'd have a hard time walking down the aisle. Not to mention dancing barefoot."

"HA! I KNEW you were home," Sherry said, sweeping into the living room where Jay sat alone and miserable in the semidarkness. He watched with resignation while she switched on lights until it seemed like high noon instead of early evening. "What did you think? That I'd go away if you didn't answer the doorbell?"

"The thought never occurred to me," Jay said dryly. "But I did wonder why I was dumb enough to give you my house key. How 'bout giving it back?"

Sherry clutched the key to her chest in drama-queen fashion. "No way. If you're going to ignore my calls and refuse to answer the door, I need some way to flush you out. Lace Foundations needs you."

"You can handle Lace Foundations on your own."

"You must be joking. I do fine on the business end, but we both know the future of the company hinges on your creative genius. You've built a better bra. Think what you could do with girdles and slips and panties."

Despite himself, Jay found himself growing enthusiastic at the prospect. He already had an idea about how to transfer the lift and thrust technology to the backside of underwear. He purposefully reined in his excitement. "I thought you decided Lace Foundations should specialize in bras."

"For now, but there's no reason we can't branch out into new products once you've come up with prototypes." She moved into the living room as she talked, stopping abruptly shy of the sofa where Jay sat with his right ankle elevated on pillows. She gestured at the injured limb. "Did you hurt yourself?"

Jay rubbed his brow. "Let's just say I had an unfortunate encounter with a bedpost."

She narrowed her eyes. "Why were you sitting here in the dark anyway?"

"I was thinking," he said shortly.

She tugged down the skirt of her business suit, sat on the chair adjacent to the sofa and gave him her full attention. "Why do I get the feeling you weren't thinking about all those messages I left asking in what colors we should carry the Impeccabra?"

"I was thinking about Tara," Jay admitted because she'd worm it out of him sooner or later anyway. "She's getting married on Saturday."

"She can't get married. You told Mr. Patterson you'd stop her from getting married. We owe him, Jay."

"I know that," Jay said, sweeping a hand across his brow. "I've been racking my brain trying to come up with a way to stop her from going through with this, but I'm coming up blank."

Sherry pressed her lips together, crossed her arms over her chest and furrowed her brow. "If you were somebody else, I might suggest running the other guy off," she said after a moment. "But, considering the way you are, that won't work."

"Why not?" Jay asked, insulted. He'd intimidated George Merrimack and Robby Fairchild, hadn't he? Never mind for the moment that Billy Trotter didn't find him the least bit threatening. "And what do you mean, the way I am?"

"You're a softy, Jay. It's simply not in you to hurt anybody. Sure, you look like a man's man, but you're not."

"You think people can tell I'm not a man's man?"

"Of course they can." She must have noticed his hurt

expression, because she rushed to reassure him. "But only people who know you. You can't fool them for long, little brother."

"I was afraid of that," Jay muttered. "But maybe I could change. Billy's a nice enough guy, but when I think about him touching Tara..." His voice trailed off as his hands clenched into fists. "I think I could hit him. Maybe."

Sherry whistled long and low. "Oh, my. And the plot thickens."

"What do you mean by that?" Jay asked irritably.

"You've gone and fallen for her." Sherry leaned back against the sofa cushions, a knowing smile on her face. "Don't bother to deny it, because I can see the truth on your face. You never could hide anything from me, little brother."

"I wasn't going to deny it," Jay said, because it would be hopeless anyway. "You should meet her, Sher. She's smart, beautiful, loving, caring and—"

"Hell-bent on getting married to somebody who isn't you."

"I don't know if I'm ready for marriage," Jay said, even though he wasn't entirely sure that was still true. "I want to be with her. And the funny thing is, I thought she wanted the same thing until a couple days ago when she suddenly announced she was engaged."

"The way you feel about her certainly changes things," Sherry said slowly. "I assume you've told her?"

"Well, yeah, I told her not to marry Trotter."

Sherry shook her head. "No. I meant did you tell her why?"

He nodded, amazed that she'd ask. Did his sister really think he'd neglect to tell Tara something so important? "Sure, I did. I told her I didn't want her to."

Sherry groaned, got up from the chair, walked over to her brother and whacked him on the shoulder.

"Hey, that hurt," Jay said, rubbing the sore spot. "What'd you go and do that for?"

"To knock some sense into you. You love this woman, don't you?"

Jay's inclination was to protest, but the words wouldn't come. Instead, he thought of the way he felt around Tara. Their relationship was still new, certainly, but his heart had already identified her as the woman for him. No other woman could make his heart pound with her smile or send warmth cascading through him with her kindness.

"Yeah," he said with wonder in his voice. "I do."

Sherry thumped him again. "Then tell her."

He felt a slow smile spread across his face. "Yeah," he said aloud. "I'll do that."

Sherry sat in the chair again and leaned forward, her hands on her knees, her expression intent.

"Now that we've gotten that out of the way," she said, "suppose you tell me if you think we could sell purple Impeccabras."

TARA'S ARMS ached from the effort of carrying three-inch-thick bridal magazines to the front desk of the hotel the next afternoon.

"For cryin' out loud, T.P.," Sadie Mae said, rolling her eyes. "Don't you think you're carrying this too far?"

Tara dumped the magazines on the counter, nearly sighing aloud over the beauty of the sleeveless satin wedding dress with the scooped back that graced the cover of the magazine on the top of the stack. She felt a pang of envy for the bride who would be wearing that dress while she walked down the aisle to marry the man she loved. But then that bride probably deserved her happiness. *She* hadn't allowed herself to fall in love with a lying snake.

"I'm not carrying anything too far," Tara said, massaging her aching arms and wishing she could do the same for her heart. "If I want Jay to believe I'm getting married Saturday, I need to scatter evidence about to make it seem like it's true."

"But it's not true," Sadie Mae said, her red hair swinging as she shook her head. "Even if you loved Spud, which you don't, he's married to Roxie. And you know what she's like."

"Roxie's not so bad."

"Not if she likes you, she isn't. Don't tell me you forgot what she did when she caught Norma Jean with Spud at the high school prom?"

Tara winced, because nobody could forget that. No matter how hard they tried. "Norma Jean's pretty white prom dress didn't look so good with red punch all over it."

"Exactly."

"But it's not Roxie I'm trying to fool. It's Jay."

"I've got news for you, sister. You've already fooled him. When I was helping him fix that slow-draining tub in room two twenty-six today, he was positively morose."

"If he were a real maintenance man instead of a civil engineer, you wouldn't have to help him with the plumbing," Tara said tartly. "And the only reason he's morose is that he thinks he's failed in his mission to stop me from getting married."

"He hasn't failed yet," Sadie Mae said, glancing toward the elevator. Jay stepped off it and turned toward the front desk like a bat locating his prey before striding purposefully toward them. "That sure looks like a man on a mission to me."

"Sadie Mae, Tara," Jay said as he approached them. Although he addressed them both, those dratted, wonderful cream-soda eyes were focused only on Tara. "Could I talk to you a minute in your office?"

"No," Tara said, remembering what had happened the last time she was inside a confined space with him. Sexual disaster. "Whatever you have to say, you can say out here."

Jay glanced around, his gaze taking in Sadie Mae and the guests milling about the lobby. He put his elbows on the desk, leaned forward and gave her a beseeching look. "This is kind of personal."

"How personal can it be?"

He lowered his voice. "It's about why I don't want you to marry Billy Trotter."

The same white-haired lady who'd scolded Tara for kicking Jay out of the maid's closet suddenly appeared at the front desk. Ignoring Jay, Tara addressed the lady. "Can I help you with something, Mrs. Tobago?"

"That's Tabasco, dear. Like the sauce, not the country. Did you ever do that name association thing to remember people's names? I used to be one red-hot mama. That's how people remember mine. Although you probably don't believe that. You probably think I'm an old geezer."

"I do," Tara said, then realized with horror what she'd implied. "Believe you, I mean. I didn't mean I thought you were a geezer." Although she was ninety if she was a day. "Now, what can I help you with?"

"Nothing," Mrs. Tabasco said. "I just wanted to hear what your young man had to say."

"He's not my young man," Tara refuted.

"I could be if you don't get married on Saturday." Jay cut in.

"What I'm wondering," Mrs. Tabasco said, "is what you were doing necking with him in the closet when you're marrying somebody else."

"You were necking with Jay in the closet?" Sadie Mae asked Tara, her green eyes wide and speculative. "How interesting."

Tara felt her face flush. "What Jay and I were doing in the closet isn't anyone's business."

"Which is why I wanted to have this conversation in private," Jay reminded her.

"I don't want to go inside my office with you," Tara said.

"Oh, I get it," Mrs. Tabasco said. "She doesn't trust herself behind a closed door with you." Mrs. Tabasco gave Jay the up-and-down. "Not that I blame her."

"I do, too, trust myself with him," Tara denied heatedly even though she didn't believe it. Not for a second.

"Then let's go," Jay said, gesturing toward her office.

"Do you have to?" Sadie Mae wailed. "I wanted to hear why you don't want her to get married."

"I'll tell you later," Jay said.

"But who's going to tell me?" Mrs. Tabasco asked. "I want to know, too."

Convinced of the need to take their conversation private, Tara marched into her office, her back stiff. Jay followed her inside, then she shut the door and leaned against it. "So talk."

He took a step toward her, and she sidestepped him, putting as much distance between them as she could. He let out a heavy sigh. "You're not making this easy on me."

"Good," she said.

"I messed up in the closet. I should have told you then why I don't want you to marry Billy." He leveled her with a look she'd have sworn reeked of sincerity. If she hadn't known better. "I love you, Tara."

Joy radiated through her, but it was quickly diluted by doubt. Tara crossed her arms over her chest and laughed softly, without humor. "That's the best you can come up with?"

His brows drew together. "Didn't you hear me? I told you I love you."

She swallowed the lump in her throat. "I heard you, all right. I just didn't realize you'd stoop this low. You should be ashamed of yourself."

He shook his head, his confusion palpable. "I got to tell you, this isn't quite the reaction I expected."

"What did you expect me to do? Fall into your arms and say I love you back?"

He tipped his head and gave her a half grin. "That's kind of what I was hoping for."

"Admit it. You want me to call off the wedding, don't you?"

"Yes." He agreed readily, stepping forward. She stepped backward. "There's nothing I want more."

"I knew it," she said, jabbing her finger at him.

"I'm missing something here. You act like that's a crime, but why should I hide the fact that I don't want the woman I love to marry some other guy?"

"You've certainly hid a number of other things," she said tightly.

THE FIRST SLIVER of unease skittered down Jay's spine. Her brown eyes looked cold instead of soft and warm the way they got when she was happy.

"What things?" he asked.

"Oh, let's see, how about the little fact that you happen to be in cahoots with my father? Or the only reason you're working here, posing as a maintenance man, I might add, is to stop me from getting married?''

The bottom slid out of Jay's world and he cursed himself for not having explained everything before now. ''You don't understand.''

''I understand plenty. Sadie Mae and I followed you Friday night to the Occoquan.''

Jay snapped his fingers. ''I knew I heard something out there.''

''I know what I heard, too. And it wasn't anything good.''

''You've got to let me explain. I told you about my family's lingerie company. If your father hadn't given mine a loan, there wouldn't be a Lace Foundations. My dad paid back the money but died before he could repay the favor. What was I supposed to say when Cliff asked me to help him?''

''How about, 'No, you crazy old coot.' ''

''I had a responsibility to say yes. Don't you see? When my dad died, his debt came to me.''

''What gives you and my father the right to interfere in my life? *My* life, Jay, not my father's. If I want to get married, that's my business. Not his. And certainly not yours.''

She was right. He'd known it from the beginning, but still he'd done Cliff's bidding. At first, it was because he owed him. But later the reason had changed. He'd interfered in Tara's life because he'd wanted to be part of it.

"I was a fool," she continued. "A stupid little fool to think you were attracted to me—"

"I *am* attracted to you."

"When all the while you were trying to keep other men away from me." She finished as though she hadn't heard him.

"I love you, Tara. If you give me half a chance, I'll prove it."

"You still can't stop. You'll say anything to fulfill that debt you think you owe my father, won't you?" Tara swept past him, pausing at the door. When she looked at him, he felt as though he'd been blasted with frigid air. "Well, I have something to say to you.

"You're fired."

10

AS HE SQUARED his shoulders and rang the doorbell on Cliff Patterson's tony Colonial in suburban Prince Edward County, Jay reassured himself that he was doing the right thing.

His family was still indebted to Cliff for pulling their business from financial ruin, but Jay would have to pay back the debt another way.

His allegiance was no longer with Cliff, but with Tara. Yes, she'd refused to take his phone calls for the past day and a half. And yes, she'd had Sadie May relay the message that she'd have him arrested for trespassing if he stepped foot in the hotel.

But Tara needed a champion, and he was determined to give her one.

Before he could sound the summons a second time, the door sprang open and Cliff grabbed him by the arm and pulled him inside the house. The older man looked up and down the street before shutting the door.

"What are you doing here, Conner James? I can't believe you took such a chance. What if Tara shows up?"

Jay's shoulders rose and fell as he took a fortifying breath to get him through the conversation to come. "It's over, Cliff. She followed me to the Occoquan the other night. She knows about our pact.''

Cliff swore and raked a hand through his snow-white hair. "So that's why she's dodging my phone calls. I haven't talked to the girl in nearly a week."

"So you don't know," Jay said flatly.

"Know what?"

Jay sighed, wishing he didn't have to be the one to tell him. "Tara's getting married Saturday."

Cliff shook his head, defiance written on his broad, handsome features. "No, she's not. Saturday's in two days. Tara can't get married for six more years."

"She's determined, sir."

An indentation appeared between Cliff's eyebrows as he seemed to ponder that. Then his chest puffed out and his eyes blazed. "Not as determined as I am to stop her. With your help, of course."

"That's what I came here to talk to you about." Jay dragged in a deep, laborious breath. He'd reached the most difficult part of the conversation. "I came to ask you not to interfere. Tara's an adult. She has a right to decide when and—" he winced "—who she's going to marry."

Cliff shook his head, the determination in his expression not abating. "You're not making sense, son. You're on my side. Remember our pact."

Jay raised his chin and stood up straighter. He had an inch or so on Cliff and needed every advantage he could get. "I know my family owes you, but—"

"What do you mean, your family owes me?" Cliff interrupted.

"My father. He never got a chance to pay back the favor after you gave him the loan to keep Lace Foundations going."

"Sure he did," Cliff said. "Who do you think introduced me to my beloved Hildegarde?"

"My dad?" Jay shook his head in wonder because the information didn't compute. "Then why did he always say he owed you?"

Cliff shrugged. "An expression of speech, probably. If anything, I owed him. You can't put a price on love like you can on a business."

The whole situation still didn't make sense to Jay. "Then why did you ask me to stop Tara from getting married?"

"Because you're the son of the finest, most trustworthy man I ever knew. What better man could there be for the job?" Cliff answered. "Besides, I didn't know you thought you had to do me a favor. I thought you wanted to help me because we see eye to eye on this marriage business."

"Not anymore we don't," Jay said, giving his head a vigorous shake. "Not if it's at Tara's expense."

"Are you quitting on me, Conner James?" Cliff sounded incredulous, as though the very notion was ludicrous.

"I'm afraid so. If Tara wants to marry Billy Trotter, she should be able to."

"Billy Trotter? Sadie Mae's brother?"

"He's not Sadie Mae's brother," Jay denied even as he finally figured out who **Billy** looked like. "This guy's a burly redhead a couple inches shorter than me. He sells potato chips for a living and misquotes Shakespeare."

"I know who he is. I had the misfortune to go to a community play in Pennsylvania last year where the main Hamlet was sick and Trotter was the understudy. You don't forget a guy who says, 'To be or maybe not, that is the question.'"

"Then he *is* Sadie Mae's brother," Jay said, wondering why nobody had told him. He'd been under the impression Tara had met Billy only recently, and here they'd known each other for years.

"It doesn't matter who he is," Cliff declared. "I'm stopping the wedding."

"No," Jay cried, putting a restraining hand on Cliff's arm. "Let her be, Cliff."

"Fat chance of that happening," Cliff said before he shook off Jay's grasp, dashed out the door and hurried to his car.

Jay swore and followed him, thinking it ironic that he was headed to the Excursion Inn to fight for the right of the woman he loved to marry another man.

TARA PULLED a short-sleeved sweater over her head and positioned herself in front of her dresser mirror so she could repair the damage to her long hair. Now if only she could do something about the sadness in her eyes. In the reflection, she had a view of Sadie Mae sitting cross-legged on her bed, looking unusually contemplative. Alley was curled up beside her.

"I can't believe you didn't tell Tool Man you weren't marrying Spud," she said, repeating her mantra.

"I already told you, Sadie Mae, it didn't come up," Tara explained again.

"You know he's going to find out, don't you?"

It wouldn't change anything if he did. The man she loved would still be an underhanded rake who'd say anything to get his way. Her chest tightened until it hurt. "Not if I never see him again, he won't," Tara said.

"Your father will tell him, for sure. Then Tool Man will show up here, mark my words."

"He better not," Tara said and tugged hard on the sliding door of her closet. She succeeded only in pulling it off its tracks. "Darn it. This blasted thing never works right."

"Let me take a look at it." Sadie Mae got off the bed and bent down. After a few seconds, she said, "I could fix that easy. I'll pick up a part and do it first thing tomorrow."

"You wouldn't mind?"

"Nah. I like doing stuff like that," Sadie Mae said. "But we're getting off the subject. You never told me what your father had to say about this fake marriage business."

Tara slipped into a pair of low-heeled pumps, avoiding her friend's eyes. "That's probably because I didn't tell him."

"What?" Sadie Mae's exclamation was so loud that

Alley jumped off the bed and dashed into the next room. "Why not? What is this? Selective revenge?"

"I never got around to it, is all."

"But your father's the one who has the crazy wait-until-thirty rule. He's the one you should be mad at, not the Toolster."

Strangely, that wasn't the case. Tara expected her father to be irrational and even devious in getting what he wanted. She'd counted on more from Jay because she wanted him to be the kind, moral, upstanding man she'd thought he was. It hurt her heart that he wasn't.

"Have you seen my yellow sweater?" she asked, rifling through the stack of sweaters in her dresser drawer. "I wore it the other day and now I can't find it."

She thought Sadie Mae winced before her friend shook her head. "You're changing the subject again. We were talking about how unfair you're being to Tool Man."

Tara forced herself not to react to Sadie Mae's choice of the word "unfair." Her friend already knew her position. "Could we please drop it? Billy was supposed to meet us in the lobby five minutes ago."

Sadie Mae followed her to the door. "Have you at least told *him* there's not going to be a wedding on Saturday?"

"Very funny," Tara muttered and didn't speak again until they were in the nearly deserted lobby. Billy was nowhere in sight. She sat next to Sadie Mae on a flowered love seat, wondering if she'd ever be happy again. Even the fresh daisies on the end tables didn't cheer her up.

"Wonder what's keeping your brother?" she asked after a moment.

"You're kidding, right? We're talking about a man who refuses to own a watch. So don't be surprised if you're waiting at the altar Saturday." Sadie Mae snapped her fingers. "Oops, I forgot. If he shows up Saturday, it'll be bigamy."

Tara rubbed her lower face. "How long are you going to keep this up?"

"As long as it takes to talk some sense into you. Jeez, Tara. You are the most pigheaded person I've ever met."

No sooner had Sadie Mae uttered the statement than Cliff Patterson burst through the doors of the Excursion Inn, his face taut and his brow furrowed. He immediately located his daughter and strode toward her.

"I take it back," Sadie Mae said under her breath. "You're only the second most pigheaded."

"Tara Hildegard Patterson, I demand to know what's going on," Cliff said, nearly breaking her eardrums with his command. He stood over them, a formidable frown marring his features.

"Hello to you, too, Daddy," Tara said, rising to kiss him on his cool cheek. He remained perfectly still.

"Don't you hello me, young lady. I hear you think you're getting married on Saturday." He shook a finger at her. "What were you going to do? Spring it on me when it was a done deal?"

The front door opened once more, diverting their attention. This time Jay came through, slightly out of breath as though he'd been running. He was wearing a brown Henley and khaki pants, but even without jeans and a tool belt he still looked wonderful. Disgustingly, marvelously so.

"Stop yelling at her, Cliff," he demanded, looking every bit as formidable as her father as he crossed the room toward their unhappy little circle. His handsome features were more serious than she'd ever seen them.

"What are you doing here?" Tara challenged before he could say anything more. "What are you going to be? The good cop? You'll let my father yell at me not to get married for a while, then you'll try to reason with me."

"Sounds good to me," Cliff said, puffing out his chest as though settling in for a long fight.

"It's not like that," Jay said. "I didn't come here to stop you from getting married."

"Because I don't need either of you telling me what to do," Tara insisted, then glared at her father. "I know you want me to wait to get married, but this is my life, Dad. You were a wonderful father. You *are* a wonderful father. But you have to trust the way you raised me and stand aside.

"I'm not like you. Career's important to me, but I don't want to manage a big resort with lots of prestige. I want to stay right where I am. I want other things, too. A husband who loves me. And babies. Two or three of them. Heck, I even want that house in the suburbs. And if I choose to have them before I'm thirty, you'll have to live with it. Either that, or live without me."

She transferred her glare to Jay, giving her anger free rein to override her heartache. "As for you, I've had enough of you roaming around my hotel scaring off the guests. If I choose to get married, you'll have to live with that, too.''

"I know," he said softly.

The softness, more than anything, got her attention. That and the way the corners of his mouth drooped. She eyed him suspiciously. "You do?"

"You haven't been listening. I'm not trying to stop you from getting married. I'm trying to stop your father from stopping you."

"Why?"

He sighed, looking terribly sad and impossibly dear. "I already told you why. Because I love you."

"You love me?" Tara asked in wonder, but she saw the answer in his cream-soda eyes. This time she couldn't doubt him, because the truth was shining there, bright and timeless. Wonder filled her, along with a life-affirming joy. Jay loved her.

"You love her?" Cliff repeated, sounding irked. "When in the dickens did that happen?"

Tara felt Sadie Mae poke her in the ribs through her haze of happiness. "See, T.P.? I told you the Toolster loved you."

"Hey, what's going on here?" Billy walked into their midst, and Tara saw resignation fall over Jay's face. Oh, no. He still thought they were engaged. Jay stepped away from her at the same time Billy noticed her father. "Hey, Mr. P. It's been a long time." Billy put his hand over his heart. "O! Call back tomorrow, bid time return."

"That's call back *yesterday*." Cliff scowled at the redhead. "It hasn't been long enough for me. But considering you're about to become my son-in-law, you better start calling me Dad."

"That's not necessary," Tara began, but all three of the men were focused on each other.

"Yeah, congratulations," Jay said, giving Billy a hearty handshake at odds with the grimace on his face. "I'm sorry I didn't tell you that before."

Billy bit his bottom lip as his gaze ping-ponged from Jay to her father and then finally to Tara. "I suppose this means you haven't told them?"

"Told us what?" Cliff asked.

Before Tara could speak, the lobby doors burst open for a third time.

"Surprise!" an excited voice squealed. All eyes swung to the front of the lobby, where a woman at least eight months pregnant dropped her bags and ran full tilt toward them.

They parted like the Red Sea, all except for Billy, who opened his arms. Just before the pregnant woman reached his embrace, Tara recognized her as Roxie, Billy's wife. Billy laughed as she peppered his face with kisses.

"Oh, Billy, I missed you so," Roxie said.

"I wear my heart like a sieve," Billy said.

"Upon your sleeve, not like a sieve," Tara corrected, but she was touched by the reunion nonetheless. Oh, to have a husband who would greet her like that after only a few days apart. Especially if that husband were Jay.

"Trotter, if you don't have a good explanation for who

this woman is," her father said in his roaring voice, "I'm going to rip off your sleeve. And your arm with it."

Roxie broke off the embrace, her eyes a bit wild when they focused on Cliff. "Don't you threaten him. I'm no woman. I'm his wife."

"You're married?" Jay focused on Billy as his blood rushed through his veins, thick and boiling. The two-timer had been toying with Tara's affections! He moved toward the other man. "How dare you string Tara along like that!"

"Tara?" Roxie asked. "Tara Patterson? From high school? But I don't understand. How could my Billy be stringing her along?"

"Tara and Billy are supposed to get married on Saturday," Cliff announced.

Roxie's cry of rage momentarily diverted Jay's attention from Billy. On the heels of it came another wail, which sounded more like a shriek of pain than anger. Billy rushed to his wife's side and put an arm around her.

"What's wrong, sweetheart?" Billy asked anxiously.

"I think she's in labor," Sadie Mae said.

"I refuse to be in labor when another woman is messing with my man," Roxie wailed.

"Calm down," Sadie Mae told Roxie, for once sounding like the voice of reason. "T.P. is not messing with Spud. They've been pretending. Tell them, Spud. Tell them it was all an act."

"Of course it was an act," Billy said. "All the world's a stage, and all the men and women merely playing."

"Players, not playing," Sadie Mae corrected.

"I couldn't turn down the role when Tara asked me to convince Jay I wanted to marry her," Billy continued.

Roxie let out another great cry, and Billy's eyes turned desperate. "Please believe me, honey."

"I do," she said, gasping. "But Sadie Mae's right. I *am* in labor."

Jay was barely aware of the married couple rushing out of the hotel as he turned toward Tara. He thought the ache in his heart must be as intense as any labor pain. "Is this true? Was it an act?"

Wordlessly, she nodded.

"But why?"

"Revenge," Sadie Mae answered for Tara. "She figured if you and Mr. P were dumb enough to believe she'd marry the first guy who came along, you deserved everything you got."

Jay tried to dredge up some anger at the game Tara had been playing, but it wouldn't come. Not when the blackness that had been cloaking his heart was finally lifting. "So you were never going to marry Billy?"

Tara shook her head. "It's not Billy I love."

"This is wonderful news, simply wonderful," Cliff announced, but Jay couldn't turn away from Tara, not when hope was welling in his chest, not when she was looking at him with that soft light in her eyes.

"Oh, Jay," Tara said, coming to stand in front of him. Her hand cupped his cheek, and her lush lips trembled. "I've been so stubborn, refusing to see what was right in front of me. I love you, Jay. Only you. Can you forgive me?"

"I guess I can promise to stop telling you to wait until you're thirty to get married, Tara," Cliff said, obviously oblivious to what was happening between his daughter and Jay, "but I can't pretend I'm not happy you're not."

"Who says she's not getting married?" Jay asked Cliff, but his eyes never left Tara's. He leaned closer to her, speaking words from his heart. "I didn't think I wanted to get married for a long time, but now I see I was waiting for you. I'm willing to wait another six years if that's what you want, but say you'll marry me, Tara. Please."

"Marry *you?*" Cliff asked, finally tuning in to what was happening between them. "You can't marry her, Conner James. You were supposed to *stop* her from getting married." Abruptly, Cliff broke off his tirade and spoke thoughtfully. "Although I do like you. You'd make a fine son-in-law. And a respectable one, too, with you being a civil engineer."

"Mr. P., I hope you don't take this too personally, but you need to put a sock in it," Sadie Mae said. "Now if you'll excuse me, I've got to get to the hospital. I have a niece or nephew on the way."

Tara blew the departing Sadie Mae a grateful kiss, took Jay by the hand and pulled him past her dumb-founded father into the room Mrs. Burnside used to prepare continental breakfast. She shut the door, hooked her arms around his neck and gazed into his handsome, beloved face.

"Now where were we?" she asked, smiling. "I seem to remember you mentioning something about marriage."

"Before you say anything, your father was wrong out there. I'm not a civil engineer. Not anymore. I've decided to join Sherry at Lace Foundations permanently." He smiled crookedly, and she could tell he was completely sure of what he wanted to do for the first time in his life. "So I'm a Bra Prince."

Happiness radiated through her. "I think that's wonderful, although I did like the way you looked in a tool belt. Replacing you will be awfully difficult."

"Not if you hire Sadie Mae. That woman might not be able to drink a cup of coffee without spilling it, but she hasn't met a leaky faucet she can't fix."

"Sadie Mae? Why, that's perfect. Why didn't I think of that?"

"Because you've had other things on your mind." Jay grinned long and slow as he buried his hands in her long, loose hair. "Such as how much you want to marry me."

She tipped her head. "I want nothing more than to marry you, but I think my father's right, after all. Six sounds like a good number. Now that you don't work for me anymore, I want to date you."

Disappointment descended over his features like fog on a shrouded night. "You want to date me for six years?"

"Not on your life, Bra Prince. Six *months*. The bridal magazines say it takes at least that long to plan a decent wedding," she said as she rose on tiptoes to meet his mouth in a long, sweet kiss that was going to make waiting any time at all very difficult indeed.

If you enjoyed what you just read,
then we've got an offer you can't resist!

Take 2 bestselling
love stories FREE!
Plus get a FREE surprise gift!

Three of romance's most talented craftsmen come together in one special collection.

New York Times bestselling authors

Jayne Ann Krentz

Tess Gerritsen

National bestselling author

Stella Cameron

in

Stolen Memories

With plenty of page-turning passion and dramatic storytelling, this volume promises many memorable hours of reading enjoyment!

Coming to your favorite retail outlet in February 2002.

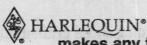